SHE WAS AFRAID AND DEFIANT . . .

Cenred seized her wrists with his big hand. "Countess, why do you tremble?" He looked down at her with his crooked grin. "Tell me, Countess Moon, what makes you so afraid of me?"

Constance stared up at him. "I had you chained once as prisoner," she said. "If you touch me now, I swear I will . . ."

He shrugged off his shirt and threw it into the room's dim corners, then jerked her to him. Before she could struggle, his lips covered hers. His fingers began the slowest of seductive circlings in her hair, the warmth of their touch flowing into the back of her neck.

She made a small sobbing sound. Dear heaven, perhaps if she had not drunk so much wine she would be braver, more able to resist. "You're pulling my hair," she managed to murmur.

"Forgive me." He had unraveled her braids. The shining, black mass spilled over her shoulders.

"Ah, Constance," he whispered. "You have put a spell on me. What is this magic? Why can't I get my fill?" He dug his face and mouth into her shoulder, his arms embracing her fiercely. "Look at me. Say you want me."

Her eyes met his.

His arms tightened. "Say it for me."

"I want you," she whispered . . .

Books By Maggie Davis

Writing as Maggie Davis:
EAGLES
ROMMEL'S GOLD
THE SHEIK
THE FAR SIDE OF HOME
THE WINTER SERPENT
FORBIDDEN OBJECTS
SATIN DOLL
SATIN DREAMS
WILD MIDNIGHT
MIAMI MIDNIGHT
HUSTLE, SWEET LOVE
DIAMONDS AND PEARLS
TROPIC OF LOVE
DREAMBOAT

Writing as Katherine Deauxville:
THE AMETHYST CROWN
DAGGERS OF GOLD
BLOOD RED ROSES

Writing as Maggie Daniels:
A CHRISTMAS ROMANCE
MOONLIGHT AND MISTLETOE

KATHERINE DEAUXVILLE

THE AMETHYST CROWN

ZEBRA BOOKS
KENSINGTON PUBLISHING CORP.

To my editor, Ann LaFarge,
with my greatest thanks for everything.

ZEBRA BOOKS are published by

Kensington Publishing Corp.
475 Park Avenue South
New York, NY 10016

Second Printing: March, 1994

Printed in the United States of America

Prologue

The lead horseman broke into a clearing where beams of sunlight splayed through a canopy of oak leaves. Very deliberately, so that Constance could see, he put his mailed hand on her daughter's leg, bared where Hodierne's dress hiked up as she rode before him.

Constance trembled as the cold hand of terror gripped her. The gesture was a warning of what the knight could do to her child if she, Constance, did not submit. A threat well-calculated to freeze any mother's heart.

He could snap her child's neck between his hands. Or, God help her, he could do even worse.

The knight held her mare's reins, and Constance fought to wrench them free, her arm around her baby, Beatriz. They were on her land; they must be mad, whoever they were, to think they could do this! They would never get past the village.

At the bridge, she saw a figure coming toward

them in the harsh sunshine, a tall man with bright hair in shabby clothes. And fancy boots.

At that moment Constance's face, her body, her thoughts were frozen. Then, just as she would have shrieked to warn Cenred, he saw them.

The troop of white-clad knights never faltered. They bore down steadily on the figure before them. Constance was sure they would kill him. She could see he knew what was happening.

She remembered screaming like a madwoman. He was defenseless, unarmed against a troop of knights. He didn't even have a sword. He was going to die—the brave, mad fool—sacrifice himself to save them! They would slaughter him where he stood!

The knight holding her mare jerked at the reins and her horse stumbled. Clutching Beatriz, Constance tried to keep from sliding from the saddle. When she looked up Cenred had run to one of the knights in the fore, reached up and dragged him from the saddle, knocked him to the ground, kicked him, and wrenched away his sword.

The column reined in. The little mare slammed into the horse in front of them. In her arms, Beatriz squalled hysterically.

Constance would have screamed herself but her breath was coming in hard, hurting gasps. She wanted to close her eyes. She wanted to pray.

She watched as Cenred swung the sword, shouting in some strange tongue, wading into the horsemen. They began to slide, or fall, from their saddles. The strange knights lay in the muddy road in their glittering mail, and white tunics, facedown before him. Cenred struck them broadside with the sword, kicking and cursing, and they did not move. He strode to the biggest horseman and dragged Hodierne from his arms. The knight fell heavily onto the ground.

"You damned swine!" He was speaking German Saxon; she understood that much.

Holding a wailing Hodierne in his arms, Cenred took his booted foot and put it on the big knight's back and pushed him facedown into the muddy earth. He gave him a kick on the side of his plumed helmet for good measure.

Dazed, Constance walked her mare through the dismounted knights groveling in the road. She didn't understand any of this. Barehanded and weaponless, he had conquered an entire troop. Beatriz, her fingers jammed in her mouth, was still shaking and sobbing.

Constance reined in her horse and looked down at Cenred. He was as she always remembered him: his big body, his gilded hair, his blazing eyes, handsome as a god. The murderous rage that had gripped him was only just ebbing away. A moment before he would have killed them all.

He tried to put Hodierne on her feet but she clung to him, screaming. He lifted her back up.

"I was coming back to you," he said over her oldest child's howls. "I was coming back, Constance."

How princely, how courageous, what a soldier.
I can believe him in the line of gods.

The Aeneid, Virgil

One

There had been no rain since the first of August, which was Lammastide. The villeins at first said it was no great loss, as a dry spell was good for the corn harvest and the last crop of hay. But by September's Feast of the Archangels the dry weather had become a drought. At Morlaix village the pastures were cropped bare, the cattle already feeding on new haystacks.

Constance slowed her mare to a walk, looking at the ruined kitchen gardens with their stunted stalks of cabbages and leeks. This was her demesne; she was responsible for her people, and the drought boded ill for the winter.

The villagers came out of the low-roofed cots and nearby fields to see her and her household knights as they arrived with pennants fluttering. She was not yet notorious here, even though the Bishop of Chester preached that she was no better than the Whore of Babylon. There were even a few scattered cheers.

Under the hot silk of her veils Constance's

lips twitched. King Henry was still more powerful here than the Norman church. Besides, her Morlaix people knew the truth about her husbands. There was even a song about her. Something about her beauty, hair as black and soft as a summer's night, her eyes dark pools of love. One had to laugh at its silliness. Especially the refrain of, "Moon, moon, beautiful noble lady like the moon. So young, so fair, so faaaaar above us!"

She'd heard the thing only once, in Wroxeter at the wool fair, and thought it an abomination. Fortunately, none of the villagers at roadside were singing it.

Behind her the retinue of baggage wagons, mounted servants, and the knight escort raised a cloud of dust that stank of chamberpots and the village ditch. She could hardly breathe. In the rear of the column her children wailed with discomfort and boredom.

Here in Morlaix the harvest had been short for the past two years, with famine and sickness in the spring. This time, Constance told herself, she must sit down with her steward and examine the tallies. Piers de Yerville, son of her father's old friend, was not proving the best of her knight *dapifers*.

The roadside cheers grew louder. Constance bowed graciously from the saddle. She seldom lived at Morlaix, preferring her more comfortable manor house at Bucksborough in the east country. But she was popular here, as her father had been.

At the market cross, wagons piled with wine-barrels for the castle blocked the road. The knight captain, Everard, urged his horse up, shouting for the crowd to give way. The drovers turned their mules to one side and Constance's mare clattered onto the planks of the bridge.

From the river, the woods fell away. In the distance Castle Morlaix stood with its back to the wall of Welsh mountains. On the meadows in between there had sprung up a virtual city of tents, guests for her sister's wedding.

To ease the knot of traffic, fifty of her knights bypassed the bridge and forded the river. Some stopped at its edge to water their horses. Her new confessor hesitated, then followed Constance on his donkey. She heard him mutter under his breath about their lateness.

Constance walked her mare behind merchants trundling a pushcart filled with sheep carcasses. She did not have to be reminded how late they were. By now Castle Morlaix was jammed to the walls with people who hated each other. Including her sister, Bertrada, who had wanted to be a nun, a bride of Christ, and not married to some mere mortal man. But she was to be married, a merciful God willing, before the day was over.

She watched her new confessor saw at the donkey's reins. Father Bertrand did not ride well. At St. Botolph's Abbey someone had told her he was a merchant's son, more accustomed to walking than riding. Still, she thought, he was not bad looking for a priest, and near her own age, which was two years over twenty. And he was yet another confessor, because the last two hadn't suited.

This one might not suit, either, she thought, watching him. All her confessors came to be obsessed with her notoriety, over-eager to reward her with penances. As a result, it had been a long time since Constance had told her confessors much of anything.

The castle road ascended the slope, cutting through the bright-colored tents. A burst of autumn wind, following the course of the river, shook the trees. Everard and the jingling column of knights rode at a trot, clearing the way. Constance thought of her father, the late earl. Gilbert would be amazed, if he were alive, to see an encampment as big as a town in the castle meadow. From their banners she recognized several earls and a smattering of west country nobility including the groom's family, the de Clintons.

Oh, Papa, she suddenly found herself thinking, *for better or ill, after today we have all been married off.*

At the top of the road the drawbridge spanned the castle ditch and under the lifted portcullis stood the castle steward, Piers de Yerville, with his bailiff and reeves. On the wall walk above them, trumpeters scampered to take their places.

She kneed her horse into a trot. Behind, her fretful children were screaming. She brushed at her filthy gown, thinking of a quiet room, a bowl of hot water to wash, a moment's rest. She wondered where her steward had put Bertrada and the nuns who had brought her sister from the convent. The Old Tower, probably. There was a good room there, away from the rest.

Banner carriers hurried into place on the walls beside the trumpeters. Constance held her mare to her gait. She was tired, and wanted to ride into the ward without stopping.

The knight Everard trotted his big horse up beside her. He touched his thumb to his helm. Constance threw back her veils to look up at him.

Everard had been in her service seven years, a lean and sinewy Gascon with black eyes that glittered behind helmet and long nasal. People called him her watchdog. But not to his face.

He put one hand on his thigh and leaned down. "Milady, the villagers say your other sister, the lady Mabele, came to Castle Morlaix yestereen with her husband. And the husband's family."

She stared at him. Her sister Mabele had been invited but not really expected. The de Warrennes hated Everard. They would kill him if they could.

Would kill me as well, she reminded herself.

There was no sign of the de Warrenne standard among the tents. She saw a flag for the bridegroom's family—the de Clintons, used a running bear as their device. The purple flags denoted the Abbot of St. Botolph's.

A crowd lined the road. Constance lifted her hand to wave. Behind, her daughters were squalling at the top of their lungs. She said to Everard, "Holy Mother, send a knight back to see what those cursed women are doing to my children."

He wheeled his destrier and cantered off as they passed under the banners of the king's royal envoy to the wedding. A figure came to roadside, shrugging into a knight's padded coat, and the crowd parted to let him through. She recognized Robert fitzGilbert, the royal treasurer's son; she'd met him in London the year before, when she was newly widowed.

She drew the veils back over her face. Last year in London young fitzGilbert had wanted to woo her, but by that time she'd petitioned King Henry not to have to marry for three years. Another heiress widow, the Countess of Warwick, had pleaded first. Surprisingly, Henry had granted them both.

FitzGilbert's hunting dogs ran underfoot, making the horses shy. The welcoming fanfare for the liege lady of Morlaix blatted from the castle walls. Everard, holding her daughter Hodierne in front of him, trotted his horse up to the front of the column. She had only a glimpse of Hodierne's triumphant, tearstained face and then they were on the drawbridge, the horses' hooves loud on the wood. A fresh blast from the trumpets made the horses rear. The knights cursed.

Piers de Yerville waited for them under the arch, solemn as a priest in a black tunic. She didn't want to talk to him, didn't want to hear complaints about how late they were. Two days. And her own sister's wedding.

Behind de Yerville she saw several young men she recognized as the groom's brothers. They stepped forward to greet her. Constance kept the mare at a trot, not stopping. Their faces fell.

The Prior of St. Aidan's in the village came alongside her horse and seized her stirrup. His words were drowned by another blast of trumpets.

The old prior held onto her stirrup. Father Maelchlan had not been well; his skin was grey. In the noise, his mouth moved to tell her something. A group of children came forward with flowers. She leaned down from the saddle to take them. Castle women in aprons hurried toward them through the crowds. The prior was saying something about prisoners he had brought to the castle, that St. Aidan's Priory could not send them to the bishop's courts in Chester.

She promised to see to it. She dismounted in front of the stables, so stiff with travel that she had to catch the old prior's arm. Some of the women pushed through the knights and dropped to their knees, wanting to kiss her hand. She waved them to their feet. Last year she had sent grain to the castle when they were in a winter famine.

"Witchcraft," the old prior was saying in her ear. "The woman is charged with witchcraft and worshiping the old pagan gods. As for the man, you must see for yourself."

Constance followed his eyes. There was a wagon by the kitchen house door and she could make out a very tall man with bright, fair hair sitting in it. She did not see a woman.

A nursemaid came up carrying Beatriz. Hodierne squirmed through to take her mother's hand. At her elbow Piers de Yerville was complaining that important guests had asked why she had been delayed, and that it had been hard to make excuses.

Constance handed Hodierne over to the nursemaids. "At the ferry the drought had dropped the river so low the boat could hardly pass."

She wanted to say more—that it had been too dangerous to cross until Everard ordered his knights to swim out and stand ready to pull the ferryboat off the sandbars, but she could see they were only interested in their complaints. She rubbed her face tiredly. She could taste the village dust on her lips.

A page appeared with a silver cup. Constance reached for it and drank the sweetened wine, thirstily. Beyond the crowd a group of women were trying to catch her eye, jerking their heads toward the Old Tower.

She handed back the cup. Everard dismissed the knights. Her confessor, Father Bertrand, hesitated, then followed the knights to the kitchen. The castle women pushed Constance through the crowds in the ward, Everard stalking in front. The nursemaids trailed with the children, waiting to be told what to do.

At the tower door the guard knight didn't recognize Constance in her dirty clothes and tried to stop her. The other saw Everard and dropped to one knee. "Milady," he exclaimed hastily.

She stepped around him, motioning to Everard to stay below. She could hear screams in the tower stairwell. In the nursemaid's arms, Beatriz began to cry.

Constance ran up the tower stairs. One of the kitchen maids leaped ahead to open the door.

The room at the top had once held hostages. Before that it had been the apartment of the castle's lord and lady. The big wooden bed had an embroidered spread, and furs were heaped on the rush-covered floor. The room reeked of vomit. A tin tub for a bath was turned over on its side. A girl with long disheveled hair stood in the middle of the room, clad only in a light undershift which showed the points of her young breasts and budded nipples, the delicate shadow of hair in her crotch. A handful of nuns in black habits stood against the wall, some weeping.

Constance's sister Bertrada held a small dagger to her breastbone. In the other hand she waved a silver crucifix. "I will kill myself rather than marry!" she screamed. She appealed to the nuns. "By the Holy Virgin, do not let them take me!"

She fell to her knees, both knife and cross at

her breast. "I am sworn to be the bride of Your Son, Jesus Christ, in a holy order of women devoted to His perpetual glory!"

Constance stepped into the muck of rushes and bathwater. "You are not going to be Christ's bride." She had to raise her voice; Hodierne and Beatriz were howling in sympathy. "King Henry has chosen your bridegroom," she told her sister. "He is waiting below."

"Constance." Bertrada's eyes slid past her. "God has not made me a whore for King Henry, like you," she said sullenly. "Why do you speak to me at all—my sister who is given like a common thing to those men the king must reward."

Constance leaned over her and pried the knife from her hand, resisting the temptation to slap her. Bertrada's eyes rolled, then with a gasp she hurled herself onto her face and began sobbing.

Constance gestured to the nursemaids to carry the children out. Someone came to the door. One of the kitchen women called, "A knight is here with a message about the Lady Bertrada."

Holy Mother, Constance realized, it could only be the de Clintons, wanting to begin the customary viewing of their son's bride.

Constance looked down at the milky skin of her sister's back, the rounded knobs of her spine showing through the thin shift. She had seen the bridegroom—he was young and rather nice-looking. She'd been told he'd ridden past her sister's convent several times, hoping for a glimpse of her, so one could say he was not indifferent. Also, his family looked upon the marriage as a stroke of good fortune. The father was a revenuer whom King Henry boasted he'd "raised from the dust," common-born, but capable and ambitious. Sheriff de Clinton would settle two manors on the couple and a dozen knights' fees. For her dower Bertrada had some Welsh marcher lands and property in Putanges in Normandy, awarded to their father, Gilbert de Jobourg, for service in arms to the king.

Constance's knees would not sustain her any longer. She sat down on the bed. "Take the nuns to the ward," she told the women, "and give them beer and food." She told the nursemaids to go to the manor house in the bailey, find Sir Everard and see that the children were put to bed. Hodierne and Beatriz were as worn and dirty as she, and Constance was tired of their howling. "I will come as soon as I can," she promised.

Wincing, she lifted her feet onto the bed as the kitchen women herded the nuns to the door. Bertrada remained on the floor, sobbing. The women righted the tub and went to fetch more hot water. Watching her sister, Constance tried to remember what it was like to marry someone you'd never seen.

Three times, she thought. She'd had three husbands by King Henry's order. Except for the middle one, Odo Waiteville, she couldn't say it had been all bad. And Bertrada, in spite of her whining, was much too pretty for a life in the convent. In that, she supposed King Henry knew what he was about.

Besides, she thought wearily, what could they, the heiresses of Morlaix, do about it? The king used them to reward his barons, his knights, even appease his enemies. She had been married three times since she was fourteen, and widowed three times. Each time she'd wed, the groom had become rich and powerful with the wealth his bride brought him, and did not even have to be pleased with her. Although she supposed, from what they'd said, some of them were.

Her sister had a very tidy parcel of dower lands, her portion of their mother's jewels, and a fortune of two hundred silver marks.

Constance sighed. With that, her fifteen-year-old sister had no chance whatsoever of becoming a nun.

Two

The tub had been filled again and two maids were trying to force the screaming Bertrada into it.

Constance hiked herself up on the bed, against the cushions. A castle page brought her another cup of wine. After a few gulps she remembered she'd had nothing to eat since breaking her fast at the ferry. She set the cup down on the floor.

She watched as the women held her sobbing sister down in the bath. Bertrada had been at St. Omer's convent school for almost five years. Constance knew the abbess there would like nothing better than a Morlaix heiress, even a younger sister, to become a nun and enrich their coffers. All little girls played at being nuns at one time or another. Her youngest sister with her mopish ways was always the nun in their childhood games. Mabele, the middle sister, was the fair lady in need of rescuing. Constance, as the eldest, was always the knight who could do it.

Constance sighed. She would have to see her sister dressed and ready for the bridegroom's mother and father when they came. The de Clintons had agreed to limit the viewing to themselves and Constance, as Bertrada's nearest relation, out of respect for her sister's convent upbringing.

By mid-afternoon, God willing, Wulfstan de Clinton and Bertrada de Jobourg would be wed on the chapel porch before their assembled guests. The Bishop of Chester had come himself to do the marrying; it was his purple-clad knights who took up most of the space in the ward. Then there would be the feasting for the bride and groom in the great hall. Then the bedding.

She bit her lip, thinking she should speak to the sheriff about the groom's brothers. They looked ready for a rowdy rush from the hall with the newlywed couple held aloft and bounced about to cheers and shouts, followed by the usual more-or-less public disrobing.

On her own wedding night, Constance had been carried up from her feast by a drunken crowd of both men and women and thrown on the marriage bed. Her bridegroom, a knight three times her age, had landed on top of her. She'd begun her wedding night, a maid of only fourteen, with bruised ribs and a wrist that ached relentlessly. For Bertrada, she had to see if a gentler handling than that could be had.

She watched the women holding her sister in the tub. Once in bed it was the bridegroom's business to make her happy and content. It was the only thing they could hope for.

At that moment her sister jumped from the tub, slipped through the women's grabbing hands, and snatched the silver crucifix from the table. Naked and dripping, she charged the bed.

"Save me, I implore you! I pray you, Constance, save me!" She fell to her knees. "I cannot give my pure body that belongs only to God to him, no matter what you do! He will rape me! You must save me! Oh, blessed Jesus." She turned to appeal to the women. "Will no one among you help me remain pure?"

Constance could guess what the nuns had told her. "Get back in the tub, you are drenching me. You know I cannot save you from the king's order. God's wounds, three times I could not save myself!"

Bertrada stared at her, wild-eyed. Constance brushed her wet dress with both hands. "Come," she said more gently, "I was wed when I was fourteen and my husband was forty-two. He treated me like the child I was, gently and with kindness."

What she did not say was that Baldric de Cressy had a mistress in his train when he arrived at Morlaix, a leman he brought with him and later kept in a house in the village. Once Constance had ridden down just to see her, a big, sun-browned woman with bold eyes, a serf's daughter, in the yard tending a garden. She had thought of de Cressy, a big man, and his strapping leman in bed like two huge beasts, snorting and straining at each other.

Nine months later Constance had given birth to a daughter, Hodierne, to de Cressy's vast disappointment.

She studied her sister kneeling before her. Bertrada was long-legged, with pointed breasts and a small waist.

"Help me," Bertrada moaned. "I do not want him to touch me."

Constance stroked her sister's wet hair, pulling it back from her face. "Come, it is nothing. The bridegroom will do it all, anyway." She swung her legs over the bed.

Bertrada wiped her eyes. "You did not have to do it. You could have killed yourself."

"Hah! And then what would have become of us?" She went to the table and put down the empty wine cup. "Take my advice and just lie there and let him poke at you. Believe me, it is such a pleasure for men that they are transported, and pay you no mind."

Someone scratched at the door. A castle woman went to open it a crack. It was one of the St. Aidan's monks with a message about the prisoners.

Constance put her hand under her sister's chin and lifted it to look into her eyes. The holy church preached that one did not marry more than one time. To do so was a sin against God. Because she, Constance, was King Henry's ward and England's richest heiress, she had been married three times. This was not King Henry's sin, according to the Bishop of Chester, but her own. With a dispensation rarely granted to heiresses, the king had granted her boon—she was free for three years. But Bertrada, instead of taking holy vows, would be forced to wed with her de Clinton knight.

"Milady?" One of the maids touched her arm. "Do not be sad, all will turn out well for the girl."

She wished she could believe that. The other women pulled Bertrada to her feet and she watched them take her back to the tub. Her sister got into it and sat quietly crying while the maids washed her hair.

One of the maids came up to show the robe Bertrada was to wear for the viewing. It was silver-embroidered red English wool woven at Morlaix, so soft it billowed like silk. Constance held it up for Bertrada to see, but her sister kept her tear-swollen face turned away.

She shrugged. She told the women to take up the wet rushes and put down fresh ones, and went down the stairs and out into the bailey.

The inner courtyard still teemed with people, even though most of the highborn guests had retired to the hall for midday meal. She knew she should be there, too, but she couldn't go in her filthy gown, her hair a dusty rat's nest. She started across the ward. Prior Maelchlan was waiting for her just beyond the steps, a young monk supporting him. "I inconvenience you, countess." She saw again how ill he looked.

She murmured something. Without the young lay brother, old Maelchlan looked too frail to stand. A page came up, marvelously dressed in a tabard of rose satin. In a piping voice the child told them that the king's sheriff and his wife awaited the Lady Constance in the knights' barracks with their son, Sir Wulfstan de Clinton, for such time as it would please the countess to join them. He bowed.

Constance and the prior looked at each other. The old man hid a smile. The de Clintons would have the whole world know the way they celebrated their riches.

"Come with me." She took the prior's arm. "I need another to witness."

He grimaced, but nodded. As they walked he explained to her that St. Aidan's had received two prisoners, a witch woman accused of practicing the old pagan religion, the other a renegade jongleur or troubadour, who had caused so much trouble that the Welsh prince, Daffyd ap Gwyllim, had thrown him in prison.

They skirted a group of archers at the ale butts. "A jongleur? What has he done?" Constance asked.

"What has he *not* done! They call him 'devil singer.' It took the men of two Welsh towns to chase him down and capture him for singing blasphemies and other nonsense. For a wandering singer, he fights like a Crusader. He was then thrown in the prince's dungeons to await judgment but raised a riot among the other prisoners with his songs and his wicked, subverting tales. And when the guards sought to beat him into submission, he only shouted defiance."

He stopped to rest for a moment. The lay brother bent to him, solicitous, but the prior waved him away.

"The prince sent him to Abbot Rhys at the monastery of Rhydich," he went on, "as the man is attractive and winning in his ways, and no one wishes to punish a troubador, most of all not among the Welsh, who prize them so. But it was not long before the monks cast him out, saying he corrupted the brothers. They complained of him again to Prince Daffyd ap Gwyllim, who washed his hands of the matter. The prince now wants no part of him."

They were in front of the barracks. The sheriff, a tall man in green velvet, waited with his wife, who wore rose satin like her page. The de Clintons stared at Constance as though they could not recognize her, dirty as a serf.

"The minstrel is mad," the prior was saying. "Even bound hand and foot he recites and sings that which is not fit for Christian ears. Your knight captain moved the prisoners' wagon behind the dog pens, and the woman, too."

Constance pushed back her hair where it had escaped from her coif. Coming forward, the sheriff remarked on her delays. Constance presented the prior. The sheriff's wife snatched at the old man's hand to kiss his ring, but he hastily pulled it away. St. Aidan's was an order of strictest poverty; its priors wore no rings.

They went up to the barracks, the prior trailing them on the stairs. The second floor of the keep was the knights' living quarters with the armory above. The room was dark as a barn, the only light falling through arrow slits in the walls.

Wulfstan de Clinton sat on the nearest bed, clad only in his hose. His brown hair was sunstreaked, his face sturdy, his shoulders and arms well-muscled. His brothers stood around him. As Constance came in they suddenly fell silent.

Wulfstan quickly put his cup of ale on the floor and stood up.

"Milady," the bridegroom said. He abruptly dropped to one knee and bent his head.

Constance hadn't expected that, even though it was her due as an earl's daughter. She touched Wulfstan on the shoulder. Under her fingers he was solid, his bare skin warm and smooth. She felt his body quiver. He was only several years older than she, twenty-six to her twenty-two.

The bridegroom got to his feet. Boisterous, the brothers rushed to pull off his boots. The sheriff's wife chattered loudly with the prior about altarcloths for her village church. The big sheriff stared into space. The brothers almost took the groom off his feet in their rush to yank off his chauses.

Constance told herself she couldn't laugh.

Once she got started she wasn't sure she could stop. The brothers stumbled into each other as they shook the bridegroom out of his hose. Wulfstan turned and faced them. He kept his eyes fixed on a point on the barracks' far wall, his cheeks faintly ruddy. She found she liked him more and more.

Wulfstan de Clinton was well-made, not so tall as some of his brothers but graceful. He had smooth skin, a few respectable scars. The de Clinton sons had trained as knights; Wulfstan de Clinton had fought in King Henry's campaigns against the French king. Between his legs was a healthy mat of dark hair from which projected his shaft, rather embarrassingly half-erect, a blunt weapon with foreskin slightly back so that the tip emerged.

At least he wasn't ugly there, Constance thought. But he was big, and would be more so when fully aroused. Fate was not making this easy.

The brothers were staring openly at her. The sheriff was studying his son. The lay brother looked doggedly at his feet. The sheriff's wife explained to old Maelchlan the superiority of Yorkshire embroidery when used in church altarcloths.

Wulfstan turned to present his back. More scars. When he turned again, he looked at Constance and smiled, rueful.

"My sister needs wooing," she said to him, low enough so the others could not hear.

"Milady." For a moment she thought he was

going to drop to one knee again. He said fervently, "I swear I will make her love me."

He has a passion for her, she thought, surprised. God knows how—he had only seen Bertrada from the convent road, if then. Or over the convent wall if he'd been bold enough to climb and look. She thought of Bertrada with her brown curling hair, her narrow waist and long legs. If he took time and was gentle, perhaps a miracle would happen.

"God willing," she said. Beside her the sheriff's hand rose as if to clap her heartily on the shoulder but stopped, thinking better of it.

He cleared his throat. "Then there remains only the viewing of the ah, fair and lovely bride."

Maelchlan lifted his head, smiling. The lay brother looked longingly at the door. Constance reckoned the time. By now the servants had dressed Bertrada, cleaned the floor, straightened the tower room. She thought of the red robe, and tried to fight off a new attack of worry that they would never marry, that Bertrada would bolt at the church porch.

She made herself say, "May God bless your future happiness." She lifted her muddy skirts and turned to lead the way. After her sister's viewing, if Bertrada did not threaten again to kill herself, she would at last go to her own room, her own maids, her clothes, her bath, her comforts. The prospect was so promising that she stumbled on the uneven stairs. The sheriff gave her his arm.

I will never last through this day, Constance thought. I am hungry and tired and dirtier than I deserve to be. *Countess Moon–so pale, so fair, so faaaar above us!*

She snorted. The sheriff gave her a startled look.

Constance made her face smooth again.

Across the ward a figure sat up in the prisoners' wagon and looked over the side. She watched the sheriff of Doncaster and his party step into the crowded ward. Llwydd of Aberdaron poked the form stretched out on the slats beside her.

"Lift your head," the witch-woman whispered. The garrison knights were turned away from the wagon, watching a dancing bear in a leather muzzle and pointed red cap. "You wanted to see the liege lord here," Llwydd hissed. "Well, lift up your head and see, if you can. That's her, coming out of the keep."

There was no answer for a moment. The big man lay on his back, still numbed from the beating the knights had given him. Llwydd watched him as a soft, sibilant sound escaped his lips. He shook his head to clear it. The movement loosened a sheath of thick, pale yellow hair spattered with blood.

"You're a tough one, you are." Llwydd bent over to help him haul himself to one elbow. The wagon bed was lined with emptied grain sacks from the priory, and his dried blood made them stick to him. "Why did ye do that, curse them and fight them?" she scolded. "It's mad you are. Then that big one, the lady's watchdog, he would just as soon have ripped all the skin from ye."

The prisoner didn't answer. His eyes were badly bruised, nearly shut. He shook his head again and hoisted himself to the wagon side, one battered hand clenched on the slats. He put his face to the open space.

"Where?" he croaked.

The witch-woman looked around. The bear shuffled in a circle, waving its paws haplessly. The crowd and the guard yelled at it and threw coins.

"The lord," he insisted, hoarsely. "Where?"

Llwydd cast her eyes sidewise. "Shhhh. No lord but a lady," she muttered. Her eyes darted around the crowd. "The Countess of Morlaix. The tall, pretty lady in the green dress."

He pressed his face up against the slats, peering to see across the ward. "A countess."

Llwydd reached out and took him by the shoulder. She pulled him back down in the wagon again. He offered no resistance. He groaned. When she took her hand away from his shirt it was sticky with blood.

"Lie there and be still," she whispered. "Don't look at her, don't say nothing. If you do, they'll beat you again, maybe this time cut the tongue from your head."

He rolled over to lie on his back, his face

turned up to the bright sky. Surprisingly, he managed to laugh through his swollen lips.

"What will they do with you, Llwydd?" he rasped. "When they take you to trial in the bishop's court."

The witch-woman, her pale eyes rimmed with charcoal, looked away. "Do with me? Ah, these Roman priests—if they have their way I'll die soon enough."

"Look to yourself then." He closed his eyes. "Die here in the courtyard of a devil bitch's castle or die later—what does it matter?"

The bear had finished performing. The knights walked back to the wagon. Llwydd quickly sank back into the corner, head bent; and gripped her knees. The prisoner closed his eyes.

Three

"I recollect your father very well," the Bishop of Chester said. A server knelt by the bishop holding up a platter of boiled beef and onions. "Had it not been for your father's support and that of the first earl, Fulk de Jobourg, your grandsire," he said, taking up the spoon, "our blessed King Henry, may God shower him with everlasting wisdom and great fortune, could not have succeeded on his glorious and rightful path to the throne."

Constance knew why the bishop was suddenly reminded of her father. They were watching his bastard, Julien of Nesscliffe, make his way through the wedding feast and past a group of St. Botolph's knights who were holding a wrestling match in the aisle. Julien and his brother, Ivor, were the late earl's living ghosts, with their father's prominent nose and the telltale de Jobourg hair. Her father had had two fine bastard sons who could not inherit Morlaix. And three daughters, all legitimate, who could.

Heiresses that King Henry had married off—*was* marrying off—to his deserving subjects. Bertrada was the last.

The young server holding the platter of meat scrambled on his knees toward Constance, dislodging one of the bishop's hunting dogs asleep in the rushes. Snarling, the grey alaunt would have thrown himself on the boy except that the bishop handily caught him by the collar. In the uproar Constance ordered the boy to pass the beef down the table to the de Clintons. Below them Julien had stopped to talk to the king's envoy to Bertrada's wedding, Robert fitzGilbert.

Constance took a sip of her wine, watching them. More than twenty years ago the Clares had conspired with her father and other Welsh marcher nobles to put King Henry upon his throne, a thing that had certainly not worked to their disadvantage. A grateful prince had made Gilbert de Jobourg an earl. Now, under Henry, the Clares, as the fitzGilberts were commonly called, were enormously rich and all-powerful.

Looking at Julien it seemed that God had made him in the perfect image of Morlaix's rightful lord. Her father had provided reasonably well for his bastard sons; Julien had a manor and lands at Nesscliffe, east of Eccleshall, and seemed content.

A squire came up at Constance's side with a pitcher of wine. The boy fell unsteadily to his knees, then put his hand in the rushes to keep from falling over. Wine sloshed out of the ewer onto her skirt.

Exclaiming, Constance brushed at the stain with her fingers. Another server brought her a napkin but she waved them both away.

She looked around the room for de Yerville's ushers. No one could keep servers from drinking at wedding feasts, particularly the half-grown squires, but there was no reason to tolerate it at the high table.

The bishop put his hand over hers. "My Lady Constance." His cheeks were flushed and when he spoke he breathed fumes into her face. "God put King Henry's bravest subjects, like your own father, to support him in New Forest that fateful day."

Constance murmured something. The Bishop of Chester repeated old stories when drunk as though she'd never heard them before, especially how Gilbert de Jobourg and her grandfather earned Prince Henry's everlasting favor by conspiring to put him on England's throne.

She slid her hand out from under his under the pretense of straightening her coif. She'd dressed in haste for Bertrada's wedding ceremony. There'd only been time for a bowl of hot water for washing, and her dress was wrinkled from having been taken straight from the trunk. But she felt more like herself in a velvet gown with sleeves slashed to show the red silk beneath. A scarf of crimson silk was held in place by a gold circlet studded with amber. Her hair, looped and braided with gold beads, hung below the veil. She knew how she looked; the women at the nobles' tables had been studying her all during the meal. Coifs and veils were the new fashion in London. She was sure they'd memorized everything.

The front tables below them were filled with nobles and high-ranking churchmen. Behind the delegation from St. Botolph's were her two confessors, then a row of St. Aidan's monks in their order's ragged brown habits. The prior, Maelchlan, was not among them. The heat from so many bodies made the hall overwarm. There was a constant crush of people coming and going.

Beside Constance, the bishop droned on. Not even he could make pretty the true story of how Prince Henry had seized the throne on his brother's death in New Forest. Murder was not a word anyone now used, but William the Second had been shot through the breast by an arrow that day in August, and his companion, Walter Tirel, the Count of Pois, had fled back to France, claiming innocence. Three days later the king's youngest brother, Prince Henry, after having raced to seize the treasury at Winchester, crowned himself King of England.

Constance leaned forward to look down the table at her sister and the bridegroom. Bertrada and Wulfstan sat beyond the Earl of Chester, the sheriff and his wife on their far side. Minstrels had been coming up to the high table all evening to sing songs and recite poems dedicated to the groom's handsomeness and valor, the bride's incomparable beauty. Thankfully, the songs had not been vulgar. Constance had told Piers de Yerville to see to it.

After the minstrels, noble guests came to the high table to toast the married couple. Bertrada was not drinking. Nothing marred her pallor as she sat beside the groom.

Watching them, Constance was hard put to know what her sister was thinking. Wulfstan lounged back on the bench, talking over his shoulder to one of his brothers.

They are married, she told herself for the thousandth time. A small voice nagged that things could still go wrong. Everyone knew the story of young Desmond fitzWalter who, on his wedding night, preached to his young wife with such fervor about denying the world and living only in the spirit of God that he convinced her to join him in holy orders before dawn broke. On the first day of their marriage he went to a monastery, she to a convent.

They were still there.

Constance took a deep breath. *God's name, what would any one of them do if Bertrada wheedled the sheriff's son into something like that?*

With a trembling hand Constance lifted the wine cup, knowing she was torturing herself.

The ushers moved the trestles back to make room for dancing. People screamed at each other over the din.

Constance gazed out over the crowd. The walls of the feast hall were lined with Everard's knights. Mabele and the de Warrennes were halfway down the hall, a handful of black-browed men with her sister in their midst. The de Warrennes were not as powerful in England as they were in Normandy. Constance longed to talk to her middle sister. She'd never wanted Mabele to marry into the family; they had a reputation for abusing their women. But the marriage had been part of the king's plans to strengthen ties to his Norman allies, and brought the de Warrennes some much-wanted dower lands in Aumale. She still hadn't been able to forget what Mabele had looked like at Michaelmas. Hubert de Warrenne had beaten her enough almost to cripple her. Now Mabele was carrying his child. None of it made any sense. Hubert de Warrenne turned, and Constance looked quickly away.

She saw her half-brother Julien approach the high table. He was wearing a knight's short coat of blue silk that made his hair look even redder. He bowed to the sheriff and his wife, then leaned over the table to kiss the bride. Bertrada looked up at him.

Julien's eyes met the groom's across the table. They gingerly clasped hands, barely touching. Julien said something to the bridegroom, then started down the table. Wulfstan de Clinton stared after him. Julien spoke cordially to the Earl of Chester, then to the bishop.

Constance sat back down again. Holy Mother, she was a bundle of nerves. It had never occurred to her that they wouldn't like each other. She let out her breath when Julien stepped in front of her. He bent to kiss her cheek. "A fine lot of parvenus," he whispered in her ear.

"Shhhh." She looked around. "I believe de Clinton will have a care for her."

He snorted. "Care is not what he needs tonight." He leaned one elbow and picked up her wine and sipped it. "Is my sister resigned to her fate?"

She had seen Julien at the back of the crowd at the marriage ceremony. She could not resist another look down the table at Bertrada's bent head. She said, "Yes, well enough."

Julien referred to the viewing of the bride that had finally taken place. The red robe had been whisked off; Constance had taken her sister's hand to turn her so that the de Clintons could see the unblemished state of Bertrada's body. Then the robe had been flung back on. The sheriff had been stiff-faced, but he looked. The sheriff's wife had heard of Bertrada's lifelong wish to be a nun, and pulled a long face.

A knight came up and threw his arm over Julien's shoulder. He would have pulled him away, but Julien held back. "Rest easy, dear Constance." She saw he'd been drinking; he swayed as he talked. "Know that my sister thinks herself a holy sacrifice to the marriage bed."

Constance looked down the table. She knew the bishop had overheard. He swiveled on the bench to look at them.

"De Clinton will have a suffering saint in his arms for the rest of his life." Julien put her empty cup back on the table with a bang. In spite of her warning stare he winked. "God's wounds, we cannot all be as sworn to our duty as you, bedding every noble lackey that King Henry is pleased to send."

"Julien, go away," she said.

He threw back his red head and laughed. "Bold de Clinton will doubtless storm the walls and breach them. Who knows, if he is passing skillful, he may be for pious Bertie the Second Coming."

The knight pulled him away, shushing him. But his words rankled. She knew they all thought her cold and unfeeling, sworn to be dutiful. But she hadn't been so faithful in her duty to King Henry when she went to her marriage bed at fourteen, only terrified. It had been King Henry's knights who stormed the high table to carry off the bride and groom, his knights who staggered up the tower stairs with de Cressy, tearing at his clothes, followed by a howling crowd of court ladies who did the same for Constance.

She looked around. The bishop and the Earl of Chester were deep in talk. The noise in the hall was deafening.

At her second marriage there had been no viewing. At thirty-five, Odo de Waiteville had been younger than her first husband, but no faithful knight commander that the king wished to reward. On the contrary, Morlaix's heiress was a prize awarded an enemy: de Waiteville had been an Angevin lord wanting some settlement in one of Henry's wars in the Vexin.

She had been seventeen then, a young widow, already a mother. The king had given them a large wedding at Winchester. She couldn't believe, even now, that Henry did not know what happened to young women in Count Odo de Waiteville's bed.

A blare of noise made them all start. Bagpipers made their way into the space cleared for dancing. Everard's knights moved slightly away from the walls. At that moment women burst shrieking from the back of the hall, their arms full of dried flowers and sheaves of grain.

Constance came to her feet. She saw Wulfstan de Clinton rise and pull Bertrada up from the bench, his brothers closing around them. They started toward the back of the hall. The tables of nobles below joined the yelling. The castle women with flowers and sheaves had reached the high table. Some knights thundered toward the back after the bride and groom. At the rear door a de Clinton brother made a stand with sword in hand to hold them off.

Constance backed away from the table as Everard appeared at her side.

She looked at the feasters streaming past, picked up her cloak and let the surge of the crowd carry her under the torn and dangling arras at the table's back. With Everard holding her arm they went through the rear door and into the ward.

The castle people greeted the mob with a roar. The air was filled with the smoke of roasting meat. Everyone seemed drunk. As the wedding party rushed past the ale tuns and roasting spits were overturned. Barking dogs added to the din. Constance followed Everard, who made a way for her, shoving and shouting. The bride and groom had reached the Old Tower. They wrenched open the door, and disappeared inside.

A wedge of Everard's knights and the de Clintons threw up a guard. The wedding mob hurled itself against them, jeering and showering them with beer and food. Women threw the flowered wreaths and grain sheaves at the knights, who threw them back.

Constance sat down on the wheel of a wagon, her arms and legs trembling. The sun was just setting over the battlements of the keep. The air was frosty but some last rays of warmth touched her face. She was reminded that in a short while it would be the October's end. All Hallow's Even. She felt exhausted.

She looked at Everard. "Did you know he would do that?"

He bent to her. "Yes, de Clinton talked to his brothers. We heard them."

It was very clever of the bridegroom to pick that moment to escape, with the aid of his brothers. Constance suddenly felt better. Perhaps Bertrada would never convince someone as daring as Wulfstan de Clinton to take holy orders. Or deny him her body. She'd been foolish to make herself nearly sick with worry.

She got up and gathered her cloak about her and walked toward the feast hall. Everard strode in front. Two figures rose from a bench: the young St. Aidan's monk, supporting old Maelchlan. "Countess," the young brother said.

She had almost forgotten the prior's prisoners. She looked over her shoulder. Everard's knights were in place in front of the Old Tower. The Morlaix constable had called up his men-at-arms, who were now running to stand beside them. The de Clinton brothers, swords still drawn, were talking among themselves and laughing. A light appeared at the grilled window above. The bridal chamber. The crowd cheered.

"It will be but a moment," the old man said.

She managed a smile. In the gathering dusk the young monk and Maelchlan led the way across the ward to the priory wagons.

Llwydd the witch-woman peeped through the wagon's slatted sides. She'd been watching the ward even though they could not see it well where they were. One of the guard knights had thought to bring the prisoners a piece of mutton, and she was hoping for more. Perhaps a bit of the ale.

After a crowd had rushed from the feast hall the bride and groom had gone to their marriage chamber. The close-packed mob in the ward was rowdier now that the nobles had come out. The ale barrels were put back on their trestles. Those who had been at the feast stayed to drink with the common folk. The bagpipers marched out into the ward. The air was brisk, as the sun was going down.

When she shifted her eye at the slot Llwydd saw the countess's mail-clad knight captain coming toward the priory's wagons, escorting two monks. The castle's lady came behind him.

Alarmed, Llwydd poked the man lying beside her. "Ah, look, summat's happened. Rouse yourself!"

The big man lay staring up into the sunset sky and did not answer. The knights guarding the wagon walked up and looked over the sides. "Get up," one of them said. "Get to your feet."

The big man did not move.

Four

It had been a long time, the prior was saying as they made their way through the ward, since the Irish chapter house in the Morlaix valley had held ecclesiastical court. Perhaps not since the days of the countess's sainted grandmother, Lady Alwyn, who had encouraged and supported St. Aidan's founder, the great philosopher Bran of Dunlaith.

However, the prior pointed out, this was not due to any unwillingess to try offenders such as heretics and blasphemers under church law, but the jealousy of the great Abbey of St. Botolph's in the Bishop of Chester's see. The Norman bishops wanted only Norman monks and priests in England, and the supremacy of Norman monasteries. They would drive out the Irish monks in Morlaix as they had the English monks and their houses.

"So we have been prudent and modest," the old man explained, "and have not tried a case in church court for many years."

Listening to Maelchlan, Constance was seeing again the gorgeously dressed Abbot of St. Botolph's and his companions at the wedding feast. And at the table behind them, the Irish monks in their ragged brown habits dictated by their vows of poverty. One could see why there was discord over more than just the Norman's desire to gobble up everything, although Norman greed was notorious. And it did not help matters that St. Aidan's was well endowed; both St. Botolph's and the Bishop of Chester would like nothing more than to have a foothold in her demesne.

"The chapter has agreed we cannot hold the prisoners," the prior was saying. "Remember, we did not seek out these people, they were brought to us. They are in our care now, until we can dispose of them. The woman is charged with traveling about the countryside urging the herders and the lowborn peoples of the Welsh to follow the old gods. The local priest sees it as devil worship."

"Devil worship?"

"The priest at Rhynbach had the villagers bring her. The charges of witchcraft are his, not ours."

The young monk who was supporting Maelchlan murmured something. He nodded. "Yes, the woman is a Celt, as are we all at Saint Aidan's, the same blood, nearly the same speech. So it does not serve us well that when the witch talks of the spells of Lugh and Morrigan that our brothers are well aware of what she is saying, many having heard their own grandmothers in Eire, may God save their souls, raise incantations to the same."

"Is the witch-woman innocent?" Constance asked.

The old prior gave her a strange look. "Innocent or guilty, it does not matter. We cannot try her here."

She sighed. "What is it you wish me to do?"

"Come." The old man tugged at her hand.

They made their way to the priory wagons near the kitchen. A black-haired woman sat in one with a shawl pulled over her head. When she looked up they saw she had startling charcoal-rimmed eyes in a white face. Not young, but still comely.

So this was a witch. Constance didn't know what she'd expected.

The knights sprang to attention. Everard said something. One reached into the wagon and pulled at a rope. "Get up, you crazy bastard," he ordered.

The man who had been lying on his back in the wagon bed lurched to his knees. He held onto the rope around his neck with both hands.

Although he was chained hand and foot, with the choke rope about his neck, Constance and the prior stepped back. One could not help it; some raw force leaped out at them as he got to his feet.

The prisoner was a big man, powerful of body, so beaten that his face was purple with bruises. His velvet shirt had been all but torn away; it hung in dirty rags from one arm. Blood streaked his bare chest and matted in his long, fair hair.

For a moment Constance could only stare.

The young monk said, "The villeins say he is a jongleur, a devil singer who tempts them with words and vile tales and lures them to sin. In one village he was stoned. In another he caused a riot."

She could well believe it. As they watched, the prisoner seemed to sniff the air, turning his head. The sheaf of wheat-colored hair, the golden gleam of his body, the remarkable battered face were astonishing. If there could be said to be a male perfect in face and form, this ragged, giant prisoner would be it.

"Milady, have a care," Everard said, stepping in front of her. "He is mad, just as Comel—"

At the sound of Everard's voice the prisoner lunged for him. Just as quickly, the others flung themselves on the rope and dragged it tight about his neck.

Even then they could not hold him. Roaring, he almost tore the chains from the bed of the wagon. As the noose tightened he reached out clawing hands toward Everard.

"The whip," the captain ordered.

A knight tossed it to him. Everard lifted the whip, the length snaking out on the grass, then brought it down over the jongleur's head and face. Streams of blood cut through his forehead, his cheeks, and dripped down his chin. Everard lashed him again. Still the big, fair-haired jongleur bellowed curses, straining to get Everard in his grasp. The two guards shouted to the captain to have a care.

"Mother of God." Constance stepped forward. They would beat him to death in their zeal. "Leave him," she said. "Stop beating him."

Her captain turned burning eyes to her. "Milady, we beat him before when we chained him, and he was like an animal in his defiance. He knows no stopping, this lunatic."

"Lunatic?"

The shouted word in French made them jump.

The jongleur grabbed the rope at his neck with both manacled hands. Prying it away, he fixed his blue glare on the prior, addressing him in a stream of unknown language.

It sounded like Latin to Constance. Latin had no meaning for her, but beside her the prior turned pale. So did the young monk.

"St. George save us!" The old man was flustered. "I have never heard such fluent Latin tongue. A marvel! And all *vile!*" he spluttered. "God preserve poor Christians from a mind and tongue like that. He is wicked—he speaks of evil, blasphemous things!"

"What did he say?"

"Ah, dear lady, you do not wish to hear it! He spared none of us. He—"

"You!" Dragging his manacles, the jongleur heaved himself against the wagon's side and fixed his bruised gaze on Constance. "Yes, *you,*" he panted in French, "King Henry's willing,

ever-ready widow. Not married yet, sweetheart? What's the delay? Has your precious cunt, jam-packed with wealth and treasures that all the noble Norman pricks pursue, cooled too much in this fine autumn weather?"

It took a moment to understand. Constance gasped. The two knights dove for him, but she flung out her arm.

"And he speaks perfect Latin?" That was what the prior had said.

Maelchlan pursed his lips. "Aye, you are gazing upon a new thing, these minstrels and wandering scholars. They come from the Paris schools and after learning Latin and Greek there go on to Aquitaine, where the land is overrun with them. They study more of the troubadour nonsense there. They are the new plague, they think themselves wonderful. But all are scandalous and provocative, and corrupting."

The big man leered at her with his swollen face. "Who will diddle you tonight, countess?" he rasped. "And storm your hot sweetness for what reward? A village? Your castle?

She frowned as she studied him. He was once well-dressed—the shirt had a band of gold embroidery, and he wore fine boots. The tight-fitting hose were ragged but made of good wool, sheathing his thighs and legs and displaying to good effect his crotch, where the bulge testified impressively to the fact that he was big in every way.

Perhaps he is a ruined monk, Constance

thought. No, not a monk; she thought of the prior and the young Irishman beside him, all her confessors. They did not look like that. A ruined knight?

Well, not many knights were learned. She had no knowledge of the other—the wandering singers and scholars from France. Whatever he was, it was a puzzle.

He had gone still, watching her. He looked down, grasping the chains that held him in the wagon. "Ah, lady," he said silkily, "if you let me into your soft bed tonight, could I—" He used a blistering obscenity. "And if I did that to you, would that win my release from your dung pig knight and the chains he put me in?" He whirled, his long hair whipping, to face the two monks. "And these churchly cretins who brought me here in the first place?"

Beside Constance, Everard shivered with rage. She quickly touched his arm.

The prior said, "If this jongleur is truly mad and has lost his wits, poor soul, we cannot give him to the bishop in Chester."

Her lips twitched. It was hard to feel Christian charity—the jongleur's scurvy mouth wouldn't let you. The bishop would surely burn him as a heretic.

Still, she thought, there was no need to kill a madman for being mad. She found herself staring at the bloodstained expanse of chest heaving with each breath. She stood close, but not so close that he could reach out and grab her. She was disturbed to find that when she looked at this man a strange feeling assailed her. A trembling excitement that was not all that pleasant.

Whatever it was, Constance swallowed it. Chin lifted, neck arched under tight-fitting coif and veil, she met his gaze. Up close his slits of cobalt eyes were flecked with yellow. No, gold specks. It fitted his gold hair and skin.

"Take the prisoners with you when you return to your manor at Bucksborough," the prior urged her. "There in the east country you may try both the jongleur and the witch in your own manor court."

Suddenly the jongleur threw back his head and began to sing. Not a wonderful voice, but fair. The tune was very stirring.

When she turned to the prior he rolled his eyes. "It is Saxon. I do not have much of that tongue—I am Irish. I would say, though, from what I know, that it is some song of battle."

The jongleur was truly mad. If he could get free she had no doubt he would attack Everard. Certainly it made no sense to shout vile things in scholarly Latin. And now he was singing some Saxon defiance. But Constance knew if she did not take the prisoners with her, the bishop and the Abbot of St. Botolph's would no doubt claim them.

The prior said, "Countess?"

She looked at the woman huddled in her rags at the other end. The madman had not bothered her, apparently. "Is he securely fastened in the wagon?"

The two knights exchanged glances. Everard said, "Countess, do not think to take this violent lackwit into your care. You have not heard even a little what his mouth spews forth in speech and singing, truly—"

"I will not be where I can listen to him." She looked up, knowing he was furious with her. "If he's not quiet you can put a gag in his mouth."

The prisoner abruptly stopped singing. "Bitch! You give orders to gag me?" His big hands reached out for her, futilely. "Listen, cut me loose and I will buck between your legs hard and long as none of the others have done. But Christ crucified, you have your black mongrel dog gag me and I will ram my cock where you—"

The guards jerked hard on the rope and the rest was a strangled sound. The jongleur's face turned to Constance.

"I'll make a song for you, Whore of Babylon," he croaked. "I swear to you, I'll kill your black-hearted bastard with his own damned whip. But you—you I will—"

The horrified prior pulled her away. "Countess, have your knights deal with him at all times. Do not subject yourself to this on the road east."

The jongleur was truly a lunatic, Constance had decided. A good mind, it would seem, gone bad. When they reached the east country she would see about sending him to some far-off monastery in Scotland. There was no need to punish anyone else with his insane temper.

As they walked away the jongleur shouted something and Constance heard the sound of a blow. She kept on going. The young monk helped the prior the few steps to the wagons where the brothers had hitched up the mules. The monks would return to St. Aidan's; it was already growing dark in the ward. Crowds milled around them. The wedding feast would go on all night.

Constance made her goodbyes. "I must go now and see if I can find my sister Mabele." The prior let her kiss him on the forehead. "I have not seen her for a long while and she is carrying a babe."

She did not know where to begin to find the de Warrennes, but she started across the ward, Everard following. She knew that he was angry that she was taking old Maelchlan's prisoners with them.

In the crowd around the ale barrels they found one of the Welsh chiefs, Maredudd ap Givanwy, turned out for the wedding in all his furs and bones and gold jewelry. He grabbed Constance by the arm.

"Here there, girl," he boomed, "I see you flitting about with your nose in the air, taking care of one thing and another." He put his massive arms around her and kissed her. Maredudd, a prince in his own country, smelled of bear grease. "But not a buss nor a squeeze have you had for your father's old friend! Never forget, daughter of Gilbert de Jobourg, I dandled you on my knees when you were a babe."

He gave her a familiar slap on the rump and Everard stiffened.

Constance pried herself out of Maredudd's arms. "I look for my sister Mabele, with the de Warrennes. In all that had to be done here I fear I have not had a chance to see how she fares."

He squinted at her. "She fares well," he said in a different voice, "for all that one can tell. My wife Branwen had a word with young Mabele, but you'll not find her here now. The de Warrennes called their horses and knights and left not long after the bride and groom went to their nest."

Constance was dismayed that she hadn't been able to speak to Mabele. The de Warrennes hadn't wanted them to meet: They'd brought her sister to Morlaix and then whisked her away to show that Mabele, for better or ill, was theirs.

"I acted too hastily," she said. "There's no help for it—they will not let Mabele see me again. It's the de Warrennes' revenge."

"Nay, girl." The Welsh chieftain fingered his beard. "You did what your father would have done, God rest his soul. A woman has but one protection, her menfolk, to see that she is not done ill when she marries. Gilbert de Jobourg would not have stood for yon lass's mistreatment at the hands of such like. He would have defended the honor of his family." He looked over her head at Everard. "You did well when you found out that Hubert de Warrenne was serving the girl too roughly. You only gave him a touch of what he well-earned."

A touch? When Constance had seen Mabele after her beatings she, too, had only thought of what her father would do. She'd sent Everard with a troop of knights to find Mabele's husband hunting in the Ruabon forest. Everard was good at that sort of thing: his knights had held de Warrenne's kinsman at bay while Everard took him barehanded. Hubert de Warrenne was not permanently marked, but he'd had punishment enough for what he'd done to her sister to spend a sennight in bed.

"Don't fret, de Warrenne's more tender with her, now that she's carrying his babe," the Welshman rumbled. "Yours was a sound message, one that the husband understood well enough. The lass was not marked today, now was she? And seemed happy enough. Or so said she to my Branwen."

Constance would rather hear that from Mabele. They challenged me, she thought, as a mere woman to do what my father would have done. Old Maredudd, her father's friend, had said Hubert de Warrenne had well understood.

Perhaps he had, but she did not think he'd soon forgive. She was suddenly tired. She wanted to see her children, and knew they were probably asleep by now. She bade Maredudd good night and dismissed Everard by the door of the castle's manor house, telling him that it was cold and to see that the prisoners had a cover. He stood in the ward, staring after her.

The Morlaix manor was built against the curtain wall in the northeast corner of the bailey. It was a small house, and the downstairs room was filled with pallets that had been laid down for noble guests. It was early; only a few of the older women had rolled up in covers to sleep. Constance tiptoed to the back, but the elderly Baroness of Glendeagle sat up and called to her.

"I am just going up to my bedchamber," Constance whispered.

The old woman smiled. "It was a fine wedding. Your father would be proud of you."

"I was late. We should have come yesterday."

"No matter. You are quite the chatelaine, as your grandmother before you." The old baroness hitched the blankets around her. "Well, now you must marry again, to match your sisters. The bishop preaches against it, you know, women who don't have husbands. One is damned if one marries and damned if one does not."

Constance knew the church's views on the subject too well. "I have dispensation, my lady, from King Henry not to have to marry for three years, granted me this last Michaelmas. The same as he gave to the lady of Warwick."

The sharp old eyes looked skeptical. "Hah, even my village priest rails against your scandalous estate. But not loudly enough to reach the ears of the king." She reached up to clasp Constance's hand. "Listen, girl, run from trouble! Get King Henry to get you another husband quickly. They call you Countess Moon, do they not? It is a good name. You are fair like your grandmother—I remember her here at Morlaix. She would say the same thing to you, mark me. That a fine, pretty thing like you should be giving some good baron a houseful of heirs!"

Constance thanked the baroness, although she could not wait to get away from her chatter. She made her way among the pallets to the stairs. At the top a squire put there to see to the fire and keep them warm was asleep on the threshold. She stepped over him. More pallets had been put down beside her curtained bed for her servants; maids and the nursemaids were rolled in coverlets across the floor. One of them, a Saxon girl, lifted her head but Constance waved her back down. She did not want the women up and stirring just to undress her. She did not know how she had managed to keep going this long.

She leaned over the bed where her girls were curled together like kittens in the covers. The nursemaids had washed their hair. Beatriz's baby curls were a tangled mass, but Hodierne's flaxen mop had been neatly plaited. She never looked at her oldest daughter without seeing Baldric de Cressy. They both had the same long nose, same grave, faintly calculating look.

She smoothed back Beatriz's tangled, damp hair. To her second husband Odo Waiteville she had given nothing, which was only just: she would have hated any child of his. But to young

William of Hersey, she had presented Beatriz. Her baby. And William's great sorrow. She remembered how he had looked after being told his much-wanted heir was a girl.

Constance tucked the covers around her children's shoulders and began to unlace her gown.

There had always been something desperate about William. She'd been widowed twice, not a good omen for a new husband, and King Henry always used him in the perilous vanguard in his wars against the King of France. William had died in the spring in a battle with the rebellious lords of the Vexin. Beatriz was then only one month old.

She stepped out of the gown and placed it on a chest. The room was freezing; the fire had gone out. She thought of the squire, asleep on the threshold. No matter. In the morning, when they were all rested, she would put them to work on everything that needed to be cleaned or mended.

She took down her hair and shook it out, a long, silky, dark mass. She remembered what the old Countess of Glendeagle had said—that she looked like her grandmother. Black hair, pale skin, silvery eyes.

In her underdress, Constance went to the windows and threw open the shutters. The room smelled of the fireplace but the air outside was clean and cold. The manor house had full windows, unlike the rooms in the castle, which had only arrow slits. In spite of the cold she leaned her elbows on the sill.

The back of the manor house overlooked a grassy lawn and the curtain wall. A full hunter's moon, newly risen, rode low in the sky. By its light she could see dark figures, at least half a dozen, clutching each other in the shadows. A wedding brought out that sort of thing. Even at her third marriage it had been like this, drunken crowds and coupling among the castle folk in spite of the chamberlain's watchfulness. The villeins might drink and rut, but the babies born nine months after were always the subject of much argument—at least among the married.

She leaned out to let the cold night wind touch her face. Just down the castle wall in the old tower, Bertrada was being bedded by Wulfstan de Clinton. Even now, a touch of fear gripped her. She had given her promise to King Henry—she could do no more. She knew he would blame her if anything went awry.

It will go well, she tried to assure herself. Young de Clinton was no aging knight commander like Baldric de Cressy, bedding a terrified maid of fourteen. Nor cruel, like Odo de Waiteville. Nor some dour, newmade baron of Hersey desperately wanting an heir. Wulfstan de Clinton was handsome, engaging, beguiled—hadn't he ridden to the convent by all accounts, wanting a glimpse of Bertrada?

She couldn't shake her mood. *We are all sold like chattels, nevertheless.* She put the thought out of her mind. It was only the bright moonlight filling her full of fantasies. She could not bear to be at Castle Morlaix too long—it was filled with ghosts.

As long as he does not hurt her, she thought.

She had looked hard at de Clinton's sex at the viewing, and found him well-equipped, with a strong, sturdy shaft. She thought of narrow-hipped Bertrada, her vapors, her maidenly fervor for the cloister.

Perhaps Wulfstan de Clinton would be sensible, take his time. It had taken Baldric de Cressy nearly all night to penetrate her, Constance remembered, aided by gentle talk, and a dish of warm oil.

God's wounds, her thoughts were rambling and worse, filled with what men and women did to each other in bed. An act she'd found awkward, sometimes embarrassing, and that left one wondering why men and even women pursued it so avidly. The saints in heaven knew she had found no satisfaction in it.

Below her, one of the shadows divided itself into a man and a woman. Arms entwined, they staggered across the grass to the ward.

Everyone wanted what was called "the delights of the flesh." It was no wonder she couldn't stop thinking about it. Lust was everywhere. Even in the prisoner below in the ward in the monks' wagon. It almost leaped out at one, along with the passionate violence. She remembered him with head thrown back, singing out some unknown Saxon battle song. It was said that idiots and addlewits were particularly well endowed.

Considering the great bulge in the jongleur's breeches, this was obviously so.

Sweet Jesu! Her breasts were tingling madly. Not only that, but there was a hot, swollen feeling in her private places. She tried to shake the image of the big, golden-haired madman from her thoughts.

She leaned out and caught the shutters and closed them with a bang. In the bed, Beatriz woke with a whine. Constance kicked off her shoes and, wearing her shift for warmth, crept in beside her.

In only minutes, they were both asleep.

Five

The displaying of the bedsheet with the virginal bloodstains had been held early, and only for the families of the bride and groom. The success of the physical union had already been well-announced. At midnight or so the four de Clinton brothers, prompted by some unknown signal, had burst into the feast hall with the news.

Probably a candle at the window, Constance thought, watching her sister. She supposed it was all right; she just did not like the style of it.

Across the room Bertrada sat in her bridal bed, flushed and pretty, surrounded by wedding guests who made a constant flow of traffic on the tower stairs. She wore the attractive morning robe of red wool, her long hair brushed to fall about her shoulders and arms, topped with a woven wreath of bearded wheat, dried flowers, and ribbons that the Morlaix villagers had fashioned for her. Wulfstan, the new husband, sat on a nearby chair, smiling, with a wine cup in his hand.

I shall have to get used to him, Constance thought. Wulfstan's brothers were clustered around him. They were still drunk, not yet sobered from the night's feast. The bridegroom's smile irked. For some reason she found that in the morning she liked him less.

Her half-brother Julien inclined his head toward the ribbon-strewn bed. "And how is the bride?" he murmured in her ear. "Did she reveal to you the night's marvels?"

Constance beckoned to a page. When he came she gave him a message to tell de Yerville to move the musicians out onto the stairs. The room was too small for loud music. It was giving her a headache.

"The night's marvel is that it was done at all," Constance said. "Yestereen she was threatening to kill herself."

Constance looked around the room. Wine cups were scattered across the floor and those in the room trod on them or kicked them out of the way. De Yerville had castle servants coming and going with food and drink but no one was tidying up. To one side of the groom the Earl of Hereford and his wife, who held a small curly dog fashionable in London, talked to the de Clintons about King Henry's demand that his nobles support his daughter, who had been married at twelve to the German Emperor of the Holy Roman Empire, as his successor to the English throne.

"Normans will never be ruled by a woman," the sheriff declared. The earl made a shushing gesture. A moment before the room had been crowded with de Jobourg cousins from Fontrevault in Maine. Magnus de Bocage, Constance's distant cousin from Wroxeter, was still there with Robert fitzGilbert, the two sleekly handsome young men seemingly oblivious to the looks the Earl of Hereford's daughters were sending their way.

Julien nudged her. "And?"

And what? Constance thought.

She had spent a restless night, waking several times to wonder if Bertrada's marriage had been consummated. She'd been the first to arrive at the bridal chamber after the bridegroom had made his appearance in the ward, where his brothers boisterously carried him off to the jakes, and more wine. Constance had made her way up to the tower room with her maids. She remembered thinking all was well, or the de Clintons would not have been so happy.

Still, she'd gone up the stairs with her heart in her mouth. One could find anything. One could find that the new husband, provoked beyond reason, had beaten Bertrada into insensibility.

Instead she'd found her sister in bed eating from a plate of sausage that had been brought up with their breakfast ale. Bertrada had been mulishly silent on all that had happened on her wedding night. After all her worrying Constance could have slapped her, but she consoled herself that it was done. She'd pulled the sheet with its stains from the bed herself.

"She talked of serving God," Constance said, "through her devotion to her lord husband. And the sublime happiness of bearing him many children."

Julien hooted. Heads turned to them as he said, "You see, it was a marvel after all. Regard—does my sweet sister think now she has truly become the bride of Christ?"

She followed his eyes. Bertrada sent her new husband a melting glance from her perch in the bed. Wulfstan was talking to his brothers and did not notice. Certainly it could be said something had transformed her sister's passion for the spiritual.

"He has swived her silly," Julien said in her ear. "That is your miracle."

Unwillingly, Constance laughed. "You are blasphemous." She was telling herself she should have had more faith in these things. God knew the groom had had confidence enough for all of them.

Some Welsh chiefs came up the stairs, Maredudd ap Givanwy with them. In spite of the crowd, Maredudd came to Constance, wanting to bargain over some cattle.

It was no time to do that; more people were pushing into the tower room. "I am hearing a petition by the village weavers," she said "in the great hall after. My chamberlain, Piers de Yerville, will see to it."

"We will deal with you now, girl, and not

later." The other Welshmen gathered around them. "There has been drought to the south as well as here, and cattle will be scarce after Yule for lack of grain to feed them. It is best to buy what will be needed now."

Constance sighed. Maredudd dealt with her as he'd dealt with her father. The Welsh had no problems with it; they allowed their own women to do business freely. On the stairs outside, the musicians, joined by the bagpiper, struck up another loud tune. Hurriedly, Constance bargained for winter supplies.

When the Welsh chiefs had gone off, Robert fitzGilbert came up with Magnus de Bocage.

"Lady." The Clare picked up her hand and kissed it. Constance pulled her hand away. The king's envoy smiled, showing even, white teeth.

"Magnus," he said, turning, "even though she is the most beauteous of all here, we have just seen how your cousin deals with the unruly Welsh. Shall I flatter her? Isn't it what all women would hear—that they have wit and intelligence?"

Over his head Constance looked at Magnus, who raised his eyebrows. "Lady," Robert fitzGilbert said, "I am your slave. I throw myself at your feet."

Constance thought of the Clares' huge demesnes in England and Normandy. Just because they were enormously rich did not mean they were not interested in becoming even richer.

"Milord, restrain yourself." She touched him on his velvet sleeve. Robert fitzGilbert knew she had the king's permission not to have to wed again for three years; the Clares thought they could do anything. "I do not wish you at my feet. It is to curb such enthusiasms that I travel at all times with a troop of a hundred knights."

Magnus burst out laughing. Constance was not sorry she had mentioned her escort. If one was the richest heiress in England one lived in some danger of being waylaid, kidnapped, carried to the altar, and married to some enterprising noble before King Henry in France could know of it.

Robert fitzGilbert looked pensive. Constance asked after Magnus's brothers and sisters. The brood of de Jobourg cousins in Wroxeter was large and if rumor was right, somewhat odd. She'd always heard there was Jewish blood in the family. It was even rumored some of the girls had made marriages in far-off Denmark.

Magnus sent his mother's regards, and reported on his father's scholarly work for the king. Constance's attention wandered. *Bertrada is married,* she kept thinking. She beckoned a page and sent him for a cup of wine. Across the room a group of young women around the marriage bed burst into laughter. There was a heavy tread on the stairs and the Earl of Chester came in followed by his countess, their rough-looking sons bundled in furs, and a daughter.

Constance looked around for a chair. She didn't believe her legs would hold her up any longer.

The wedding was over and guests were leaving Morlaix. Most of them would be gone by vespers. She planned to leave for Bucksborough in the morning. Before that she had to spend time on the affairs of the castle with Morlaix's chamberlain, the steward, and the constable, and she had to settle an urgent dispute with the weavers. But for now, she told herself, she was going to rejoice that Bertrada was married. She would send a letter to King Henry as soon as her clerks could make it ready.

She moved a plate of bread and cheese from a stool and sat down. FitzGilbert appeared before her again, asking her if she had seen the latest dance from the London court.

He was very handsome, she thought, looking up at him. Young and good-looking and rich and determined to press his suit even if he had to wait three years. She smiled and told him that she hadn't.

Constance met the weavers in the great hall. Servants carried out the table trestles to clean them, and put down fresh rushes. The group of men and women stood back out of the way.

She came in and seated herself on the bench at the high table with Piers de Yerville, the castle clerk and a tally reeve. This was but a hearing of a dispute, not full court, so there was no swearing of oaths.

The weavers were from the south, from the old Danelaw, and looked it, for most were tall and fair. They had come to Morlaix in her father's time to card and spin Morlaix wool, and make a serviceable cloth which was factored very profitably in London. They had a reputation for being clannish.

"Who speaks for these people?" Constance asked.

The chamberlain indicated an older man, heavyset, who stepped forward. His name, he said, was Torquin.

The complaint concerned some boundary dispute one of the weavers had with Morlaix's miller. The weaver, Gundar Harefoot, came forward, as did the village's miller.

She looked, curious, at the weaver's foot, neatly covered in leather wrappings. It did look like a hare's foot, straight up and down, as the heel was contracted and did not touch the ground. Behind Gundar Harefoot the thirty or so weavers listened intently.

The dispute was quickly settled. The village was castle property, and the writs had been found by the clerk. The boundary lines were read at length, Gundar Harefoot agreeing to pay the miller for the extra ground. So it was not so urgent. She was puzzled. Petitioners with minor complaints usually waited for manor court in the spring, following Easter.

"There is something more," Constance told her clerk. Julien of Nesscliffe came into the hall and took a place at a table in the back. He smiled at her.

As she suspected, there *was* more. Speaking

for all the group, Torquin the weaver petitioned to buy grain in the coming winter from the castle, and not at the grain market in Wrexham.

She thought that over. The weavers, like the rest of the villagers, believed that there would be a winter famine and that she would take care of them. If they went to Wrexham for their grain the speculators would beggar them.

She studied Torquin. The weavers were not popular with the villeins. They were craftspeople, guild members, and kept to themselves. They were said to be strange in their ways, preferring to meet and pray in their houses. There had been friction last year with the priest, and finally the bishop in Chester had a paper read in all the parish churches condemning groups worshipping outside the mass.

It was also known the weavers' girls did not marry until late, sometimes into their twenties. An odd custom. When they did, the women suckled their children long, not permitting their men to sleep with them until the child was weaned.

She thought a moment. "You have another petition."

A low sigh leaked out of the group. The leader, Torquin, looked about him.

"It's with the knights, milady." When she looked up, he said, "Not all of them, milady, but a few. In the garrison."

The castle knights, under the constable, Longspres, were not as well disciplined as those under Everard. Constance leaned forward and looked down the table to her chamberlain. "There has been no trouble," he assured her.

"Nay, milady, no trouble as yet." The weaver pulled his fingers through his beard. "But what can we do? We do not force our women to marry."

The chamberlain made a shocked noise. The clerk stared at him. De Yerville barked, "Hold your ignorant tongue! The Lady Constance—"

"The Lady Constance only wishes to know the nature of the complaint." It was an effort to hold back her smile. The weaver looked dumbstruck; he hadn't thought to offend. But then, who could forget the circumstances of her own marriages? "What is it you want to say?" Constance asked.

He hesitated. Behind him the younger women looked down at the floor. They wore their heads bound in kerchiefs and their faces could only be glimpsed, but for the most part they were tall and well-made. If one wanted a strong, healthy-looking wife one could do no better.

"We do not give our women to men without marriage," Torquin explained, "unless there is an unfortunate happening such as war. It cannot be helped, what happens then, although we pray to God it will not occur." His eyes met hers. "But here, even if the young knights should approach with offers to wed, it is not our way to bargain for our daughters. Either our daughters desire to marry, or they do not."

As he spoke, Constance could see that marriage, if proposed by a garrison knight who had little to offer but his weapons, his horse, and the clothes on his back, was not as desirable as one might think. Not for prosperous weavers.

"Not many have desired to marry?" she asked.

He did not answer.

She sat back on the bench. What could she say to these people? It was useless to forbid the knights the village. It was rare enough that they talked of marriage. Or perhaps it was just a trick, to get the weavers' girls to sleep with them.

"I will tell the constable, Longspres, that no knight shall address your daughters unless they give sign that they welcome it." When Torquin opened his mouth to speak, Constance went on, "If, as you say, you would do nothing without your daughters' consent, then they must manage it. That is, to keep the Morlaix knights at bay."

"Milady, they are threatened," he protested. "The knights come, and if the girls do not talk to—"

She would stop that game, too. "No woman shall be threatened, or the knight will be disciplined. You have my promise to Longspres on it."

That seemed to satisfy them. The weavers filed from the hall. As they got up from the table the chamberlain leaned to her, arguing that strictness with garrison knights over village girls would bring on disorders.

"God's wounds, would you have me give them license to rape?" The weavers did not look as though they would forgo vengeance. And knights could be found mysteriously drowned or with their necks broken in "accidents" in the fields.

On her way out Julien joined her muttering, "You will get in trouble with this." He had heard everything there in the back of the hall.

She flashed him a look. "Garrison knights do not marry—they are poor as church mice. It is only a trick to swive the weavers' daughters."

He smiled. "That is not what I meant." He looked around. "Where is your watchdog?"

"In the stables with my knights, making ready for the journey tomorrow."

He put his arms around her and kissed her on the forehead. "I will be in Nesscliffe tomorrow. Those of us who are not rich must work, and I must do something about the damned drought. My villagers are talking of building a pond." He shrugged. "First, of course, we must have something to put in it. I think it has forgotten how to rain."

She watched him walk away. Even from the back her father's bastard looked the image of him, the swing of his shoulders, the late sun striking his russet hair. She didn't want to argue with Julien. He had listened to her bargain with the Welshmen for their cattle, then hold court for the weavers' complaints. This is what he meant by trouble. As far as she knew no one criticized her for managing Morlaix's estates, trading for cattle, or holding a hearing for the villagers. What they condemned her for, particularly the church, was her wantonness in having more than one husband. For being sought-after even now.

She walked across the dry grass of the ward. Little puffs of dust rose from the ground where she put down her feet. It had not rained in more than a month. She saw the prisoners' wagon had been moved to the kitchen house door. The tall, gilt-haired jongleur knelt in it, shoulders hunched against the drag of the chains.

Constance walked to the wagon. A knight in full mail squatted by the wagon's side. He sprang up at once.

The prisoner looked worse, if anything, since last she'd seen him. The jongleur's stubble of beard was blood-spattered, his mouth and lips split and swollen. Dried spittle had formed at the corners. Someone had tied his hands behind his back; the wagon stank of urine. The Welshwoman huddled in the far end, her shawl drawn over her head.

"Why has he not been given water?" One could not ignore the misery of both of them. Or the stink. "Why is there only one of you here?"

The guard knight, young with a freckled face, mumbled something about the other guard gone in search of orders from Sir Everard.

"The prisoner won't take water, milady, nor food," he told her. "He curses us, curses Sir Everard, too. He'll fight like a madman. Before we bound his hands behind his back he threw everything that was given to him. Sir Milo took a blow on his nose from the water cup that was like to break it." He looked at the big man. "It's the truth, milady, what the common folk say. He's devil-possessed."

The jongleur did not look so fierce now. From the condition of his lips and his bloodshot eyes he was in need of water. So was the woman, probably.

"Milady, don't go near that witch-woman," the knight said behind her, "for she's just as bad. They say one look from her eyes and she can ensorcell—"

"Fetch water," Constance ordered. God's blood, they would do that much for their horses. "And bring whatever it is you feed them."

The knight slouched off. She moved closer to look into the jongleur's battered face. Without his wounds, he could be even more handsome than Robert fitzGilbert. She saw there had been a necessary bucket in the wagon but it was overturned. How could he use it, anyway, when his hands were tied behind him?

"Come," Constance said to the woman, "you can aid me." She looked closer. "How is it you cannot help yourself?"

In answer the black-haired woman shifted and mutely showed her hands bound behind her. Constance made a click of annoyance. The prisoners had been rebellious and they were being punished. Or the guards were afraid of them. Or both.

The young knight came back with a water

bucket, a loaf of oat bread, and a cup. Constance started to order him to untie the prisoner's hands, then saw the look in the jongleur's eyes. She decided against it.

"Give him the water," she said. He looked at her, alarmed. "Sweet Jesu, put the cup to his mouth!"

The knight reached into the wagon and gingerly touched the rim of the metal cup to the prisoner's lips. He waited, but nothing happened. The jongleur, kneeling in chains in the wagon bed, stared malevolently at Constance. Slowly, the guard tilted the cup of water. The jongleur drank, his eyes still on her. The guard took the empty cup away.

The jongleur lifted his head, his stare never wavering, parted his lips, and sprayed the cup of water back at Constance.

It hit her full in the face. For a moment, she could only blink. With a growl, the knight lunged for the whip on the wagon's gate.

"Stop!" She was too stunned to be furious. She took her sleeve, green silk edged with marten fur, and wiped her face with it. Out of the corner of her eye she saw the witch-woman in the end of the wagon cringe back in fear.

The guard edged up, holding the whip. "Milady—"

"Put that down," she said through clenched teeth. Streams of water made their way down her forehead and onto her cheeks. Her cloak and the front of her silk gown were soaked. The jongleur regarded her with gleaming eyes.

"Fill me a cup and give it me," she said. When the knight opened his mouth to protest she silenced him with a look.

Cup in hand, she went to the wagonside and reached in. She said nothing, only held out the cup. Still watching her, the man in chains bent his head and touched his lips to it. After a moment, he drank greedily. Constance waited until he was through, then she held out the cup for the knight to fill it.

She held the second cup of water to the jongleur's mouth. His blue eyes bored into hers. She could not tell what was in his mind. Not anything pleasant.

She handed the empty cup to the knight and told him to cut the woman's bonds. "When you bind her hands, tie them before her. In that way she can fend for both of them."

Constance took up the loaf of oat bread and broke off a piece. The knight had handed the Welshwoman the water cup. She was drinking from it, holding it with both hands and making small moaning noises of joy.

The jongleur was silent, his eyes still on her. He stank so badly Constance turned her head. She held up the bread.

He opened his mouth to say something, perhaps to curse her, eyes gleaming in the soft light. She suddenly jammed the bread in his mouth. It stuck there between his teeth.

Constance stood for a moment observing him. She had not planned to do it—she didn't know what had come over her. But it was the most satisfying thing she'd done all day.

If the jongleur could manage to dislodge the loaf, he made no move to do so. He knelt in the wagon with it jutting from his jaws, watching her.

She turned away and started across the ward. The knight giving water to the witch-woman called out to her, but she kept on going.

The sun was down and it was cold. A sharp north wind blew around the bailey, trapped by the encircling walls. Constance pulled her cloak around her. By the kitchen house she saw the green and white tunics of her household guard bringing their horses out from the stables to exercise them. She looked for Everard but did not find him. She skirted a large pile of dirty rushes that had been carried from the feast hall.

She suddenly felt old and tired. Her feet hurt from wearing fancy silk slippers. She tried to remind herself that she was still as young and pretty as any of the maids who had hung over Bertrada in her marriage bed that morning. In the deepening twilight, castle people hurried past, not recognizing her in the hooded cloak.

She looked up at the window in the old tower and saw candles had been lighted. Bertrada and her new husband would leave with the de Clintons in the morning.

Now we have all married, Papa, Constance thought. She remembered Robert fitzGilbert, and sighed. Three years was not long enough.

Tomorrow, Constance told herself. Tomorrow we will leave Morlaix behind us. Tomorrow we will be on our way to Bucksborough. And home.

A few moments later two shadows joined in the deeper dark by the wall overlooking the kitchen house. "Christ's bones," one said, "I have drunk enough this wedding to make my brains fit to burst. I can hardly talk, much less think."

The other shadow watched as a second knight joined the other at the prisoners' wagon. The knights picked up a whip and hung it at the back of the wagon, disposed of a cup and water bucket, then leaned over the wagon's sides, adjusting the chains of the man who knelt in the wagon bed. "She goes east on the morrow by way of Wrexham and Holt, and then through Kidsgrove Forest. With the full hundred escort, none to be left here at Morlaix. Four wagons for her household, and the wagon you see yonder, the one with the prisoners."

The other grunted. "They will have trouble passing the ferry, as they did before." He paused, then said, "And the watchdog?"

"With her, as always."

They were silent as a third knight joined the others. The newcomer seemed to deliver a message, for the countess's knights listened intently, then saluted him with their knuckles pressed to their helms. The third knight left.

The knights went to the back of the wagon, let down the gate, and hauled out a woman, bundled in a black shawl and wobbly-legged from the confinement of her fetters. She looked over her shoulder pleadingly at the fair-haired man chained in the wagon bed. But she made no sound as the two knights dragged her off.

After a long moment the first shadow said, "Kidsgrove Forest."

They watched as the two knights, the woman prisoner between them, disappeared among the sheds behind the kitchen house.

"The forest, then," the other answered.

He melted into the dark. A moment later, the other followed him.

Cenred shifted his weight against the chains, throwing back his head to look at the dark sky above the castle. The steady wind had scoured the night of clouds and the cold, distant stars were out. He took a deep breath and shivered. The wind pushed the chill into his bones, and he no longer had a shirt; it hung in shreds around him. Nor had they thought to bring the blanket back after they'd sloshed water in the wagon to clean it.

From somewhere in the shadows behind the kitchen house Llwydd's screams were lifted by the wind, an unbearable squalling of terror and pain. It had gone on and on and he was trying not to hear it. Poor woman, she had done nothing to deserve what they were doing to her.

Cenred yanked against the chains, thinking futilely what he could do to them if he had them within reach. The same thoughts he'd been thinking for days.

God rot their souls.

With his eyes closed, Cenred shut his mind to the Welshwoman's screams. *Embrace the mind's darkness. It is the only way not to go mad.* He reached for the Latin like someone fishing in a black pool. Reeling it in. Bringing it up from his unfailing memory.

Men of the line of Cadmos, you who live
Near Amphion's citadel: I cannot say
Of any condition of human life "This is
 fixed,
This is clearly good or bad." Fate raises up,
And Fate casts down the happy and the
 unhappy alike;
No man can foretell his Fate.
Creon was happy once—

He heard a noise, and the Virgil faded. Cenred cursed. He opened his eyes to see mailed knights coming to him out of the darkness, carrying torches. Before he could move they were upon him. Seven of them. Seven knights to hold down one beaten man.

Working rapidly, they freed him from the chains, keeping his hands and feet manacled, and dragged him out of the wagon. He felt the skin of his shins crack as they dragged him over the tailgate. He cursed them in Norman French. In Saxon. Intent on what they were doing, they didn't respond.

He could hear Llwydd's shrieks growing louder as they hauled him, heels dragging in the dirt, behind the kitchen house. It was dark back there. He lashed out at them wildly with his fettered hands and someone hit him. Another knight shouted for that to stop. When he fought back they all shouted and cursed at once.

Cenred bucked in their grip. Hands clutched at him. A burst of cold wind on his flesh made him realize they were yanking off what was left of his clothes. His chausses. His boots. He stumbled, barefoot, on the cold ground. Before he could fight back they had thrown him, naked, against a log wall. Gasping, he turned to face them.

The knights, helmed and mailed and fully armed, confronted him. Any two or three of them he could have taken, but not all. He shook his head to clear it. Better to fight than submit to torture.

He saw a half-dozen buckets lined up on the ground. Sweet Christ. What were they going to do?

"Here, madman," one of the Normans yelled. He picked up a bucket. Nearby Cenred could hear Llwydd's screams, the low voices of women. In a long swinging motion the knight threw the contents of the bucket over Cenred.

The icy water hit him. He fought for breath. Then another. Water drenched him. There were many forms of torture; he could not think of one that began like this.

He reeled toward them, half-blinded. They circled him.

The water was coming from all directions. Cenred lurched back and hit the wall, his shoulder, his bound hands.

"Compliments of Countess Moon!" he heard the knights shouting. "Here, madman! Here's your bath!"

Six

Traveling eastward beyond the village of Chirk, the road ran for several leagues beside a shallow river called the Tow. Here the countryside was open and rolling, good grain country, although the stubble of the corn harvest was already a sere, wintry brown in the drought. The fields, Everard had noted, were unplowed even in late October; the only green was that of water-loving trees that hugged the riverbank.

In a half-league, the knight captain decided, squinting at the sun, they would halt for midday meal here along the grassy banks. He watched his serjeant, Carcefou, riding along a double column of knights, fifty in the vanguard, fifty in the rear behind the wains, dressing the lines. Even in the countryside where there was no one to watch save a few villeins working in the fields, Everard kept his men smart and soldierly. Behind his back some of the knights cursed the iron discipline, but when they were with other troops, as at the wedding at the castle, he knew they bragged about it.

He guided his stallion forward, past the cook wagon and the wains with household baggage. He hated wagons, as did any good soldier; they tied down a column to a crawl and were always breaking down. But they were a necessary part of travel for a noble lady—the servants she must have with her, and her household. Besides, at least one good came of it: with a cook wagon and several cooks in attendance the knights could look forward to better meals than saddle rations and any game they could catch.

Everard pulled his horse up on the road's high bank and passed down the line, noting the appearance of the English. Their set faces under steel helms gave them a properly forbidding look as they rode past: Edwin of Hastings, Harold Waitson, two Edmunds, two Edgars, even a Hrolf. The English fighters were steady and brave, with the well-made bodies that one came to expect, particularly those from the Saxon lands to the south.

However, to anyone who knew them, even these pledged to Norman service, the English still regarded their conquerors with a fine, simmering hate. It was well hidden; above all else the English were unshakably faithful to their oaths. But Everard had put himself in their place, and asked himself how he would regard it. There was no other answer.

Still there was no doubt that of all those recruited, the English were among the best. Too many of those coming from Normandy now for knight service were looking for their fortunes, reckless greed driving them more than duty at a time when the fortunes to be had, almost sixty years after the conquest, were small indeed. Unless one married one.

Reluctantly Everard's eyes sought her out. *The countess.* He dared not allow himself to think of her by any other name.

She rode astride her mare in the first line of knights, her oldest child up before her. She was, he knew as he watched the two heads bent together, encouraging seven-year-old Hodierne to read. A peculiar conceit. But there was no judging her according to other women, he thought hastily: the countess was much too different. Too fine, too rare. He saw she had thrown back her hood. Her dark, unbound hair flowed about her shoulders and down the back of the crimson gown. When the wind lifted it one saw her long, elegant neck, proud chin. She was as delicate as an ivory statue. But he had seen, in those precious moments when he had been close to her, the warm blood pulse in her temple, in her narrow wrists. She was real. A living woman.

Six years ago the first husband, de Cressy, had given him his place over the household knights at the castle. Everard had been back from the Holy Land after a siege of Saracen castles in Syria, too restless for Gascony. Too restless for anywhere—until he'd come to Morlaix and seen *her.*

Fifteen she was at the time, heavy with her first babe, and yet already marked with the cool beauty of the woman that she was to be. De Cressy had died in the Avranche pursuing Robert de Clito, the old Duke of Normandy's son, and the king had soon married her to the Frenchman, de Waiteville, one of his former enemies to be pacified with a beautiful wife and English lands.

Everard couldn't help it—his heart tightened painfully. Christ in Heaven, there was nothing he could do for her then to ease her misery, short of murder. And the saints knew he had thought of it many nights, sitting alone on his bed in the barracks, considering what vast good a blade would do placed in the back of de Waiteville. If he did it, if they caught him and charged him with murder, it did not matter. But what if vicious tongues linked the two of them, he'd asked himself, and found that he loved her? And brought her down to scandal, and unjust disgrace? It was the only thing that had stopped him.

By then the ears and eyes of castle gossip had reached far. He didn't have to hear it; he'd known before the stories began. Just watching her.

De Waiteville died on the battlefield before he could kill him. The next husband was William of Hersey, who had hardly bothered to know her, he had been so busy rutting on her to get an heir.

Everard swallowed, hard. He was torturing

himself. But sometimes, when he was dizzy with the pleasure of just looking at her, he could think of nothing but taking her soft, slim hand in his. Holding her in his arms. Even kissing her sweet, soft lips.

Sweet Jesu! A dangerous idea. She was his liege lady—he had sworn his sacred oaths to serve and protect her. Worse, he was a man of thirty-two years, and no lovesick calf to moon over what he could not have. She was not his even to desire from afar. As the song went, "Oh, fair lady of the moon, so fair, so pale, so faaaar above us . . . ."

A miserable ditty. He detested it. And yet—

And yet it did not keep him from madly loving her.

At that moment he saw the countess look up, frowning, as an angry bellowing from the prisoners' wagon started behind them. The little girl said something, and the countess looked around. Looking for him, to see if he was attending to it.

Muttering curses under his breath, Everard started for the rear.

A few minutes later Llwydd said, "Now see what you've done. You can't say you didn't ask for it, *bach.* If you'd stop harrying them to bring back your clothes, you'd not get beaten."

She sat with her feet and legs dangling over the tailgate. Her forced bath had wiped her face clean of charcoal and the red stain she used for her lips. Her dark hair was clean, a wild bush of tight curls. She looked considerably younger.

Llwydd watched the big, dark knight captain ride away with narrowed eyes. The Norman's answer to the jongleur's shouts had been quick and harsh, using the butt of the whip to knock him in the skull a few last times for emphasis. Now the jongleur was holding his head, groaning.

"He fair gave it to you this time, the big, black brute," she clucked. "Ay, *bach*—what difference does it make? These clothes they gave you, they're not so grand, mayhap, but they're not so tattered as the old ones you wore."

Llwydd hitched over to look at his back, the shirt oozing blood where the whip had striped him. She had more freedom of movement than the jongleur, as her wrists were shackled to a chain which passed through one end of the slats.

He did not lift his head. "I'm not a serf," he snarled. "I want my hose and my Paris boots that some bastard Norman is wearing by now, and what's left of my shirt. Not these damned grain sacks."

She sighed. Some one of the knights had doubtless taken his boots and his hose. But she knew that if he didn't stop provoking them, especially the captain they called Everard, he would bring down worse punishment on them both. Ever since leaving the castle the man in the wagon with her had bawled his complaints about the rough villein's clothing they'd given him. And each time someone had come back to lash him.

"I can't say it's a thing worth getting whipped for, boots and a pair of wool hose." She was thinking the clothes did not diminish his looks. In the shirt and rough breeches, even barefoot, he was still wondrously handsome with his sapphire eyes, his pale silver-gilt hair. But his anger at his clothes, the icy bath at the hands of others at Castle Morlaix, were nothing to the greater misery she knew he always carried with him. He did not have to tell her.

She poured some water on his back and watched it soak through the shirt. "Consider," she tried to soothe him, "that what you have on is sturdier than what you lost, and warmer. It will be cold on the morrow—you'll be glad for a thick shirt and trews then."

He lifted his head to stare at her. "How do you know that?"

"Know what?"

"That it will be cold weather on the morrow."

She smiled her witch's smile. It would be easy to tell him some foolish thing to see if he believed it. She decided not to.

"There will be a storm first." It was warm now with the false mildness of the long drought, but if one looked for it the clouds were in the west, over the Welsh mountains. In autumn, the change came from the west.

And it was Samhainn, the fire feast that the Christians called All Hallow's Eve. The old gods would be walking. All day there'd been a hot wind, and flocks of birds had streamed across the sky. She'd even seen an owl, the ghost bird that avoided the sunlight.

She only said, "After a hot spell with no rain there's always a storm. You can see it in the beasts. The cattle are laggard—if they graze at all it's quiet-like. But sheep and swine are restless, and hard to calm. And if you look at the trees—"

He was no longer listening. He had hitched himself to his knees as far as the chains would allow. In this position he could see over the sides of the wagon, over the servant leading the wagon's mule. His eyes were fixed on the Countess of Morlaix riding in the vanguard of knights. At the moment, she was giving her attention to her oldest daughter in the saddle before her. Only the back of the lady Constance's head could be seen as she bent to the child.

The expression on the jongleur's face made Llwydd start. "Ah, you mustn't," she warned. "If you look there, at the one your eyes are on now, it will mean more trouble for you, *bach.* Not only for now, but for later."

His gaze did not move. "She sent her dung pig back to shut me up."

Llwydd closed her eyes. No wonder they thought him mad when he could look and talk like that.

The road cut close to the riverbank and they both ducked as the wagon lurched through a stand of trees that brushed them with their long, leafless twigs.

"Look, willow," Llwydd said. Someone would notice if he kept staring at the noble lady that way. "The alder, willow, the hawthorne, rowan, birch—and there's a seventh but no one knows it, 'tis the secret of wizards." She added, somewhat slyly, "They say the willow's a favorite with witches, too."

"Do they." In spite of the wagon's jolting he rested his head against his arm on the rail.

She nodded eagerly. "Oh yes, the willow is for Monday, moon day. The moon owns it. It's hers—the lady's—too. The lady of Morlaix is the willow maid. Look at her, the pale, fair face, the beautiful eyes like light on the sea. The countess of the moon, just as they say."

He raised an eyebrow. "She's no maid."

She frowned. One could not mock the old ways, that was dangerous. "The willow maid is *moon-blessed,* man! Look, it be right there." She lifted her bound hands. "Here's the forefinger, he's the oak god, big and full of power. The middle finger, it belongs to the Christmas fool—if he doesn't watch out, they'll put him in the fire and burn him with the Yule tree on twelfth night. And here," she said, hiking toward him so he could see, "is the fourth finger that worships the sun, the birch tree, Mother of us all."

He shook his head. "Careful, Llwydd, it's a pagan litany you're saying."

She didn't know what that was. "And the little

finger is for the ash tree whose mysteries cannot be told. But here she is." She thumped the heel of her palm with her thumb and looked up at him through her hair. "Hark now, my mother was Cerridwen's servant, and her mother before her. There are many of us among the Cymry, although your Christian church does not see it. I tell you, here is where the willow rules. The lady moon rules, right here in the heel of the hand. It's sacred to the old goddess."

He lifted the corners of his battered mouth, wryly. "There is no old goddess, Llwydd. And if you tell the priests that, they will let you go."

She brushed back her curls to stare at him. "No, I will not tell the priests that. It is not true!"

"Don't say I didn't warn you." Then he added, somberly, "But we are all fools for one belief or another. Christ was not the only god to die on a tree." He changed the subject. "Why do you say the Morlaix bitch is the willow maid?"

Llwydd eyed him cautiously. She did not know how much she should tell him. There was much about him that showed in the sacred signs of divining, about those that followed him, and wanted him, that had nothing to do with why he had come there, to be where he was. She could not see beyond that. But yes, he would have his revenge, she thought, staring at him. For all the good that it would do.

"One is not a fool to believe," she murmured.

"Tell me what it is you believe. And how it has made you a fool."

"What? My faith as a Christian?" His eyes glinted. "Little witch-woman, I believe in nothing."

"Nothing?" She was taken aback.

He turned his head to watch the wagons pull up under the trees on the riverbank. The knights circled their horses, trampling down the long, dry grass, making a place where they would water the horses and take the midday meal.

"In philosophy, I am a Platonist like—" He stopped. "—like someone I once knew." He thought on it for several long minutes. "And I believe in Death," he said in a different voice. "That is enough."

Llwydd looked away. She was not educated in the way that he knew; she was a simple woman. She followed the old gods in the mountains of the Cymry, which people called Wales, and because of it the Christians called her a witch. Perhaps the priests would even burn or drown her for it.

She hunched down in the wagon and closed her eyes, thinking that she believed in many things. They might kill her for it. But it was better than his nothing.

They rested on the banks of the Tow for several hours while the knights diced and talked and the servants climbed into the wagons to sleep. The confessor, Father Bernard, came with the clerk, Brother Welland, to say a blessing over their midday food and then they went away to sit on the riverbank some distance apart. Constance kept her girls with her on a blanket the maids had spread. The sound of the water rushing over stones and the whirring of locusts in the long grass was peaceful. For a while Beatriz chased butterflies, small white ones, which were plentiful. Constance read to Hodierne from an illustrated Book of Hours the monks at St. Aidan's had made for her. Hodierne asked endless questions about the monks' pictures: Why were there doves and what did doves do? Why was the Serpent of Temptation blue, and were there real snakes that color?

After a while, after Beatriz had become hot and tiresome and there were no more butterflies, the two little girls curled up on the blanket and napped. Yawning, Constance lay down beside them.

When they woke she had a slight headache. The columns of knights formed before and behind the wagons and they moved back to the road. The air was hot and oppressive. A low line of clouds had crept in from the west and covered the sun.

Beyond the village of Holt the fields were full of people looking for the last grains of the harvest after the villagers had done their gleaning. Many of the serfs wore nothing but ragged shirts. The children, even some well-grown boys, were naked. They were a silent lot, staring at them from the fields.

Hodierne gawked at the naked boys. She twisted in the saddle, trying to see her mother's face. "Who are they, Maman?"

"Poor people." Even as she spoke some of the serf women came to the edge of the road and held up their babes. They kept holding them up, mute as beasts, as the column rode past.

Hodierne leaned forward to stare. In her green-dyed linen gown with a belt of silver links, her hair braided with ribbons, she must have looked like a doll, a vision to these barefoot brown people with their lined, sullen faces. "Why are they doing that? Holding up their babes? Do they want us to bless them?"

Hodierne raised her hand but Constance quickly pulled it down. She signaled to Everard to ride forward. He trotted his stallion up beside her.

"Give them half the bread," Constance told him. "And a share of the cheese and meat. One-quarter share."

"Milady." Behind nasal guard and cheekpieces his face was disapproving. "That will short us badly for the journey."

"God's wounds, do as I say." Abruptly, he wheeled his horse and rode away.

"Maman." Hodierne strained to look up at her again. "Why are we giving them our food?"

Constance hauled her around again to face front. Her headache pounded. "Sit still. You ask too many questions."

She knew that desperate, yearning look on the mothers' faces and it set her teeth on edge. The serfs feared the coming winter. The women held up their babes in the hope that she would take them with her, but there was nothing she could do. This was poor country under the heels of the Earl of Chester. And had always been.

Hodierne squirmed. "Your baby is very pretty," she called out to one of the women.

Constance shushed her. The babes were not pretty, they were wizened gnomes. Not the fat, handsome children her own had been. Constance couldn't bear to look at them.

The people at roadside were silent as the food was given out. The knights rode among them to keep peace, anyway. When the last of the food was gone the homeless folk went back to their gleaning. They carried leather sacks, some small baskets made of leaves, to carry away the kernels they might find.

"But why did we give them food?" Hodierne wanted to know as the columns started up again. "They are not our people here, are they?"

Constance closed her mouth on the proper retort. Which was that they were the Earl of Chester's, homeless folk for most of the year. And he starved them. She said, "They are God's people. And as such we must treat them as our own."

"Why—"

Constance put her fingers over her daughter's lips and pinched them together. Hodierne was more like Baldric de Cressy every day. The same look, the same long face. Her first husband, too, had been full of endless questions that cut as sharp as a blade for a fourteen-year-old wife. *Why, Constance? Why not a well-made meal? A clean bedchamber? A thrifty accounting? Why not?*

And why the daughter she'd given him, instead of a son? She could never answer that. But God's truth, she wished de Cressy were there now to answer his daughter's endless inquiries!

Hodierne's shoulders were stiff. Contrite, Constance stroked her fine brown hair and put a light kiss on the top of her head. She worried about Hodierne and Beatriz. Some said schooling daughters was foolish, a waste. But many knight husbands were unlettered, and could neither read nor cypher. And Hodierne would have to run her household.

Her own father had felt strongly about it; he'd given Constance tutors when she was not much older than Hodierne. The Earl of Morlaix could not himself read nor write. Which, she supposed, was the reason behind it.

Hodierne's endless questions meant a bright mind and Constance wanted a good schooling for her, but not the convent Bertrada had attended. The nuns there practiced weeks of fasting and bouts of frenzied weeping that spread from one to the other like the plague, so that last year even the bishop had had to call for their disciplining.

So, *not* the convent. She would not choose that for her children. One must face the world, not fly from it, as her father had often said.

Some good young knight, Constance was thinking as she pulled back Hodierne's hair, the long strands wet with heat where they'd lain against her neck.

Her daughter needed a knight fair and open of face, an honest man, not a bully or one coarse with women like so many of the young ones. A good husband, a good father for her children. A sigh escaped her. Hodierne was not an especially pretty child; it was to be hoped she would be handsomer as a young maid. But one needed to be practical. An ugly man could be admired, could woo a beautiful woman and win her, especially if he were rich and powerful. But a maid's looks were everything.

Of course, Hodierne would inherit a goodly lot as her portion, and that helped. If, Constance thought, she should marry again, and she had no doubt the king intended her to, and had male children by her next husband, then she had to provide well for her orphaned daughters. Good dowers were laid down for both of them against abandonment or widowhood or other misfortune. Hodierne, if she was not pretty, would need a clever husband. Someone who would talk to her. A friend.

Constance knew she was asking the impossible. In three marriages she had not had any of that for herself!

She had decided the best was to send Hodierne for her tutoring to St. Hilda's near Bamborough, to her great-aunt, the Abbess Alys. Her father's sister had taken holy orders after a bad marriage, but she remembered her as a person of kindness and the finest intelligence. It had been years since she'd seen her.

The road descended to a thick wood ahead. For the first time they smelled the burning.

Pagan fires. Constance wrinkled her nose. She had forgotten it was All Hallow's Even. The old gods' Samhainn. In the month of June, on midsummer eve, and at Samhainn at the end of October, it was not uncommon to find the villeins building bonfires on the tops of hills. Many spent the night of the pagan fire feast drinking and carousing and having wanton sex. The church railed against it to little avail. Especially here in the grain country, where the people were more observing of pagan ways than they were in the east.

The sun was going down. She looked around. The knights ahead were entering a deep woods. It was Everard who had thought it better to avoid the towns and camp in the countryside for the night. Now Constance was not so sure.

In the rear, Everard urged the column to close ranks. There had been some straggling at the ferry and men and horses were tired, but he blamed himself for the long rest at midday on the banks of the Tow. The countess had slept, the two little girls beside her, and he had hated to wake her. By this time, though, they should have been on the far side of Kidsgrove wood.

He kicked his horse into a fast trot, making his way up the shoulder of the narrow road. There was only a slim hope they would be out of the forest before the light faded. He passed the kitchen wagons, then the wain with the prisoners. The man faced forward on his knees, shackled to the wagon bed, his eyes fixed on something ahead. When Everard saw the object of his stare, he cursed under his breath.

He cut the stallion between the row of knights and pushed it close to the wagon. Leaning, he reached out to bring his fist down on the side of the prisoner's head. With considerable satisfaction Everard saw him fall sidewise.

The gilt-haired jongleur lay unmoving in the bottom of the wagon. It was no more, Everard told himself as he rode away, than he deserved. For looking at her.

Seven

The wind began after sundown, as the knights were picketing their horses. A crack of lightning and a sprinkle of rain sent the servants scurrying to make their beds under the wagons instead of in them.

In her tent, Constance looked up as the wind suddenly billowed the top and then sucked it inward. She remembered that Everard had seen that there were guy ropes tied to the trees in the event of a storm such as this.

The knight posted outside stuck his head in and looked around.

"Yes, it's all right," Constance told him.

She was seated at her small table with a tin lantern at her elbow, the reports of her Morlaix steward spread before her. Hodierne and Beatriz were asleep in the back of the tent, in the small room made by the hanging partition.

He hesitated. She could not remember all her knights, but she thought this one's name was Gervais. "There's a disturbance," he said.

She nodded. They had all heard the noise from the Samhainn fire feast that had started at sundown—in a clearing in the woods nearby, someone had said. Now the wind carried the singing and shouting and the smell of smoke.

She wished they were out of the forest. Trees drew lightning; being camped among them was almost as bad as being on a hilltop. She couldn't help thinking the whole journey had been cursed with lateness, beginning with the travel to Bertrada's wedding, and now coming back.

"A disturbance with the horses." He was still there. "Because of the storm, some of them are loose, milady. Sir Everard wanted me to see that you were safe."

"I am safe." Constance winced as hard, drumming rain hit the fabric above her. She waited, listening for her children to wake. "That is, if the tent holds."

He looked up at the ceiling. "Oh, it will hold, lady. We ran extra ropes to the trees, all sturdy oaks."

There were shouts outside, over the roar of the wind, and he turned to go. At the tent flap he paused to say, "I will be outside. But if all the horses go free, it will be the devil's own task for us to find them in Kidsgrove wood."

He left and the rain began in earnest. Constance picked up the candle in its tin cylinder and went to the back of the tent. The room there was snug and tight, with an oiled ground covering and hides on top of that. The girls slept on small pallets next to her own.

She bent over her daughters, warm and rosy in their sleep, and pulled the covers up around their necks. The wind battered the tent again. A flash of lightning sliced the dark.

Thank God and the saints they were blessed with good shelter. Outside, her servants and the knights would make a poor time of it. She thought of the serfs they had passed and their children. Where did they go in a storm like this? Into the forest, one supposed. But the forest around them was being deluged; water had begun to drip down the tent's center pole.

She carried the lantern back into the front room and sat down at the table. She could not go to bed in the storm—it would only keep her awake. She thought of the horses. If the storm had stampeded their mounts they would have to stay in Kidsgrove forest until they were found. She hated to think of yet another delay. She wanted desperately, now, to go home.

She propped her head in her hand and turned the sheets of Piers de Yerville's report on the revenues of Morlaix. The steward's grandfather, Hugh de Yerville, had come to the Welsh marcher country with her grandfather in the days of Duke William the Conqueror. Piers' father had served under her father, Gilbert de Jobourg. But that was not to say that this de Yerville was the man she would pick to administer her castle's affairs. Yet how in the name of the Blessed Virgin could one make him more able?

She bit her lip. Under de Yerville, who was earnest but never seemed to know what to do, Morlaix revenues decreased every year. Another bad harvest was expected and another poor wool crop. She was glad she'd bargained with the Welsh chiefs for grain and meat at Bertrada's bridal viewing. If the famine was bad by midwinter she would have to send grain from her manor at Bucksborough. Perhaps even from her other fiefs in the south.

Another torrent of rain hit the tent. Water had collected on the roof and was seeping through. A drop fell on the table. She wiped it from de Yerville's accounts with her finger and suddenly remembered the prisoners.

Both the woman and the man were shackled to the wagon, unless someone had thought to move them. The prior of St. Aidan's would never forgive her if something happened to his malcreants before she could get them safely to Bucksborough. She thought of the fairhaired jongleur and his angry shouting all day about his clothes.

She got up and went to the tent flap and lifted it and looked out. The knight Gervais was not there. A lightning flash showed water pouring down in sheets, horses and men milling among the trees. Then it was dark again.

She stepped back, her face and hands wet. She was not usually afraid in storms, but she cringed as another bright blast of lightning shook the ground.

At least the rain had put out the Samhainn fires. There was no noise of it now, only the wind and thunder and the shouts of her household as they chased the horses.

She went back to the table and stood, not wanting to sit down again to the steward's accounts. Sweet Mary, it sounded as though the storm was tearing up all creation! Perhaps the only safe place was bed, after all.

She reached out to pick up the lantern. A gust of wind made the light flicker. She looked up.

A figure had stepped inside the tent, naked to the waist, glistening with rain.

Constance could only stare.

It was the fair-haired jongleur, she realized, rain-soaked, without his fetters, although each arm was marked where they had held him. The bright blue eyes were fixed on her, lips pulled back in a grin.

"Countess," she heard him say, "I have come to take my gracious leave of you."

She put her hand on the table to steady herself. She was too astounded to be afraid. She could not believe he had escaped, but there he was. Her mind turned with frustrating slowness. It was useless to call for help—no one would hear her above the storm. Oh God, her girls were asleep in the room beyond!

Perhaps he meant to kill her.

She made her lips move. The only word she could utter was, "Why?"

"Why?" He moved toward her, his big, gleaming body circling the table. "Why, to thank you," he said hoarsely, "for all the many pleasures you have bestowed upon me while you had me in your care."

Holy Mother in Heaven. She remembered the beatings. Her breath came quickly enough to make her heart race. Her eyes fell on her dagger on the table among the sharpened pens.

He followed her look. Before she could move he reached out his hand and swept the knife to the floor. He moved in front of her, blocking her way.

Even in serf's rough woolen braies and barefoot, his beauty leaped out at her: wet, golden body, gilt hair, the cobalt eyes, the stubble of beard. He stood before her savage, glistening, dangerous.

"Before I take my leave," he said, "you must allow me to give you something in return for your—ah, hospitality."

She backed a step, the stool behind her, and put her hand to her throat. She knew what he wanted now. Her only thought was for her girls—that they should not wake up and see him violate her. Or kill her, if that was the way it was to end.

Constance's courage had not deserted her. With an effort she drew herself up and lifted her chin, telling herself no matter how he looked, he was a madman. "You risk much.

Consider that when you are found, my men will kill you."

He tilted his head back to look at her with something like admiration.

"Brave countess. What cause would there be for such a rash move?" He reached out and took her trembling hand in his, eyes never leaving her face. "Have I not said I am here to repay you sweetly for all that you have done for me?" Slowly, he pulled her to him. "Surely you know your kindness begets kindness. What then can you fear?"

She took a deep, shuddering breath. He mocked her. She—that is Everard—had been anything but kind to him; it was the way one treated prisoners. At this moment, she thought, agonized, surely the knight Gervais would return to his post in front of her tent. Surely Everard would come in. Surely something would happen.

Instead, a cracking flash of lightning turned the night pale around them. A cry burst from Constance. In the back of the tent there was a rustling sound. Hodierne's voice called out sleepily, "Mamma?"

The jongleur watched her.

She took a deep breath. "It is nothing," she called. Her voice shaking only a little. "It is the storm." She suddenly felt his hand on her bodice front, at the laces. "Go back to sleep."

His cold fingers touched warm flesh and she swallowed a scream. She tried to break away but he held her, both her hands now gripped in one. With the other he pulled her gown open, his eyes on her white, thrusting breasts.

"Wh-what is it you want?" Her teeth were so clenched she could hardly speak. "Is it riches? Let go of my hand and I will give you my rings—"

He lifted his eyes to her face. "Lady Constance, you do not have to pay me to do what others before me have done." His fingers, cold from the storm, cupped her breast and she shuddered. "Lying in the wagon I have thought many times of how I would reward you for my sore ribs, my face, my striped back, my gracious bath—and oh yes, my wondrous new clothes. I have thought long and hard on what I could give you in return. Something," he said as his thumb rubbed across her nipple lightly, "that would gift you with the same feelings I have rejoiced in these past days."

"Then not only my rings," she blurted. "Wait, I have gold and—"

He put his hand over her mouth. Holding her tightly, his hand rucked up her skirts, then dragged her underbritches down to her knees. He lifted her so she half-sat on the table. The table wobbled and two pens rolled off onto the floor.

Constance was rigid, not breathing, as his head bent and his mouth touched hers. She clutched at him. He said against her lips, "Dear countess, I have promised myself I shall hear you scream for me."

She held her breath. Looking up, she saw his

slitted eyes like blue stones. Now that she knew what he wanted she could not cease trembling. "P-please don't hurt me! My children—"

"Hurt you?" That fierce, cold mouth touched hers again. The caressing tip of his tongue slid against hers. "Lady, that would be a poor reward for your highborn favors that are, we must admit, not exactly fresh, but still surpassing fair." He pulled back and gave her a searing, deliberate look. He held her propped against the table with her skirts hiked up, her underclothes stripped away, her sex thoroughly exposed to him. "No, I want something far finer." She felt his hand between her thighs. "I will hear you sob, I will hear you scream. And before that, I will hear you beg."

For a moment she thought she would faint. Her legs stiffened around him. *"Don't!"*

In her ear he said, "Sweet countess, that's not what I want to hear."

She felt the air cold on her naked legs. Lightning crashed, and rain thundered on the roof of the tent. His touch penetrated the folds of her feminine places and stroked, softly relentless.

Constance tried to pray, but no words came. This could not be happening to her. She was sprawled against the table with her legs spread, her skirts up, her bodice open to bare her breasts. He was doing what he pleased, his hand between her legs, and she was powerless to stop him. She gripped his arms to keep from falling. His fingers found a small button of flesh. The nerve there shot through her body and she cried out.

He thrust himself over her, his mouth seeking hers, a strange fire in his lips. Constance jolted and almost slipped from his grasp. At the same time she felt him shudder. Something strange was happening. A bolt like the lightning flashing around them seared into their kiss. Deep in his throat, he groaned. When he drew back she saw that his eyes had changed. He was breathing hard.

"I—" he said huskily. Abruptly, he buried his head in the valley between her breasts.

Dazed, she stared up at the swaying tent above them. From the moment his hands had touched her she had been helpless, a prisoner of terrible sensations she could not explain. He was not the only mad one, she thought with a sob. She felt his mouth softly nuzzling her aching nipples.

She had lost her senses. All she could think of was the image of him, wet and golden, as his hands slipped down her thighs. Her knees went wide, waiting for him. Unwillingly her hips pushed against him. He fumbled at the front of his clothes.

He lifted his head and she saw his bruised face, his brilliant eyes. There was a devil in him, she thought wildly; he made her do this against her will. He bent and his warm, wet mouth was on her breasts, sucking, biting, teasing. The fire between her legs had become a vortex shaking her, devouring her. Constance bit back a scream.

God in heaven, this was what he wanted! He said she would scream for him. Beg for him. She squirmed against him. Her body had gone mad. Her hands pulled urgently at his bare hips, holding him to her.

"Shhhh." He bent over her, pressed against her. She could feel his hard, naked shaft, his bare legs against hers. He bent and kissed her, his tongue into her mouth. "So sweet, so sweet," he muttered against her lips. "Ah, countess, moan for me." He put his mouth against her cheek and she felt the stubble of his beard. "Beg me," he whispered into her ear.

She babbled something. The tip of his hard flesh was at her opened body. Straining, she hiked her hips closer, trying to touch it. He growled, softly. She was frantic, she hardly heard him. He pulled back and that viselike hand slipped into her warmth, fingers penetrating, then pulled out. She stiffened and cried out, her hands clutching his bare shoulders. Then with one heavy stroke he was inside her.

She went rigid under him. "Be still," he said through clenched teeth, "and I won't hurt you." She heard a moan from deep inside him. "Ah, God!"

His body contracted against hers. Sheathed tightly in her, he moved with shuddering slowness, kissing her face, her eyes, her lips, the curve of her ear. The center of Constance's body was in flames. She writhed under him, matching his motion.

"Feel me," he groaned. "Take me deep."

He lunged heavily into her. The table shook, spilling sheets of vellum to the floor. The lantern teetered. She heard her own frantic cries, dimly aware they would wake her children. She could do nothing; the feel of him in her body destroyed the last of her reason. A terrible ecstasy poured from his pounding; she sobbed that she wanted him, hearing his wild words—that she was precious, beautiful. That he had burned for this moment.

The heat built from his frenzied battering. She dug her fingers in his tangled, wet hair. She pulled at him, sobbing, straining for something unknown, until at last his body clenched in convulsions. At the same time Constance's world exploded. As the firestorm peaked, she shrieked. He gave a low, tearing moan, arms wrapped tightly around her.

"Mamma!"

A second's pause. Then, dazed, they fell apart, gasping. He stared at her with the face of a tormented angel. Constance slid from the table to the floor.

"Mamma, what is it?" her oldest child called.

"Christ!" He looked around wildly as he hauled at his braies.

On her knees, Constance looked up. She saw him stumble to the tent flap, pull it aside and disappear.

"Mamma." It was Hodierne, at the partition

to the back. Long-faced and solemn. "You were making a lot of noise."

Dear saints in heaven. Constance tried to get to her feet, but her shaking knees would not support her. She was cramped painfully in her thighs and crotch, the wetness spreading. *His* wetness. Hodierne was staring at her gaping bodice.

"I was getting undressed." She did not recognize her voice as her own. "I'm looking for my pens."

She groped across the floor, picking up the quills. Some other woman was doing this. Her mind and body was still full of a bursting, sensuous heat. I ought to be weeping, she thought dully.

She grasped the edge of the table and pulled herself to her feet. Her hand held the edges of her bodice together. "Go to bed, now," she told her daughter. "I will be with you as soon as I put out the light."

"My lady Constance!"

It was Everard's voice, harsh with worry. Without waiting he crowded in, the knight, Gervais, behind him.

"Milady, are you safe?" His eyes swept the tent, the disorder of the accounts on the floor, the spilled ink and pens. "What has happened?"

Constance put her back to the light. Sweet heaven, she was not going to tell the world! They could not see her clearly; if Everard saw her face, he would know. Her legs were trembling so she had to sit down. She pulled the stool toward her.

"I am undressing." She saw the doubt on his face. "Why have you—why have you burst in on me like this?"

"The prisoners have escaped." His eyes roamed the tent, not satisfied. "While the horses were loose in the storm they broke their shackles. In the storm, in the woods, it is not likely we'll find them."

Constance drew Hodierne to her. She held her tight by her side. "The woman, too?"

"Both of them." He waited, hands at his sword. "We were not alone here in Kidsgrove forest. I have looked at them and it is clear the shackles were cut. Whoever would come here to do this picked their time well."

"Yes." She was not paying attention. He had escaped; she knew that when he came into the tent. Her mind was a muddle, her nerves screamed. Her traitorous body ached, sensually.

It was the first time this had happened to her, this mystery of what really transpired between women and men. When she closed her eyes, she could see only the jongleur's face bending over her. Feel again the hot thrusting of his body in hers.

God in heaven, she had to stop thinking about it.

Everard had motioned the younger knight to go out. "Why would they want him?" he said half to himself. "A common troubadour, of no concern to anyone save a jailer and the dungeon that's meant for the likes of him."

When Constance did not answer he gave her a last, fierce look, and left the tent.

Eight

The next morning, as the column splashed its way out of Kidsgrove forest, the knights talked about the prisoners' escape. There was a good deal of arguing. The English claimed to have seen the footprints, even in the dark, of ten or so men and horses before the deluge washed them away. Other knights hooted. Outlaws and bandits had been after their horses, and nothing more.

After the prisoners' escape Everard had given out punishments and stiff fines that left the hundred-man escort smouldering. The discussion turned to how, even if the prisoners had accomplices, they had managed to outwit the pickets, turn the horses loose, assault the two guards and, most difficult of all, sever the heavy leg and arm shackles that chained both the jongleur and the witch-woman to the wagon. That meant considerable forethought and the proper tools to break the chains and locks, so it was not just a random attack. The raid was meant to set the prisoners free.

Constance, whose nerves were on edge, didn't want to listen. Surprisingly, neither Everard nor the knight serjeant gave the order to be quiet. For miles the knights argued as to why such a daring attempt would be made for a wandering troubador and a witch from the wild Welsh hills.

She gritted her teeth. Household troops were big gossips; when there was little else to pass the time they pursued a subject until it drove one mad. It was all she could do not to call Everard to make them cease.

She'd chosen a place to ride in the middle of the column where she was more or less by herself, but she could not get her worry out of her mind. Losing two prisoners that had only been taken as a favor to old Prior Maelchlan was nothing compared to what had happened to her. Constance felt as though she would burst if she had to listen to any more.

She'd spent the morning fearful that someone had heard something, even in the storm, and knew what had taken place in her tent. If the story went abroad, the mad jongleur's assault would only serve to turn scandal against her. She was notorious enough, a woman who had petitioned the king not to have to marry. Every day the church preached against what they termed women's animalism, and the lust of their base bodies. God's wounds, with the stories they already told, it would be said she invited him!

Under her lashes Constance studied the faces of the knights riding around her. No one looked at her in any way differently except for Everard: now and then he gazed at her in a manner she could not fathom.

At last Constance called for the nursemaids to bring Beatriz. She rode with the baby in the saddle before her, finding too late that the maids had given Beatriz a handful of honey-cakes to keep her from fretting.

"Maman, eat." Beatriz twisted to stuff a cake into Constance's mouth and smeared her cheek with sticky honey.

"Bébé, not now." Constance felt tears welling up again. She bent her head to hide her face in her daughter's hair.

God help her, one could not call it rape. Not when she had consented! The world might think her proud and unfeeling, but she was a woman, as vulnerable as any. No woman could take lightly the assault of her body.

None of it made any sense. When they, she thought feverishly, whoever they were, had set the jongleur free, one would have thought he'd make haste to leave the camp while he could. Instead, he had come boldly to her tent to have his revenge.

Revenge. It was as simple as that. What he had done to her was in return for the beatings Everard and the guards had dealt him.

She wanted to scream. To think that he would

do it, that he would dare to approach her! He was truly a lunatic. With a troop of a hundred knights guarding her, he'd come to her tent, forced his way in and had his way with her with no thought of his possible capture. He'd taken his life in his hands!

"Look, Maman," Beatriz insisted. She forced a piece of cake between Constance's lips. "Eat, Maman. It's good."

Constance stared at her daughter. By the Cross, she'd kill him herself if she could find him. *I'll make you scream for me, countess,* he'd said. *Make you beg me.*

A roiling in her belly made her clamp her lips together. She was sick just thinking of it. Had she really screamed out in her lust, as he'd promised? Holy Mother, she couldn't remember!

She did remember, though, his rain-wet body gleaming in the lantern-light. There was no denying he had a power over her; she'd been like a bird held in the stoop of a hunting hawk. She thought of his face as he leaned over her, his rough trousers pulled open to expose his great, swollen shaft. His soft, taunting words.

Why hadn't she shouted for help?

She told herself for the hundredth time that it would have done no good; in the storm, no one would have heard her. And it would have only wakened her girls and terrified them. She remembered thinking that, about her frightened children, even as he thrust into her, the pumping of his hard body inflaming her.

What had happened next was not her fault, she told herself. If anything, the jongleur was the true Serpent of Temptation, wickedly knowledgeable about fleshly pleasures, just like the Serpent in Hodierne's book of devotions. And she had been the stupid innocent, a woman grown who should not have been so easily tricked. The disgrace of it, to convulse with passion for the first time, unexpectedly, like any servant girl taken up against a wall!

Or across a table, she thought, her lips trembling.

"Maman, look." Beatriz patted her face with a sticky hand. "Ev'rard coming."

When he pulled his horse up beside her she snapped, "Make them stop talking. I'm sick of it."

He gave her a surprised look but touched his fingers to his helm and rode off. She called Uma, the nursemaid. When the girl came running up she handed Beatriz to her. Her daughter screamed that she wanted to ride. Ignoring everything, Constance turned her horse and rode to take a place behind Father Bertrand and the clerk, Brother Welland.

Back there with only the rearguard of knights she could at last be alone. She must stop thinking or she would start weeping again. *It will be all right,* she tried to tell herself. *No one knows.*

After the storm, the day was clear and windy. It had turned much colder. Constance wore a deerskin cape lined with marten fur. It had a hood which pulled up to hide her face.

The holes in the road were filled with water and the horses' legs were splashed to the knees with mud. That one storm was not enough to break the drought. If rain came later the winter grain would be planted.

She shifted in the saddle. Dear Jesu, but she ached. It had been a long time since a man had ridden her so hard. She would not think of it, the possibility that she could carry his seed.

She felt a moment of sheer terror. To carry a wandering, nameless beggar's child was madness. She, Constance, Countess of Morlaix, who had petitioned King Henry for her freedom!

She fought down her panic. She knew that for flouting him the king would kill her. Imprison her. Cloister her for life in a convent. *It will be all right,* she thought frantically. *It must be.* It was surely too early to worry about it.

She'd vowed the secret of what had happened to her at the hands of the lunatic was forever locked within her. Heaven help her, she could not even confess it; she would have to stay away from her priests. And if that was a sin, too, she would gladly burn in hell for it.

She stared at the two clerics before her, riding their mules. The scribe, Brother Welland, had a theory that the witch-woman and the lunatic had escaped because the night just past was All Hallow's Even, the pagan Samhainn, and the witch-woman's fellow demons had come to carry her off. The young clerk was an earnest, towheaded boy not yet out of his teens, the son of poor serfs from Lincolnshire.

The educated young French monk, Father Bertrand, snorted. "Pah, it was mounted men that came under cover of the storm and let the horses loose, did you not hear the knights talking? As for the witch, what would anyone want with her, a little Welsh beast that worships rocks and trees?"

"Her demons wanted her," the lay brother insisted. "They would come for her, for their unholy ceremonies at the fire feast of Samhainn. And the madman, too. Lunatics and witches, they have common cause."

Father Bertrand snorted again. "He's no lunatic. I knew him in Paris, at the schools of Notre Dame."

"You knew him?" The other gaped. "You mean you knew him, the prisoner, and said nothing?"

The confessor shrugged. "For what purpose? Cenred is much changed, not the student I knew. Then he was called *le beau,* the beautiful. You see how he looks—a golden Apollo. And brilliant, a firebrand in the schools. There was not a one of us that was not jealous that Peter Abelard, the magister, gave him favor—although at first it was thought he was Peter's *amour.* But as we learned, Abelard was no lover of boys; when he became unchaste he did it by falling afoul of that slut of a nun at Argenteuil. And then, Jesus help us, the world collapsed."

"Slut of a nun?" The lay brother stared. "Who is Abelard?"

The monk fixed his gaze on the knight riding in front of them. "Who is Abelard? Sweet Mary, I had forgotten we are at the far reaches of Christendom in this rude country, where nothing is known."

"Well, I have heard of him," the other said defensively. "I just do not recall his fame."

The confessor rode for a moment in silence. " 'Who is Abelard?' A god. That is Abelard. When I was there in Paris as a student he was at the height of his glory, the famed young magister of Notre Dame, the cock of the walk with his black curling hair, his fine big body. He was then only in his thirties, a prodigy of the schools, a Breton knight's son, the firstborn who should have been a knight himself, had he not renounced arms to follow philosophy."

"Oh, I have heard of him," Brother Welland said, "I just did not remember. Abelard the philosopher."

The confessor was not listening. "We used to crowd the lecture room and hang in the windows. When you walked the Isle de France and saw the colleges of Notre Dame, there were Abelard's students like crows on every windowsill, their backsides overhanging the street. It was the only way we could hear him, he attracted such crowds. And God is my judge, he held us spellbound! The greatest teacher, the greatest speaker, the greatest mind of our times. Even the Pope himself has said it."

There was a another silence. "But another

Lucifer," the monk added. "That is what some now call Abelard. A magnificent mind, but one cannot preach Aristotle and reason as a tool to approach God instead of blind faith. The church condemns it. They have already forced him to burn his latest book."

"The slut of a nun," Brother Welland murmured.

Father Bertrand turned to look at him. "Ah, at that time she was a postulant, a student, whatever they call the girls who board there for their studies. She is the niece of Fulbert, a canon of the cathedral school. The convent of Argenteuil is very fashionable, admitting only girls from good families. The nuns let the girls have their ponies, even pets such as birds."

The confessor looked out over the fields. "Heloise, of course, was beautiful, although the nuns extolled her learning. Beauty, and her learning. A seventeen-year-old virgin, a student of Greek and Hebrew, of Livy and Ovid and the other Latin masters—a fatal attraction for a god like Abelard. He had always boasted that he was chaste, and why not? Peter had everything, he was above other men at the top of the mountain of Notre Dame, at the pinnacle of his pride. He did not need a woman to destroy him."

The scribe scratched his head, confused. "The prisoner who escaped, the jongleur, was his student in Paris?"

Constance had not really been listening.

Now the repeated word *jongleur* penetrated her thoughts. They were talking of the escaped prisoner who was, astonishingly enough, some student her new confessor had known.

She brought her mare up behind the two on their donkeys. Her heart had begun to pound. She could not believe the French monk from St. Botolph's had known the man who had taken her last night. There must be some mistake. She dared not speak to them. She could only listen.

"I do not doubt that Cenred is mad," Father Bertrand was saying. "For if he lost his wits it is because he loved Peter Abelard. We all worshipped our god. The night when what was done to him—"

His voice dropped low so that Constance could not hear. She strained to catch it, but only heard the lay brother gasp.

"We all went mad," Father Bertrand went on. "The news spread throughout the city of Paris. Abelard's students—all Notre Dame students, all of us—rioted in the streets. Cenred was the leader, I thought him a lunatic then when I saw him, wild with grief. He and the others who had been Peter Abelard's favorites were only intent on seeking out Fulbert, and the servant. The servant they caught. You do not want to know what was done to him."

God in heaven, Constance was thinking, what were they talking about? The name Peter Abelard she knew dimly, the center of some great scandal with a young girl from a convent. Distant Paris gossip; she thought they'd had a child. It was the sort of thing Bertrada, her sister who had wanted to be a nun, would know. The revelation was that his name was Cenred. He'd been a student in Paris!

Her hands were shaking. She could have screamed with frustration at their mumbling. She couldn't hear what they were saying, only the scrivener's shocked exclamations.

Finally Father Bertrand said, "If Cenred took to wandering across the face of the earth, it is fitting. They say that when he left Paris he was a wild man, that his heart was broken, that he cursed God for what had happened to Abelard."

The clerk said something.

The monk shrugged. "Who can say? Cenred was—is—a fair poet; Abelard thought well of his verse. And God's truth, he burns with a bright white flame. They are from the same mold, those two. I saw Cenred's temper, once. You could never say he suffers of a mild Christian spirit. Neither does Abelard."

The scribe was studying him. "You did not like him."

The monk shrugged. "Who can dislike another god? Even a mad, fallen one? I wish him no harm. May the angels protect Cenred's soul, wherever he shall wander."

The scribe began to discuss some academic point in atonement for sins.

"You mean Peter Abelard? It is an interesting theory, Conceptualism," the other responded.

"In the cloister schools at Notre Dame they argue Universals, or concepts in the abstract—it is all the rage. And the Realists attack them. But Abelard confounded them by teaching that Universals are neither Realities nor mere names, but the concepts formed by the mind when abstracting similarities between perceived, individual things."

"That is—ah, interesting," the clerk said.

"Interesting? It is dazzling. Abelard is a champion of *disputatio,* that new school of teaching that poses a problem and discusses it by means of question and answer. We loved it, all of us who had been driven to a death in life with the boredom of lectures, lectures, lectures by droners such as old Anselm."

Constance sat back in the saddle. They were talking of philosophy, religion, and were not going to talk any more about the jongleur. She bit her lips in frustration. She must be careful; if she questioned them she knew they would not tell her anything. It was not seemly that she, a woman, should discuss church scandal. Little Father Bertrand would take delight in censuring her.

Her head was pounding; she'd had a headache since she'd wakened. They had one more day of travel before they would reach Bucksborough. At least they would not camp by roadside or in the forest. She had already told Everard they would stop the night at the inn at the hamlet of Roverly.

In spite of herself, hot tears came. It was

tiredness, Constance told herself—she had to cease this silly weeping. But how she longed to be home!

The girl Uma came to run by the side of the mare, her hand on Constance's stirrup. "Milady." She was breathless. "Should you care to come, the little one has puked. She cries for you."

Damn them, they *would* gorge Beatriz like a pig on honeycakes to keep her happy.

Constance touched her eyes with her fingertips, wiping away the telltale wet. She turned her horse in the direction of the nursemaids' wagons.

Not too far away two men stood in the dappled light and shadow of Kidsgrove forest, facing the half-circle of mailed knights on horseback.

"What do they mean, they lost him?" the first one said. "Tell him Kidsgrove was where we said they'd find him, and they found him. We can do no more than that. Not for what they paid us."

The other man looked somewhat worried. The sun picked out the knights' polished-steel chain mail, the lances with the white guidons hanging limply in the still air.

"They say since they lost him in the storm, when he escaped, that we're supposed to find him again."

The other gave a croak of protest. "Find him

again? When they can't keep their hands on him? Listen, we've got better things to do than follow some singer over the countryside." He nudged the other man sharply. "Go ahead, tell them you speak their language. If they want him again, they'll have to pay for another go at it."

The knight with the crowned helm and white plumes had listened to them in silence. Now he pushed his massive horse forward. The riders behind him were all the same in their handsome steel hauberks and peaked helmets, their plain white tunics over mail.

When the second man started to say something, the huge leader lifted a mailed fist.

"Spies," he said, contemptuously, in guttural Norman French.

He reached inside his white tunic and pulled forth a leather pouch. He held it in his hand for a long moment, studying them with pale blue eyes. Finally he tossed the pouch at their feet.

"Find him," he said.

As if at some silent signal, the knights behind him turned their horses and started away.

The first man bent and picked up the purse, opening it so that gold coins spilled out into his palm.

"Is it enough?" the other one asked.

"More than enough." He turned to watch the knights moving their horses out of the clearing. "If it wasn't, I'd just as soon wash my hands of the silent, arrogant bastards."

The other man put his hands on his hips.

"Well," he said with a sigh, "that's that. Now, where do we begin?"

No man can foretell his fate.

Antigone, Sophocles

Nine

It was cold in the timbered manor hall. There was no fire, but a brazier of coals had been put under the table so that Constance, Brother Welland, the bailiff, and her steward for the Bucksborough fief, a former knight who had lost one arm in the Holy Land, could have some heat. Most of those gathered for manor court had not bothered to take off their outer clothing. They stood in heavy furs and sheepskins, growing wet and fragrant as the snow on them melted.

Because of the dim light the hall was lit by rush dips, bunches of reeds stripped and then soaked in mutton fat which smoked and stank. A constant stream of people came and went, leaning to whisper and leave messages with their kinfolk before departing. The noise made it hard to hear the testimony, which in itself was not easy to follow. Most of the witnesses were villeins speaking the local East Anglia dialect of English, which only Constance and

Brother Welland the scrivener really knew. Some, overseers and knightly vassals, used Norman French. Father Bertrand had been keeping notes in church Latin. All they needed, Constance couldn't help thinking, was the Welsh. Fortunately, they were too far east at Bucksborough for that.

She shifted, moving her feet closer to the brazier, and drew her fur-lined cape over her knees. For manor court and its hours of chilly sitting she had dressed in tunic and several underdresses, a beltless coat with panels of coney, and a warm woolen coif with the same fur covering her hair. From the appearance of the clothing of those who had just come in, it was still snowing heavily. In the back of the hall someone coughed with a deep, hacking sound, reminding them of the ailments that would plague them before spring finally came.

The dispute being heard was in answer to a petition for marriage between the daughter of the smith from Constance's village of Neversby and a young huntsman from one of the sheriff of Repton's hunting lodges. The burly headman of Neversby had been saying that the English did not look with favor on more classes to divide people, such as the Normans were bringing to England.

"Sokeman, villein," he rumbled, "maybe a merchant or two is good enough for us. That is, free men. And then them villeins what is tied to the land by order of the liege lord with one law or another." He bent a look from under craggy brows on Repton's bailiff. "English do not recognize serfdom here."

Constance rubbed her hands together, wishing she had worn her mitts. Brother Welland, she noticed, had his hands clamped for warmth between his knees when he was not writing.

Villein was not as easy a term to mark in the testimony as Norman *serf.* In the country around Bucksborough there were villeins in such varying degrees of servitude, or freedom, that one could not say what was the rule. As the headsman had said, "tied to the land by one law or other" made some villeins not serfs, but not entirely free, either, while others were as unencumbered as sokemen.

The Normans' serfdom was far different. The English saw it little better than slavery. And in all truth, if one were to take the serfs' poverty as a measure, it was.

She studied the smith's daughter, thinking that the girl was pretty with her fresh, smooth skin and brown hair. She wore a rabbitskin cloak with the hood thrown back, covering a homespun gown and apron. The young huntsman, born a Norman serf according to the bailiff and brought from Coutance in Normandy to serve in the sheriff's game woods, was tall and broad-shouldered with a headful of black curls. A good-looking fellow, in spite of the fact that he had made the mistake of wooing a freeman's daughter in another fief. She wondered how they had met.

The bailiff was saying that the sheriff of Repton did not give his serf permission to marry outside his lands. The bailiff had brought a priest from the sheriff's village of Ledburgh to testify that Ralf the serf was to marry one Elen, Hedwig's daughter, also a serf, said Elen also belonging to the sheriff of Repton.

While the bailiff was speaking the huntsman, on his other side, had darted the smith's daughter a quick look.

Constance caught something in the air.

She's carrying, she thought. *And he's worried for them.*

Sweet Mary, as well he might be!

From the testimony that had been given there was no way that she could see to join the smith's daughter with the sheriff's comely serf. Even if she had wished it, she could not buy him; as a serf, Ralf belonged to the land. Even the sheriff could not sell him separately.

It had already been mentioned that if by some chance the sheriff agreed to let them marry and the smith's daughter left Neversby, that she would, by wedding a serf, become a serf herself—And therefore also belong to the sheriff.

That had raised an uproar. The smith's daughter become a serf? Never! The whole village of Neversby, it seemed from the crowd that jammed the manor hall, felt strongly about it.

Bad enough to lose one of theirs to the village of Ledburgh, in another lord's fief, but to lose her to a Norman *serf*? They were all opposed to a condition that robbed a man of everything, even his children if his lord so desired. In the villagers' eyes serfdom was not so different from slavery. The English hated Norman laws.

Banastre, the steward, leaned to Constance. He said behind his hand, "There is no way to get the fellow here, my lady. It may be he will have to marry his serf girl that the sheriff has picked."

Constance looked down at the surface of the table, thinking about the smith's daughter and that she could be carrying a babe. A dull pain in her own belly answered, the same grinding ache that came when she was reminded of her own condition.

Every morning she examined herself for signs that she was carrying the jongleur's child. She had missed her monthly flux in November and now it was December and there was still no sign. Desperate, in the freezing dimness of her room before her maids woke, Constance held her hand mirror up to examine her body.

She could not understand it. To be so late with her womanly flow could mean only one thing, but her breasts were not tender and her belly was not even slightly swollen. She still had not bled. It was almost two months.

There were women, she knew, who could advise her. She could even seek out her old nurse who had been with her since she was born. But somehow she could not bring herself to speak of it—that she had been taken by an escaped prisoner, a mad wandering singer, on the journey back from Morlaix Castle. And that she might now be with his child.

Now everyone complained of her uneven temper, and that she had taken to screaming over small nothings. But by night she was tormented by dreams that she was already in prison, that King Henry had cast her into a dungeon below his White Tower in London and left her there, alone in the darkness with the rats, in a terrible black stone room like the ones in the dungeon at Castle Morlaix. The world had forgotten her. Hands passed her food through the opening in the barred door, without speaking to her. She never saw faces. The solitude, the shame, was soul-destroying, and she woke, sobbing.

Then there were dreams that the king had sent her to a convent. The prayers, rising in the middle of the night for masses, the meek despair, sent shivers of dread through her.

Worse, no matter what happened Constance knew she would lose her children. In some dreams she strove to get to the sea with her daughters and take a ship to Denmark, or the lands to the south like Spain or Italy. But each time when they were about to set sail the king's knights came riding up to capture her—and drag Beatriz and Hodierne, screaming, from her arms.

She awoke from these nightmares bathed in sweat. She could have killed the lunatic jongleur then with a dagger through his heart and been glad of it. Whatever the mystery about him, whatever he seemingly had suffered, did not matter. She only wanted to make him pay for what he had done to her. And was doing to her.

However, there were other dreams, she thought, guiltily. Dreams about *him.* Thinking about them made her flush hot with shame.

Once Constance dreamed she was dancing naked before him.

The jongleur was lying on a couch as unclothed as she, his hands behind his head and watching her, his golden body lithe and powerful against fur coverlets, his big shaft in his crotch rigid and aroused. She couldn't take her eyes from it.

Wild music played. The things she did in her dance were unbelievable, things she'd never dreamed of even with her husbands. Even the depraved de Waiteville. She flung her legs about so that he could glimpse her most secret womanly places. She held her arms above her head and turned her back to him, shaking her bottom at him wantonly until he groaned. Then she approached him and bent over him to teasingly brush the tips of her breasts, her tightly budded nipples, to his opened lips. And he—

"Milady?"

The hall was filled with angry shouting. Constance shook herself. The young huntsman, between two sheriff's men, was being held back from the smith's daughter. She stood with her arms outstretched yearningly.

"She says she will go with him," the steward

said. He had to raise his voice over the noise. "The sheriff of Repton will be generous and let them marry if they wish to concede the first-born child to her father, the smith." He bent forward to look at her. "Milady?"

Constance stared down the hall. She'd been far away, wrapped in shameful visions of lust. It was as though she was under some form of enchantment.

She shook herself. The smith's girl was being told to give up her firstborn child? Holy Mother, she could never give up Hodierne, or Beatriz! This was the sort of thing men would think of.

She lifted her hand and the gesture brought some measure of quiet. At least the shouting in the back of the hall died down.

"The serf—" Sweet heaven, in her lewd musing she had forgotten his name. "Where was he born? On Norman lands?"

The bailiff looked uneasy. "In Coutance, milady."

"And," she wanted to know, "he is tied as a serf to the sheriff's lands in Coutance?"

The bailiff nodded.

"In France, then, he is a serf." She knew the huntsman's burning eyes were on her. The girl's, too.

"Milady," Banastre said, leaning forward, "perhaps—"

Constance waved him silent. "Tell me, bailiff, what is the huntsman's condition here?"

He answered, somewhat testily, "He is still a serf."

"I do not understand. This is not Normandy, this is England. Are there no English lands the sheriff's huntsman is tied to?"

The bailiff scowled. "That is beside the point. Lands here or in Normandy, a serf is still a serf."

"We do not have your serfs here," the Neversby headman shouted. "English law does not say a man is a serf, the sole property of his lord, forever tied to his land!"

None of them, including Constance, knew every detail of the law. But at least English law was English law and not Norman. From the back of the room where the villeins stood came a cheer. Everard's knights along the wall stirred at the outburst; and touched their swords.

The bailiff turned to consult with the sheriff's men. It took some time. They turned their backs to the table while they talked.

Brother Welland said to the steward, "What do you think they will do?"

The one-armed knight shook his head. Constance ran her fingernail along an old groove in the top of the table, wondering if the huntsman had met the smith's daughter at the Michaelmas fair. If so, he had wandered far from the sheriff's demesne.

The bailiff turned back to them. "The serf," he said, "will return to Repton and will not come to your lands again, countess. He will obey his lord, and marry the serf girl picked for him."

The smith's daughter made an agonized sound.

Constance regarded the sheriff's man thoughtfully. "But it is a point, bailiff, is it not, for future argument? Is a Norman serf a serf on English soil? To come and go quickly, as in travels with one's lord, as if for example one were a body servant, I think that would be so."

The bailiff wanted to interrupt her but she went on. "To stay and live here when English law and custom do not provide for serfdom in the Norman manner, however, is the question."

She was thinking now that the sheriff's man was only a bailiff, his liege lord only one of the king's tax-collecting officials, yet they thought they could challenge her, an earl's daughter, in her own manor. It suddenly occurred to her they wanted money, and that if they were adamant enough about the girl marrying their serf she would ransom him. They knew she took care of her people. Angry, she wondered how long it had taken them to think of this.

The bailiff said, "Ralf will not marry your girl now. If the question is put, that is the answer—no marriage at all."

She rested her chin on her hand. Everyone in the hall was silent, straining to listen. "The next time I am with our glorious king," Constance said, evenly, "who is a lover of the law and revels in its conundrums, I will put this interesting question to him. 'When is a Norman serf not a serf on English land?'"

The bailiff opened his mouth, but she went on, "King Henry is forever eager for scholarly debate on points of law. Perhaps in his goodness and wisdom our glorious king will debate this with your lord the sheriff."

The bailiff was beginning to look harried. "As you say, our lord King Henry is a scholar of such matters." He looked around. "Neversby's girl might live with Ralf the serf until such time as the sheriff should decide whether she is a freewoman or a serf. That is, by reason of her marriage."

Constance was not going to let Repton's sheriff decide that. And the bailiff well knew his liege lord did not want to take the question of whether the Norman huntsman was a serf or not on English land to the English king. In the past few years, since the death of his only son, Henry had grown even more cruelly unpredictable.

Beside her, the steward Banastre coughed behind his hand. Constance knew young Brother Welland was staring as though he expected her to turn into a harpy before his eyes and fly out the door.

"I think the king will be well entertained," she said, "to study whether the smith's daughter would be free or serf when married to the sheriff's serf."

The bailiff waited a moment, scowling. "Yes, my lord sheriff would desire that."

In the back, someone groaned.

"But this is a minor matter," he added quickly. "A serf's marriage is not of the greatest importance to my liege. He is a man busy with most important affairs."

There was another pause while the sheriff's men whispered something into the bailiff's ear. Under his breath, Banastre the steward said to Constance, "Milady, that was well played. They are changing course, it would seem."

The bailiff stepped forward. "Lady countess, I speak for my lord the sheriff of Repton when I say it is his wish to keep peace and amity always between you. My lord the sheriff of Repton, as he has said in the past, desires only to know your gracious wish."

Constance didn't look at Brother Welland or Mallory Banastre. "Perhaps soon the king will be prevailed upon to give us his thoughts," she agreed. "That is, on the laws concerning marriage of a freewoman to a Norman serf living in England. And the estate of their children. The sheriff and I would profit much to know this."

At the end of the table, Father Bertrand asked, "Have the banns been read?"

Constance sat back on the bench. The bailiff grudgingly promised that they would be. She saw the huntsman give the smith's daughter a triumphant look. Father Bertrand was writing it all down, that the sheriff of Repton's serf, Ralf, would marry Edith Smithsdaughter, freewoman of Neversby, a sennight after the banns, henceforth to go to live in the village of Repton with her spouse.

Running her finger in the groove on the table, Constance told herself she had done nothing except match wits with the bailiff, and through him the sheriff of Repton, over a village marriage. It was what Julien had warned her about. When Ralf and his sweetheart wed they would be out of her reach. And no doubt the sheriff, who was a grasping man, would test them all someday. She could sit in manor court forever, she thought with a sigh, and learn that nothing was really settled. But the sheriff of Repton would think twice before he challenged her again.

The Neversby villagers and the sheriff's men left the hall. The next hearing concerned a boundary matter. Constance had never held manor court where there was not at least one boundary dispute. Her attention wandered. She was not surprised to see a messenger from Piers de Yerville come from the back.

She ducked her head to say to Mallory Banastre, "I had not expected to hear from Morlaix so soon."

When his turn came the messenger addressed her with her vassal Piers de Yerville's respects and his plea for her to send such provisions as could be spared to her subjects at the castle, as there was a shortage there now.

"The fool," her steward said under his breath. "Did you not leave there but a few weeks ago?"

Constance had known this would happen. She questioned the messenger about the Welsh cattle and grain she'd bargained for, but he did not seem to know of it.

She did not want to go back to Morlaix for the Yuletide, as Christmas at her manor was much pleasanter, but there wasn't much choice. There was little way of relieving de Yerville of some of his duties; his family was as old in England as hers. She must think of something.

She motioned for Everard and questioned the messenger about the castle's needs. Her captain was at her elbow as the messenger produced de Yerville's list.

The full troop, Everard told her in a low voice. They would need the hundred knights and perhaps more to escort that much food through the countryside at Yule.

She couldn't spare the full troop. Constance handed the list to Brother Welland, who began to read it aloud. He did not get through five items when she said, "Mother of God, where does he think we will get all this?"

They looked at each other. Temper short, Constance got up and walked down the hall to the door, leaving Everard and the steward to attend to it.

Outside the door the guard knights, standing with sheepskins thrown over them, looked frozen. They brought up their swords in salute.

The villagers had gone, as had the villeins with their boundary dispute; there was no longer need for the guard. Constance told them to go to the cookhouse, and they grinned and hurried away.

She stood watching ragged flakes spin out of the sky to fall on the fields around the manor. Cattle huddled by a rail fence. A wagon was coming down the road from Neversby, the villein hunched under a cowhide.

She put her hand under her clothes, at her belly. The thought of a child was never far from her mind. She remembered the golden madman who had taken her in her tent that stormy night, his mocking words, his brilliant eyes.

She found herself wondering what it would be like to have his babe. A boy. She had never had a boy. She supposed it would be beautiful.

She turned and started across the yard to the manor house. She knew what it would be like, she told herself. A disaster. Her downfall. She was a fool even to think it.

They had planned to travel to Castle Morlaix some four days before Christmas. In a short time Everard mustered fifty knights for the journey and Mallory Banastre had partially filled de Yerville's list of supplies. Then a messenger came from the king.

Constance took the message from the royal courier on the stairs of the main house. She had been directing her maids cleaning the great hall and her arms were full of brooms and rags. She could barely manage a free hand to take the parchment and roll it open.

His Most Royal Majesty Henry, Sovereign King of England under Christ, commands Constance, Countess of Morlaix, to join King Henry and his family at Winchester to observe the Yule season.

Constance stared at the knight who had brought it, not able to speak.

She had a feeling the worst had happened.

Ten

"You have picked a poor time to visit," the Abbess of St. Hilda's told Constance. "If you were not my own lovely niece I would turn you away."

"I sent a messenger ahead—I thought that would give you forewarning," she said. "And we bring our own provisions." Constance hadn't intended the abbey feed her household and half a hundred knights.

She kicked her feet free of the stirrups and slipped down the side of her mare, stiff with travel in the biting cold. There was hardly room for the Bucksborough party in the convent courtyard, it was so filled with wagons and horses and weeping, expensively gowned women and their servants. She stared about her, curious.

"Where are the children?" her aunt wanted to know.

"In Bucksborough. I go to Winchester for Christmas with the king by his order." Even as she spoke she felt a pang. She seldom traveled without her girls. Everard, too, was missing, gone to Morlaix with the wagons of supplies and half her household knights.

The mass of women pushed forward to see a somberly dressed female come out of the convent chapel and walk toward them. She was followed by a maid carrying a small fluffy white dog.

The little abbess looked resigned. "Tell your knights to picket their horses and camp outside the wall. The guest house is overfull as we are having an enclosure. The bishop will be here tomorrow for the ceremony."

Constance looked around, then back to the pale, reedlike figure in penitential black velvet with the women, obviously her friends, clustered around her.

She said, "Surely not—"

"Oh, but surely *yes.*" The abbess looked impatient. "Diane of Dol, Countess Merwick, desires to be an anchorite in her widowhood. We will enclose her in the courtyard at sext tomorrow."

At the look on her aunt's face, Constance nearly laughed. "The little dog, too?"

She shot her a sharp look. "No, we are having the parting ceremony for Trou-Trou now. That is what the weeping is about."

She took Constance's arm. Behind them, the Bucksborough servants took down her baggage and the knights unsaddled the mare and led it away.

"She is endowing us richly," the abbess went on. "For what the countess's enclosure will bring we can pay off our debts to the episcopate and have food for a year. Come." She steered her to the middle of the courtyard. "Look what a fine domicile our lady has had built."

The little wood and plaster house, or more correctly the anchorite's cell, had been constructed in the middle of the convent yard. It had only one door, still open to show the spartan furnishings inside.

Constance looked in and saw a wooden bed, a table with a candle on it, a bowl and spoon, and a necessity chair with a bucket under it. The far wall had a large, shuttered window where the anchorite could stand and receive the world after she was formally enclosed, accept food and alms, and dispense compassion and wisdom.

But not that much shut away as one might think. And no pet dogs.

The abbess said, "Enclosure has become very fashionable, especially for widows of a certain age. There has been a rash of it in the south. I give this one six months."

Constance spluttered, swallowing her laugh.

"Hush," her aunt told her, "such levity is unseemly. Besides, we are not laughing here. The chapter does not fare well, neither do the monks in our sister house."

Constance turned to look down the hill where St. Dunstan's monastery sat among the winter-bare trees. St. Hilda's convent and St.

Dunstan's, with its lazarhouse where the monks cared for lepers, was one of the few sister establishments remaining in England. The Norman clergy did not look with favor on the old Anglo-Saxon-style monasteries with nuns and monks living in separate chapter houses and often working side by side.

They walked to a less crowded part of the yard. The new anchorite was holding up her dog in both hands and kissing it farewell to the accompaniment of her friends' and her own loud sobbing.

"Tell me that you do not fear you will be put out," Constance said.

The other woman shrugged. "I have gone through all of my own money here. I can do no good." At Constance's look of concern she waved her hand. "Ah, don't fret, I am not sorry to welcome Diane of Dol. Before she tires of her saintly life we will have wealth enough for our own pressing needs."

They went across the yard and into St. Hilda's chapter house. In the main room there was a small fire on the hearth. They drew stools up and sat down.

Constance reached up and threw back her fur-trimmed hood. The room was not warm but it was not uncomfortable, either. Bunches of dried herbs hung in the rafters, giving the air a faint fragrance.

"I came to ask about placing my eldest child for her education," she said.

Her little aunt, hands clasped before her, regarded her stilly. The ghost of her prettiness was still there in her bright eyes, her heart-shaped child's face. Constance remembered the old stories. That her father's sister had been mad for love of a childhood sweetheart, a knight who had gone on crusade, but had been married off by her family to a French nobleman, regardless—a marriage that did not survive. It was said Alys of Aubigny had entered the religious life while her husband was still alive, after the death of a son.

"If your child is the age I remember, she is too young," her aunt was saying. "We can take her at twelve, but not before."

"And my youngest, Beatriz," Constance said, "both of my girls. I want them to have your best, some deportment, music, and needlework, Latin at the very least, Greek and Hebrew—I don't know. And numbers. You know I am no scholar, but my arithmetics have always been good."

She had never regretted her lack of convent school. Being the oldest girl, her father had had her tutored by an old monk at St. Aidan's. But it was more fashionable now, especially if one was high-born, to go to a convent for one's learning.

The abbess kept her eyes on Constance's face. "Why," she said, "has the king sent for you?"

Constance looked away. Her abbess aunt had vast experience reading faces.

"It has been some time since King Henry has

seen me," she said carefully. "In the last year, I petitioned him not to—"

Her aunt cut her off. "Yes, I know of it, the dispensation. You do not have to tell me again."

A young girl in a postulant's habit came in with bowls of hot broth. Her aunt took hers in both hands and blew on it.

Constance balanced her bowl in her lap and took up the spoon. "Tell me, aunt, what do you know of the nun Heloise? And Peter Abelard?"

The little abbess looked at her over the rim of the bowl. "Has this to do with why the king has sent for you?"

Constance put her broth on the floor beside the stool. Her face was burning. She felt like one of the convent students. "Perhaps."

"Hmmm." The other woman studied her as she spooned her soup. "I can tell you of Heloise. We are all Benedictine, the same order, and Heloise is one of our own. The Holy Mother in Heaven knows there has been enough to gossip about."

"I do not ask for secrets."

"Hunh!" She looked sour. "Nothing in this terrible business is a secret now. Although the marriage was, at one time. They say that was the beginning of the trouble."

"Marriage?" She'd not been told that.

The abbess stood up and walked a few steps away from the fire, her hands clasped before her. "Afterward, you will tell me why you wish to know it."

"I don't know that I need—"

The other woman made an impatient sound. "Come, you said Heloise and Abelard, did you not?"

In the hidden corridors of the convent they heard the sound of young voices. She turned back to the fire.

"Heloise is Canon Fulbert's niece, although not many at Argenteuil believed that was true. Fulbert is a churchman, a canon at the Cathedral of Notre Dame. When I was at St. Sulpice, before I left France, I had always heard that Heloise was Fulbert's illegitimate daughter. The mother's name was Hersinde. There was never any mention of the father, who would have been Fulbert's brother. There is no denying Fulbert was enchanted with the child, proud of the intelligence the nuns, in their mistaken pride, cultivated. Because it was this, Heloise's gift for learning, that attracted Peter Abelard to her. He suggested to Fulbert that she become his pupil."

Constance murmured, "A great elevation for a convent student."

"Oh, Fulbert wanted it for her. She was his pride and glory, all Paris—all France—talked of beautiful, learned young Heloise. Fulbert basked in the triumph of what Abbess Bertholde and the sisters had done at Argenteuil, all those years of teaching. All of them so proud of their brilliant darling, wanting only the best for her."

She turned and walked back. "Then we have the famed young philosopher, a canon, the *ma-*

gister scholarum of the cloister schools of Notre Dame, a *clericus,* not a priest but a tonsured holder of minor orders, Peter Abelard. Someone has called Abelard an attractive, unbearable man. He destroyed his teacher, Anselm of Leon, when he was at his school by brilliantly exposing poor Anselm's dull wits. He ousted William of Champeaux at Notre Dame the same way and took his former master's place. He is a marvel of a teacher, and as master of all the cloister schools he has raised Notre Dame to the heights of any college in Italy or the German Emperor's domain. He has admitted to the world that lust was his only interest in Heloise, that there were no worlds left to conquer except those he had denied himself. Fulbert took Heloise from her convent at Argenteuil and brought Abelard to live in his house so that they could be together while Abelard taught her. I am sure this was Abelard's idea." She raised her clasped hands. "Mother of God, I cannot think Fulbert could be so deluded."

Constance watched as her aunt paced back again.

"Yes, you see it is upsetting even to speak of it. I knew many of the sisters at Argenteuil who had taught Heloise. They had seen her as a prodigy, her future perhaps as a famed scholar in all Europe—and a *woman!* So they agonized, helpless, when the inevitable happened. Abelard and Heloise fell madly in love. Oh, I know Peter said it was lust that spurred him, but he was a victim of his own wicked cleverness. They made love in his room when he was thought to be teaching her. He was besotted, so carried away as to be quite reckless in his personal behavior. He neglected his pupils, abandoned all effort at serious teaching, paid no mind to the gossip which raged through Paris, and wrote love poems and songs to Heloise that were read and sung all over the city. He taught his classes in a stupor of sleeplessness; his students made merciless fun of him when they saw the great Abelard engulfed in his first taste of passion. And then, of course, Fulbert found them together."

The same student came for their soup bowls and took them away. Abbess Alys waited until she was gone.

"There was a terrible uproar. The uncle, Fulbert, parted them at once, and Abelard left the house. But Heloise wrote him joyously soon after that she was carrying their child. They left Paris—some said he abducted her she was so unwilling to go, and he dressed her as a nun so she wouldn't be recognized and took her to his family fief, to his sister and her husband in Brittany. The baby, their son, was born there."

She sat down on the stool. "I think they were happy for a while," she said in a different voice. "Abelard had retired once before to the Breton country for six years, after the episode of Anselm of Leon. *Six years.* Overwork, some said then. A malaise of the soul after so much early ambition."

There was a silence.

The abbess sighed. "But Peter Abelard, the genius of the *disputatio* schools, missed his far-off Brittany, where adoring crowds of young men had followed him everywhere. Abelard made Heloise leave their baby behind—with his sister and they returned to Paris. The rest I know only as what the nuns at Argenteuil have made known to the rest of us. The uncle, Canon Fulbert, pressed for a marriage to ease his disgrace. He was not happy nor satisfied with Heloise living as Abelard's mistress. Some say the notion was Abelard's. It was disastrous, this fancy—a mistress for a canon of Notre Dame is not uncommon; the church would have tolerated it far better than they imagined."

Constance rubbed her brow, thinking that the story was much more complicated than what she had overheard the monks discussing. One never dreamed that these things could happen.

"Heloise, brave and sensible young woman that she is," the abbess continued, "pleaded against marriage. They were in no danger living as they were, she argued, as man and mistress. She was so loving—she thought only of Abelard, and was sure that a marriage would destroy his career in the church. But Abelard has never turned from the provocative or the dangerous. Fulbert pressed for marriage and Abelard, with one of his strange turns of mind, agreed. They would marry, but secretly."

Constance sat staring at her. "A secret marriage?"

"An insane idea. Heloise despaired. She had been forced to leave her babe, she was in Paris living in Fulbert's house once more, a married woman with no way to live as one. I do not know what happened. Once before Abelard had put her in nun's clothes to take her to Brittany to have her babe—a strange conceit. No one will tell me why they were persuaded at Argenteuil to take Heloise back with them. Although Abbess Bertholde, Anne the prioress, and the nuns so truly loved her they would have done anything for her. It was Abelard who insisted that the marriage be secret, and that Heloise leave Fulbert's house and live at Argenteuil convent dressed as a postulant—as one who desires to take holy vows."

The convent bells began to ring for nones, and the abbess paused. She turned to Constance.

"I have told them at Argenteuil that they had taken some of the others' madness into the convent. For the story of the secret marriage was out, as all secrets will, all over Paris, and at the same time Heloise was living by some insane fancy of Abelard's dressed as a postulant at her old convent school. Worse, Abelard would come out from Paris—it seemed he could not stay away from her. Once, having no better place for their passion, he took her on the table in the convent's refectory while the nuns were at mass."

The little abbess turned to pace the hearth. "What was in their minds, these two? Why did not the sisters at Argenteuil do something? Alas, Heloise would do anything Abelard told her—she put her god before herself, always. And Fulbert, beside himself now that the story of the secret marriage was all over Paris, heard that Abelard had persuaded her to return to Argenteuil dressed in a nun's habit!"

"Why—" Constance began. At that moment a nun came to the door and caught the abbess's eye.

She nodded and stood up.

"Do you read Greek? No, I don't suppose you do. In Greek, it is said that whom the gods would destroy they first make mad. Canon Fulbert was convinced that Peter Abelard intended to set his wife, Heloise, aside. Why else would she be at Argenteuil, dressed as a postulant? Imagine Fulbert's rage—his beautiful, learned, brilliant Heloise he had adored from childhood. He had watched Abelard destroy her from the moment he'd brought him into his house—and now she was ruined and cast aside in a nunnery.

"Fulbert bribed Abelard's servant, Thibaud, who opened the door to Abelard's rooms one night. Canon Fulbert and his servants and some others came in and found Abelard in his bed, and castrated him."

She took Constance's arm and pulled her up from her stool. "Don't look like that. We have all felt like that. It is all over—there is nothing to be done."

Constance could not move. Stunned, she

fixed her eyes on her aunt's face. "Holy Mother save us," she whispered. "What happened to them?"

The little abbess pushed her toward the door. "I will tell you the rest after prayers."

Eleven

Constance did not sleep. The bed was hard and the unheated room, the cell of a nun who had died, was bitterly cold; even her fur-lined cloak pulled over extra bedcovers brought from the wagon did not keep her warm.

Just as she was retiring the knight serjeant, Carcefou, came to the convent gate to ask that the troop of knights be allowed to camp in the village. Constance granted their request, although she knew the reason for it. The men would be better entertained close to the village ale house than against the convent wall.

After she crept into bed she lay listening to the loud talk and coming and going at the guest house where Diane of Dol's friends were spending the night. When that had quieted, the convent pupils at the end of the building embarked on a whispered, giggling journey through the corridors which she could only guess was some of the younger girls on a trip to the jakes. Probably a nightly ritual.

After that the hours dragged on. She needed sleep but it would not come; she was near to exhaustion with the long trip from Bucksborough, anxiety about her summons to Winchester, and her secret worry, that she might be carrying the jongleur's child. But her mind, churning with what her aunt had told her about Abelard and Heloise, would not rest.

God's face, she thought, rolling over in the comfortless bed and yanking the covers around her, how could anyone not be haunted by such a tragedy? When her aunt had come to the end of what she knew, Constance had wept for Heloise, and her child. Even for Peter Abelard.

She had not dared ask if there had been any mention anywhere of a student of Abelard's by the name of Cenred. Yet the story her aunt told matched in most ways that of Father Bertrand's.

In the morning when it was discovered that Peter Abelard had been attacked in his bed, all Paris rose up in shock and anger. A mob led by his students found Thibaud, the treacherous servant who'd let the mutilators into Abelard's rooms, and blinded and castrated the man. Canon Fulbert, Heloise's so-called uncle, took refuge in the cathedral.

Even now, lying awake in the dark at St. Hilda's, Constance could not hold back a shudder. From what Father Bertrand had said, Cenred had been one of the frenzied avengers. It sickened her just to think of it.

There had been no one to keep the mob from carrying out its wild vengeance; even if Peter

Abelard had wanted to stop them, it was beyond his power. Lying feverish and in great pain, he had been overcome with revulsion at what had been done to him. In his own words, he had become the Hebrews' "unclean beast" of the Bible. A eunuch.

The uproar of students rioting through the Paris streets, the confusion of his helpless friends coming and going in his rooms that terrible first day, had not comforted Abelard, only plunged him into wild despair. Abbess Alys thought Heloise had rushed to him from the convent at Argenteuil, but that he had rejected her grief and care for him. So great was Abelard's shame that what happened next was almost unbelievable.

There seemed nothing left for the Notre Dame school's great idol to do but take holy orders, become a priest, and retire to the monastery of St. Denis. Abelard had been honest, saying it was not a call to God that moved him but the wish to escape, in his misery, from the world. So powerful friends made arrangements that waived the usual proper time for a novitiate at any monastery. Then, finally, he had one last cruel task: to make Heloise take holy vows and enter Argenteuil as a nun.

Abelard took days to persuade her, threatening, arguing, pleading. When the world found out what he intended Heloise to do, her former teachers at Argenteuil—those who knew her from as far away as Provence, some who did not know her at all—sent messages to Heloise. Because of her youth—she was only nineteen then—her beauty, and her intellectual promise, they begged her not to shut herself away.

But Abelard prevailed. Heloise said she was not becoming a nun for the love of God, but for love of Peter Abelard.

"*He* was her god," her aunt had said. "Abbess Bertholde at Argenteuil put into words what we all knew, that Heloise would follow Abelard to hell. And for their beautiful Heloise, who did not want to enter the cloister, did not want to remove herself from the world and her child and her lover, the convent *was* hell."

What drove a knife through Heloise's heart was that Peter Abelard insisted that she enter the convent first. Intent on seeing that she was his alone and that no other man would ever have her, he stood in the back of the church and watched as Heloise took her vows. Only after seeing her safe within the cloister did Abelard take his own holy orders and enter the monastery of St. Denis.

"It broke her heart," the little abbess said, "that as much as she loved him, Peter Abelard did not trust her."

Abelard's jealous mistrust would have been no more than Constance would have expected. But why, she wondered, had it all happened in just that way? Even her aunt acknowledged the irregularities—that it had all been done so swiftly—so many of Abelard's powerful friends had arranged to have the church swallow them up, he to St. Denis, Heloise to her old convent of Argenteuil.

"You ask why?" Her aunt raised her eyebrows. "To my mind too many of those high-placed in the church were eager to be rid of them both. Heloise is even now seen as the instrument of Abelard's downfall. Are we not familiar with the church's teachings—St. Jerome, St. Augustine, St. Paul—on the sinful temptation of women's vile bodies? Besides, Abelard has many enemies as well as friends. Abbot Bernard of Clairvaux considers him if not exactly a heretic then at least wild, uncontrollable, a menace to the faith of the holy church."

"Is he?"

"Hah." The abbess had made a face. "I don't think Abelard himself knows. His last treatise, *De Unitate et Trinitate Divina,* was burned, and now he's causing trouble at St. Denis, the very place which took him in."

Peter Abelard had not waited long to recover the powers of his formidable intellect and begin to challenge authority. At St. Denis, he said his study of the historian Bede confirmed his suspicion that the abbey had been named for the wrong St. Denis—not Dionysius the Areopagite as they believed. And if that were not enough, he issued an angry denunciation of the abbot and the monks for living unclean and dissolute lives.

Probably true, Abbess Alys admitted, shrugging. There is always some of that when men live together, and monasteries are no exception.

But the monks at St. Denis apparently had seen Abelard, a handsome man even in his infamous condition, and were attracted to him, perhaps even because of it. The abbot, particularly. That had been five years ago. Peter Abelard had since left St. Denis after a hearing on the monastery's alleged depravity in which nothing had been proved, and gone back to teaching.

His many students in Paris had been waiting for his return and even more arrived in the city hoping he would set up his school again. A rich and important friend had given Abelard some land for a retreat in the east, near Burgundy, and hundreds of his former pupils followed him there to camp in the fields and help him build an oratory.

And what of Heloise?

The abbess turned her face away. "When she was to take her vows and enter Argenteuil she asked to see her babe one last time. And she wept."

Heloise was now prioress of Argenteuil, still not reconciled to her fate. Still loving Peter Abelard.

Constance sat up in the bed. There were noises in the corridor outside. She listened, her heart beating loudly. Then she realized it was mostly older nuns who, the abbess had told her, rose for matins. It was three hours after midnight.

She thought of the women in the icy chapel praying in the middle of the night. And of Heloise.

Suddenly she could not help it—she began to weep. Silently at first, as some strange knot of misery grew down inside her and made her very heart hurt, then with large, gulping, despairing sobs, as a child cries.

She wept for a long time sitting in her bed in the dark, hands covering her face. Sobbing for Heloise and her babe, for broken Abelard. Even for mad Cenred, wandering the countryside and shouting his rage and grief to the world at the loss of his god, and for Cenred's babe she might be carrying. It was as though a wave of something unknown had begun there in Paris and swept on, reaching out to touch all of them.

When she lay down again Constance was exhausted, empty of tears. She suddenly knew something had happened. She sat up and pulled back the covers to look at her gown, and saw the red stain. Her courses had begun.

In the morning her eyes were swollen and she plainly looked as though she had not slept. As usual with her flux Constance felt listless; she struggled through lauds in the convent chapel trying not to go to sleep where she stood. After prayers her Aunt Alys walked with her to the horses. Her servants were loading the wagons with baggage, bundled to the ears in the cold, their breaths puffs of steam on the air. The knights had come from the village and waited outside in the road. A fog hugged the ground and swirled as high as the horses' hocks. They heard the convent pupils singing at mass. There was no sign of the new anchorite or her fashionable friends. At the gate a ragged villein was standing with a rail-thin child.

"Go away," the abbess told them. "Why do you keep coming here? I told you, I can do nothing."

The child shrank back, but the man said something Constance could not catch, and held out his hand, pleading. Her aunt turned away.

"What do they want?" Constance asked.

The abbess made an angry gesture. "He cannot feed her. The drought has been bad and there are more at home just as hungry. The father wants me to take her into the convent. God's faith, we are having a hard time feeding our own!"

Constance thought of her own girls. Hodierne was about the same age.

"I could only put her in the kitchen," her aunt went on. "Pupils pay for their schooling."

"Then put her in the kitchen," Constance said. "I will send you some money for her."

Her aunt turned to her. "Hah, would you bring down a flood of starvelings on us? That is what would happen, niece, if I take Durand's girl. The village has a surfeit of children; every day some are taken into the forest and abandoned."

"Then I will endow five," Constance said, stubbornly, "for a year." She told herself it could not take that much money to feed and clothe five little girls.

"Give me your word on it," the abbess said.

"You have my word." Her aunt held her stirrup as Constance hauled herself into the saddle.

The little abbess stepped close, looked around to make sure the others were not near enough to hear, and said, "Now what was the trouble that made you come to ask about Peter Abelard and his wife?"

Constance managed a pale smile. "There was no trouble. I was only curious."

Her aunt frowned. "I do not expect you to tell me lies. There is only one thing to make a woman so unhappy she cannot speak of it to anyone, and that is a man."

Before Constance could say anything, she went on, "I am not unaware the king has given you this dispensation not to have to marry. You remind the world of its constantly."

Constance flushed. She jerked in the mare sharply, which made it snort and back. The abbess let go of the reins. "I'm telling you the truth, there is no trouble now. Besides, what does it matter?" She knew she was giving herself away. "I will never see him again."

She walked the mare to the gate and out into the road to the column of knights. They made their goodbyes, Constance leaning down for her aunt's blessing and kiss on her cold cheek. The fog was beginning to lift. By noon it would be a clear winter day.

Once away from St. Hilda's and St. Dunstan's they turned south. The knights were sluggish after carousing in the village ale house all night. Carcefou rode up and down the lines cursing those that dozed in the saddle. He shot furtive glances at Constance, but she could hardly keep her head up herself.

She missed her children, she thought sleepily. There was no one to talk to unless she wanted to travel in a wagon in the rear with her maids. She preferred to ride her mare.

The road dipped into a marsh, the fog thick in the low places. Suddenly they heard horses' hooves and the sound of jingling gear. Carcefou shouted for the column to fall to the right.

Strange knights rode at them out of the mist. Constance's troop had reined in on the side of the path. The others kept coming, all in silence. They wore polished steel helms and bright steel chain mail with white tunics over them. Each knight carried a lance with a white guidon.

A ghost troop. In the wagons the servants gaped and a few crossed themselves. There was no sound but the horses' hooves and the dripping fog.

The strangers kept their eyes stonily ahead as they passed except for the huge leader, who wore a helmet sprouting white cock feathers. His pale eyes passed over Constance, then looked away.

Someone swore. The ten ghostly knights passed down the road and the fog swallowed them.

Carcefou trotted his horse up quickly to Constance. She managed a laugh. "Holy Mother, were they real?"

"Germans." He looked back down the road. "They are the emperor's men or I am a Martinmas pig. But what do they here?"

Constance suddenly yawned. "Well, thank God and the saints they are not looking for us."

She nudged her mare with her heels. If they could keep going until the sun had warmed the air then they could stop and make camp, perhaps at noon. She felt swollen, uncomfortable—not so happy, after all, that her monthly flow had come. She would not have minded another baby, she thought wistfully; now that there was no chance of it she felt safe in thinking that.

In the front of the column, a knight had begun to sing. The sun came out in brilliant, sudden light, making the marshes glisten.

Perhaps they would camp earlier than noontime, Constance told herself. She didn't know if she could keep awake that long.

She yawned again.

The little group of entertainers stood huddled outside the great hall of the Earl of Hereford's castle. Some, like the lightly-clad acrobats, hugged themselves against the wind that laced across the bailey and around the castle's stone walls. The sun was going down and it was cold.

The tall, fair-haired man in a green satin shortcoat skipped a copper coin back and forth across the knuckles of his hands to keep them warmed and limber. Then with a quick movement he palmed the coin out of the ear of a dwarf standing with the acrobats. The dwarf swatted the side of his head without turning and cursed ill-naturedly.

Inside the hall a burst of laughter greeted a band of mummers, rouged men in wigs and long gowns who were about to perform a bawdy farce called "The Trojan Women."

Thierry de Yners had watched the coin disappear between the jongleur's fingers, then come back again. "Well done—you are very skilled at that," he said, admiringly. "A coin trick will beget coins in plenty for you, but take my advice and don't try Hereford with that bit. The earl hates tricks. It's the countess who will warm to you. Pull two or three out of her bodice, if you can. She's old enough to like it immensely."

The tall man had been studying him. Then he said, "De Yners?"

The other leaned forward. They were standing in the light that spilled from the open door; part of him was in shadow.

"I know that voice." The scholar moved toward him eagerly. "God is my judge—Cenred? *Cenred?* It *is* you! St. George save us, what do you here so far from Paris?"

The jongleur said, "I might ask you the same."

"God's truth, man, seeking to feed myself, no less than you!" Thierry pulled out several vellum rolls from the front of his long grey gown. "They are thirsting for this stuff now here in England, anything that smacks of the cultivated mind, even when it bores them. Which it usually does. I am giving a bit of the Metamorphoses, Jupiter and Europa, first in Latin very quickly, then in Norman French which the gentry love, with dramatic embellishments. And finally, Saxon English for the back of the room. You are looking prosperous." His eyes roamed over the silk jacket paired with rough woolen braies and fancy red boots. "What do you do tonight besides the coin tricks?"

"My prosperous clothes are a gift from a Welsh friend," Cenred told him. "Stolen from somewhere before the friend departed for the Welsh mountains. And as for what I do tonight, if the hall is quiet enough I will sing parts of the Song of Roland so that those who are already drunk will celebrate their bravery and get even drunker. But none of it is as difficult, I imagine, as holding them with Ovid."

Thierry shrugged. "I pick amorous lines only." He hesitated, then said, "You know, do you not, that Peter Abelard is building an oratory he calls the Paraclete, and his students have flocked to him by the hundreds. It is a great vindication. Abelard has never been more popular in spite of the enmity of Bernard of Clairvaux and the others. Have you seen him since—since that night?"

The blue eyes were distant. "I saw Peter before I left Paris. He did not have much to say to me then, nor I to him." He said in a different voice, "Tell me, de Yners, what do you know of her? How does she fare?"

The acrobats had just gone inside for their turn and the entertainers' line at the door moved forward. They moved with it.

Thierry saw the light strike his face. With those vivid eyes on him he blurted, "She is prioress of Argenteuil now. She is still beautiful. Still in love with him. Still unhappy. They tell me he does not write, has not seen her; it is as if he plans never to think of her again."

Inside they could hear the cheering for the acrobats. Thierry took him by the sleeve. "They said you disappeared, vowing never to return. You, the shining star to whom we all looked, after Abelard. That you—that you—"

The other's eyes glinted. "That I am mad."

Thierry shuddered. "Believe me, I shall put the lie to it when I go south. I swore it couldn't be true. Those of us who knew you at Notre Dame never believed it."

Cenred pulled another coin from his jacket. He juggled two of them across his hands. "But I *was* mad. I am a lunatic now." He smiled, wolfishly. "You have just not seen it."

The young scholar looked uneasy. "Ah, one never knows when you are joking. It was the same in Paris." His manner turned brisk. "Listen, after this feasting here at Hereford's you must come with me. All the troubadours, the mummers, and comedians on God's earth are going to King Henry's court at Christmas.

There will be enough of us and more to go around—the court's Christmas lingers on past Epiphany unless the king is attacked again with a fit of melancholy." His eyes sized him up. "You are big and strong. You can earn good money at the revels if you can hold up under rough treatment. Can you play the Christmas Fool?"

The other put his coins away as they moved to the door. "Thierry, you are an innocent. How do you know I am not mad?" He laughed at the expression on the scholar's face. "Nay, be easy, I play a perfect Christmas Fool. And I am big enough to take the beatings. Where does the court go this year?"

Thierry, vellums in hand, moved toward the entrance to the Earl of Hereford's hall. "We will talk of this later, and plan it together. But this year the king goes to Winchester."

Twelve

Everard was standing in a sunny spot of the outer bailey drinking a tankard of Morlaix ale when one of his English knights sidled up to him. "There's something wrong here," the knight said out of the corner of his mouth.

Everard nodded, and lifted the cup again to his lips. The knight's name was Hrolf, a good sort and sharp-eyed; it was just unwise at that moment to talk. He had been watching the tallying by the castle reeves for some time. There were three of them at the table with Piers de Yerville, the steward.

It was clever, Everard had to admit, this tallying by notched sticks and knotted string. It was complicated enough so that the castle clerk was having trouble keeping up with his transcribing.

As well he might, Everard thought. Unless he was losing his good Gascon wits there were two sets of accounts going on and no one, apparently, the wiser. Unless the Welsh were in on it.

He hadn't been able to decide. The grain wagons from Bucksborough had gone through the tally earlier and the sacks were being unloaded. For the sake of Sir Everard's convenience, the steward had explained, the tally for the Welshmen's cattle had been interrupted to do the Bucksborough supplies, and now was resuming again. Although, Everard was sure, not in the same place.

According to his calculations the gap left thirty, perhaps as much as fifty, head of cattle unaccounted for. The Welshmen, clumped by the cattle pens, looked unconcerned. *Unconcerned* or *unknowing?* Were the Welsh being duped, or were they a part of it?

It was a good question. The reeves and the steward were not at all alarmed that he was there, or that he might suspect their intricate tallying. One would take them for the very picture of industrious innocence.

On the other hand the Bucksborough wagons, as far as he could tell, were tallied fair and honestly. It was just the damned Welsh that bothered him. They had furnished a lot of cattle to the castle this year—it was not like them to be so lax.

And not only the Welsh and their cattle, he thought, scratching his jaw with the rim of his cup. De Yerville never showed a profit here, and God knows the people were poor enough from their look. Then there were the demands on the countess every winter to supply the castle with provisions. One had to be both blind and stupid not to suspect something was going on. Hrolf was not the only one.

He handed his empty cup to a stable knave and walked to the herders gathered at the cattle pens.

"Pick me a good cow," Everard said to the old man in a bearskin.

Maredudd squinted at him. "Cow?" he said. He thought about it. "What kind of cow?"

"One of those." Everard pointed to some longhorned cattle clustered at the far end of the pen. "A heifer ready to calve."

The steward, de Yerville, had been watching them. Now a tally reeve got up from the table and hurried over.

"Sir Everard." The tally reeve smiled from ear to ear. "What is your wish?"

"Cow," the old Welshman said. He pulled at his nose hairs with thumbnail and forefinger, his eyes on Everard. "Is it a gift you want it for? Those are fine cattle there."

"A gift, yes." The tally reeve glared at the old Welshman. "A nice gift for someone, Sir Everard?"

"I will pay for it," he said. "How much is a brown cow ready to calve?"

Maredudd lifted his arm from the fence rail and straightened up. "Two silver pennies," he rumbled. "Two and a half and I'll pick you a good one."

The tally reeve looked back at the table. His smile grew pinched. "No, no, a gift for *Sir Everard,* don't you understand?" He pushed the old man out of the way. "Will you be riding away with it, Sir Everard? If so, I will have the herders find you a rope."

Everard nodded. "Yes, I need a long lead."

Shrugging, the old Welshman let himself into the pen and cut out two heifers. He drove them, waving his arms, toward their end of the pen.

Both of them looked good. Everard chose one with a white blaze on her face and went to get his horse. The cow ready to calve was worth a penny in these drought times—not two nor two and a half as the old man had told him—and less in the late winter when feed was short. Still, although he was knight captain to the countess and accustomed to gifts, a good, healthy cow without cost was too generous. He couldn't bring himself to believe that they were trying to bribe him. Again he wondered what they were doing with the provisions they had bargained for, and those that had been sent from Bucksborough.

He led the cow out of the castle portal gate and down the hill. She was balky. When she stopped, Everard jerked on the rope and she fell down. He had to wait for her to get up again as he didn't want to drag her; it would injure the calf. Leading the cow behind his destrier, Thunderer, was awkward enough; he knew they were watching from the castle. He had a certain reputation and most of the Morlaix people were afraid of him; now they were doubtless enjoying seeing him leading a fractious heifer down the road to the village.

He brought the animal toward the river and the bridge where some boys who were fishing gawked at him, openmouthed. It took longer to reach the weavers' cots than he'd thought. The settlement was beyond an oak woods on the far side of the others. He chose the last house at the end of the lane, bigger than the rest. They had seen him coming. Children who had been playing in the road ran inside and slammed the door.

A moment later the door opened and a man appeared, wiping his hands on his apron. He squinted up at Everard on the big destrier. From his expression the weaver knew who he was.

Everard told him what he wanted. A woman came to the doorway behind him. "No," she cried. She was tall, with some grey in her fair hair. The weaver's wife. She put her hand over her mouth and looked at the cow.

"Yes," Everard said. He dismounted, the cow's lead rope in his hand. "Take me inside—I want to look at them."

The man stood with his feet planted, face stubborn. "Sir Everard, you know we do not give our women to the knights."

Everard held out the cow's lead rope to the woman. She took it, her mouth trembling, not looking at him.

Three girls appeared in the doorway behind the woman. He knew they'd been listening. They were tall like their mother, their heads covered with scarves, but he could see strands of light brown hair. They were pretty girls. They kept their eyes downcast.

At least the girls knew what he wanted; that was why he had brought the cow. Simple bargaining. No force. No unpleasantness.

"Lord sir," the weaver said. He stood with his arms outspread, blocking Everard's way. "Sir Everard, you were there at the hearing when I told the countess that we do not give our women this way. Please—"

Everard moved toward the door.

"No!" The woman threw herself in between. She dragged her husband to one side. "Go—do what you want," she said hoarsely.

Everard went into the house. The girls led the way into the cramped front room, full of bales of cloth. When Everard came in they were standing together against one wall. The mother put her hand to her mouth and moaned.

He had seen them before in the village. The one in the middle, the long-legged one, he thought. She felt his eyes on her and looked up. He liked the shape of her face, her mouth, the eyelids delicate over wide brown eyes.

He reached out and took her hand. Her fingers were shaking. The mother gave a loud cry and began to weep. The father stepped forward to stop him.

Everard lifted his hand. He still wore his mailed gauntlet. The weaver saw it and stopped short. One of the girls went to her father and put her arm around his shoulders.

He said to the woman, "We need a room."

She held her hands to her mouth, sobbing, as he followed her toward the back of the house.

From the look of it the room was the one used by the mother and father. He supposed the girls and other children slept above in the loft. The lintel was low. He had to duck his head to enter.

The place was not large but it was clean, with no chickens or other animals. The bed was big and covered with white linens. He was surprised at the fineness of the coverings until he remembered they were all weavers. Cloth was their craft.

He let go the girl's hand and bent and punched his fist down on the bed, testing it. It was an excellent bed, with rope springs. He sat down on it and took off his gauntlets, then his helmet. His hair was sweaty, and he ran his hands through it. The two women stood watching him.

Everard stood up and unbuckled his sword belt and put his sword and scabbard on the floor by the bed. The mother said something in their Saxon dialect and they both went out. He was pulling off his hauberk when the mother came back with a basin of water and a cloth. She held it out to him.

They wanted him to wash. He liked that.

He took the basin and cloth and put it on the floor. He shrugged out of his padded jacket, his tunic and chausses and sat down on the bed to pull off his boots. Then he picked up the bowl of water and cloth and began to wash his face and arms. His body smelled of sweat.

He was washing his groin when the girl came in, barefoot, wearing only her shift. She stopped short and stared at him. She had taken off her headcovering and her hair was loose and unbound, the color of dark honey. The points of her young breasts thrust out under the clinging shift. He could see the swell of her rounded hips, the outline of her thighs.

He turned his back to her, already aroused. "Get into the bed," he said in Saxon.

He heard the creak of the ropes as she settled herself. He turned and made sure his sword was where he could reach it before he got in beside her.

She was under the white coverlet. He pulled it back and motioned for her to sit up. He stripped the shift over her head and knelt beside her in the bed, looking at her.

Naked, she was even prettier than he had expected, with smooth, butter-colored skin and long, waving brown hair. Her arms were slender and round and her breasts full with tight, pouting pink tips. A small waist, and the long slender legs were perfect.

He found he wanted her right away. "Have you had a man before?" he asked.

She stared at him as though she didn't understand. He repeated it in Saxon. She bent her head and shook it, no, her long hair sliding silkily over her breasts and bare shoulders.

That also pleased him, although he was not

one who insisted on virgins. His need, however, was growing pressing. He was ramrod stiff, beginning to hurt.

Carefully, he turned her over on her knees, then took her arms and propped her elbows on the bed. Her long hair fell away, exposing the back of her neck. He heard her breath, quick and frightened. Her spine dipped into the small of her back in a graceful curve; below that was the full, creamy swell of her backside. He put his hand between her legs, into the soft furry warmth there and his fingers spread her flesh apart.

"Be still," Everard murmured, moving himself over her.

She was tight under his touch, and dry. He stroked his fingers into her, first one, then two together to stretch her. When he put both fingers in her she gasped loudly. He moved them in and out. Slowly, she became wet.

His own body was hard, his groin cramping. A pulse pounded in his head and his very skin seemed on fire. He hadn't been like this since he was fourteen. He knew that his hands shook as he guided his shaft toward the tight, sweet opening between her legs. It had been a long time.

Constance. My beloved.

"It will hurt a little," he said hoarsely.

He held her hips in both hands and pushed into her. She tensed, her back and shoulders stiff. Pushing against her hot tightness was agonizing. He pressed against the barrier of her maidenhood and saw her take a deep, shuddering breath. When he broke it she gave a muffled scream. Trembling, he slid to the hilt in her.

He stopped, closing his eyes, needing control. He didn't know why he was suddenly like this. Sweet Jesu, she set him on fire!

Under him was the length of her curving body, then his own, darker, more powerful, his legs and groin pressed tight to her buttocks, his flesh buried in her.

He tried not to think of the weavers' girl he held beneath him, but of his own love's cool beauty, dark hair. Her crystal eyes.

Constance, my love.

He plunged into the girl, feeling her clasped tight around him. He ground his teeth, trying to maintain the movement. *Honey-brown hair. Long beautiful legs. The girl panting under him.*

The vision he was trying to hold failed him. Faded completely away.

Bloody hell.

Everard pulled out of her and sat up. There was a blotch of red on the weavers' white covers. He sat on the edge of the bed, cursing himself, nerves raw, shaking and unsatisfied. Sweet angels in heaven, he could hardly think! He was hard as a rock and in pain—he needed release. He wanted to think of his love, bury himself in sweet Constance, that was the accursed reason for all this. He looked down at the girl on the bed. This brown-haired weavers' daughter had fuddled his mind.

She looked up at him, her hand pressed between her legs. He knew how he must look to her. A fighter, a knight with scars on his body. Swarthy, not like her people with his black hair and olive-skinned body. A man from the south.

Still, he thought as he watched her, she had made only that small cry when he took her maidenhood. He remembered her standing with her sisters in the front room. Looking at him.

Was it true, he wondered, what the weavers said? That only their women could choose who would bed them? Under his breath, Everard cursed.

She drew in her breath sharply when he bent over her. He put his mouth against hers. For a moment she lay still, then she moved her hand to the back of his neck. With a groan he opened his lips and tasted her. She was sweet, shivering, excited. Curious.

God help him, perhaps it was better that he took her where he could look down at her flushed face, those heavy-lidded eyes. The first time he had taken a woman that way since he had found his Constance.

The girl's hair spread out on the sheets in a spill of dark gold. Her body under him was lithe, soft, fiery. He parted her lips and thrust his tongue into her mouth. He saw her eyes open, then close again, and she moaned.

The sound excited him. *She* excited him with her warm, willing softness. He moved her legs apart and drove into her. He realized at once he was not going to be able to hold back. Her hands on his neck, clutched in his hair, drove him to a wild need. He felt her flinch, then lift her hips to him and move. Awkwardly at first, then with sounds of pleasure.

He was too consumed with his own frenzy to heed anything. He lunged into her and she stiffened and closed tightly around him. In a moment she shuddered, then squealed, legs kicking, crying out.

Dimly he knew she had reached her peak. Waves of fire rushed over him and he jerked like a rag doll in the throes of his own. Drowning in flames. He buried his head in her tangled hair and bellowed out his release.

Everard fell heavily on top of her as someone came to the door. He quickly dragged himself to his elbows, saw the sword still within reach.

The footsteps went away.

The girl put her hand in the small of his back. Her fingers moved, stroking his sweat-slick skin, then shyly across his hip, down to where they were still joined. He heard himself sigh. He lifted his head and saw her eyes were closed. Her long hair was wet and matted, flung against the bed.

She opened her eyes and looked up at him. For a moment they stared at each other. He still lay between her legs, breathing hard. He started to speak but the footsteps came back again and the door opened.

Everard rolled off the girl and reached over the bed and picked up his sword. When he looked the mother was standing there, a half-loaf of bread in her hands and a bowl of meat.

The girl quickly scrambled out of bed, picking up her shift. The woman thrust the food at Everard. He put down the sword and took it as she put her hands out, holding her daughter at arm's length.

They said something he could not understand. The woman looked over the girl to see if she was hurt. Well, they had been noisy. He remembered his bellow, her loud cries.

He swung his legs back into the bed and broke off a piece of the bread and stuck it into his mouth. It was fresh-baked and good. Amazingly, he was hungry.

The mother said something and looked past to Everard, staring at his nakedness. The girl came back and got into the bed beside him.

The weaver's wife said, "Her name is Emma."

He said, "Let her say it for herself."

The girl turned and looked at him. She was not small; he was big, broadshouldered, sinewy, and sitting in the bed she looked level into his eyes. "Emma," she said softly. She reached for his bread and broke off a piece.

Emma, Everard thought. He watched her nibbling at the bread. Her thigh rested against his. He suddenly wanted her, as hot and urgent as before. Wanted to pull her under him and drive into her and listen to her squeal. His groin drew tight.

He put the bread into the bowl and put it on the floor. He leaned over Emma and moved his hands to cover her breasts. He heard her sharp intake of breath. Not so used to him after all, he thought, pleased.

They heard the woman go out and shut the door. Everard did not look up.

It was dark when she let him out of the weavers' house. The rest of the family was asleep. Whispering for him to be quiet, Emma led him to the door and then out into the yard.

His destrier, Thunderer, stood hip shot, dozing in the moonlight that filtered through the tree where he was tied. Everard drew Emma into his arms and kissed her again. She was warm and soft. They both smelled pleasantly of musky sex.

He tried to think of something he could give her. He finally pried off a Saracen ring from his little finger that he had had since the Holy Land. It had never been off; he had to use his teeth to do it.

She held the silver ring up to the moonlight, smiling. Then she kissed him again.

Everard could not believe he was so entranced with this fair weavers' girl. She set him on fire, she was warm and gentle, she pleased him just being near him. It was all he could do not to take her right there, standing up against the oak tree. He was aware that she was swollen and sore, but it still excited him to think about it.

"When will you return?"

He looked down at her. They all asked that. Until now he had only wanted to serve one love, so it hadn't mattered.

But now he realized he wanted to tell her when he would return to Morlaix. His troop of Bucksborough knights were due to take to the road early on the morrow; there was no way he could think of to delay it. To stay another night was impossible.

"Soon," he murmured against her lips.

He mounted the destrier and turned its head in the direction of the castle road. He had taken many farewells in his life—family, sweethearts and friends, and knew it was best not to look back. But he broke his rule to turn in the saddle and see her. She stood before the weavers' house, a still figure in her white shift, one hand before her eyes against the bright moonlight.

God's wounds, he was besotted, Everard told himself. He tried to feel disgusted and instead thought of how soon he could come back to Castle Morlaix.

The warhorse had not been watered since the noon. Everard took him from the road and down through the trees to the riverbank. He dismounted, and the big horse shouldered him aside, eager to drink.

Everard ducked under the low-hanging oak limbs. It was thick dark there, but beyond the moonlight shone on the surface of the river.

He heard the rustling only a second before the blow fell. He still gripped the reins. Thunderer reared and whinnied, lashing out with his hooves.

A hail of blows beat on him. The reins were pulled out of his hands and he heard shouts as his destrier galloped off, thrashing through the bushes.

They beat him down expertly. He put his hands over his head but he fell to his knees anyway. They beat him so that he fell forward on his face. They closed on him, kicking him. He felt his ribs snap. He was battered so fiercely about the head blood ran in his eyes and he couldn't see.

When he was nearly unconscious they turned him over on his back. They stripped off his mail, his helmet and gauntlets, his padded knight's shortcoat, then his chausses and boots. When he was naked they hauled him through the bushes onto the road where they beat him some more. He thought they had sticks, the branches of trees. He could not tell how many of them, he drifted in and out of a swoon.

Later they tied him naked to a rope and dragged him down the road. He knew his jaw was broken, shooting pains went into his skull.

Being dragged over rocks and ruts in the road made him scream with pain. He fainted again.

He revived when the horses clustered in a yard somewhere. He was cut loose, a length of rope slid down to lie on the frozen ground beside him. He struggled to one elbow, blood flooding his face and eyes. He was lying in front of a house. Christ's wounds, the weaver's house. It was dark, they were all asleep.

Emma, he thought. He tried to shout but no noise came out of his damaged throat.

An icy wind was blowing. The cold had penetrated his body and the numbness lessened the pain. Lying on his back, Everard looked up and saw the moon. With his broken jaw, he could not cry out. In the cold, by morning, he would be dead. Blood seeped into his mouth and he choked.

He knew he was dying.

Hail Caesar

Tacitus

Thirteen

Over a hundred of England's greatest nobles crowded into Winchester's ceremonial hall for the king's annual oath-taking. Constance, standing flanked by her vassals from her Sussex fiefs who themselves had come to Winchester to take their own oaths of loyalty to her, William de Crecy, and a new knight *dapifer,* Earnaut fitzGamelin, watched as the great and near-great vied with each other for a place closest to the monarch's seat. Henry was due to arrive shortly.

Constance was not all that anxious to be up front and capture the king's attention; time enough when the herald called her name. In the meantime she searched Winchester's vast hall for the de Warrennes and, she hoped, her sister Mabele. Newly-married Bertrada would not be there; the de Clintons were not important enough to warrant a summons for the king's Christmas. But she wanted to see Mabele.

When she had first arrived in Winchester she'd sent Father Bertrand to the de Warrennes' house in town to inquire about her sister, and he had come back to report that the de Warrennes, traveling in the Earl of Hereford's train, were indeed in the city, but no one could tell him whether or not Mabele was with them. It was possible, her confessor suggested, the Lady Mabele was too near her time to travel.

That was probably it, Constance told herself. She hoped her sister, if she were being at all mistreated, had wits enough to send a messenger to her.

It was Christmas Day. The court had been to mass at noon at the cathedral, followed by the king's annual visit to the shrine of St. Swithin's, and inspection of the cathedral construction that had begun under Bishop Walkelin over forty years ago and was still going on. With, from what the king had seen today, no doubt another forty years to go. The cathedral had been packed with canons, secular priests and monks and lay orders, along with several bishops, led by King Henry's adviser, Roger, Bishop of Salisbury.

The gold and silver embroidered robes and mitres had sparkled like living jewels in the cathedral's vast gloom as the churchmen had taken their places around the altar during mass.

Since Roger of Salisbury was now the king's justiciar and ruled in his place when Henry was in Normandy, one could not easily tell the bitter schism, the Investiture Controversy, that had existed between the English church and the king—

a schism that Henry had inherited when he came to the throne.

After Archbishop Lanfranc's death, the Prince Henry's older brother, King William Rufus, had delayed appointing a successor to Lanfranc in order to waste the resources of the archbishopric's provinces—something that King William was very good at, and widely censured for. Finally, when he appointed Abbot Anselm of the monastery of Bec, in France, to take the archbishop's place, he found a stern adversary in the unwilling Anselm. The first thing the new archbishop insisted upon was that he not receive the symbols of his office from King William Rufus, but from the Pope himself.

From the times of the Old Conqueror and even before, Norman dukes had been appointing their own churchmen to high office. Some of them, like William the Conqueror's brother, Odo, were more warriors than bishops, and like Odo again, had mistresses and children. The new archbishop, a very saintly man, was determined that the church, not a king or a duke, should appoint its archbishops and bishops. The investiture was complicated by the fact that at that time there were two popes—Urban II and Clement III, the latter an antipope nominated by the Holy Roman Emperor Henry the Fourth. Anselm finally got his pallium of office from the hands of a cardinal legate sent from Rome by Pope Urban.

Nevertheless, the fight between Lanfranc and King William Rufus over the issue led to Lanfranc's exile in France until after King William the Second's violent death while hunting in New Forest.

Anselm returned to England only to lock horns with the new king, William Rufus's younger brother, Henry, over the same issue: whether the church and the Pope in Rome, not kings, would appoint bishops and archbishops. Again, Anselm went into exile. After a long struggle and many delicate negotiations, a compromise was reached—King Henry was good at compromise. The king would surrender investiture in return for an agreement that the king would supervise the election and take homage from the candidate before investiture. It was not until some time later, when this had been in effect several years, that it was realized that canny Henry had as usual given up little, if anything.

After the ceremonies in the cathedral there had been the usual Christmas procession through the streets. With the king had ridden his sisters, the last of the old Conqueror's nine children. They were old women now—Adelaide, Adela the Countess of Blois riding with her handsome, popular son, Stephen, and Constance, Countess of Brittany. Cecily, abbess at Caen, had died some years past.

The weather was bright and cold, the court magnificent in gold and silks and furs. Two knights with leather bags full of coins rode before the king, tossing handfuls into the crowds. The king's generous brother, King William

Rufus, had thrown silver coins to his subjects. King Henry's largesse was copper, and only farthings at that. A daring few in the crowd threw them back.

Constance had ridden behind the king and his sisters with her Sussex vassals de Crecy and fitzGamelin and her escort of household knights. She was dressed in a double-skirted red silk gown trimmed with gold with a red, fur-lined cloak over it. Her hair was twined with gold beads and red ribbons and piled high upon her head, showing her long neck. Along the way there had been scattered cheers for the Countess of Morlaix, which surprised her.

The king had entered Winchester Hall for the oath-taking. There was a sudden rustling and turning of heads. Henry's stocky figure came down the hall surrounded by his treasurer, chamberlain, an army of clerks, his remarkably able, bastard son, Robert of Gloucester, and his adviser, Roger, Bishop of Salisbury, now the most powerful man in all of England except for the king himself. The nobles remained standing as the king took his seat on a carved stool under the running leopard of the Norman banner.

Constance thought the king looked weary under the weight of his ermine cape, jewel-studded sword and scabbard, and the Old Conqueror's crown studded with sapphires and polished diamonds. Clerks with their rolls of vellum, the writs and summonses King Henry had made increasingly popular in his reign, clustered around him, talking earnestly.

In the crowd behind Constance, someone sighed. She felt the same way. It was hours past noon and the court had not yet broken their fast. Lesser nobles could slip away unnoticed to buy pastries and meat from the vendors outside, or to go to the horseracing, the mystery plays, or to Winchester's Christmas fair that would continue through Epiphany. But those who were required to swear fealty to the king were obliged to stand there in the ceremonial hall for hours.

In years past the oath-taking had frequently dragged on into the night as England's magnates, Montgomerys—the "mad butcher," Robert of Belleme, had been imprisoned by King Henry for more than a decade—Beaumonts, fitzGilberts, Montforts and l'Aumaurys, fitzOhers, fitGeralds, fitzOsberns, Taillebois, Bigots, d'Aubignys, and the Clares were called to wait, more or less patiently, in a line by the clerks. Then they made their way down the hall to kneel before King Henry, place both their hands clasped between his, and take their oaths to support him and England under Almighty God.

Constance would not have been there, a lone women among men, had she not been ranked as an earl's daughter and a countess, and, just as importantly, heiress to the Morlaix fortune.

In the back, young pages were bringing out

cups of wine. "Milady?" De Crecy wanted her to know he would fetch her a cup if she wished.

Constance nodded, and he went into the crowd. In the back of the hall the king's clerks had set up a table. The king was listening to Robert of Gloucester and two of his other illegitimate sons who bent to him, one on each side.

Her vassal fitzGamelin said in Constance's ear, "Would that the king could use his bastards to good effect. The country would follow that fine knight, Earl Robert of Gloucester, instead of the king's arrogant, argumentative chit of a girl raised among the Germans."

Constance knew most of Henry's illegitimate offspring. They ranged in age from adolescents to grown men who had provided the king with grandchildren. It must have been galling to the king to know that his bastard Robert of Gloucester was so well respected by his nobles.

"But the people say," fitzGamelin went on, "that some devil's vengeance has been wrought in our time. The good King Henry has no legitimate heirs for England's throne, while his father, the great Conqueror, as all England knows, was merely a bastard himself."

Constance shook her head. It was dangerous to talk of the king's misfortunes. But it was true—a perverse fate hung over the old Conqueror's family. Two of the king's brothers, Prince Richard and King William Rufus, and a nephew, another Richard, had been killed while hunting in New Forest, although there were many who claimed that William Rufus's death was no accident. King Henry's only legitimate son and England's heir had drowned three years before.

The king had been in France, Prince William with him, when the roistering seventeen-year-old youth decided to return to England ahead of his father. The king had provided the young prince with his own ship, companions, and crew. When the violent storm struck, it was said all on board were too blissfully drunk to man the vessel and it sank with only one survivor, a lowly sailor.

Since then King Henry had been subject to fits of melancholia and erratic tempers, and the court had learned to dread them.

De Crecy had returned to Constance with her wine. She stood sipping it, watching the nobles lining up to wait for the clerks around the king to call them to the oath-taking.

There was a substantial de Jobourg city house in Winchester where she and her servants and knights could stay in comfort, for which Constance was eternally grateful. It was not uncommon, if one followed the king, for noble ladies, maids and pages to have to sleep ten to a room, frequently without enough beds or even pallets to go around. Mealtimes for the court were always uneven, as they were discovering. Even with such public living, the amount of licentiousness was amazing. After the feasting each evening it was not uncommon to see people one knew very well coupling in dark places. And some not so dark.

King Henry, of course, had been notorious in his youth and was, according to current court gossip, not all that much changed. Before she married, Constance had nearly lost her virginity to Henry during a hawking party. The king had chased her through the woods, dragged her down from her horse, and would have assaulted her then and there had not the entire hunt come riding up.

Pages and clerks had cleared a space around the king. For the first time Constance saw the Earl of Chester, her own liege, and the Clares, Robert of Meules and his powerful brother William, now the greatest magnates in England and Normandy. With the Clares was their nephew, Robert fitzGilbert, who had been the king's envoy at Bertrada's wedding.

Constance quickly turned her head. In the crowd across the aisle the Earl of Essex's wife and daughter were talking to a young man in a scholar's long gown. This Christmas in Winchester it was all the vogue for noble ladies to entertain poets and scholars in the style of the courts of Aquitaine and Provence. The corridors were full of good-looking youths with rolls of verse under their arms hurrying to their next appointment. She had heard the rage was for Peter Abelard's love poetry, since the scandalous story had crossed the channel from France some time ago.

Constance declined the ladies' assemblies,

where they sewed and gossiped and listened to scholars and troubadours. She preferred her own house. Fingering the gold chains and beads at her throat, she realized how much she missed being at home with her girls. Christmas at Bucksborough was a simple affair, but lively. Villeins and shepherds from outlying cots came to camp in the fields, hold their animal fairs, and dance all day and into the night. On Christmas Day all crowded into the manor yard for the liege lady's feast. This year she would not be there; her steward and his wife would oversee it.

The king's court at Christmas was far different. Here all who could jostled shamelessly for the king's favor and looked with ill-concealed contempt on those who could not. And all the shocking things whispered of Henry's court were undoubtedly true—there was much roaming from room to room at night, so that one could never be sure whom one would encounter under cover of dark. Or in what condition. Current gossip said a minor noble's young daughter had been raped and that it was hushed up by order of the king himself.

The herald began to call out the names of those nobles present who were to swear fealty. England's most powerful men wore rich silks and brocades, gold chains and jeweled belts, and mantles that swept the floor and trailed behind them. Most were knights, fighting men; many had fought under the king's brother, King William Rufus. Constance craned to see the Earl of Chester, florid and heavyset. Then the Earl of Hereford, the Welsh marcher lord, one of Henry's closest friends. Then the Earl of Norfolk.

She fiddled with her heavy silk skirts while she waited. She was the only heiress there. The king had not summoned the other, the Countess of Warwick.

She felt a queer sense of panic. The sight of Robert fitzGilbert had unsettled her. This was the way one came to feel at court, she told herself; people around the king were always plotting.

She patted her jeweled necklaces in place. When she looked up her half-brother Julien was coming through the crowd. She was glad to see him. She said, "I thought you were with the king's sons."

Julien gave her a dutiful kiss. "I am doing my best. King Henry's by-blows are much sought after. Last night I bought Aimery de Courtney enough wine to fill the Thames. Now he is talking about how much he likes a Flemish stallion that Hugh of Lacy has for sale."

She lifted her eyes to him. She was tall, but Julien overtopped her. More than ever he looked like her father when Gilbert de Jobourg had still been a handsome, impetuous young man. "Mother of God, you can't afford that."

He looked gloomy. "I have petitioned the king to be Sheriff of Wrexham. This year I will have something out of all this, Constance, I swear to you, even though it is clear I have no favor with the Bishop of Salisbury. He sits on top of the king's awards like a churchly lizard, hoarding all."

Julien and his problems with money, Constance thought impatiently. It was a good thing the other brother Rannulf was in the Holy Land, because he was no better.

Julien read her thoughts. "Come, we are not all so tidy with our fortunes as you, sweet sister." He gave a strand of her beaded hair a tug. "They tell me you grow richer day by day."

"Whoever 'they' are, they lie." One of the king's heralds had found her in the crowd. Constance picked up her skirts, careful of the dirty floor. "If I am given time enough I will speak to the king for you. If I ask, perhaps he will make you the Wrexham sheriff."

She thought he lifted his hand in assent. But when she turned and looked back Julien merely stood there, watching her.

She made her way through the crowd and, at the herald's cue, down the aisle. The Earl of Hereford knelt before Henry with his hands clasped in the king's, but the Earl of Chester stood where he was, red-faced, gnawing his lip. Two magnates, Norfolk and Wrexford, were in deep conversation with the Bishop of Salisbury.

The Earl of Chester took Constance by the arm. "There is to be another oath. The clerks will tell you of it. Do not look surprised."

She pulled her hand from his. The Baron of

Huntingdon and Lees came up and drew Norfolk away. Constance followed the herald as a buzz of muffled conversation ran through the hall.

The herald stepped back to call out Constance's name. She had to wait, listening to all her titles to her possessions: Castle Morlaix, Bucksborough and the Sussex fiefs, the York and London and Winchester properties. All hers and her family's by the grace of God and his servant on earth, Henry fitzConqueror, King of England.

She sank to her knees before him, her red skirts spreading across the wooden floor. The king hitched himself forward and took her hands, holding them clasped between his own.

She looked up into his face. Henry, the youngest son of the great Conqueror, was three years past fifty, squat and broad in the shoulders, still a vigorous man although his sorrows and disappointments showed in his narrow, beak-nosed face. All that he was—intelligent, greedy, crabby, shrewd, suspicious, bad-tempered—was there. And in his eyes the look, dark and hot, that told of lifelong lechery.

"Sweet child," the king said. "Constance, Gilbert's daughter. Sweet, beautiful child." He turned to the Bishop of Salisbury. "Attend, Roger, isn't she lovely?"

The bishop looked down his nose at Constance. "Her admirers would agree, milord. They wait, burning with little patience, to hear your wishes about the countess."

She could not pull her hands away—they were held tight in Henry's. She could feel the stares of the court. The king could not break his word to her, Constance told herself.

Henry looked into her eyes. "You must keep your suitors' longings in your prayers, sweet, lovely lady. The countess," he said to the clerk who hovered at his elbow, "will be with us for the oath-taking to the Empress."

She bent, her knees shaking, to kiss Henry's hand, and got to her feet. Roger fitzGilbert was at her elbow. She brushed past him.

A clerk was in her path. Someone took her arm to steer her away from a Wessex baron on his way to the king. The clerk was saying that King Henry would be pleased to have the Countess of Morlaix entertain the court on the third day of Christmas.

She hardly heard him. Dear God in heaven, why had the Clare nephew been there as soon as she turned? She was shaking, ready to believe anything.

The clerk followed her, insistent, and Constance stopped. He wanted her to pledge an entertainment on the third day of Christmas.

She stared at him, remembering she had paid months before for a day of the king's Christmas at Winchester, as had all the magnates. One full day's expenses and food and lodging for the king and his retinue. Now Henry would have her levied for an extra entertainment.

"It is an honor, milady." The bishop's clerk held up his list.

"I am aware of the honor." There was nothing she could do. "I will send my vassal, Sir William de Crecy, to the bishop."

"The third night of Christmas," he reminded her.

She had a sick feeling in the pit of her stomach. The money for an entertainment was nothing, but the king could not withdraw her marriage dispensation. He had given his oath on it.

Robert fitzGilbert came up to say, "My lady Constance, tell me that you support the king in this."

Constance looked around for her vassals, de Crecy and fitzGamelin. She had little stake in this issue that the king pressed so hard upon his nobles, the swearing fealty to his daughter the German empress. Now that his legitimate son was dead, the king was determined that Matilda, married at eight years of age to the German emperor of the Holy Roman Empire, should succeed him. The idea of a woman succeeding to the throne was massively unpopular; not many of King Henry's nobles in either England or Normandy supported it. And then there were the Germans to consider. What if Matilda became Queen of England and Normandy while she was still Empress of the Holy Roman Empire?

"I don't know what I support." It was too much to think about, and she didn't like the Clares' handsome nephew following her about the hall where all were watching.

He took no offense. "As you wish."

The king stood up. The trumpeters blew a fanfare that made a great racket in the crowded hall. People stopped talking. The herald called out loudly for King Henry's noble vassals to come to him and swear to support the Empress Matilda as heiress to England's throne.

It would be a long afternoon, Constance thought with a sigh.

The day dragged on. Those who would not be sworn grew tired of watching and left to find food and a place to rest. After her name had been called, Constance went to the king to swear to the special oath supporting the Empress Matilda.

De Crecy and fitzGamelin joined her afterward and they walked outside. The sun had disappeared in a bank of clouds. A band of shouting youths, mostly apprentices, chased a man dressed as the Christmas Fool to the market cross in the middle of the square. He climbed on top and hung there, gesturing defiantly, a tall, muscular figure in motley wearing the black mask of a gargoyle.

A Morlaix knight brought up Constance's mare. With him was the serjeant, Carcefou, and another knight, dirty from the road. The courier knight dropped to his knees in front of Constance.

"It is bad news, milady," Carcefou said quickly. "Gisulf has just come from Castle Morlaix. Sir Everard has disappeared."

Fourteen

"The great stallion, Thunderer, too," Carcefou said. "Vanished, both of them, with no trace."

Constance couldn't believe it. A pair of the Clares' knights rode up to the steps leading Robert fitzGilbert's mount. *Not Everard.* Not her shadow, her protector.

She made herself say, "He's not dead."

The serjeant spread his hands. "It would seem foul play, my lady. When last seen Sir Everard had taken a cow from the pens at the castle and was going to the village. The cow was found wandering by the river."

"A cow?" That didn't sound like Everard.

"He was her knight captain," de Crecy explained to Robert fitzGilbert. "Everard Saujon, a Gascon."

Constance shuddered. *Was?* They were so quick to believe him dead. She knew Everard had many enemies. She turned to the courier, who was still on his knees. "How long was this?"

"Three days, my lady." He looked up at her. "The constable, Longspres, has lodged your household knights with the castle garrison, and asks further orders."

Three days. It took more than two for a courier at full gallop to travel from the Welsh marches south to Winchester, so at least they had not waited to let her know.

He is not dead, Constance told herself. It was a mistake. Something had happened to Everard, but he was like a rock, invincible; the others were always in awe of him. Perhaps he was being held for ransom by outlaws.

She said, "I must send someone. Do they continue to search for him?" She knew they did, but wished to be sure of it.

The young knight frowned. "Mightily, my lady. The village and the countryside has been turned out, but all say they know nothing. Since the cow was found unclaimed, this may be true."

She motioned him to his feet and tried to think. The cow puzzled her. What was Everard doing in Morlaix village? Was the cow to be sold to some villein? She could not imagine it. Everard was no cattle trader.

Ostlers' grooms brought up horses for de Crecy and fitzGamelin. People from the hall came out and made their way around them, looking curious. Beyond them, on the market cross, the Christmas Fool was holding his howling tormentors at bay.

Constance drew her cloak about her. A cold wind scoured the market square and the afternoon sun was behind grey clouds. Carcefou and the courier were waiting for her.

She could not leave Winchester until after the king's third night entertainment. Her vassals, fitzGamelin and de Crecy, would help with it, but the loss of Everard, if indeed he was lost, was something she could not put aside.

There was no need to hold half her household troops at Castle Morlaix; she would have to go there herself to attend to matters. But first home to Bucksborough. She needed her children, needed to be home for a while.

"We must leave here in the morn after the king's entertainment." She moved to her mare to mount and Carcefou handed the reins to fitzGamelin, who bent with clasped hands and gave her a leg up into the saddle. She leaned down to say, "Who is in command now of my household knights at Morlaix?"

The courier said, "Under the castle constable, Sir Belinus is second in command, my lady."

"Good. And I will send someone—" She stopped. The unexpected oath-taking for the Empress Matilda and Robert fitzGilbert's unexpected appearance had made her forget to ask the king a boon—to award Julien the post of Sheriff of Wrexham. Nothing was going right.

"Send this courier back," she told Carcefou, "with the message that I will send my brother Julien of Nesscliffe to Morlaix to help search for Everard."

Robert fitzGilbert pulled his horse alongside hers, smiling. "You put mere men to shame, beautiful lady, with your fine gift of command. Give me your orders and I, too, will be your brave, parfit knight."

Carcefou and the courier knight turned to stare at him. Constance bit back a sharp retort; the saints knew she did not wish to offend the king—there was too much going wrong as it was.

She managed a stiff smile. "Come," she told the Clares' handsome nephew, "ride with me as far as my house."

The horses moved away from the hall. At the market cross the Christmas Fool had beaten back his attackers. Most of the apprentices and beggar children were leaving, shouting parting insults and taunts.

Constance gave them only a distracted glance. She had heard that in times long past the fool at Yuletide was sacrificed to the old pagan gods. Burned, if she remembered the story right.

Of a sudden she looked back. He was still in the square, a tall, graceful figure in a suit made of bright cloth patches, a cap with a dangling peak, the Rod of Misrule in his hand. The leather gargoyle mask was turned to her as though he watched her.

She turned back, uneasy. For a moment something about him had seemed familiar. She rode again for several moments, then turned to look.

He was gone.

* * *

A knight, Ivo, was provided with a fresh mount and sent back to Morlaix with Constance's messages. She still worried about the mystery of Everard's disappearance. Surely a knight captain did not ride his horse into Morlaix village and disappear. Even if Everard had many enemies who wished to harm him or even kill him, she felt they would know better than to challenge Constance of Morlaix by attacking one of her knights in her own fief. And her villagers had always been loyal. She'd never had an uprising or disorders such as were common on Chester's lands.

Also, she was sure Everard would not leave her service without telling her. Besides, where would he go? In the north and west, at leas he was known as her man. People respected him. Feared him. Marked him as her captain.

The household knights under Carcefou seemed dutiful enough but she sensed that Everard's disappearance had unsettled them. The serjeant made no secret of his worry.

That night Constance could not sleep. Her stomach pained her. The rich food served night after night at the long Christmas feastings was not good for anyone's digestion. And although the house in the High Street was comfortable, she longed to be at home with her own things.

She crept late into bed and lay awake in the dark listening to the noisy crowds in the streets and thinking of her girls at home in Bucksborough and the nursemaids who looked after them. She could not stop worrying, fretful about everything. Winter was always worrisome, the time of smallpox plagues and lung fevers.

She sat up, punched her pillows, and lay down again. God's bones, it was no wonder she found it hard to sleep! Since she'd been in Winchester she dreamed strange, restless dreams. Once about the little Welsh witch who'd been prisoner with Cenred, the mad jongleur.

She woke up abruptly. She'd been dozing. Her stomach still burned. The room was pitch dark, and empty. Her maids did not sleep in her room in Winchester, preferring the kitchen and the hallway below.

She got up and used the chamberpot and then went back to bed, but she still did not feel any better. The room was cold, the floor icy in spite of the sheepskins scattered on it, and her belly hurt. In the name of God, where could Everard be? She could have howled it.

When she finally slept she dreamed again. This time about the jongleur, Cenred, dressed in a suit of motley like the Christmas Fool, cavorting and dancing and mocking her, calling her by name in the wintry streets of Winchester town.

The Earl of Hereford provided the second evening of the king's Christmas revels. A procession of wrestlers, mummers, dancers, and singers in Hereford's own manor and hall in Winchester's High Street were followed by a troupe of rope walkers. Since the founding of Christian states in the Holy Land, Saracen entertainment had become very popular.

The earl, a little unsteady from the day-long drinking, made his way down the high table to Constance, "How do you like my heathen? The Saracens cost me a pretty lot, girl. I brought them all the way from London."

He looked around the hall filled with a hundred and more Norman nobles, and then to the king, sitting with Roger, the Bishop of Salisbury. "Pity the poor devil who has to entertain Henry the last nights of Christmas. Winchester will have been picked clean by then of every dancer and troubadour able to squawk or hobble."

She managed a smile. Her stomach was rebelling at the sight of yet another whole roast oxen carried by staggering servers, deer with their antlers put back on after cooking and piled around with boiled eggs, braised doves, coneys and fowl, mounds of peas swimming in lakes of gravy—the displays of food seemed endless.

She watched the sweating kitchen knaves and cooks carrying in the feast and wondered how ordinary people would fare there in Winchester after Christmas. She'd had enough trouble with her own fief's shortages.

Beside her Robert fitzGilbert held up a bowl of honey-boiled fruit, apples and plums in a nest of roasted hazelnuts. "Such food stuns the eye and inspires the soul," he intoned. "Does it not?"

She couldn't think of anything to say. *Stuns the eye,* she thought, studying a green apple in a puddle of syrup. Perhaps it was his own poetry. She waved the page away.

They sat a few seats down the high table from the king, Roger of Salisbury, and the king's bastard, Robert of Gloucester. From time to time Henry bent forward to look at Constance with fitzGilbert beside her.

She had not lacked for attention even with the king's eye on her. Two barons from the north and several knights had come up from the lower tables to stand and lift their cups to her. Constance was obliged to match them drink for drink. Or in her case, sip for sip of well-watered wine.

Most of the nobles were drinking wine whole, or the strong Wessex ale, and had been all day. Even King Henry was flushed and more talkative than usual.

So much drinking, though, had set Constance's head to spinning. An older baron, Thomas Moreshold, brought a young scholar up to the high table to recite a long poem dedicated to her silver eyes and hair that rivaled the night.

She sat through the tributes, knowing the king was watching. It was the vogue lately to be courtly in the French fashion and single out noble ladies at mealtime with poetry and compliments. As she matched her courtiers drink for drink, Constance wished she knew what was in King Henry's devious mind. Perhaps the barons and knights of the court dedicating poems and songs to her knew more than she. Perhaps it was not Robert fitzGilbert alone wooing her. Perhaps in some way her position had changed.

She choked back her fears. Two and a half years were left of the king's dispensation. Only six months was spent, and the only thing she could think was that the king might break his word. Robert fitzGilbert filled her wine cup. She drank deeply before she realized the wine was whole.

The Earl of Hereford's stewards cleared a space on the floor below for a singer. After some fussing to select the right stool at the right height, the troubadour lifted his harp and launched into a song about two maids on their way home from Kensington Fair.

Constance barely listened. She told herself she could not lose her freedom so soon—not when the king had promised her a precious three years.

She thought of the entertainment on the morrow and hoped Hereford was right and the choice of entertainers was still large and varied. By now she dreaded the whole affair. King Henry was very clever at extracting expensive gifts from his nobles. There was no way out of it.

De Crecy had already sent for his steward and cooks from his Sussex fief, and the bakers in Winchester were preparing the bread and meat pies. Both her young vassals had spent large sums of her money hiring performers, but with great success, they swore, in taking away entertainers from other lords-hire not willing to pay as much as she. FitzGamelin had spoken with enthusiasm of fire dancers, all women, all in scandalous dress. The king, they assured her, would rejoice in it.

The crowd in the hall had quieted for the singer. He was telling of how the two maids on their way back from the Kensington Fair had chanced upon a tall, pretty youth, a herdsman, asleep under a tree.

The fair youth had been swimming, the troubadour sang, and lay asleep under the oak tree with only his herdsman's hat laid low on his belly to cover him.

FitzGilbert leaned to Constance and said behind his hand, "Look at the king."

She glanced at Henry who was leaning forward, elbows braced among the dinnerware, listening intently.

The troubadour sang in a high treble to imitate a female voice. Ah, said the first girl, what a pretty man. Shall we see what's under the hat?

Yes, we shall, replied the second.

Full of mischief, the girls removed the hat ever so softly and were amazed at what they found there.

Constance felt the king's eyes on her. When she turned, Henry looked away.

The fair maids fell to giggling, the troubadour sang, at the sight of the comely youth who, after his bath in the river, had so sweetly fallen asleep under the oak. The youngest girl took off her red hair-ribbon and so stealthily—so gently—

Here the harp trilled dramatically. The singer paused as a ripple of laughter ran around the room.

The girl tied the ribbon around that which both maids had so greatly admired, and put the young herdsman's hat back on top of it. And then the waggish, prankish, roguish girls coming back from Kensington Fair went on their merry way.

Robert fitzGilbert picked up Constance's hand and held it in both of his. She sat for a long moment before she tried to pull it away, but he held tight.

The troubadour sang. He looked around, drawing out the moment.

And then our pretty youth did awake. The first thing he knew was of some slight difference in feeling under his herdsman's hat and he lifted it. And started in surprise.

Lo! What had by magic appeared? The fair young herdsman stared, and scratched his head in wonderment. Then after long thought he declared, "I don't know where you've been, Tom, but from the looks of you, you've had yourself a right rare time. For to judge by yon red ribbon, you've won yourself *first prize!*"

The room burst into thunderous laughter. Constance struggled to free her hand from fitzGilbert's grasp. There was a loud bang that made them all start. The doors of Hereford's hall burst open. A shouting mob spilled into the hall.

The knights of the king's guard sprang forward. Beside the king, Robert of Gloucester jumped up, dagger drawn. The crowd pressed as far as the back trestles, carrying a man who bounced shoulder-high in their midst like flotsam caught on the crest of a flood. Howls for the Christmas Fool suddenly came from all parts of the room.

There was a pause. The mailed knights of the king's household stood with their swords drawn, waiting for orders. In the Saxon past a Christmas mob might burst in upon a king, proclaiming the Christmas Fool and Lord of Misrule, but it was not so common now under the Conqueror's sons.

The king, holding a wine cup, surveyed the riffraff from the streets for a long moment. He made a dismissive gesture. The knights stepped back.

The figure in bright patchwork clothes jumped down and landed on his feet with a broad flourish and bow to the king. A sudden silence fell.

From behind the black gargoyle mask the Christmas Fool addressed England's Norman nobles, welcoming them to the rule of disorder of the season. A few at the back tables laughed.

Then the Christmas Fool advanced and began to declaim in sonorous Latin.

Constance sat frozen, not able to drag her eyes from the broadshouldered, narrow-hipped form, graceful in its glittering motley. Or the fool's demon mask. The mouth was cut large in black-painted leather so that one saw his lips moving. And the eyes were like azure jewels in the beast's face.

She was suddenly deathly afraid. She reached for her wine and witlessly drank several gulps, her hand shaking.

FitzGilbert turned to her. "Does the fool frighten you?" He patted her captive hand with his other. "Ah, gentle Lady Constance, let me offer you my protection. You can fear nothing when I am by your side."

Now that Constance saw those eyes, that long, lithe body, heard that voice, she knew that the masked Christmas Fool was the same man who had invaded—assaulted her—in her tent.

Mother of God save her, he was *there,* speaking before the king!

Her hand was shaking so that when she put the cup to her lips it rattled against her teeth.

A few nobles at the high table were clapping for the Latin recital. "The fool speaks Virgil, milord," Roger of Salisbury called. "And speaks it well!"

"Yes, yes." Henry looked impatient. "Anchises, speaking to Aeneas. I know it."

From behind the mask the fool said in Norman French, "Then I speak this for your subjects, my lord." He recited in the same language:

"Here is Caesar, and all the line of Iulus,
All who shall one day pass under the dome

Of the great sky: this is the man, this one,
Of whom so often you have heard the promise,
Caesar Augustus, son of the deified,
Who shall bring once again an Age of Gold
To Latium, to the land where Saturn reigned
In early times. He will extend his power,
Over far territories north and south
Of the zodiacal stars, the solar way,
Where Atlas, heaven-bearing, on his shoulders
Turns the night-sphere, studded with burning-stars."

"Well done, well done." Roger of Salisbury turned to the king. "It should please you, sire, to be so skillfully exalted in the company of Virgil's Caesar Augustus."

Before King Henry could answer the fool bounded past the knights, reached over the table, and pulled a coin from the bishop's open mouth.

He held it up at arm's length so that everyone could see.

"Only a farthing, your grace, from your lips," he shouted. "Not the pure churchly gold, alas, that we are accustomed to!"

Henry barked his laughter. "He makes sport of you, Roger. But his Latin is good."

"Nay, my lord king." The voice behind the mask was smooth. "I make no sport, only do justice in the spirit of the season." He rolled two coins across his fingers, made them disappear, and then pop back again. He held them up for the benefit of the back of the hall. "Now come let us honor Old Winter's hard reign. See—here! For our blessed sovereign King Henry let us render to Caesar the things that are Caesar's."

Before the knights nearest the king could stop him his hands had roamed over the king's hair and jeweled jacket. At each lightning touch coins rattled from his fingers and onto the table among the wine cups and bread and meat.

Hereford lifted his wine cup. "Beware, Henry, the fool is impoverishing England."

There was quite a mound of coins in front of the king. The demon-masked fool pulled more from King Henry's long nose and lank black hair. The laughter which had begun in the back swelled to a roar.

The king's person seemed to be spewing money. Henry sat, glitter-eyed, as farthings fell onto the table and rolled off onto the rush-covered floor.

Constance sat open-mouthed. Dear Jesus, she had never thought to see him again. The madman was more dangerous to her than anything that walked the earth. He had taken her against a table in a burst of lust which she, in her own madness, had wickedly desired. And if King Henry ever learned that this ragged fool from the streets of Winchester had engaged in suchlike with his ward and the foremost heiress of his realm, he would kill them both. When she looked down she saw, surprised, she had drunk all the wine in her cup and someone had given her more. It was no wonder she felt flushed and dizzy.

The jongleur gave Robert of Gloucester a quick glance, then moved to the bishop. Leaning over the table he pulled spoons and cutlery out of Roger of Salisbury's embroidered robes, exclaiming in shocked tones over each as though the king's advisor had intended to steal them. The crowd was howling. After one look at the bishop's face the Earl of Hereford collapsed, helpless, tears streaming down his cheeks. Beside him, Chester scowled.

Constance felt Roger fitzGilbert's leg pressed up against hers under the table. He turned his handsome head and whispered something in her ear, still holding her hand captive.

She didn't hear anything. Her eyes were fixed on the madman who could destroy her. If only he failed to see her. She prayed for it; there surely was no place there, in front of the king and everyone, where she could hide.

At that moment the black-masked face turned in her direction. She felt a wave of dread move down her spine.

The jongleur jumped down from the table. In front of King Henry he scooped up the pile of copper coins as though they were a fountain running backward into his hands.

While the high table was still gaping he moved, catlike, down to Constance.

"Milords," he cried in his ringing voice.

The hall fell silent.

"Caesar Augustus ruled Rome wisely and well as good King Henry now rules England and Normandy. But true treasure, as all men know, lies with the goddess who rules both love *and* money." He opened his long fingers and copper farthings dropped onto the table in front of Constance. "Mark you, milords, and let us pay our tribute to the king's own Venus!"

Constance looked somewhat tipsily down at the pile of coins. The lunatic had done this to humiliate her. *Venus. Love and money.* She knew he thought her no better than a whore.

She looked up. The blue eyes blazed at her through the gargoyle face. They passed to fitzGilbert fondling her hand, and back again. Then with a swift movement the fool jumped down and made for the rowdy mob that had carried him inside.

"Hail, King," the Christmas Fool shouted. He took up his rod of misrule and brandished it. "Hail Caesar!"

The hall roared again. A king's knight came through the mob and tossed the fool a small leather pouch. Waving the king's purse in one hand and the rod in the other, he let the crowd boost him to their shoulders and carry him out.

Constance stared after them. She could not believe he had gone. It had been like a dream. She was still shivering. And, she realized as she looked around at the wavering faces at the king's high table, she had drunk too much.

She knew she was going to be sick.

* * *

As soon as they were outside the doors, Cenred jumped down and took to his heels. The crowd of Winchester's apprentices and tavern loafers was not in a mood to let their Christmas Fool go so easily. They chased after him, shouting and whooping.

Past the market square he pulled off his mask and ducked into a refuse-filled alley. He pressed against the side of a house, gasping, as they searched in every side street with curses, threats, and even honeyed wheedling for their Christmas Fool to come out and join them. They meant no harm—there were even better revels to visit.

He smiled, sourly. One took one's life in one's hands to play the fool on the streets of any town at Yule, but it paid well. The rougher the play the more was given in coin, but broken bones were not unusual.

So far, he thought, tossing the rod of misrule into the dark, he'd done well. It had not been his idea to confront King Henry as he sat at his feast, but the half-drunken mob had thought it the greatest of games in the old style of Yuletide. Fortunately, Henry had been in a good humor. The king's purse was the best of all.

The sounds of the mob drifted closer and Cenred climbed over a wall and dropped into a yard with a stinking midden pile. And beyond that, with dogs barking, into another alley. He knew he was somewhere near the butcher's quarter. He stopped to get his wind and wipe his face.

Sweet Mary, he told himself, he hadn't believed his own eyes at first, but it was the Morlaix bitch there at King Henry's table, looking inhumanly beautiful, not like the much-married king's prize that she truly was.

When he had seen her seated next to the popinjay fitzGilbert, so coolly imperious with her jeweled hair and fur-trimmed gown, the picture came to him of the Lady Constance half-naked that night in her tent, her beautiful breasts bare and warm under his hands, her skirts up around her waist showing her long legs and her sweet secrets, trembling and moaning in his arms. Oh, so unwilling. And oh, so lusciously tempting.

And that doe-like look of surprise in her eyes when she reached her peak.

Good Jesu. Even standing freezing in a Winchester alley he was aroused just thinking about it. She was fire and ice, honey and vinegar, she was a part of everything that he hated, and she drew him like a lodestone. He'd never had another woman like her.

And much too good, he told himself, to let go to waste on the Clares' lackwit candidate for her next husband.

He stuck the king's purse in his shirt and started back to the square. The evening was not over. The place to seek out the rest of it was in the High Street where the nobles' houses were.

The market square was empty. There was little light and what moon there was rode behind cold clouds. He was at the far end of the square that emptied into a narrow street when he heard the horsemen.

Cenred stepped quickly into the blackness of a doorway.

There were ten of them in the emperor's white tunics, carrying their white gonfalons, one each to a rider. Their horses' hooves made sharp, hollow sounds on the stones.

As they passed, a stray beam of light struck the head and shoulders of the leader, who was wearing a great barrel helmet with a plume of white feathers. Cenred did not have to see his face. He knew him by his size, and the way he sat the massive Swabian war horse.

So, they have sent only the best. The emperor's knights rode under the command of Sigurd of Glessen, the great Crusader. And yes, there tied to the saddle's pommel was the telltale leather bag the size of a human head.

They passed within touching distance in the narrow street. He watched them, motionless, pressed back into the shadows.

Now that he had seen them, he knew he would have to leave Winchester before the morning sun. But not, Cenred told himself, before he had seen to another matter.

He set off in the opposite direction, a moving shadow in the dark, toward the High Street.

And one particular house.

Fifteen

Everard tried to open his eyes and couldn't. It was as though a weight had been tied to his lids and, struggle though he might, he could not force them apart. But he could hear.

What he heard were shuffling, bumping noises and the sound of voices. With other voices answering.

Slowly he became aware that he could not move his mouth or his chin. Something had been tied around the lower part of his face. When he tried to reach up to touch it he found that his hand—both hands—were bound. He could only make a low, groaning sound of despair.

Immediately a voice said in his ear, "Shhhhh," and then something he could not understand in Saxon.

God's face, where was he? He quickly realized there was no need to struggle; whoever held him captive had him bound and helpless, and for some reason he couldn't even open his eyes.

But he was alive. He let his body relax, warily, to listen. And to feel.

The last thing he remembered was being beaten half-dead and then dragged at the end of a rope into the weavers' street and left in front of a house.

Well, he was *not* dead, he told himself. Although with the pain that was throbbing through his face and his ribs he might yet wish to be. How badly was he damaged? he wondered. And where was he now?

His head, he was gradually aware, was pressed against something soft and warm. And something soft and warm held up his back and shoulders.

He lay for a long moment, puzzling it over. The noises overhead continued. There was an odor of something in the place. Helpless, blind and virtually gagged, it was good to know his nose still worked.

He lay still, assessing the pain that wracked him. Broken ribs. Knives stabbed him when he breathed. Perhaps broken bones in his wrist. He could tell more when he had a chance to move it. And most probably a broken jaw. That was why his face was bound—not to keep him from crying out so much as to hold his jaw bones in place.

As the sense of it came to him—that someone had bound up his face—it was hard to fight down his joy. It was too accursed early to be hopeful; a life of soldiering had taught him hope was dangerous. But, carefully, Everard took a shallow breath.

The pain of his broken ribs almost made him scream. He found wherever he lay smelled of dirt, and mustiness. Not too big a place, either: the tip of his bare toe was rammed against something.

When he tried to move the voice whispered, "Shhhh," again. Something touched his face. Something light and warm. A woman's fingers.

By all the saints, what was this?

Everard tried to lift his right hand, and ground his teeth against the pain. That wrist was truly broken. He could not help it as a groan tore out of him.

The fingers clamped over his mouth. "Be still, be still," the voice whispered in his ear. "They are above, in the house, searching for you."

Christ crucified, he knew that voice.

Emma. The weaver's girl of the long legs and the soft brown hair. He'd come with a cow as a price to take her to bed, and somehow it had all changed. He suddenly remembered everything.

He felt her fingers stroking his brow. His eyes were swollen shut, that was why he couldn't see. The softness was her body. She was holding him, to keep him quiet, her arms around him. Someplace, Everard thought, his mind racing, someplace under the weavers' house. The weavers' root cellar. He would swear the musty smell was turnips.

For the first time he allowed himself to drop his guard, to stop fighting the pain. He took another cautious breath, careful of his shattered ribs.

By all that was holy—he could not believe it, but he was in a root cellar, he was alive, and sweet Emma was holding him in her arms.

The weavers were hiding him.

"Yes, the oaths were taken today," Robert fitzGilbert was saying, "but not willingly. You had only to look at the faces of the nobles of England and Normandy, my uncles among them, when they placed their hands within the king's, to see how they feel."

William de Crecy said, cautious, "But no one will defy King Henry, will they? The magnates will swear to accept the empress to keep peace with the king."

They had been arguing the king's oath to recognize his daughter as his heir, all of them full of praise for Robert of Gloucester, the king's bastard son who would have solved all England's problems had he but been a legitimate heir.

Constance was not much interested in the argument. She and her Sussex vassals were riding toward her house in the High Street with Robert fitzGilbert, who was in his cups and did not seem to want to bid them good night.

It was possible the oath-taking for the king's daughter was still going on in Winchester's great hall, although she doubted it. The sun had set hours ago, and the bell in the cathedral had rung for compline long since.

The other vassal, fitzGamelin, snorted. "But after the king is dead? We all know how much faith to place in oaths beyond the grave."

They all spoke at once. "What of Robert Clito, Duke Robert's son?" de Crecy wanted to know.

"Yes, there are still many," the Clare nephew put in, "who say that the Conqueror's oldest son should have had the throne to England, and that Duke Robert's son Clito is a worthy heir. No, no—not my uncles," he added hastily. "You know they supported King Henry against his brother, William Rufus. But King Henry has been fighting Clito in Normandy for some long years and has not been able to dislodge him. Many nobles are saying, why not Clito instead of this half-grown daughter the king sent to marry the German Emperor?"

"Hah." FitzGamelin made a disgusted noise. "Can't you see what the king is doing? He has Salisbury ruling England for him when he is pursuing his war with Clito in Normandy, and his army of officials that he alone has created—this great crowd of bailiffs and clerks and writ servers and justiciars and tax collectors that King Henry boasts he has raised from the dirt and educated so finely to tend to the affairs of the kingdom! Norman barons and earls no longer are called to royal councils; they cannot get past the writ-carrying, ink-stained rabble, the Curia Regis, the money-counters of the Exchequer, and all the rest the king has placed in between. These are the nobles, truly."

De Crecy nodded. "But it is all done cleverly, is it not? When King Henry defeated his brother Robert, the Conqueror's oldest son, the Duke of Normandy that many thought should have been England's king after the death of King William Rufus, the king did not raise men's tempers by killing his brother. No, King Henry put poor Robert in a soft prison where he has been many years, and where he will remain until he dies."

"Like Robert of Belleme," fitzGamelin said. "Although *there* is a fiend that deserves to die in hideous agony, like the brave knights he tortured for his pleasure, and not loll about with his luxuries in his prison tower."

Constance did not want to hear any more. She pushed her horse ahead to join the serjeant, Carcefou. "I am much grieved to think that something has befallen Sir Everard," she said to the small, swarthy knight. "Tell me what you think has happened."

His face was cautious. "Mayhap Sir Everard has enemies. An able knight such as he is not often well-loved."

"Then you believe with the others that someone attacked him?"

He looked away. "Let us say I do not think Sir Everard would leave your service willingly, lady."

There was something in his voice that made

her pull back her hood to look at him. "Carcefou, what has happened? What do you think Sir Everard would need with a—a cow?"

"There is no guessing." He sounded genuinely puzzled. "A fine cow would be a great gift for some villager, if one was wanting a boon."

She could not think of any favor Everard would want from the Morlaix villagers. She wanted to ask him more, but they were at the door of her house. The porter came out shouting for a stable knave to see to milady's horse.

De Crecy and fitzGamelin were drunkenly arguing whether to go back to the inn with Robert fitzGilbert for more talk and ale, or proceed to their lodgings.

Constance lifted her voice to bid them good night. At that both vassals quickly dismounted and helped her down from her mare, then went down on their knees before her to kiss her hand. She looked over their heads at fitzGilbert, who smiled at her.

She followed the porter inside. Several maids were in the back of the house, talking and laughing. She did not bother to call them. If she was still hungry later she would have them fetch her some food.

She took a candle from the wall and climbed the stairs. She had drunk enough wine so she had come full circle and was almost sober, although she had a slightly aching head.

In her room a fire had been lit on the hearth, but the shutters were wide open and the room was cold. She muttered under her breath about her servants as she put down the candle and went to close them and draw the hides to keep out the wind.

Before she turned she sensed someone was in the room. She whirled.

By the light of the candle she saw the jongleur, Cenred, lying on her bed, his arms folded behind his head. The light picked out the colors of the Christmas motley that hugged his long body.

He grinned at her. "What," he said, "no lisping fitzGilbert with you and hot for your bed, Lady Constance?"

She couldn't move. The wine still fuddled her. She was assailed by the same wild confusion that attacked her whenever she saw him. Now he had invaded her bedchamber.

"H-how did you get in?" They were two stories up.

"By the window." He took his hands down and stretched, catlike. "There are footholds in timber and plaster if you know where to look for them."

She gaped at him. She could well believe that he had climbed the wall outside to come in her window. He was reckless, a lunatic. She had seen him taunt King Henry himself.

She looked past him to the door. If she moved carefully, she could slip by the bed. She knew she couldn't show fear. He was a madman; all was lost if she did.

"If you have come to—to avenge yourself," she croaked, "know that I hold you no ill will for what has—h-happened." Blessed Mother, perhaps with his uncertain wits, he did not even remember what had happened All Hallow's Eve. "I know your—ah, mind and soul have suffered much over the tragedy that has befallen your Paris friend."

He sat up in the bed. "My friend?"

She eyed the door, desperate. "Y-yes, Peter Abelard. I was told the sad tale by my—by someone who knew of them both."

He swung his legs over the bed. "And they told you of me."

On his feet, the full effect of his indolent, dangerous beauty made her shudder. He had held her over a table that All Hallows Eve in her tent, and taken her while she struggled. She could not get the picture out of her head. Even now, deep in her body, her traitorous flesh tightened sensuously.

She licked her lips, thinking she had drunk too much wine. Should she scream and rouse the household? If she did perhaps he would leave the way he came, by the window, before anyone could reach her room. Then there would be no scandal. The king would never hear of it.

He came around the bed. "Sweet countess, no matter what you were told, I am no friend of Peter Abelard."

She backed away. What was he talking about? Everyone knew the story of his tragedy.

"No, that cannot be, Abelard was your master—don't you remember? Alas, your wits were unsettled in Paris because you were there when—"

"You know nothing of me. Nor of Abelard." He followed her until she bumped into the far wall.

She put up her hands to ward him off. "But I *do* know," she cried. "I have heard your story, that you were a student in the Paris schools, th-that you studied under the master philosopher, Peter Abelard. That when—when what was done to him, ah—was done, you—"

He seized her wrists in his big hands. "Countess, why do you tremble? Come, put aside your maidenly terror—it ill befits you. I prefer you as you are, cold-eyed and lofty as at the king's feast, with one of the Clares fawning at your side. Like the cruel goddess Venus. Like King Henry's own plummy pudding of wealth and beauty he dangles before his slavering nobles." He looked down at her with his crooked grin. "Tell me, what makes you so sore afraid of me?"

Afraid?

Constance stared up at him. He made her shake with terror every time she thought of what it had been like to be in his arms. He would not let her forget it—he taunted her and reviled her. She knew suddenly he wanted to make her grovel before him, to beg him for more of what he had so shamefully done to her!

She jerked her hands, trying to break his grip. "You—you street offal!" she burst out.

"Go! Out! Leave my house before I raise a cry that will bring my servants!"

He waited, eyes gleaming. "Do it, then."

She stopped, panting. They glared at each other.

"I will," she said.

He laughed as he pulled her to him. "Ah, sweet countess, my fabled lady of the cold, peerless moon, have you forgotten it was you I held writhing and squeaking, with your claws digging holes in my backside in your eagerness to have me—*all* of me—" he murmured, drawling the words, "—inside you? And that we were not even decently in a well-cushioned bed as with the gentlefolk, but rutting noisily over a table like—how did you call it? As the 'street offal' do?"

She gasped. "You raped me!"

"Unfair and untrue, as you well know." Holding her with one hand, he began to unlace the front of his shirt. "Your eyes tell me even now that you would like me to do it again."

"I had you chained once as—as a prisoner," she spluttered. "If you touch me now, I swear I will—"

He put his finger on her lips. "No need to beg me, dear countess. In the absence of the Clares' ambassador to diddle your peerlessly political purselette, I will make the sacrifice myself."

He pulled off his shirt and threw it into the room's dim corners.

"You are mad!" she cried.

"So I am told, constantly."

He jerked her to him. Before she could struggle his lips covered hers, forcing open her mouth. His tongue plunged in deeply. Her sense of outrage was complete as her indignant cries were swallowed in his mouth.

While his lips took her, his fingers began the slowest of seductive circlings in her hair, the warmth of their touch flowing into the back of her neck and her straining body.

She couldn't move. His kiss moved roughly, making her aching lips open even wider to him.

Constance moaned. She was aware of the bulge of his aroused body that pressed against her, the hard band of his arms, his tongue's thrusting invasion. All meant to drag her with him into his mocking, sensual fire.

She dug her fingers and nails into the muscles of his arms and clung to him. With that plundering kiss, wave after wave of surrender swept through her. This was the madman who terrorized her dreams, groaning with hunger for her.

A hard, rebellious ache flared between her thighs. The blood rushed into her breasts and her nipples tightened painfully. When he pulled away from her he was breathing hard, the wide curve of his lips wet with her taste.

"Ah, sweet countess," he murmured huskily, "this is what I've wanted since that night I first had you." He held her while his hips circled back and forth to press the stiff bulge of his shaft against her.

She made a small sobbing sound. Dear heaven, perhaps if she had not drunk so much wine she would be braver, more able to deny him. She struggled, but he only brushed her hands away.

"That's it, sweeting." His fingers were working at her bodice. "This time I want you naked."

Naked. Some of her reason returned to her. She managed to pull back enough to swing her fist at him.

He ducked. The blow glanced off his shoulder. Before she could run for the door he grabbed her by one arm and dragged her toward the bed. He pushed her backwards into it and she fell, sprawling.

He leaned over her. "Has he had you?"

"Had me?"

"The Clare. FitzGilbert."

"God's wounds, but you think me a slut!" She punched him in his face as hard as she could, wanting to hurt him. Heedless, he held her down with one hand and with the other stripped away her bodice, then the silken mass of her skirts.

She kicked at him. When he backed away she gave him another kick to the belly that broke his grip. Panting, Constance rolled to the edge of the bed. He quickly dumped her remaining clothes on the floor and caught her by the sleeve of her shift. She heard the thin cloth tear.

He fell on her, to hold her down. "I remember the scent of you, like flowers." In spite of her thrashing he lifted a handful of her hair and buried his face in it.

She stopped, panting. He lay on top of her, holding her down, his mouth buried in the warm curve of her neck.

She took a deep, sobbing breath. What was she going to do with him? Why did he humble her like this? He had already had his revenge. He was so handsome, so sure of his sensual magic. Now, as he held her captive on her bed, she was fearfully attuned to the sound of his breathing, the insistent stroke of his hands in her hair, the warmth of his big body. That hard, sculpted face, the shock of gilt hair, the gleam of sapphire eyes.

She licked dry lips. "You're pulling my hair."

"Forgive me." He had unraveled her braids. Strings of beads were all over the coverlets. The mass of her loosened hair spilled across her shoulders. He murmured, "Ah, Constance, I don't know what spell you have put on me, but I am here."

She lay perfectly still. He was dangerous and cruel, he lived to torment her. Even now his hands explored her breasts, his thumb stroking the hard points of her nipples. She was terrified of her own quivering expectation of his mouth against her flesh, of his tongue ravishing her, burning her, making her want more.

"Let me go," she quavered. "I don't want you to touch me. You're mad—your wits are addled by your misfortune!"

He laughed again.

Her torn shift was gone, pulled away. Her bare, taut breasts thrust out wanting him, aching for him. He pulled back to look at her and drew in a sharp breath. "How can you deny me when everything I do makes that lovely body want me? This, and this—" He nuzzled her nipples with his lips, the flesh of her breasts hard and swollen against his mouth. "Give me your softness, your fire that wants me so much."

He lifted himself over her and his mouth found hers.

Constance drowned in the sudden dark seizure of his kiss, that slow, savoring possession that stroked and caressed her with all the desire of his words. Her head was spinning as she fell deeper under his spell.

She struggled against him with the last of her resistance and wrenched her mouth away. "Holy Jesus in heaven," she breathed, "let me go! It is mad and dangerous for *you*—for *me*—"

"No." His legs clamped her body against him. "I know you know you want me." His mouth moved across her breasts, pulling and nipping softly. "What is this magic? Why can't I get my fill of you?"

She felt the knowing touch of his hands as he spanned her waist, outlining the naked curve of her hips. "I'll have you, Constance, I swear it." His tongue licked her skin with tender, persuasive caresses. "I'll kiss you all over your beautiful white body and be gentle. I promise."

He held her down with one hand while he

pulled off his boots, kicked them to the far corners of the room, then removed his hose. "I want my mouth on you, I want to kiss you and stroke you." The silky growl was urgent. "I want to get inside you—sweet Christ, but I need to lose myself in you!"

She was faint with desire. Her body could not stay still—it writhed beneath his fingers. His husky purr filled her mind with the words of how much he needed her. Wanted her. Her hips arched to him, and her thighs opened. Then his fingers were inside her in a flaming rush. "This is where I want to go," he growled, "to feel you so tight and hot around me."

A moan burst from her. She didn't know what she was pleading for, head thrown back, nails biting into the skin of his forearms. In another moment she knew she would be lost.

"I want to put my mouth on you, I want to kiss you, stroke you." His hand pressed against her moist cleft, moved to find the hard, erect nub of flesh, and pressed again. "Don't say no to me, Constance."

He dug his face and mouth into her shoulder, his arms fiercely around her. "Sweet Constance." His hands slid under her to cup her bottom. His hips moved against her. "Don't you want me?"

His lips brushed hers, then tantalizingly withdrew. He ran a wet tongue against her left breast and then the right. She cried out, fingers clutching his hair.

"What do you want? Show me."

Constance spread her fingers against the back of his head and drew his face down to her.

He moved with sudden savagery to seize her open mouth. "Say that you want me inside you," he mumbled against her lips. "Look at me."

He lifted his body over her and settled into the cradle of her thighs. "Open your eyes," he said hoarsely. "Say you want me as I go into you."

She felt the first thrust of his flesh part the tender folds of her body and gasped. She was terrified to give herself over to him like this. It was like being lowered into leaping flames.

The muscular body pressing down on her was drenched with perspiration. He ground out, "I want you to give yourself to me. Look at me."

She lifted her eyes to him. The moment was so fiercely lustful she felt like screaming. If he did this now there was no escape.

His arms tightened around her. "Say it for me."

"I want you," she whispered.

She cried out as he stroked into her. As she quivered under him he thrust into her again and again, rough, caressing words tumbling from his mouth. Then his lips closed down over hers.

As her body jolted from the fierce impact, he repeated his total possession of her, his tongue thrusting to fill her mouth completely.

Constance took his weight, his raging need, as his fingers dug into the flesh of her bottom to hold her. She arched under him, bursting lights ripping through her with a release that made her cry out. She felt him pull out of her and thrust against her thigh, his hoarse, bursting groan against her lips.

After a few moments, she drifted back. Her mouth, her breast, her whole body hurt. Wet stickiness spread over her thigh. The beautiful man who held her was still in the power of something so violent that he could no more than bury his face against her shoulder.

Constance put her hands to his hair and held him until finally he lay still against her. She stroked his shoulders, down to the curve of his buttocks, and heard him grunt softly.

His fingers tightened around her hand. Then he rolled slowly to one side and pulled her to him. Still breathing hard, he flung one arm over his eyes.

Slowly, very slowly, Constance's body stopped its trembling. She looked up into the candlelit dimness of her bedchamber thinking she hadn't wanted to lie with this dangerous, half-mad man. And yet, as she lay in the curve of his arm, she realized with dismay that she loved him.

It could not be true, she thought. Yet the evidence was a warm golden wave of tenderness, of love, rising inside her.

It didn't make any sense at all. Love couldn't be built on this powerful rutting that swept them together. But dear saints in heaven, how could one deny it when it was *there?*

She lay in the dark with her lips against his

bright, damp hair. Her own tresses were wound around them, binding them in its dark tangles.

She could not tell him that she loved him; she could hardly believe it herself. Anything more unlikely she could not imagine. She, Constance, Countess of Morlaix, who had had three husbands, and who had felt nothing for any man until now!

Her fingers stroked his shoulder, tracing the powerful muscles under the silky skin. With the weight of his body resting so heavily on her she felt a strange melting, not unmixed with despair. How had she come to feel so deeply—*wondrously*—for a beggarly wandering singer?

She knew nothing about him. Even with the story that she had heard, and there was no reason for her aunt and her confessor to lie, he'd denied this night that he was a friend of Peter Abelard. Yet somehow she knew that was not all of it. She had seen the pain in his eyes at the mention of Abelard's name.

Looking down at him she realized he was asleep.

Sweet Jesu, he had fallen asleep on her breast as fearlessly as he had climbed in her window! Never worrying that she would make good her threat to call her servants. Or perhaps not caring.

She pulled the damp, bright hair back from his face. He twitched, and mumbled something.

He was the most beautiful man she had ever seen, and she had called him mad, but now she truly did not know. Perhaps he was sane. Sane as any of the king's court this Christmas in Winchester. Sane enough, at least, to pull out of her this time so as not to get her with child.

Dear God, what was to become of them? In her heart, she was afraid she knew the answer.

She lay quietly, not wanting to disturb him. And after some time she, too, slept.

When Constance woke, dawnlight was in the room, the candle burned out. The shutter was open and the room was freezing.

And he was gone.

Sixteen

The king did not come to Constance's feast on the fourth night of Christmas. A council of England's nobles was suddenly called to confer yet again on the problems of the succession. No one, it seemed, not even the esteemed Roger, Bishop of Salisbury, could convince the king that his Norman magnates would not willingly accept a woman as legitimate heir to the English throne.

As a consequence it was said the king was in a roaring bad temper, suspecting secret support among his subjects for his nephew, William of Clito, who currently ravaged Henry's duchy in Normandy and proclaimed himself England's rightful heir. Constance had decided it was better, perhaps, that the king did not come to the feast in such a mood.

The weather that night was cold and rainy. Many of the lesser nobility were slow in arriving because of the downpour. The hall was not even half-filled when the first serving began.

Even Robert fitzGilbert had stayed away, no doubt to attend his powerful Clare uncles as they argued with England's nobles about the king's determination to have his daughter inherit the throne.

King Henry had himself sent several gifts with apologies to his favorite ward, Constance of Morlaix, for his absence: a gold circlet from Spain, studded with rubies and pearls, a bolt of embroidered French silk, and a long-legged puppy from his kennel of hunting alaunts.

Still, Constance thought, watching a troup of London comedians her vassals had obtained for the feast at an outrageous price, her glorious evening for the king could not be called a success. With Henry and all of his magnates sequestered in the king's council, her efforts amounted to a far-too-lavish feast for most of the minor nobility and the middle church.

But worse things had happened, she told herself. Considering what had occurred all Christmas season in Winchester, including finding Cenred the jongleur in her bed, one would hardly call the king's absence the greatest catastrophe. And, thank the saints, this year she could afford the expense.

After the meal William de Crecy and Earnaut fitzGamelin left the high table to drown their disappointment in the company of some of the Earl of Leicester's vassals in the back of the hall. Constance was fairly sure from their talk they'd been with whores the night before.

Both her vassals were older than she: fitz-

Gamelin was more than thirty, and William de Crecy was twenty-seven, with a wife, two little girls and a baby boy at home. When she was with them, though, they often acted like swaggering boys.

Baron Thomas Moreshold, who had earlier brought a poet to the king's table to compose a tribute to her, asked if he might sit with her. "I have seen you with your pretty girls," he told Constance as he settled himself beside her. "You are a fine mother."

She studied him, a big knight with graying hair, as he told her he had three sons, none as yet old enough to train as squires, and how much he missed his dead wife's tender care. In court circles Moreshold was known as a just and honest man. Perhaps too honest; Constance had heard he owned a great deal of land in the north of Lincolnshire, but it was riddled with debt.

She sipped her wine, watching a pair of sword swallowers, man and woman, stick flaming pokers into their mouths. Of all her would-be Christmas suitors she liked Thomas Moreshold best by far. She fiddled with the idea that if she married a man with children of his own and settled into a tranquil and orderly life, that she would not be so unhappy. She could have more children. It was something to consider. Perhaps she wouldn't dislike having them with a good, steady knight who seemed to care as much for his boys as Moreshold did.

Even while she was thinking, Constance

searched the crowd for a tall figure in form-clinging motley. It was madness to think she was in love with Cenred. Would she be this way for the rest of her life? Looking for a glimpse of him in crowds and places of entertainment like any besotted chambermaid or kitchen girl?

She was a grown woman and England's richest heiress. It was the worst sort of empty-headedness for her to be bound in helpless passion for a street jongleur, a wandering singer who held her fate in the palm of his hand whether or not he chose to climb in her window or assail her in her tent while she traveled.

Why could she not have fallen in love with someone else? Constance asked herself as she motioned for a server to fill the baron's wine cup. For example, with handsome and willing Robert fitzGilbert?

There was no denying the Clares' nephew's attraction at court. He was the most popular of all the young knights this Christmas, and the girls followed him around when their mothers were not watching, sighing and making sheeps' eyes behind his back.

And, no doubt, Constance thought wryly, when they saw fitzGilbert's pursuit of her the girls told themselves that the notorious Constance of Morlaix was unspeakably old at the ripe age of twenty-two, and unbearably worn. It was what she would have thought when she was their age.

The sword swallowers had gone. Now brightly-dressed Saracen dancers rushed into the center of the hall, yipping and shrieking, clashing small cymbals in their fingers. Constance bent to Thomas Moreshold. "My vassals tell me King Henry dotes on entertainment such as you see."

Her voice trailed away.

The Saracen women were bold-eyed and muscular, and wore gold coins in their long, trailing black hair. They danced barefoot on the muddy planks of the feast hall's floor and wore, as de Crecy and fitzGamelin had promised, costumes of alarming brevity: tight, spangled bodices that barely covered their breasts and transparent silk skirts that whirled about their ankles and knees and showed the outlines of their bare legs. It was what they did when they raised their skirts in both hands and whirled by that rendered Constance speechless.

Thomas Moreshold quickly turned so that part of her view was blocked, and began to talk of the heavy wagering that had gone on all week at the nobles' horseracing in Winchester fields.

It didn't help. Constance could still peer around him.

Holy Jesus in heaven, these women wore nothing under those skirts! When they lifted them in both hands and shook colored silk in the faces of the nobles and their wives, it could be seen that their private parts were not only naked but lasciviously *shaved*—smooth and plump like so many pale flour rolls pressed together. Constance couldn't stop staring. Neither, she saw in something of a daze, could anyone else.

"I do not wager at races," Moreshold was saying rather desperately, "although I have run one or two mares."

He stopped when Constance turned a flaming face to him. "My vassals," she choked. "They have done this."

"Yes, I know," he said quickly. "I heard them boast of a special entertainment for King Henry. But my Lady Constance, they could not know what they bargained for." Unaccountably, the corners of his lips began to twitch. "Although I see it is true, as de Crecy maintained to me, that had he been here King Henry would have doted on it."

At that moment a buxom dancer leaped to the dais and lifted her skirts in front of Moreshold. He was taken aback for a moment, his eyes widening at the view so vividly displayed.

At the look on his face, Constance began to gurgle.

The baron raised his hands as if to ward off the dancer. This only seemed to encourage her. She grinned, displaying a mouthful of white teeth, and clashed her finger cymbals. Then she dropped her skirts and reached into her skimpy bodice and pulled out a dusky bosom. The Saracen leaned over the table, cupping her flesh in her hand, and shook an olive-tipped breast at Baron Moreshold.

Constance was suddenly strangled with laughter, although she knew it would not do to burst out in front of poor Moreshold. She waved her hand at the dancer helplessly and managed to say, "No—no, go away!"

A knight stationed behind them heard and took it for an order. He jumped over the table and seized the dancer by both arms.

Before Constance could do anything, Carcefou had given the signal and surged onto the floor below with his knights to chase the suddenly-screaming entertainers. The panicked Saracens did not seem to know the cause, if indeed there was any, for the armed interference. In their confusion they began stripping off parts of their dress and throwing them at the knights.

Constance's household guards, taken aback at a tactic that bared so much unashamed flesh, did not seem to know what to do. Only stocky little Carcefou picked up his shrieking, half-naked Saracen, dumped her over his shoulder, and attempted to carry her away.

For a stunned moment the guests sat still. Then the hall burst into roars of laughter.

Constance gasped, "Sir Thomas, I—" and could go no further. She propped one elbow on the table and put her chin on it, her shoulders shaking.

He gave her a severe look. Below them, Constance's knights were chasing a dozen partly clothed, howling Saracen women through the benches and tables.

Thomas Moreshold caught her eye. "The

king would have doted on it," he said solemnly. His face crumbled then, and he whooped.

Constance was breathless. She leaned against him, her head resting on his arm as, cackling helplessly, they gave in to it.

Finally de Crecy's and fitzGamelin's ushers cleared the floor and brought on two pairs of wrestlers, who charged each other manfully. But the noble guests jeered and threw bread at them, calling for the wild Saracen women to be brought back.

Julien of Nesscliffe came in late, his cloak soaked with rain, and threw himself onto the bench beside Constance, giving Thomas Moreshold only a nod. His tousled hair was wet and he had a stubble of reddish beard. Plainly de Crecy and fitzGamelin were not the only ones keeping late hours in town.

Constance wiped her eyes. "You do not look very merry."

He helped himself to the bread and meat. "God's face, is this all you have to do, sit at feasting through day and night? I never see you doing anything else." He gestured for the server to bring him wine. "Nor do you stir yourself much to help me, Constance. You do not care how I fare here."

She stopped smiling. "It is true—I have not had a moment to speak to the king on your behalf, but I will."

He shrugged, angry. "It is the accursed Bishop of Salisbury. He hates bastards. They say he has had to scrape the treasury to provide for the twenty of them King Henry acknowledges, and damns them all. He sees it as England's vilest plague."

Constance was fond of her half brother; she did not like to see him like this. "It is my fault, Julien, I swear. I forgot, there was so much to remember when I took my oath with the king—"

"Leave it." He lurched to his feet, wiping his hands on his jacket. "I do not need your sympathy nor your gold, dear sister, although I fear you would give me neither." He picked up his wet cloak and slung it around him, hunching his shoulders. "I am one of England's devil-cursed, as Roger of Salisbury proclaims. When one looks at the good sons around King Henry who cannot be his heirs, one can well believe it."

He slouched down from the high table, shouting that he was going in search of de Crecy and fitzGamelin.

Thomas Moreshold stared after him. "He is the image of Gilbert de Jobourg. Your father had two, as I remember—there was another boy."

Constance watched Julien's tall figure weaving into the crowd. "Yes, my father and King Henry shared a like dilemma. No sons to inherit legimately, only a female."

Someone dressed in motley had come into the hall with a rain-drenched group. For a moment she held her breath.

Not Cenred, Constance told herself.

At second glance the group seemed to be ordinary players. She sat back on the bench, relieved and disappointed. She took a sip of her wine. *I am mad,* she thought.

Beside her, she knew that Thomas Moreshold had been watching her.

The rain stopped during the night. At daybreak a cold wind blew as Constance's household prepared to return to Bucksborough. They always seemed to be carrying so much more in the wagons coming back, she thought, as she made her way through the crowded courtyard. Although the saints knew they had been loaded to bursting coming south.

The scrivener, Brother Welland, who was keeping the tally, was cross enough to make Constance wish she'd brought Father Bertrand. The lay brother's haggard face told the reason.

"I have been told," she said to Carcefou, "the Benedictine brothers do not spend their nights in taverns."

He shrugged. "He is young. He is English." When she turned he added, "Well, if he were Norman perhaps he would be worse."

A groom brought up Constance's mare. She handed over her keys to the watchman and gave him instructions about the Winchester house. She had to raise her voice to be heard over Brother Welland's household tally and the uproar as the knights threaded their horses through the tangle of wagons in the courtyard, exchanging complaints and insults with the drovers and servants.

"I hope you had a good Christmas, milady." Carcefou bent to make a basket of his clasped hands and lift her into the saddle.

Had she had a good Christmas? Constance settled herself and took the reins. For a moment she couldn't answer because her head was suddenly filled with a memory of Christmas night in her candlelit chamber, her lover's naked body joined with hers. The feel of his damp skin under her fingertips, the words of passion, how much he needed her. The thrusting drive of him in her.

She sat unseeing, a hard, hungry cramp between her thighs, while her mare stamped, restless, and pulled at the bit.

"Milady?" the serjeant said.

She shook herself. "I miss Sir Everard." If her captain had been there the jongleur would never have climbed in her window. She would not be so torn, now, wanting to be another woman. A woman in love.

He squinted at her. "Yes, milady, so do we all."

She drew a deep breath. "God's blessings on you, Carcefou. Yes, it was a good Christmas." She turned the mare's head and walked her to the gate.

It took some time to get the wagons into the street between the vanguard and the rearguard.

Everyone in her household, including the knights, had bought gifts at the Christmas fair and were taking them back to Bucksborough. Constance, too, was guilty. She'd bought necklets of blue and amber beads for her girls, and linen cloth for summertime dresses.

Both Hodierne and Beatriz were growing like meadow weeds. Especially Hodierne. It did not seem possible that in only five years they would be looking for a husband for her. Betrothed at twelve, married at thirteen.

Or fourteen, Constance told herself, if she could argue the extra year to the king.

The sun had come out in a bright sky, and it was warmer in spite of the wind. It was only the fifth day of Yuletide. Crowds flocked to Winchester's streets. Constance rode with Carcefou in the front of the column. In the square they found a good-natured mob gathered for a mystery play. People surged in and out of the cathedral's scaffolding and over the piles of masonry to attend Christmas masses. Children ran alongside the horses begging for Christmas alms.

"Go away," Carcefou yelled. He waved his mailed fist. "Away with such nonsense, brats, you're not poor and worthy!"

They were merchants' children. Constance, laughing, told him to throw them some farthings. The serjeant dug into a leather purse and threw a handful. The children raced away, screaming.

Winchester's sanctuary was only half-built after nearly half a century of construction. The old Saxon cathedral had been torn down in the last years of the old Conqueror's reign to build this giant Norman edifice. The largest cathedral in England, the bishop had boasted. In all of Europe.

On the other side of the square the stage for the mystery play was the bed of a wagon with a canopy over it. A black-robed figure of Death leaned on his scythe and watched a fat man playing Gluttony and Vice tempt a man playing a young maid in a blond wig with long braids.

"Saint George save us but that is an ugly maiden," Carcefou muttered. "One would be hard-put to believe in her virtue."

Constance was watching the figure of Death. A shiver ran through her as the skeleton mask turned to look as they passed.

Her mouth went dry. The eyes behind the mask were not blue but dark, the figure stockier. Still, it had shaken her. She kicked her mare to a trot, threading her through the crowds.

"Milady," one of her knights called.

Her mare was shoulder-high in the throng. She reined in and turned in the saddle to look back.

Her knights had come to a halt. A strange knight in mail with his visor open pushed his stallion past Carcefou.

She waited for him. He was a few feet away, hampered by vendors selling meat pies, when she recognized the heavyset figure, the face under the helmet. It was Hubert de Warrenne, her sister Mabele's husband.

He pulled the war horse alongside her mare. "She is calling for you," he shouted, looking down at her. "The child is coming. Your sister will have no one but you, now."

After her first shock Constance thought, God's mercy, Mabele must be dying. Her hands clutched the reins. "Where is she?"

He looked back at her knights, the wagons stopped in the crowd. "At my mother's manor north of Basingstoke. Countess, will you come?"

Yes, of course. Her hands were wet with fear. Thank Christ Basingstoke was to the north, and not all that far away.

She reached out to grasp his reins. "Tell me of my sister. Does she—does she have trouble bringing out the babe?"

"I know nothing, God help us, except that she has sent for you. Yes, my mother says she is laboring with the babe." For once he had lost his bluster. He was not bad-looking—her sister had thought him handsome—but Constance had never liked fleshy-faced men. "I am riding north now, my father, my brothers and I, at all speed. Our wains, the rest of the slow company, will follow after."

Constance looked around. That Mabele had sent for her could mean anything. That the birth was bad, that she was in danger. That she wanted her. Dear God, Mabele couldn't be dying. Death in childbirth was horrible.

Hubert was saying that he and his father and

brothers would ride hard to Basingstoke and would make it before sundown. Constance knew she could not use the mare—the little horse was not powerful enough. She remembered the courier, Gisulf, had a fine stallion. It had brought him to Winchester from Morlaix in excellent time.

She said, "I must speak to my household." She walked the mare back to the vanguard. Her brother-in-law turned his horse and followed her.

"My sister is birthing her babe at Basingstoke at the Countess of Selford's manor," she told Carcefou, "and has sent for me." Her voice shook. At the look on his face she said, "I do not know. I can only pray God all goes well."

"I shall pray also, lady." When Constance told him she would switch horses and leave with the de Warrennes he gave Mabele's husband a quick glance. "I will split the company of knights, milady." He kept his voice low. "Half your knights will stay with the wagons and bring them north. The rest will be your guard to Basingstoke."

She took his meaning at once. In her worry for Mabele she had almost started off unprotected in the company of the de Warrennes.

"I will command the knights with you," Carcefou said. "If you will allow."

Constance watched Hubert de Warrenne slumped in the saddle, his face drawn. He and his brothers were brutes. She could not believe he cared anything for Mabele.

"Yes," Constance said, "come with me."

She slid down from her saddle and waited for Gisulf to bring up his horse.

Seventeen

The girl made a point of walking very slowly, seemingly to gather deadfalls for firewood. Now and then she stopped and looked around as if waiting for something.

She had made a circle of the clearing three times while Llwydd watched, a tall, strong girl with brown hair in long braids. She wore a gray-brown cloak that, in the late sun through the leafless trees, made her a creature of black and brown and winter light, like a forest-dweller. When she was on the far side of the clearing it was hard for Llywdd to see her.

It was the same girl, Llwydd was sure, the one whose message the charcoal burners had brought. She reminded herself she could not be too careful; it was dangerous to be in Morlaix at all. She followed the old ways, the old gods and their magic, and there were not many like her left in England. Not even now in the land of the Cymry, in Wales. The last time she'd come this far east the monks at St. David's had seized her and brought her in chains to the Irish monks' priory for trial as a witch. And then the lady of Morlaix had taken her. It had only been through all-powerful Woden's luck and the jongleur, Cenred, that she'd been able to escape.

Llwydd hunkered down in the hollow filled with dead leaves and considered the matter. The charcoal burners had told her only that the weavers' girl needed a message to go to the Countess of Morlaix, and none of the weavers could do it, nor even knew where the countess might be.

Now, Llwydd knew, she either met the weavers' girl and found what she wanted, or she did not, and turned her face toward the mountains again. This was not something that concerned her, unless she made it her own. Or the old gods'.

With a sigh, she stood up.

It took the girl a moment to see her. With her black cloak and the muted glitter of the gold torque around her neck, Llwydd was one with the winter trees and dying light.

The weavers' girl's eyes widened.

Llwydd put her finger to her lips. After her first surprise the girl was smart enough to pretend she'd seen nothing. She began to drift toward the oaks. When she was near the shadows Llwydd reached out to pull her under the branches.

"So you are the one," the girl whispered. "The Welsh witch." Her eyes swept Llwydd's face, taking in the black eyes rimmed with charcoal, the gold torque at her throat. "The forest people told me they did not know if you would come. But they said you are the only one who can reach her, that you can pass on the byroads like a shadow with your magic."

Llwydd only grunted.

"We cannot do it ourselves," the girl went on in her urgent whisper. "We have him hidden, the lady's knight captain. And his horse. It is very hard to hide a horse that big, but my father and brothers have him with cattle in a hidden byre in the woods."

Llwydd remembered Sir Everard too well. "The Gascon knight is a harsh man."

The other dropped her eyes. "He is tender with me."

So that was the way the wind blew. Llwydd snorted. "Is that why you hide him?"

The girl looked away. "Nay, the weavers remain loyal to the Lady Constance. She has let us come here to trade in our clothmaking and keep our ways. She has not taxed us burdensomely, and has been fair with us." She opened her hand. The silver Saracen ring lay against her palm. "He is ill and much disabled, but Sir Everard sends a message to the lady of Morlaix that she will know is from her loyal knight when she sees his ring. He wishes to tell her that it is a time of peril. That she may trust Longspres, the constable of the garrison here, but no other."

Llwydd made a sound between her teeth. "So

that is what it has come to. Did the Gascon see those who waylaid him?"

She shook her head. "They left him for dead on my father's doorstep, thinking that would please us. And that we would take him away and bury him for our revenge."

"But you hid him. And you badgered your father to hide his horse?"

The girl's lips tightened. "I told you, we are loyal to Lady Constance. Besides, I—*we* do not wish him to die. Listen, the charcoal burners said that only the witch-woman from the mountains would know where to find her."

"The willow maid." Llwydd turned the ring over in her fingers. "The lady of the moon. She and the oak god, they are twined together."

So he had been tender with her, Llwydd thought. And now the weavers' girl was taken with the iron-handed captain. The charcoal burners had told her about the cow and the reason for his trip to the weavers' street. On the other hand, she could not be sure the Gascon had truly given the weavers' girl the ring. Or if it had been taken from him when he was dead. It might be a trick. "What else did the lady's captain say?"

The weavers' girl wrinkled her brow. "I do not understand, but Sir Everard said to say to the countess that he would kill the jongleur if she so desired."

Llwydd held back a smile. Yes, he lived.

"Will you find her?" The weavers' girl looked anxious.

The Welshwoman drew her black cloak around her. "I do not know where she is."

The girl reached into her skirt. "You will need money. Sir Everard said you were not to be asked to do this without it."

She handed Llwydd a knotted piece of cloth. Llwydd took it, untied the knot and inside found coppers and silver pennies. It was more than enough.

"All the weavers of Morlaix gave to it," the girl told her. "You are to say to the lady of Morlaix that our message is that we are loyal, as are the castle garrison and those of her household under Sir Longspres. No matter what happens, they are ready to come to her."

Llwydd stuck the cloth pouch in her bodice. She lifted her eyes to the last beams of the sun in the black branches over them. "It is a long way," she muttered. "And to find her, first I must find *him.*"

The manor at Basingstoke was an old Saxon fortified *burh,* surrounded by earthen raths with a high wooden gate. The inner courtyard was filled with barns and pens and outbuildings. Grooms ran up to take the horses. The de Warrennes' party had made the last league on mounts nearly spent after the relentless gallop from Winchester.

Constance was stiff and sore. She hobbled toward the manor hall in the wake of the earl,

Hubert de Warrenne, at her elbow. "I pray we are not too late," he told her.

She shot him an angry look. The de Warrennes had paid little attention to her during their journey. She had ridden hard with Carcefou and her knight escort, thinking about Mabele's husband. Would it be to his advantage if her sister died? After all, he had beaten her. If Hubert de Warrenne was tired of his wife, death was simpler than setting her aside.

Servants rushed ahead of them, crying that the lord had come. Three hard-faced women met them at the door to the main hall.

"You are not welcome here," the older one said to Constance.

Hubert de Warrenne pushed past her. "Mother, God's truth, you sent for us." He waved a hand at them. "This is my mother, Lady Selford, and my sisters. Where is she?"

Before they could answer he bounded toward the stairs. The earl stopped to speak to his steward. Constance was shaking with weariness. She stared at the women, who stared back. "My sister, Mabele—"

The countess shrugged and turned away. One of the sisters leaned forward to hiss, "Mabele is decent—she can be encouraged to be a good wife to my brother."

Constance stared at her. Christ in Heaven, what did that mean?

A woman came down the stair with a bundle of soiled bedclothes in her arms. As she passed Constance stared at the bloodstained covers.

"Mabele is alive?" She was so hoarse with tiredness she could hardly speak. "My sister is not dead?"

The sister, pursemouthed, said, "Go see for yourself."

God curse them, the de Warrennes were monsters, even the women. She knew why they hated her; she had sent Everard to give Hubert de Warrenne a drubbing for what he had done to Mabele. She wondered if these sour women were beaten, too, by their husbands. For all the richness of the de Warrennes' house she would not want to live there.

She stumbled toward the steps. The manor had a vast hall with a gallery that ran around it. On the stairs a stout servant woman said to her in a whisper, "Your sister lives, lady. She had an easy time, and now they are bathing her. It is the babe."

Dear God, the babe.

Constance lifted her skirts and ran the rest of the way. At the far end of the gallery Hubert de Warrenne came out of a room and slammed the door. He bolted past her and down the steps. A maidservant opened the door and looked out.

Constance rushed down the gallery, calling out to her. Before the maid could close the door she pushed her way in.

The place was full of servants. Two were yanking fresh linens across the bed. Her sister, Mabele, naked except for a stained towel between her legs, sat in a chair with maidservants hanging over her offering warm cloths, scent bottles, and a cup of wine. Mabele was wailing loudly.

Constance pushed through them to her sister's side.

"Oh, Mabele!" Shaky with relief, she bent to kiss her sister's cheek, so close to tears she could hardly talk. Mabele looked pale but well. "You can have another babe."

Mabele looked up at her. "Holy Mary help me, Constance! Oh dear Christ, why couldn't you have come sooner?" She reached out to clutch her hand.

Constance bent to smooth Mabele's long, damp hair. "De Warenne will not hurt you, I swear it," she said in her ear. "You must be patient until I can put you in a wain and take you back to Bucksborough with me."

Her sister gave her a blank look. "Oh, Holy Mother have mercy on me, what have I done to deserve this? I have failed him! The babe is a gi-i-irl!"

"A *girl?"* Constance's legs wouldn't hold her up any longer. She sat down on the bed. Mabele was not dead. Apparently the babe was not, either. She said, "A girl?"

"A sweet little girl," one of the serving women told her. They milled around Constance, all talking at once. The Countess of Selford and her lady daughters had never seen a birthing so easy. Someone produced a linen-wrapped bundle bound in ribbons with lace. A nobleman's child. Constance looked down into the little face. It was not a bad-looking babe, red-faced and squinting. It was asleep.

She wondered if Hubert had threatened Mabele. What could he threaten her with? Even girl-children had their uses if one married them off well.

"Lady?" A little serving girl came to stand before her, holding out a cup of wine.

Constance took it and sipped at the wine as the women helped Mabele into the bed and brought a basin and began washing her hair. *Failed him,* her sister had said. Constance was so tired she couldn't think. The terrible de Warrenne women in the hall below. Their strange words.

Her hands shook with weariness. Some of the wine spilled on her skirts. The de Warrennes' servant women clustered around her, fussing.

"Leave it be," Constance told them. God knows she was filthy enough from the all-day travel from Winchester. She remembered with a sinking feeling that her trunks and boxes were with the wagons. There was no telling when she would catch up with her clothing.

She propped her elbow on the chair arm and rested her chin. Why had she done all this? Left half her knights and her household wagons to gallop across country as though the demons of hell were behind her?

She sighed. She had thought Mabele was dying.

Constance looked at her sister. The women had toweled off Mabele's hair, arranging the damp curls with ribbons that hung over her shoulders and arms. Mabele had pretty hair, dark red like Bertrada's, like their father's. Like Julien's, Constance thought. She was the only one with dark hair and grey eyes like their grandmother.

She got up and gave the empty wine cup to one of the maids. Mabele was saying something. Constance put her hand on the back of a chair to steady herself.

"They do not think much of us, you know." Mabele's voice whined, full of tears. "You do not know how hard it was for me at first. I wanted to leave, I could not bear it at Revensey," she added, referring to Hubert de Warrenne's manor. "Then I knew I was carrying the babe."

Mabele began to sob loudly. The servant women clustered around, trying to soothe her. "It is just what they expect of us, that I would not give him an heir!"

Constance stared at her. Was this what it was all about?

"I do not care a fig for what they expect!" She did not bother to keep her voice down. "The de Warrennes are nothing! They spring from hired soldiers in old William the Bastard's army. The men are brutes. They have the manners of pigs. If my father had been alive he would not have let the king marry you to Hubert de Warrenne." She suddenly thought of Mabele in bed with him, the man who had beaten her black and blue, who had rutted on her and given her a child. It made her sick.

"Hah, you say that, Constance, but they are a proud family—you know they have much land and title in France!" Mabele, dressed now in a woolen bed gown and looking pretty, had taken the baby from the nurse. She looked down at her child and touched it on the cheek with her finger. "We are rich, but not so fine a family as the de Warrennes. And we come from common folk. Grandsire Fulk de Jobourg—"

"God's wounds, who has been telling you all this?" Constance was beside herself. "We owe them nothing, these people. They have treated you basely. Did you call me here to tell me this? I thought you were dying!"

Her sister looked up. "I wanted you with me, Constance, but you did not even come in time! My first childbirthing and you were not even here! Now, you might as well take me back with you. I am nothing here. I have not even given my husband an heir!"

Constance listened with her mouth open. "If by the grace of God you were not dying," she managed, "I at least thought you might be in some danger."

"Danger?"

The Countess of Selford came in, Hubert with her. The older woman approached the bed. "Mabele, enough of this! You must let my son see his babe."

They bent over the bed. "No—no!" Mabele threw a corner of the cover over the child's head. "I have failed! It is my shame, my penance—to have only this female child."

Mabele began to sob in earnest. Hubert lifted his bearlike head and appealed to Constance. When she only glared at him, he turned back to Mabele. "Come now," he said gruffly. "I do not mind if it is a girl."

Mabele's screams woke the babe, who added its newborn squalls to the racket. The serving-women rushed around the chamber, tidying things, eyes downcast. The old countess scolded Mabele loudly, and her son for not being more forward to come take his babe.

Constance gaped at all of them. The servants' expressions astounded her. Some of them were openly smiling.

Hubert held the bundle of his girl-child in his arms. The nursemaids fluttered around him, telling him how pretty she was. The babe screamed like a trapped cat.

God's wounds, Constance thought. Her weariness dragged at her; she wondered if she could stay on her feet.

She knew suddenly that Mabele did not need her there; she had served her purpose. Her sister had sent for her and she, the head of the de Jobourg family of Morlaix, had arrived post-haste in a most respectable manner. The de Warrennes could not fault them on that.

As for the matter of the babe being a girl—Mabele was taking care of that, as Constance could well see. The hulking Hubert stared down at his howling offspring, grinning uncertainly as the nursemaids cooed over it.

Constance made her way to the door. The

old countess came to her side before she reached it. "You must stay and allow us to entertain you," she said to Constance, "and your household. You must stay with us a sennight."

The offer was no more than what was proper, but Constance wanted to be away from there and the old woman's cold-eyed hospitality. She muttered that they would stay the night but must be on the way in the morrow as her children were waiting for her at Bucksborough.

The countess studied her. "Yes, you have girl-children too, do you not?"

She was tempted to tell her that for generations the de Jobourgs had had only daughters. An ill-natured lie, but true enough in her father's case.

She went out onto the gallery and started for the stairs, then heard steps hurrying to catch up with her. When she turned she saw it was Hubert de Warrenne.

"Countess." He looked down at her. "You must not think badly of us."

Constance tried to step around him. "Sir Hubert, I am weary and must see to my knights. Lady Selford has most graciously offered hospitality for the night."

He blocked her. "I beat her because she said she would leave me. It is not as though I do not care for my wife."

She stared at him. "Care for her?"

"When a man beats his wife it is for her own good." He narrowed his eyes. "Besides, I would not let her leave me. She is a de Warrenne now."

He was right; any man could beat his wife and most did. She remembered Mabele had been a mass of bruises.

"I understand vengeance," he was saying, "and yours was misplaced, Lady Constance. Your own sister will tell you that. You should not have sent your hirelings to do something that was all unearned."

"I do not wish to speak of it." Constance was able to slip past him and make for the stairs. She said over her shoulder, "I only want to see my sister happy."

"She is happy. I have made her happy." He leaned over the railing to shout at her. "I have given her a very sweet babe!"

There was no one but servants in the downstairs hall. Constance went out into the yard. She saw her knights standing to one side with their horses, looking frozen. Carcefou came to her at once.

"Have they offered you nothing?" Constance snapped. "No food nor drink?"

He could see her mood. "The Lady Mabele?"

"Is well." She had forgotten the knights did not know whether Mabele was alive or dead. "She has a pretty babe, a girl. It was an easy birth. We will stay the night here."

The men murmured their good wishes for her sister and her newborn child, lifting their cold-reddened hands to cross themselves. Constance was rebuked by their good manners, especially since they had stood hungry and tired so long in the de Warrennes' yard.

Carcefou sent them to stable their horses. "She is truly well, the Lady Mabele?"

Constance nodded.

The little serjeant studied her. She supposed she must look a virago. For a brief moment she thought longingly of her clothes somewhere on the road. She would have to manage, dirty as she was, for the de Warrennes' evening meal and her night's lodging. Inwardly, she groaned at the thought of sitting down at table and making any sort of talk. She had not changed her mind; the de Warrennes were unbearable brutes.

"Carcefou," she said suddenly, "do I look old to you?"

He started. "Oh, no, lady. You are most young, and surpassingly beautiful. All the world says it."

He sounded sincere. She thought of Mabele upstairs in the manor house screaming over her little babe because she was a girl. And Hubert de Warrenne, who said he had only beat her sister because she threatened to leave him. Then her own daylong terror, riding at a breakneck gallop to get there.

"I feel old," Constance said.

She followed the knight serjeant across the yard.

Eighteen

Constance told herself that Mabele seemed content; otherwise she would not have left her at Basingstoke.

She rode at the head of her column of knights, and had thrown back her hood. The sun had come out and there was no wind. It was almost warm. Behind them the knights had shed their sheepskins and cloaks.

They had traveled all day and had spent the night at an inn at Twyford, near Oxford. Constance knew it was best to avoid inns in the countryside, as they were often rough and miserable places. But although they were passing through some of the Clares' land, she did not know the fitzGilberts' vassals there well enough to ask hospitality for herself and her knights. So they had stopped at the inn.

Earlier in the day Carcefou had sent Gervais back along the road to find their wagons, but he had not returned. The knight serjeant was fairly sure they were now ahead of the other Morlaix party.

The column went at a leisurely pace in the mild weather, hoping for Gervais' return. Constance had been thinking about her sister since they left the inn. Mabele was content, she told herself, but surely not happy. How could one live with the de Warrennes and find happiness? They were a grim lot. And they had made it all too plain that they thought their sister-in-law, the heiress of Morlaix, too notorious for their taste.

Still, she had to admit for all Mabele's vapors there had been something in her middle sister that she had not seen before. In the end the old countess took Mabele's side, and the lout of a husband had surrendered in the matter of a girl babe. When it was time to leave she had not been too surprised when Mabele told her that her wifely duty was with her husband and his family.

So be it, Constance thought. It remained only to tell Mabele that if she needed her she had only to send a message. Now as they traveled slowly north she couldn't help thinking that after Basingstoke—after this Christmas—she doubted everything she knew about love. And marriage.

The track that took them north was crowded with holiday traffic. Outside a small village they joined a line of wagons full of villeins and their families going to the Christmas fair. The giggling girls called out to the Morlaix knights, holding up cups of ale and honeynut cakes.

Constance watched knights and country girls flirting with each other. All morning she'd puzzled over her sister Mabele and how she could live with a man like Hubert de Warrenne. She was feeling the call to Basingstoke had been a sham, that there had been no real danger. But whatever it was, it had worked.

As for herself, she was sorely confused. Last night at the inn she'd eaten in the common room with her knights, then lain down on the benches before the fire wrapped in her fur-lined cloak, with Carcefou on one side and two knights between her and the rest. It had not been a good place to sleep. Constance had turned, restless and uncomfortable. Then a half-grown boy had come in several times during the night to tend to the fire. When he was noisy the travelers on the other side of the room woke and shouted and threw things at him.

The knights of her household troop were big, muscular young men. After their meal they went outside to the midden pile to piss, and came back laughing and joking. Then, scratching and yawning, they took off their boots and lay down on the benches. Some stripped off their mail and kept their swords by their sides, while some stayed fully mailed and armed, even to sleep. It was the first time she had slept among them.

In the dark she lay curled with her cloak drawn over her feet, her face pillowed in her hands, listening to them breathe, smelling their travel-weary muskiness, remembering their talk.

Men's bodies. The thought brought back vivid pictures of the jongleur, Cenred, and her dim bedchamber. To her surprise an unexpected heat began to burn between her thighs.

It had startled her. She lay on her bench thinking that before Cenred had taken her she had been innocent of the burnings of lust. Now just the presence of her own knights tantalized her.

She inched over on the narrow bench and thought of her sister Bertrada and her surrender to her bridegroom at Morlaix, and what unknown wiles he must have used with her. Dear God. Even Mabele lying with her churlish Hubert.

The ache between her legs had grown sharp and hurting. It was humiliating beyond belief. Under the cloak, she put her hand over it.

He had done this to her. The madman with his sapphire eyes who had climbed in her window at Winchester and enchanted her with his mouth, his beautiful body, his rod like a great sword in the fair bush of his groin. Now when her body was fiery with lust it was as though she could not live without him. It was so cruel she wanted to scream.

Carcefou said something to her.

With a start, Constance looked around. The column had left the villeins and their wagons behind.

The serjeant shouted an order and the Morlaix knights closed ranks. They approached the Chiltern hills on their way north. This part of the Clares' land was thickly wooded.

"Outlaws," Carcefou said. "They lurk in any wood, but this one is famous for it." He turned his horse's head and rode down the line.

Constance closed her eyes, the sun warm on her face. Gisulf's big horse picked its way under the overhanging limbs.

One could not be consumed with passion, she told herself. Had not Cenred's master at Notre Dame and his lover, Heloise, been so ensorcelled by their desire that it had destroyed them? Only now could she understand how that could happen.

Her beggar-lover was taunting and cruel, and filled her with unbridled appetites—to remember them afterward made her face burn with amazement and shame.

Yet that night in her bedchamber he had fallen asleep on her breast, his fingers laced in hers as though he held tight to their dream of forbidden desire. So beautiful as he lay there that she could not but love him.

Just the thought made her heart clench in despair.

And other memories. A figure of multicolored fire sheathed in Christmas Fool motley, risking his life for some reckless need to taunt the king and the Bishop of Salisbury. And making them like it. Making the crowd packed in the hall adore it. She had been there; she had been just as entranced as the rest. His lunatic wit, his dangerous laughter—she could no more resist him than his master Abelard and fair Heloise could resist each other.

And, Constance told herself, hers would be the same fate. There was no quicker way to bring about her downfall than to give herself to a wild passion for a fugitive student from Paris, now a hedgerow minstrel.

In the spring he would no doubt return to France. There was no reason why she would ever see him again. If his wits had healed perhaps then he would be a student once more. At Winchester someone had said that Abelard was teaching again.

The sun faded as the column of knights passed into the forest. The air turned cold. Constance drew her cloak close to her. With high oaks that shut out the light, the Chiltern woods were as somber as her mood.

She did not want to give up the only love she had ever known, the first tender lovemaking that only he had given her. But what she felt for him was doomed. She knew nothing about him, not even where he came from. And although he was known as Abelard's friend, for whom he supposedly had grieved enough to sink into madness, he had denied even that.

She knew she should put him from her mind. It was possible that if she petitioned King Henry he would let her marry Thomas Moreshold. A good, solid knight, with a care for children, old enough to want the comfortable life. With her money she could offer him all that.

If Thomas Moreshold could be content, she would be, too.

Content, not happy. Like Mabele.

Suddenly something unexpectedly rebellious rose up in her. The mutinous feeling did not want to marry Thomas Moreshold. It wanted, instead, to scream and rail and beat its fists against the fate that would force her to lose the one man who had made love to her.

She rode for several minutes, fighting it down.

Mother of God, what was the matter with her? She had never felt this way before. All her life she had made herself do her duty—things she had not, in her heart, wanted to do. One was foolish to long for happiness and love. Such things did not come to King Henry's heiresses.

She straightened her back and sat higher in the saddle. She had her lovely children. And if she approached the king wisely she could no doubt wed a kindly man like Thomas Moreshold.

Carcefou trotted his horse back up the line. There was something in the path ahead. In the uncertain light, it was hard to see. "Wait here, my lady," he said as he passed.

Constance had already made out shapes in the forest. They were not the outlaws that Carcefou thought, but wild charcoal burners and swineherds and their ragged families. In the winter, having no crops, only what they gathered in the woods, the forest folk fared very poorly. She had no doubt they were looking for food.

She pushed the big stallion after him. They still had provisions from Lady Selford's manor. And Carcefou had bought meat and fresh bread at the Twyford inn.

The charcoal burners stood in the road, watching them. Constance did not know their language, nor did any of the knights. The headman, if one could call him that, a grizzled elder in filthy deerskins, spoke to them in a few mangled words of Saxon.

"Lady," Carcefou said, riding back to her, "it is not wise to stop here. You cannot feed every wild pack we find in the forest."

He was as bad as Everard. Constance reined in, staring at the children. Only the monks cared for the forest people and then not too generously, as their religion was thin. If indeed they had any at all.

"Give them bread and meat, Carcefou. The sacks the de Warrennes gave us at Basingstoke."

She turned to the headman to speak in Saxon. As she did so a ripple of something ran through the band, and the old man's eyes widened. In the next instant the wild folk were melting into the trees.

"Where are you going?" Constance called. "Come back! My knights will give you bread and meat."

There was no answer. Suddenly the air around them was full of noise and motion. Riders burst out of the woods. There were warning shouts from her knights.

Constance wheeled her horse. Gisulf's stallion stumbled in the soft dirt by the side of the track. She saw Carcefou lunging for her, but two riders in face-covering hoods and dark cloaks came in between. When she looked again Carcefou lay in the road under the horses' hooves.

Before she could scream they swept down on her, one reaching out to grab the stallion's bridle. Constance flailed hearing the hoarse cries and the clang of iron from knights fighting behind them.

She did not have time to free her dagger, but it would not have done any good. Coming up beside her, a rider dropped a smothering sack over her head. She howled and struggled and tore at it with her hands, until with an oath someone brought his mailed fist down on the back of her neck.

Then there was only silence. And darkness.

Glory is never a trivial thing.

The Georgics, Virgil

Nineteen

Thierry de Yners dove headfirst into the boundary ditch and landed with a muffled yelp. Beyond the oat field he had just crossed, the villagers still searched, armed with their wooden rakes and hoes, for the source of their anger. When he stuck his head out briefly Thierry could see them outlined against the bright sky and hear their enraged shouts. Fortunately the hedgerow was thick, a tangled ironwork of beech and holly branches. For the moment, he knew he had a safe hiding place.

Thierry rubbed his head. He'd cracked it on something coming down and, examining his fingers, he saw it was bleeding. Devil take it, where was Cenred, the cause of all this?

He heard a prolonged hiss nearby and started, thinking of snakes.

A husky voice whispered, "Yners, you ass, it's me. A foot more and you'd have landed on top of me."

"Cenred." They could still hear the howling

villagers searching for them. He squinted to find him in the hedgerow's shadows. "God is my witness, I know now I've lost my feeble wits to leave Winchester with you and tread the roads to these damned godforsaken villages! Turnips and jeers is all we get for our pains—if not cracked skulls!" He took a deep, outraged breath. "What prevailed on you, man, to sing a damnable song doubting the Mother of God was a virgin? At this season, yet! Have you forgotten it's Christmas?"

Thierry could see him now, feet in fancy boots propped up against the dirt wall of their hiding place, wearing a threadbare cloak over his dirty Christmas motley. They had landed in the bottom of the ditch where there seemed to be almost half an inch of icy water. Thierry lifted his bottom, gingerly, and found it was wet. He cursed under his breath.

"It was a revolting song. No wonder those louts are ready to kill us. Which they will do if they find us." He looked around the ditch. "We'd best wait here for dark. Where in Christendom did you hear such an obscene ditty? You'd better do your best to forget it."

The other laughed, softly. "I can't forget it, de Yners, it's mine own. I composed it yestereen, on the road."

The young scholar turned to stare at him. "Christ crucified, Cenred, I do not believe it! That song that set the whole peasantry of Woosten Cross after us wanting to do murder—that is your *own*? That verse about virgins who roll and play in the hay sometimes have their hymens intact when they give birth?"

The other regarded him, eyes gleaming. "It's been known to happen."

"You can't do that!" De Yners sputtered. "Make a song like that. It's blasphemous. It's—it's *unChristian!*"

"I thought it was successful. Besides, I'm not all that Christian." He gave him his crooked smile. "At least I had their woodenheaded attention there for a while."

De Yners slid down, his back against the dirt, and stared at him with something like wonder.

"Cenred, you *are* mad," he whispered. "What sort of lunacy is this that courts death and disaster? I saw you do this same thing before King Henry. It was brilliant then, and marvelously daring, but this day you nearly got us killed." He paused and studied him. "Jesu, Cenred, is this what you want? For a howling lot of villeins to beat you into bloody shreds and end it all?"

The big man shrugged. "Your nature is too serious, de Yners. You worry too much."

"No, hear me out for once." The other hunched closer so he could look into his face. "Is this what you want, Cenred," he said earnestly, "not to live? Is this the real cause of your troubles? Not madness?"

The other still smiled. "Tell me, friend, why does any man cling so fiercely to life? What is there in this existence to makes us love it so? I ask myself this, having seen that all that one loves can be destroyed, even as one stands helpless."

"Cenred—"

"Come, you asked the question, did you not?" After a moment he shrugged. "You are right, of course, it is my own demon that drives me, not yours. Perhaps I should leave you," Cenred said, "and go the rest of the way into Wales myself. It is wrong to put you in the way of danger."

The scholar made a quick gesture. "No, no, I'll stay with you! I may take my life in my hands, you madman, but I do not know anyone's company I favor so much. Besides, I know the depths of your sorrow. That you still grieve for him."

"Grieve for him?" Cenred put his bright head back against the ditch's wall and closed his eyes. "You mean grieve for Peter Abelard?"

They were silent for a few moments as the shouts of the enraged villeins of Woosten Cross seemed to draw nearer. A voice, louder and deeper than the others, was ordering someone to go get the dogs.

"Dogs!" Thierry got to his knees in alarm. "Did you hear that?"

"Stay." Cenred put out a hand to hold him. "Serfs don't keep hunting dogs, only barnyard curs. They are hoping we hear them howling so as to flush us out."

With a sigh, the scholar sank back. They were silent, listening. Their pursuers seemed to be crossing into another field. He said, finally, "You are not at all afraid, are you?"

The other shook his gilded head. "I am thinking of Wales, de Yners. And how long it will take us to get to that country."

"Too long." Thierry shivered. "I had counted on something to eat here, Cenred. This wandering life puts no meat on a man's bones. Even one like me, who is resigned to a poor poet's hungry life. And my bottom is wet. The damned ditch is full of water. We'll freeze before sunset."

"The Welsh bards are wondrous," the other went on. "And as for singing, you cannot surpass them. The whole country chirps like a heaven full of birds at dawning."

Thierry examined his muddy boots and looked peevish. "Well, I for one will not benefit as I for one do not speak that barbaric language."

"Shame on you, de Yners, art is universal." With his eyes closed, Cenred grinned. "As is poetry.

"I am the stag of seven tines.
Over the flooded world I am borne by the
  wind.
I descend in tears like the dew, I lie
  glittering,
I fly aloft like a hawk to my nest on the
  cliff,
I bloom among the loveliest flowers.

I am both the oak and the lightning that
blasts it."

Thierry stared at him. "Mother of God, what was *that?*"

"Welsh poetry. It—ah, loses much when put into Norman French. How about this?

"Bum twrch ym myndd
Bum cyff mewn rhaw
Bum bwan yn llaw."

The scholar scowled at him. "You have a fiendish humor. Is it your purpose to drive me away from Wales rather than bring me to it? But if, as you say, their princes have been reading Virgil and Ovid and Horace and are avid for the classics, perhaps they will be generous." He sighed. "That is my trade these days, instructing the barbarian horde—my own included. God, how I miss Winchester! The noble ladies doted on me. I had messages from the sweet young Lady of Sackford, did you know that? To come and—um, read Ovid to her. And her husband a sour old dolt aged enough to be her grandfather."

"And rich enough to have you killed."

"But now here I am with you, traveling in winter across the misbegotten land of the English to an even more savage land of the Welsh, all because of your violent fancies. And," he lowered his voice as he looked away, "because you are still wild-witted."

Cenred, sprawled against the wall of the ditch with one leg drawn up, did not reply. Thierry fidgeted awhile, watching him. He started to speak several times, then thought better of it. At last he blurted, "Cenred, tell me of Peter Abelard. What happened that—that *night?*"

The other man opened those lucent eyes.

Thierry went on in a rush, "I have heard so much about those who bribed Abelard's own servant to go up the stairs into his bedchamber. The uncle, Fulbert, of course, says nothing, damn him—"

He came to a stop. Cenred's face was polite, expressionless.

Thierry licked his lips. "I know you were there, all Paris knows you and Abelard's students pursued the attackers, and what was done to Thibaud. A just vengeance," he added quickly. "I find no fault with it."

Cenred merely stared at him.

"Is it true," he plunged on, "that Peter Abelard has said he knows nothing of—what was done to him? That he says he does not remember *because he was asleep*? Dear God, how can one sleep through one's own castration?"

Cenred said flatly, "Where did you hear that?"

"In Paris. Cenred, have you no idea what a storm of talk, a whirlwind of speculation, still continues? The church and the schools are incestuous enough, and he is one of their own. Every monastery and convent is abuzz with what Abelard is doing now that he has been condemned by the Soissons Council for his heretical book, and yet is still followed by great crowds of adoring students. The story of Abelard, the great philosopher, that marvelous mind and mutilated body, goes from one far corner of Christendom to the other. Even kings gossip of it. Louis of France loved Abelard greatly, although he knew he was—is—dangerous. And *you.*"

Thierry stopped and drew a deep breath. "There was talk enough of you, Cenred, and your glory in the schools even before Abelard's disaster. Now it is as though you have dropped from the face of this earth."

Cenred looked up at him. "Peter Abelard says he remembers nothing? That he was asleep when they cut off his balls?"

Thierry winced.

Cenred laughed. "Have you never heard of Origen, de Yners? An early father of the church. Peter Abelard worships him, thinks him Holy God along with St. Jerome and Virgil. And Peter Abelard, of course."

"Sweet Mary, Cenred, that's blasphemy!"

"However, it was not what Origen preached, but what he did that left its mark on Abelard." Cenred put his hands behind his head and stretched. "The more I think on it the more I believe I know Peter's forbidden secret."

"Cenred, in God's holy name, the man has suffered horribly!"

He raised an eyebrow. "Oh, I agree. Peter had

heaven in his hands and he threw it away. Leaned out the window, one might say, and tossed it into the street to be trampled into the mud. And the queen of heaven, may God always bless her. Abelard is not content unless he smashes his gifts, his students, those who love him, his books of his own writing, his old teachers, his powerful mentors, the kings who admire him, the Pope—"

"Jesu, lower your voice!"

"Yes." He stopped, and wiped his face with the back of his hand. "You are right, de Yners, no one can castrate a man while he sleeps peacefully through it. I was there afterward in his rooms with a wailing, weeping mob, and there were people from the houses around who told me they heard the screams."

The scholar shuddered. "Why, *why* did her uncle do this dastardly thing?"

Cenred looked weary. "Castration is the punishment for adultery."

"*Adultery*? You can't mean—"

"Fulbert loved her. You have heard the gossip, that Heloise is his daughter? But he did not need to have that excuse, believe me, to attack Abelard. Heloise is beautiful—of the two she is the far better scholar, the more perceptive thinker. The world loves Heloise." The corners of his mouth turned down. "Not all the world loves Abelard."

"I—I have heard some of what they say about Heloise. Abelard's poetry about her is still sung in Paris. It is very erotic."

"God's wounds, I have already told you he had heaven in his grasp and threw it away."

"Well, yes." He asked quickly, "Cenred, tell me as his friend, do you think Abelard could have taken another woman? Is it true that he took Heloise to her old convent dressed as a nun in order to set her aside? That he—"

"Shhhhhh." Cenred raised his hand. The shouts of the villagers had come closer. And with them, the distinct baying of dogs.

"Christ in heaven!" Thierry lurched to his feet.

"Get down, you fool!" Cenred dragged him back by the edge of his cloak. "We'll know soon enough if they think to try the oat field."

They were silent. Thierry fixed his eyes on Cenred's face and drew a shuddering breath. "Ice runs in your veins, damn you. You are mad, you do not care for your life. I am seeing now that you care for nothing."

"You do me an injustice, de Yners. I care for little, it is true, but I once loved Abelard for his brilliance, his daring, his genius. I was young, and wanted to worship brilliance and genius, as the young do. I was ignorant of what one will also find."

Thierry turned his head, listening to noises coming nearer.

"However," Cenred went on softly, "I am not so afraid of heaven as Abelard. Once one has known it, heaven is worth keeping."

"I am not ready for it," Thierry said nervously, "I want to live. I swear, Cenred, I think they are coming closer."

"Heaven is a woman," the other went on. "Any woman, providing she smells sweetly and is soft and loving. And," he added, remembering, "with silver eyes and hair like the starless night, a tiny waist and exquisite breasts with satiny, rosy-brown tips. And a delectably tight, hot purse that squeezes the life juice from you in her squealing, thrashing passion."

Thierry had gotten to his knees to look out. "God is my judge," he whispered hoarsely, "they are chasing someone. The louts from the village have their dogs—they're chasing a woman! They're there, in the other field."

He turned. His friend was pursuing some vision of his own, eyes unfocused. "Cenred, did you hear me? The dogs have picked up someone else's scent. A woman, running for her life. She has drawn them off, poor soul."

He looked up. "Yes, well, stay put, de Yners. Who is it, can you see?"

Thierry shrugged. "A woman. A Welshwoman, that is what they are shouting."

Twenty

"Help me!" Constance kicked at the door. They had taken away all her clothes and she was barefoot as well as naked, so the sound did not carry too far. "Someone, please help me!"

She slumped against the wall, gasping. As usual, there was no evidence that anyone had heard her.

God help her, it was an effort even to do that much. She had been sick for more than a day. The back of her head where she had been struck still pounded, and her stomach was queasy. She had vomited several times, but in spite of her shouts and calls for help no one had come to clean it up. She was in such filthy condition she could not believe that she, Constance of Morlaix, was in a dank cell whose floor was covered with vomit, clad only in a dirty blanket, her hair stiff and matted with blood from the wound made when her captors took her.

She put her hands over her eyes and took a

deep breath. *How long had she been there?* She'd tried to keep track of the days.

The first day—she was sure it was daytime because some gray light had appeared around the frame of the shuttered window and then died away—she had lain on the cot, not able to lift her wounded head, and with barely the strength to roll to the edge to keep from soiling herself when she puked.

The second day she had been sick with fever. It was the second day she could not remember at all well. Shadowy presences, perhaps two or three, had come and tried to get her to drink from a cup of water.

Even though Constance had racked her brains since then, she could not remember who they were. Perhaps they had been nuns. This much she knew—she was in a convent or even a monastery, because she heard the bells ringing for mass. It was not a place she could name; perhaps, she had told herself, they were still on fitzGilbert land.

Now that she was no longer desperately sick and could study her cell, she still could not say where she was, nor guess who held her prisoner. And without her clothes the cold was unrelenting.

She huddled on the cot with the stinking blanket around her, feet pulled up under it, her arms clasping her body for warmth. She gathered that whatever they wanted from her, her nakedness and the filth and cold and her misery as the way they hoped to get it.

And the loneliness.

She had tried resisting the temptation to talk to herself after hours of shivering silence, but it did not work. The cold alone was enough to drive one mad. At night when it was worse she wept from the pain of her frozen flesh, her poor feet and hands especially.

At first, hearing the sound of her voice whispering her thoughts out loud had unnerved her. It had attracted the attention of others, too—she was sure of it.

There was a narrow slit in the door, covered with a piece of wood. From time to time she knew the slit opened and eyes watched her, although she was never able to turn fast enough to see. Nor hear any footsteps; whoever came and went was careful not to make noise. It was very quiet in this place, wherever it was. Even the sound of the convent bells was far away.

In the beginning she had told herself angrily that whoever they were, they took their lives in their hands abducting a ward of the king. After Christmas in Winchester with an army of suitors fawning over her, and King Henry's pointed favoring of Robert fitzGilbert, it was madness to do something like this!

But after a while her outrage faded, replaced by bouts of terrible despair. No one knew where she was or who had abducted her; those who had taken her in the Chiltern forest had worn hoods so their faces would not be recognized. Her last glimpse of her knight escort from Basingstoke showed them fighting for their lives, with Carcefou either dead or wounded upon the ground.

This cell might very well be where she would spend the last of her days.

But why?

She threw herself on the cot, wanting to scream. Pound her fists against the walls that held her. She could make no sense of it. She was sure no one wanted her dead, for the simple reason that she was worth so much more alive. For ransom, or for marriage.

So why starve or freeze her to death in some out-of-the-way convent? Did they hope that the king would forget her and make no inquiry as to what had become of her? Holy Mother, that was hardly likely; they didn't know Henry!

And her children? What was to become of her daughters? It was all very well to despair for herself, but she could not leave Hodierne and Beatriz motherless.

But who? The question tormented her.

She paced the cell back and forth, dragging the blanket around her, heedless of her feet on the freezing bare stones. When she thought of those who would miss her, who would remember to look for her, her heart sank again. Everard, her protector, her devoted knight captain who would search heaven and hell for her, was missing. Her half-brother Julien, who would do the same, had left the court by now, on his way back to his manor at Nesscliffe.

The de Warrennes might have wanted revenge for the beating she'd ordered for Mabele's husband, but she did not think that likely after her visit there. If they'd planned her any harm, they would no doubt have done it months ago.

Constance groaned. That was the damnable puzzle of it. She could think of no one who wanted her dead. Dead, her fortune and lands went to the king.

King Henry?

She stopped short, and shuddered. Great Jesu, he was capable of it. But murder was not the king's way. At least, not like this.

Besides, King Henry was rich enough. Awarding her and her fortune to one of his nobles in marriage was much more profitable.

Without realizing it, Constance had spoken out loud. At that moment the door opened and a nun appeared with a cup of water, piece of bread, and a necessary bucket. But not, apparently, to clean up the filth.

When she spoke the nun only stared at her as if she did not understand Norman French. Repeating it in Saxon was no better. Constance drank the cup of water greedily. It was the lack of water, more than food, that was the hardest to bear.

"Who are you?" she demanded. "Where is this place? Why are you holding me here?"

The little nun would not look at her. In silence she handed the bread to Constance, then went to the door. Someone on the other side unlocked it.

"Wait!" Constance lunged forward, arm outstretched to stop her, but the nun slipped under it and scooted through the door. It slammed in Constance's face.

She leaned against it, pleading with them to come back and tell her what they wanted of her, but there was no answer.

After a little while she went back and sat on the bare ropes of the bed and thought of ways to escape. The stone cell had only the door and the shuttered window. The slats, when she tried them, were tight and secure.

Then there was the door, and the nun who came with bread and water. She sat with the blanket around her, teeth chattering, planning what she could do.

She told herself she could stand to one side of the door when the nun entered, seize her, and throw her to the ground. She was strong enough to do it.

She would tell them that if they did not let her go she would kill the nun. She would choke her to death.

She could do that, too, remembering Hodierne and Beatriz. She believed that she could kill someone if it meant saving her children.

She put her back against the wall and closed her eyes. When the faint light at the window faded and dusk came, she dozed, but only fitfully. She could not sleep, she was freezing.

The sound of the bolt being drawn on the door woke her. She sat up.

Constance knew at once it was not the nun. Those who stood in the doorway held candles, tall shadows behind the light. She could not see in the brightness. She held up her hand before her eyes.

They stepped inside. Constance's heart began to race. The shadow in front, not finding her, lifted his light to peer about him. The candle's brightness fell on his face.

"You!" she cried.

Twenty-one

With a shriek, she launched herself at him, the blanket tangling around her legs for the briefest of moments, then falling away.

He seized her and held her at a distance, hands gripping her wrists. "Now, Constance, keep back, these are my good clothes. Sweet baby Jesus, but you are a stinking virago!"

Behind him Robert fitzGilbert's face was filed with horror. His eyes dropped from her matted, bloody hair to her nakedness, then the filthy floor.

"Dear, sweet lady," he blurted, "I never meant this to be done to you. Julien, in God's name—"

His voice trailed away as Hubert de Warrenne came forward and picked up the blanket and draped it around her shoulders.

She glared at them through her bedraggled hair. "I'll kill you!" She tried to wrench herself out of Julien's grip and the blanket fell again. She didn't care that they stared; she wanted to murder them.

"God damn you to suffer in everlasting hell, Julien," Constance yelled. "I wish I could bring down my dead father's curse on you!"

He jerked roughly on her wrists. "I told you we should have let her ripen a day or two more. She won't give in to us now, not in this temper."

"Julien, for Christ's sake, she's your sister!" The Clare nephew was agonized. "Let her go."

Julien gave her a vicious shake before he flung her away. Constance reeled across the cell, hit the bed, and fell on it.

Robert fitzGilbert picked up the blanket to go to her, but de Warrenne grabbed his arm. "Listen to Julien, man," he growled. "You will not bring her around by coddling. We need to do what's to be done quickly."

Constance sat up and looked at them. They were bundled in furs against the cold. Snow dusted their clothing and hair. They had planned this together. The thought sank into her mind like sharpened knives.

Julien was staring at her bare breasts. "The devil take you, Constance, are you going to be reasonable? FitzGilbert is besotted with you—he desires to marry you. I have given him my blessing."

She threw back her hair with her hands. *"Your* blessing?"

"Jesu, don't scream. As de Warrenne says, we don't have all the time in God's creation. And no one has much patience. In particular not the three years' worth of which you so proudly boast."

Constance sucked in her breath. She still could not believe Julien's betrayal. She looked from one face to the other. There was horror and shame on Robert fitzGilbert's, oxlike satisfaction on Hubert de Warrenne's. Cool calculation on her half-brother's.

Ah, they were so clever. But they were wrong if they thought they could force her to marry. Even King Henry had not done that.

"You can't make me wed him, no matter what you do!" she cried. "The king will hear that you have abducted me, and punish you. All of you!"

Julien lifted his brows. "King Henry has left for France. Robert de Clito has taken the Vexin so the king will little think of England for the while. But it is no matter, Constance, the king is weary of waiting. Did you not see it in Winchester? You think yourself surpassing clever with your damned petition, but Henry is not so eager to have all of England see him cool his heels over you, while every knightly lout in his kingdom scrambles for your hand."

He gestured to the younger man. "Marry fitzGilbert now. Another husband is nothing new to you—you can spread your legs for a Clare who is rich as Croesus, can't you? I do not lie when I say fitzGilbert wants you. He tells me he is willing even to let you keep your brats."

Constance gasped.

Robert fitzGilbert flung Julien an angry look. "You have a vile mouth, Nesscliffe." Like Julien, he could not keep his eyes from her nakedness. "Lady Constance, say you will wed me," he said hoarsely. "A priest waits outside."

She lifted her eyes to them standing there, waiting for her. What Julien had said was probably true: The king had been out of sorts with her flock of suitors at Christmas. Dear God, Henry could be capricious and cruel, he was famed for it. And he had already shown he favored Robert fitzGilbert.

Looking at them she could see they believed they could force her to marry. They were confident of it. Sweet Mary, but she hated them. "And what is your reward for your treachery?"

FitzGilbert blurted, "Nay, Lady Constance, you do us an injustice—"

"Bucksborough." Julien grinned, unrepentant. "Bucksborough is mine, and a hundred silver marks. As your dowry Robert gets Castle Morlaix."

FitzGilbert shouted, "Damn you, Julien!"

She hardly heard him. *Bucksborough.* Her rich fief, the jewel of all she owned. It was a great prize. Better, it would solve all Julien's problems. Robert fitzGilbert must truly want her to let him take it.

She did not look at Hubert de Warrenne. Mabele's husband had his revenge to see her cast down, naked and freezing and filthy in this convent cell; it was good payment for his beating. She knew he would gloat over it.

Oh God, she should have known before what was in their minds! One did not make enemies in this world without suffering for it. And she had thought all her life that Julien loved her. As she had loved him.

"No one is forcing you, sister." Julien's voice was syrupy. "We want you to desire this marriage of your own free will. We want you to sweetly implore Robert fitzGilbert to end your unhappy unmarried estate, and offer you his good name and protection, as all virtuous women rightly desire."

She could only stare at them. For all his eagerness she hated the Clares' nephew fully as much as the others.

Constance bent her head. She would not be forced into marriage. Bile rose up in her throat at the thought of it. She was nothing when she was only some nobleman's wife, object of his lusts, a brood mare for children, a wealthy, high-born prize he had caught and possessed.

Yet there were her girls, she remembered. At least fitzGilbert had said she would keep them.

God's wounds, was there no way to fight this? She was cornered, their captive. She wanted to scream her defiance. She did not want Julien to take her manor at Bucksborough from her, although no doubt Robert fitzGilbert would give it to him for his part in this. And oh, how she longed to pay Hubert de Warrenne for helping them!

"Lady Constance?" Robert fitzGilbert would have come to her but Julien held him back. "Dear, sweet lady, know that in spite of what has been done I have but the tenderest feeling for you. I have not had the favor of presenting my suit, but I want to assure you of my noblest intent, no matter what these circumstances. Pray, speak to me, and tell me that you hear what I say!"

Hubert de Warrenne looked at Julien. "Stubborn bitch," he said. "She will only sit there and not answer. I have seen that look of hers before."

Julien nodded. "I told you we had not let her cook in this stinking pit long enough to make her sweet-natured. Come, Robert." He gave the other man a tug by his jacket. "Take your mind from dreams of her cunt long enough to take a meal with us at the inn."

"But you cannot leave her like this!" The other stared, aghast. "It is colder than a tomb in here."

"Exactly." Julien took his arm and steered him toward the door. "Leave my damned sister here a few days more to compare this cloistered life to what she can have with you." FitzGilbert craned to look over his shoulder. "Julien, God's face, I don't want her starved! It is bad enough, this filth and cold, and—"

"No, of course not." He exchanged looks with de Warrenne. "She can have soup, can't she, Hubert? With her bread and drink?"

The other rumbled something. He opened the door and stood there.

"Yes, well, let us remind the prioress." Julien turned back to Constance. "Don't be a lackwit, sister, fitzGilbert's cock will have no other. Ask him and he will tell you. And, wed to a Clare, you will be richer than ever you dreamed. You know you would like that."

She lifted burning eyes to him. After a long moment, he shrugged. He turned and passed through the doorway, pulling Robert fitzGilbert with him.

Hubert de Warrenne slammed the door behind them, and the bolt shot home.

Constance went back to the cot and drew the blanket up around her and sat with her feet tucked under her, shaking as much with rage as with the cold.

In her heart she knew she would have to give in to keep her children. She could not bear the thought of Hodierne and Beatriz taken away from her for a new marriage, perhaps to be put in some convent she did not even know of. There was no way out of it. Besides, half of England would think her mad not to marry the Clares' nephew.

Still, it was hard to think of surrender. Had she been alone in this, they would not have conquered her, damn them to hell! She would have stayed in this accursed convent cell and starved, if need be!

She stopped, surprised at the depth of her hate. What was happening to her? She, who had made choices all her life according to what was expected of her, now felt an anger that shook her to the depths of her soul. At that moment her hatred encompassed them all, even the king.

Holy mother, she was a virago, just as Julien had said. She lay back in the bed, exhausted.

The light waned but no one came to bring her water and bread. Constance got up and pounded on the door but no one seemed to hear her, and she went to bed hungry.

The next morning her mouth and lips had dried out and her thirst was painful. In the afternoon she shrieked and pounded on the door to no avail. And shouting made her dry throat and swollen tongue worse. For the first time she cried.

She sat on the cot and wept for a long time, the saltiness of her tears and runny nose moistening her cracked lips. She told herself she could not understand why no one came to her, when they had given her bread and water before.

By evening she was very frightened. She racked her brains to think of anything she had said or done that would make them want to starve her. No, they had promised her soup, she remembered. Julien had said that when he left.

Thinking of hot soup, Constance was overcome with a yearning that was almost madness. If they had come then with a bowl of it she would have given them anything. She would have married fitzGilbert on the spot. She would have thrown herself at Julien's feet and kissed them and begged him to forgive her for whatever it was she had done. She knew she was thirsting badly. Her body had so little water she did not even need to use the necessity bucket. Darkness fell and it grew colder, and she lay on the cot weeping until she fell asleep.

It was dawn when she heard the voices.

Constance rolled from the cot. Her legs wobbled so she nearly fell to the floor. Reeling drunkenly, she made for the door.

Soup. They had promised her hot soup. Her thirst-parched tongue was so swollen that she couldn't cry out, only make a hoarse, desperate sound.

The door opened.

I surrender, Constance wanted to cry. She took a few wavering steps. *I will do anything you want. Only don't leave me here!*

At first she could not see clearly. It took her a moment to know it was not her half-brother Julien nor Robert fitzGilbert nor Hubert de Warrenne standing there.

Constance peered at them. She had forgotten her blanket, she was naked again, and her bloodstained hair hung in her eyes. Through its tangles she could make out a monk in a black habit, and a nun.

They stared at her, not moving. Then she heard the monk curse, vilely and feelingly.

"Constance." He reached out to steady her as she swayed. "In Holy Jesus' name, I'll kill them," he grated. "I'll make them suffer hell's own agony before they die."

She watched what they were doing dazedly.

It seemed they were not really a monk and a nun. The monk held Constance still while they put a nun's habit over her head.

"Cenred," she whispered. She would know those blazing blue eyes anywhere.

Pure, witless joy washed over her in a wave. She couldn't help laughing. The sound was terrible. She let her head loll back. The room was beginning to spin.

The woman took her by the arm. Black eyes looked into hers, ringed with charcoal. "Willow maid," she said in Welsh, "do not fear, we have found you."

Constance couldn't stop laughing. "Soup," she tried to tell them. Now that they were there soup was all she needed to make her happiness complete.

She made no resistance when Cenred bent and put his arm behind her legs, picked her up, and carried her out.

Twenty-two

"Ah, and *fight,"* Llwydd said. "I never saw the like in my life, the way he fights!"

She was picking at Constance's blood-soaked hair, trying to loosen some of the snarls. Now and then she stopped to grunt, dismayed and angry, as she worked around the large lump on the back of Constance's head where her attackers had hit her.

"There I was," the Welshwoman went on, "running from those men of Woosten Cross with their dogs at my heels, and here comes my young oak god in all his glory across the fields with a tree branch in his hand as long as I am and as thick around, that's the truth of it. Cenred came raging down on them and their dogs like the lightning from out of the sky, swinging the staff and laying about him like Woden himself. I was near my limits with running, I tell you, I couldn't do no more, and I was that glad to see him. I knew when I saw him come roaring out of the woods it was the oak and the lightning, the Old One with his eyes blazing fire, the wood in his hand."

Constance turned her head to look at Cenred by the fire. He had carried her in his arms all the way to this clearing in the woods, and there was deep snow on the ground. She hadn't realized how much it had snowed since she'd been a prisoner.

He wore a ragged cloak and the dirty Christmas Fool motley, but he still looked to her as she'd first seen him chained to the wagon at Castle Morlaix: broad-shouldered, singularly graceful for all his height, with his silver-gilt hair, his unusual eyes. She could not take her eyes from him.

She was not the only one. The charcoal burners and their families crouched around him and worshipfully watched every move as he melted more snow in a pan over the fire.

Constance still had not satisfied her terrible thirst, even though she could hold the cloth of the nun's habit to her belly and see it puffed out with all the water she'd drunk. She was no longer hungry. The forest people had given her a gruel of ground acorns which was not the worst thing she had ever tasted. It had certainly filled her empty stomach.

"You never saw the like of it," Llwydd was saying. She put down the comb and worked at Constance's tangled hair with her fingers. "Those Woosten Cross villeins lay down where they were and didn't want to get up again—not to face *him*, that is. One lick and they'd had enough. Them others, seeing their friends broken-headed and bleeding, and him standing over them like all-avenging Woden himself, took to their heels. When they were all gone, and their nasty dogs with them, he came across the field to me with his friend you see there, the young scholar, and they lifted me up and set me on my feet and he wanted to know what I was doing there so far from Wales. And I told him I had followed him the width of England looking for him, asking where a jongleur that looked a certain way, and did certain things, might have passed. I didn't have to tell him there are many across this country who have never seen him but have heard of him and his songs. Like the people of Woosten Cross."

Constance had to smile. She could imagine what he had been doing among the villagers to make them chase him like that.

The Welshwoman tugged at Constance's hair. When she winced, Llwydd made a clucking sound. "Ah, lady, this blood in your hair has putrefied, and there's no water to clean it. You'd be better off having it gone."

"Oh, no." Her hair was long enough to sit on; she could not imagine herself close-shorn. "We'll do something, we'll bind it up."

She sighed and closed her fingers around Everard's Saracen ring. She knew now Julien had tried to kill her knight captain. And that no doubt he and Robert fitzGilbert were searching for her. They would not so easily let her slip away this time.

Even worse, her household knights were scattered and out of reach. Twenty-five were on the road from Winchester with the wagons, the rest in the Chiltern woods after the ambush there. Alive or dead, she did not know. Everard's command of fifty knights he'd taken to Morlaix were in the castle with the garrison under the constable, Longspres. Everard, Llwydd had told them, was in the care of the weavers. Constance said a prayer of thanks that he was alive.

Cenred came and sat down beside her and gave her a cup of water. "Are you hungry?"

The water was snow melted over the fire and still warm. She smiled over the rim at him. "A little."

His eyes darkened. "We'll get something with meat in it to get your strength back."

He did not say how. The scholar, Thierry, had gone back to Woosten Cross to see what he could steal. They knew the villagers would not sell them anything, not after Cenred had sung his blasphemous songs and broken a few heads there.

She looked at him. "I am strong—this will not hurt me. I have fasted days before, at Lent."

"Not without water, you haven't. It's the thirst that will kill you." He watched Llwydd working at her matted hair, then took a knife from his belt.

"Oh no, please." She twisted, yanking her hair from Llwydd's hands, which hurt; the back of her head still had not healed. "I will clean my hair up somehow."

His face was grim. "It will be some time before we can bathe. We cannot do it here in the dead of winter in the woods. It is best to get rid of it."

She could not help staring. This manner was new to her. She remembered Llwydd's words, that she had never seen a man fight as he had. Perhaps, she thought, studying him, he was a ruined knight, as she had once suspected.

He waited, frowning.

"It will be easier, dear," the Welshwoman told her.

It was a hard thing to do. Her hair had never been cut. She remembered the tributes to it in the feast halls at Christmas. With tears in her eyes, Constance nodded.

He handed the knife to Llwydd. "Short, like a youth's," he told her.

"It will grow back," the little Welshwoman said as she lifted a solid mat stuck together in the back, and began to saw through it.

Constance looked down at her hands. "How did you find me?" she whispered.

"Llwydd. And the charcoal burners who were there in the Chiltern woods when you and your knights were attacked." He squatted in front of her as the Welshwoman hacked through a large piece of her hair and laid it on the ground. "Do you know the wild forest people call you 'the Norman lady who feeds them?' "

Constance looked surprised. She supposed she never traveled without giving food to someone. But she had never thought of it.

"The charcoal burners did not see who had taken you, and like most forest people they are shy of townsfolk and did not know who to tell. Then they heard the Welsh witch also searched for you. After Llwydd, it was not so hard to find me—not with all of that cesspool, Woosten Cross, chasing Thierry and me, trying to hang us." He looked away. "I gather your loving bastard brother, Nesscliffe, and the Clares have done this."

Head bent, Constance nodded. There was nothing she could say about Julien's treachery.

Llwydd leaned to murmur in her ear, "To hear him tell it you would think it was not but easy going to find you. But we searched the road north in the heavy snows of these past days, up and down, back and forth, asking for you. Then a traveling friar said he had heard there was a lady at the convent of St. Magdalene the Blessed. Ah, you should have seen this one when we went there! I thought the prioress would drop to her knees and kiss his boots before he had finished with her."

Cenred picked up the pieces of her fallen hair and threw them into the trees. "I gave her my king's purse from Christmas," he said. "It was more money than they'd seen in that place in a year. Not to mention that they were wanting greatly to get rid of you. The prioress is afraid of the Clares, but afraid of her bishop even more."

He got to his feet and looked down at her, hands clasped in his belt. "Countess, we are on foot, traveling like serfs, and there has been deep snow, with more to come. I gave St. Magdalene's prioress the last of my pence for that habit you wear, and Thierry has little or nothing. For Llwydd, it is the same. We are hard pressed even for food."

She stared at the ground. Yes, they were risking their lives for her. If they were caught, she would live—she was valuable to her captors. But Llwydd, Thierry, Cenred—as common folk they would be punished most horribly. They would suffer mutilation and torture before they died.

Constance said, "I owe you my life. I would thank all—"

"We will go north and west from here," he interrupted, "to Cirencester, and then to the Earl of Hereford's lands where, since he is your ally, it will be safer. I will carry you on my back."

On foot like serfs.

She sat thinking about it. Those who pursued them would be on horseback, well-provisioned, and with ample money.

Besides, to carry her on his back through the deep snow seemed an impossible feat. She did not know if any man could do it. She was tall, not small like Llwydd.

She said, "No, I will—I *must* find some vassal of the fitzGilberts here to take me in. Then I will write letters to King Henry in France, and Hereford and others who know me, asking them to support me."

Llwydd and Cenred stood staring at her. Her

voice trailed away. They knew that Clare vassals anywhere would not be likely to give her shelter, and certainly not there.

Perhaps they were right. She said, "Where—where are we going?"

His face was expressionless. "To take back your castle, countess, and your knights and your lands, and all that is dear to you. Isn't that what you want?"

She lifted her chin. She would not deny it, no matter what he thought.

"Yes," Constance said.

Thierry came back from the village beaming. He threw a muddy sack down in front of the fire.

"Hah, Cenred, there are villeins in Woosten Cross with broken legs who won't be chasing poor poets and scholars through the fields this winter. You had a heavy hand with that cudgel."

Cenred picked up the sack and looked into it. "What the devil?" He pulled out a square of salted beef and swore again. "How come you to steal this? Where have you been? Have you killed anybody?"

"Not *stolen*, man." Thierry scraped his hand through his thick, curling hair. "I was most craftily exploring a henhouse that unfortunately was empty of hens, when a fat widow came up behind me with a rake and threatened to brain me until I stepped out into the light. When I did so, I could see that she liked what she saw. So I put on a piteous face, and told her I was starving and would do anything for a gracious meal."

Cenred scowled at him. "And?"

His grin grew wider. "*Anything* was not too bad, even fat as she was. And, all the saints help me, it was a feather bed. I almost wept when I had to crawl out of it and return to this miserable lot."

Llwydd had grabbed the sack and pulled out a loaf of black bread. She struggled to break the tough bread in half, and stuck a piece of it in her mouth. With her other hand she offered the rest to Constance, who seized it just as eagerly.

"And there is this," Thierry said, digging into the sack and pulling out a boy's tunic made of sacking. He gave Constance a swift glance. "Does she know?"

Cenred didn't look up. "No."

"What is it I should know?" Constance asked.

The scholar went and stood in front of her, the tunic in his hand. His eyes grew wide. "Milady," he said after a long moment, "do not grieve, your hair will grow back."

Constance couldn't bear the look on his face. "Go away," she told him, "or I will hit you."

She heard Cenred laugh.

Before they left the clearing he came and helped her to her feet. "Can you stand alone?" he wanted to know.

"Yes, I am feeling better." She was afraid of

being a burden. They were doing this for her; they had no quarrel with Julien or the Clares, and God knows it would be difficult enough. "You will see, I will get stronger," she promised.

"Hmmm." He handed her the boy's rough tunic and some well-patched braies.

"I can't wear men's clothes." Constance stared at the things in her hands. She could not imagine exposing the shape of her legs for the first time in her life. "The nun's habit is warmer."

"That damned thing! I had hoped never to see another woman in it again." His voice was harsh. But his hands were gentle when he slipped the rope from around her waist, and then the black robe down her shoulders.

Constance turned her back. He had seen her naked when he took her from the convent, but it was different now, standing in the dark woods, in the cold, with snow all around them. There was still a heat between them that reached out hungrily. She pretended that he didn't feel it.

She moved away from him to step into the braies, bracing her hand against a tree trunk. "Is this what you wish, for me to travel dressed as a boy?"

There was silence for a long moment. Then he said, "Yes, it is safer. There will be many, at least at first, who will not know who you are."

She pulled the tunic over her head and down to her hips. When she turned he was staring at her, a taut line of white around his lips.

She could not read the expression on his face.

He bent and took the nun's habit from the ground and balled it up and started for the fire.

"No, wait!" She hurried after him. "What are you doing?"

She wasn't fast enough. He had hurled the black habit into the embers.

She pushed him aside. "Holy Mother, what did you do that for?" She took a stick and lifted out the smouldering robe. "We need this. It is good wool—I can cut it up and use it for a cape."

The nun's habit had almost caught fire. She knelt on the ground, her legs not strong enough yet to hold her up. Llwydd came up and stamped on the cloth until it stopped smoking.

"With the sleeves we can make boots for you," the other woman said, "and stuff them with dry grass, as the villeins wear. Then your feet will be warm."

Dear God, her feet hadn't been warm in days. When she looked up both Thierry and Cenred were watching.

Constance rubbed her hands down the front of the rough tunic. She was shivering, barefoot, and all her hair was gone. She managed a wobbly smile.

"I have never looked like this," she told them.

Thierry smiled back. Cenred, scowling, turned away.

The sun came out, warm enough to melt the snow, and it was windy. After an argument, Constance let Cenred hoist her to his back, her legs clasped around his waist. She could feel the strong muscles of his back straining under her stomach and breasts. Warmth spread along the length of her body from the heat of his under his clothes.

She knew it was not easy for him to carry her. He had to lean forward and if she shifted at all it threw him off stride. At the edge of the wood the charcoal burners turned back. One moment they were there, the next they were gone with no word of farewell.

Constance could not keep from feeling relief. They had bread and meat only for themselves, and could not feed the woods dwellers. But the wild, stick-thin children tugged at her soul.

Without turning Cenred said, "Spare some worry for yourself. We have a long way yet to go."

She stiffened. She told herself she never liked the way he had of reading her thoughts.

They avoided the road until past noon, but all were tiring except Cenred. He seemed made of iron. When they came to a small, shallow river with a bridge over it Thierry slid down the bank to the water with whoops of joy, and they followed him to drink and rest in the sun, out of the wind.

Her legs were so cramped from being carried that Constance could do no more than crawl to the water. After she'd drunk, she put her feet in the stream. The cold made her gasp, as the water had come from the snow melting around them, but it was not unbearable.

She knelt on the bank and scooped water over her head, using her fingers to work it into her hair. The others were sitting on the bank making a meal of the bread and salt beef. Constance slipped off the tunic and splashed water on her breasts and arms. Her teeth began to chatter even though the sun was warm on her back.

She moved behind a large stone and slipped off the ragged braies. When she looked up Cenred was standing there.

Without speaking he knelt beside her and pushed her head forward and poured water over it again from his cupped hands—the last of the dried blood was washing away. He poured handfuls of water down her back, making her shudder, and rubbed it in with his hands.

Then he came in front of her, pushed her into a sitting position, and pulled her legs out straight and washed them. Constance sat with her teeth clicking with cold, her skin bright red under the scrubbing.

Soap. It was but a thought. At that moment, though, she would have given its weight in gold to have it.

She felt his fingers on the inside of her thighs. Then his open hands, pouring water there, opening the soft, feminine folds. When she looked up at him his eyes were hooded.

The muscles in her thighs clenched painfully

as his touch invaded her. There was searing heat and at the same time the spill of icy water in all her tenderest, flinching places. And then the hard, lustful ache in answer.

The light, the pale sun, even the knifelike cold glowed in her throbbing body.

When she opened her eyes he was standing over her with the tunic. He quickly slipped it over her head. She got to her knees and, holding onto his shoulder, stepped into the braies.

She ached with wanting. Her private places were swollen and hurting. She turned her head away, not wanting to meet his eyes. Thierry and Llwydd were sitting on the bank, talking and eating. But she knew they had seen.

Twenty-three

"What's the matter with the young lad?" The drover was covered with a countryman's straw cloak against the downpour, and had to thrust the hood back to see. "Is he hurt?"

"Weak," Thierry said, laying his hand on the side of the oxcart, "just weak." Behind him, Cenred stood hunched over with the countess on his back, Llwydd in her dripping black cloak beside them. "He had lung fever before Christmas, but he's better now." He pulled a long face. "This terrible wet does him no good, though, poor boy. He might catch his death in it."

"Ummm." The old man studied them, taking his time. "Strolling players, is it? You picked a poor season to go north. Should have stayed south—they have a fat Christmas there, in the south. Not soon over, like it is here." He paused, then shouted over the noise of the rain, "What does the big man do?"

Christ in Heaven, Thierry thought.

They had been staying on the bypaths, under Cenred's direction, to avoid being recognized, but the rain's steady, cold torrent had forced them to the Cirencester road and the dangerous hope of begging a ride from some villein with a wagon. But this old gaffer was the only one who'd passed in all the time they'd been trudging their way north.

Thierry looked back at Cenred. The rain beat down on his head and shoulders, flattening his gold hair to his skull. He held the countess on his back by gripping her legs and one wrist. Her head lay slumped against his neck, her eyes closed. Thierry hoped she was asleep, and not in a swoon.

"He's a jongleur," he shouted back. "Juggles the balls, plates and cutlery, too, and does a bit of singing. You'd like his songs. Make you laugh." Rather desperately, he gave the old man a wink. "Jokes with a bit of naughty stuff, and all that."

"Hmmm," the gaffer said. "Don't like singing and jokes myself. But to give you a ride down the road is the Christian thing to do, what with the weather and all." He peered disapprovingly through the rain at Llwydd. "Is the woman his wife?"

"Mine," Thierry said hastily, "she's mine."

Without waiting he gestured to the others, then climbed into the oxcart among the grain sacks, the trussed sheep, and the tubs of turnips.

"She's Welsh," he said, bending to help Llwydd over the tailgate. "They have fine, obedient women in Wales, that's why I wed with her. But she has no Saxon." The Saxon tongue was what they'd been speaking.

Cenred climbed in beside them and lowered the countess onto the sacks. He bent over to shield her face from the rain. "Where is he going?" he muttered.

Thierry shrugged. "Anywhere, I care not." The cart lurched as the old man called out to his ox. "I was frozen before, in the snow. Now I am frozen and wet in this damnable rain."

Cenred straightened up. "We seek shelter," he shouted to the driver, "someplace dry. Have you a barn or a byre that could keep us?"

The old man hunched his shoulders and did not answer.

The wagon passed between open fields planted in winter grain. The weather was breaking. Through the leaden downpour the late winter light showed the corn sprouts thrusting up through the melting snow to form, in the twilight, a pleasant green haze.

Sometime later the oxcart went through the gates of a manor house side yard, the stables and outbuildings closed and deserted. The old drover got down to open the gate to a fenced pasture surrounding a stone barn.

Thierry sat up in the wagon and looked around. "Look at the size of it," he exclaimed. "And the manor house where we came in. This is no villein's holding."

Cenred got down to help the drover close the gate.

"You can sleep in the loft," the old man shouted. A veil of rain poured from his straw cowl. "Sir Ralf's in Winchester with his master, Lord Robert of Meules, swearing fealty to King Henry. There's no one about until they come back."

Cenred pulled down the tailgate. Thierry said, "Where did he say this was?"

Cenred pulled the figure dressed in boy's clothes to a sitting position. "Constance," he said in a low voice, "how do you fare?"

She opened her eyes and managed a pale smile. "Where are we?"

"You have got your wish," he told her. "It appears that one of the Clares' vassals has taken us in."

The fief's barn was built of stone with a great loft that ran the length of the building. The bottom held stalls for the vassal lord's cattle and horses. The air was warmer because of the animals, and stank strongly of manure. The old man drove his ox and wagon inside and closed the door.

Thierry quickly followed Llwydd up the ladder into the hayloft. "Dear Christ, it's almost warm up here," he called down. "Cenred, look about and see if there is sacking to put on this hay so we can make bedding."

"See to it yourself." He set Constance on her feet and turned to bargain with the drover for a bowl of soup. "My loud friend," he told him, "still has a few pence if your good wife can sell us some."

The man went out, muttering something about not knowing if there was anything such as soup to be had, and closed the barn door.

Constance started slowly up the ladder. Below, Cenred searched in the horse stalls, looking for sacks. When he had found some and a good horse blanket, he climbed up after her.

The high loft doors were warped, letting in slivers of grey light. He motioned Constance to go down to the end, away from Thierry and Llwydd burrowing noisily in the straw on the far side.

She groped her way to a corner and sank down. The air was cold but she stripped off the piece of nun's habit she had made into a short cape and spread it beside her, glad to get rid of her wet coverings. It was a new experience, to be carried in rain-soaked clothes, chilled to the bone, for hour after hour. She knew now why her heart had always gone out to beggars and other poor folk.

Cenred knelt beside her, his clothes and hair as drenched as hers. They had not spoken much the long day. She knew he was tired. She watched him strip off the top of his fool's motley, then sit to pull off his wet boots. He carefully stood the boots side by side in the hay to dry.

He had inhuman strength, Constance thought, studying his bent, gilded head, to carry her from morn to dusk almost without stopping. The muscles in his naked chest and arms bulged as he picked up a sack and rubbed at himself.

"We will stink of horses." She was only teasing; she knew as well as he that they were lucky to have the barn and dry hay to sleep in.

He shot her an azure look. "Take off the boy's garb and dry yourself." He threw her a sack. "No one will see—it is growing dark in here."

At that moment the doors opened below, and a herder drove in two cows. They threw themselves flat against the hay, not breathing, as he stalled the cattle, then took his time pitchforking fodder into the rack. When he went out they rose up again only to slip back when the door below opened once more.

The old drover looked up at the loft. He was carrying a wooden pail, and a bowl and spoon under his arm.

"Christ's balls, it *is* soup!" Cenred got to his feet, hitching up his hose, and hurried toward the ladder. "I can smell it."

The drover wanted to stay and question them some more about where they were from and where they were going, but Thierry paid him his copper and filled the big bowl and took it back to Llwydd. Cenred carried up the spoon and the wooden bucket. They heard the old man go out and close the doors.

Cenred sat down and gave the spoon to Constance and held the bucket for her. The soup was thick with barley and turnips and glistened with a deep coat of mutton grease. It was hot;

a veil of steam rose in the cold air. Constance fell on it with moans of happiness.

He sat watching her. After a minute she sat back and wiped her mouth with the back of her hand. "Never talk to me of heaven," she sighed.

"Is it good, then?"

She made a face. "No. But it is wonderful."

She picked up the big spoon and dipped it in the soup and held it out. When he would have taken the spoon from her, she held it away.

Their eyes met. For a long moment they said nothing, looking at each other. Then she held the spoon to his mouth. He swallowed, then took it from her, and began to eat. Every other spoonful he offered to her, holding it to her lips, until the bucket was empty.

Constance lay back in the hay and stretched her arms above her head. Not to be wet and cold was nothing short of a miracle, and the mutton soup lay warm in her belly. She had never felt so fine. The heavy rain thundered on the thatch above them. The light around the loft door was nearly gone. She felt much stronger. She had been able to sleep part of the time when he carried her.

Cenred picked up the shoes Llwydd had made out of the nun's habit. He fingered the sodden, feltlike black wool the nuns wore both summer and winter. From the brooding look on his face she could not tell what he was thinking. Piece by piece he pulled out the soggy straw and dropped it into a pile. The noise of the rain around them was loud.

She heard him say without looking up, "I was the one who took her to Argenteuil that last time, in nun's clothes. That is my curse: if it had not been for me, Abelard would not have destroyed her."

Constance lowered her arms and looked at him, not sure that he was speaking to her.

He turned the black cloth over in his hands, staring at it.

He said in the same voice, "I was their courier. When she had a message for him I would take it. Or I would bring Heloise to him at night, in the dark, through the Paris streets. I had been at the schools for some years—I was not a green boy like some of his students, so that is why Abelard charged me with it. And also to take her back to the convent at Argenteuil that last time, when it was thought he had put her aside."

He lifted those strange, light-filled eyes. "I loved her. God help me, so madly did I love her that I thought Peter was a fool to trust me. Then I came to think that he knew that I did, and that for me to love her served his purpose. Yet when I saw what he was doing I would have killed him, except that she loved only him; she could see no one else, and she would have hated me for it. I brought her from Argenteuil to see him that morning, after he'd been castrated. I stood in the hall at the top of the stairs at his lodgings with the mob around us, holding her in my arms until Abelard could send word that she could come in. But it never came. So I took her back to the convent still wearing this damned crows' cloth that had done so much to bring her harm."

He threw Llwydd's makeshift shoe aside. "Now, don't you want to ask me, as you did in Winchester, what has addled my wits?"

Constance pulled herself up to her elbow. There was so much raw pain in him she was almost afraid to speak. "I never asked you that."

He shrugged. "No, you are right, you did not. You are rare in that. You did not ask me, you *told* me."

She watched as he stood up and peeled down the sodden hose. As he stepped out of them she could see his shaft hung ruddy, half-aroused in the gold hair in his groin. He bent and took one of the grain sacks and scrubbed at his legs and belly. In the loft's dim light his big, narrow-hipped body was like a bright shadow.

"She loved to laugh, that was Heloise." His voice was harsh. "She was already famed—all of France had heard of the learned angel of Argenteuil. Fulbert was puffed up with insane pride in her; he would do anything to serve his own folly, including asking Peter Abelard the Great to tutor her. And Abelard, from the pinnacle of the world as the philosopher and magister of all the Notre Dame schools, looked down on mere mortals, bored with his triumphs. He had been reading Ovid, *Ars Amatoria,* that most cynical, learned Latin treatise on how to seduce a maid. Yet none was worthy of his dalliance until Heloise."

He bent to rub his legs with the sack. "Peter would never have had her if it had not been for me, their willing courier. I was a slave to him—my master teacher and the great object of my adoration. And then enchanted, besotted, in love with the fair Heloise. So nobly suffering for them both, and their love. And then mine."

Face contorted, he tossed away the sack. He lifted the blanket and spread it on the hay. "That was before the great Abelard got her with child, and by force took her away in nun's garb from Paris to Brittany, to have her babe. That was before he made her leave their child and return with him to Paris. That was before Magister Abelard agreed to marry her, but only secretly. That was before Abelard the God brought out nuns' clothing again and persuaded her to put it on. Persuaded once again to take her to Argenteuil." His voice cracked. "Holy Jesus in Heaven! I have asked myself since then—what kind of stupid, dangerous fool can one man like me be?"

Once started, the words poured out of him in a torrent of hate. After this long and miserable day a barrier had broken, but his torment was such that Constance could not bear to see or hear it. For the life of her she didn't know how to stop it.

She watched him from under her lashes. He stood with his naked body rigid, his hands clenched.

"Do you want to hear the greatest madness of all, how Peter Abelard wanted the marriage to be secret? Jesus knows Fulbert was not happy with that; he couldn't wait to break his promise and tell half of Paris! But I knew that Peter wanted it a secret because he did not want Notre Dame, the world, to know that he who preached that the intellect was everything could have fallen a slave to mere human emotion. To love. To the body of a sweet and beautiful woman. He wished still to be a chaste doctor of the church, an undying light of reason. He could not do that with a wife and a mewling babe. It put the lie to all his famed speculative dialectic."

He looked down at her and said suddenly, "Have you heard of *Sic et Non?*" When she shook her head, he said, "It was—is—a great work. Peter searched the Bible and laid down opposite to each other all the confounding contradictions that are to be found in the holy book. The purpose of it? To show that one must accept God with one's mind as well as one's faith, in full knowledge of error and the unknowable."

He abruptly sat down beside her. "God's face, Constance, do not look like that. Philosophy is of no great consequence."

She said stiffly, "I am not well read. I have no Latin."

"I know." He bent his head and rubbed it with both hands. "What am I doing, telling you of this? It was the damned nun's habit that began it. Jesu, even now I cannot think of all of this without courting the demons of hell in my head!"

She bit her lip. "I have heard most of this dreadful tale. You do not have to tell it. My aunt, the prioress of—"

He wasn't listening. "I begged her to go away with me. I promised I would not destroy her and her babe as would Abelard if she stayed with him. I told her that I loved her, adored her, and wished to live with her and cherish and protect her until the end of our lives. It only made her angry. Abelard was her god. Her *life,* goddamn him to hell forever! Yet he could not put aside ambition even in the very hour they came to defile him!"

Constance put her hand on his arm. On the other side of the loft Thierry and Llwydd were quiet, listening. "Shhh—whatever it is, it is past."

"Past?" He gave her a violent look. "I am telling you that it is still what keeps him from her! He loves her—yes, he loves her, the great Peter does, and he treats her as if she were nothing!"

She studied him anxiously. The grim, steady look of the past days had dropped away. He was the wild-eyed madman again.

"He read Ovid to seduce her, damn him," he said hoarsely. "And then, when Fulbert brought the surgeon to administer just punishment for what Fulbert thought was Peter's setting aside of his true wife, Peter thought of his great deity, Origen, who also would destroy sinful flesh to keep from being drawn from the sanctity of pure thought. And, ah, God, Peter Abelard realized he could be famous yet!"

Constance pulled him to sit down beside her. "It *is* all over," she whispered. "You are only tormenting yourself."

"You do not understand." His face was right in hers. "Origen was a famed doctor of the church of the fourth century. He castrated himself in order to preach, and not be tempted by women."

Her mouth dropped open. He said fiercely, "I know how Abelard's mind works. He was thinking he could be free of Heloise and the humiliation of the lusts of the flesh. He could have fought off Thibaud and the surgeon and Fulbert—they were no challenge to him."

He was shaking. Constance reached up and put her arms around his naked shoulders and drew him to her. He allowed it, like one in a nightmare.

"You see how he destroys everything?" His voice was muffled. "For after it was done, he knew it was a great error. Peter Abelard was not reborn as the great master of the church, the new Origen, but as Peter Abelard the eunuch, the mutilated and disgraced!"

"Cenred—"

"Yet as always, Peter is lucky. All of Paris rose up in pity and rage and made him a hero. At least for a while—there are still many like me who hate him. And then our hero turned his wounded self upon the one who loved him, and made her suffer as he suffered. He made my Heloise take vows as a nun."

He lunged forward and put his face in his hands. "Christ in heaven, but I begged her and she would not listen! I could do nothing to keep her from this living death. She did not want to become a nun—she wanted her life, her babe. Her husband. Not me."

He lifted his head and looked into the dimness of the barn. "I went to St. Denys to kill him and stood outside the gate with a knife in my hand, and could not. I could not kill him—I left him alive for her sake.

"Then I left France. No, first I stood with Abelard in the back of the chapel at Argenteuil to hear her take her vows before he took his own. He insisted on it. It was one of his cruelties that broke my beloved's heart."

It was dark now, and Constance could hardly see his face. She reached up to put her hands on his shoulders. She wanted to love him, comfort him, but she did not know how. It was as he said; he was still tied to his demons. He had locked himself away from the world in his savage wildness and mockery. She wanted to ask him, *Do you still love her?* Her mind added, *As I love you?*

It served nothing to ask. She knew the answer.

"I went mad," he said into her shoulder. "I wanted to destroy the world and everything in it. I wanted to spread outrage and ruin like the great Abelard."

She stroked the back of his damp hair with her hand. "Shhhh," she whispered.

"Christ, they say the devil seizes me. I can't help myself."

Yes, she knew all too well that dangerous agony from the times she had seen it. Constance pushed him to lie back against the straw.

He looked up at her. "What are you doing?"

"*I* will love you," she murmured. "Love is not dead, is it? I do not believe that."

She leaned over him and kissed him on the mouth slowly, her tongue tracing his lips. She felt him shudder.

"Constance." He wrenched his mouth away. "I have not been fair to you. I—"

He stiffened and groaned as her hand found his belly, then the flat plain of his flesh sprinkled with fine hair that led to his groin. There she found his shaft soft and warm, half-engorged, and wrapped her fingers around it.

"Constance, I won't touch you." A moan burst from him. "Holy Jesus in heaven—leave me alone."

She put soft kisses against his jaw, his throat, then his breastbone. She licked his smooth, damp skin like a cat, murmuring low, sweet words.

He drew up one leg, and then let it fall as her lips found their way down his chest, stopping to take his small hard nipples between her lips, then her teeth.

She nibbled at the buttons of flesh as his hand clutched the back of her hair. He smelled musky but clean; the drenching rain had been like a daylong bath to all of them. His breathing grew harsh and rapid as her mouth descended into the soft, pale curls around his manhood.

"Constance," he ground out.

He had taunted her that she'd had many husbands, that they had used her well and taught her how to please them. And in some respect this was true. It was that which Constance used, now, to make him know that love was not lost in his cruel, chaotic world.

She cupped his shaft in her hands and put her mouth on him, kissing him softly and gently, then moving her lips with light caresses to his inner thighs, then to the rough, tightening sac between them, then back to his great sword, now standing rigid and thick. She put her mouth completely over him and kissed him and sucked him, her lips circling the sensitive shield of the tip. She heard a tearing groan.

Then his hands were on her shoulders in her hair. He writhed under her, muttering garbled words until he could stand it no more.

She had skinned out of the boy's tunic; now she pulled off the ragged braies. She lifted herself over him and took him into her carefully because of his size. Then, just as slowly, she began to ride him. But he suddenly seized her arms and lunged up under her, making her cry out.

"Constance, damn you," he choked, "why do I need you? Why do I desire you so much?"

He pulled her up and down on him roughly.

His hands seized her breasts, squeezing and tugging. With the breath jolted out of her she only knew she wanted him, too. That she wanted to love and comfort him.

At the words, he shut his eyes.

Their coupling was madness. Constance was as wild as he. It was as though they sought to join themselves in a lust as keen as death. Or oblivion.

He lifted her and rolled her to her knees and took her that way. Then over to her back, her heels under his ears while he pounded her. She knew that he had reached his peak more than once and still he kept on, hard and big and relentless. And she matched his frenzy, her own passion wringing her again and again as she kicked and squealed and dug her teeth into the smooth flesh of his shoulders and arms.

At last with a bellow of release he fell on her, his big body slick with sweat. And Constance, with her hand at the back of his neck, could only sob with her drained flood of weariness and love.

His mouth burrowed into the wet hollow under her chin and softly kissed her. There was a silence, then he murmured against her ear, "Ah, sweetheart, I miss your long hair."

When she stiffened, he laughed.

Twenty-four

As they were leaving, the old drover met them at the gate with a cloth-covered bundle in his hand which he thrust at Constance.

"It's a poor day for traveling," he told her. "It's growing colder and there will be ice by evening, so have a care. They say the young lady of Morlaix is on the road, pursued by her enemies, poor lass. Although there are many who would give a hand to help her."

They stopped and stared at him, alarmed. Thierry said, clearing his throat, "Would you—ah, know her, man, if you saw her?"

The drover gave them a gap-toothed grin. "Oh, aye, I had a look at her one year when she was going to London. Travels with a hundred knights, she does, and a whole army of wagons and servers. But she's a fine, pretty lass—there's never a one that will be turned away if she thinks they're hungry and wanting. Aye," he said, nodding, "there's even them what pray to her, like a saint."

Thierry looked startled. "*Pray* to her?"

The old man slid his shrewd eyes past him to Llwydd. "The old ways don't die, or so they say. Can't tell who or what's a Christian these days, and who isn't. And there's some," he added darkly, "what seems to be both. Watch them with their Samhainn fires, and the Beltane fires in the summer and suchlike goings on, and you'll see plain enough if the old gods still live. And Christmas, too. Half the witching with the young maids wanting to see them that's going to be their future husbands in a pan of water—that's not Christian. I tell you, if sommat come to me and say the Morlaix lady is their sweet maid of the willow grove, and they want to ask a boon of her in their prayers, I wouldn't say nothing to them, that I wouldn't. Neither would Gundry, that's my wife."

"Holy Jesus." Thierry looked around for Cenred, but the tall man had started down the road. "I must go," he said hurriedly. "Listen, keep a tongue in your head, will you, for the sake of—of poor travelers?"

"Oh, that's done," the drover said. "Just this morn at cock crow I was telling Gundry, she's my wife—"

Llwydd passed him and as she did, she looked up into his face and smiled her strange smile. The old man seemed to shiver. Then he shut his mouth with a click.

* * *

The old drover had been right—the weather was much colder. There were puddles of ice in the road from yesterday's rain. Constance picked her way, still a bit unsteady on her feet.

"What did he give you?" Llwydd wanted to know.

"Food." Constance held up the cloth-wrapped bundle to her nose and breathed deep. "Oat-cakes, by the smell. Holy Virgin, and more turnips, I think. And that must be cheese. Only cheese reeks so."

The other woman watched her closely. Cenred was a dozen or more paces ahead, Thierry following. They were well behind them. She said in her husky voice, "Do you remember me from Castle Morlaix, my lady?"

Constance gave her a quick look. "Yes, you were the Welsh witch the Irish fathers gave to me to take to my Bucksborough manor for trial. They feared to leave you there among them, with the Bishop of Chester so near."

"Ummm." Llwydd kept in step. She said suddenly, "Are you unhappy now, my lady?"

Constance missed a step. Llwydd and the young scholar had heard them last night in the barn loft—how could they not? She looked at Cenred ahead, taking long strides in spite of the frozen ruts filled with ice.

How could she be unhappy, Constance thought, when the only man she had ever wanted had held her in his arms and made love to her through most of the night?

She knew in her heart they had no right to

any of it; it was passion and wonder and glory snatched from under the very nose of fate. She was a much-married noblewoman and he a wandering minstrel. They had only this time, and no more. If they arrived unhurt or even alive at Castle Morlaix it would be miraculous. And even then they would still be in peril.

But *unhappy?* By the cross, for the first time in her life she was delirious. *Ecstatic.*

"Your hair that I cut," Llwydd said. "And them shabby clothes, dressed like a boy. It's not what my lady is accustomed to, is it?"

"I—ah, it is a perilous time," Constance said earnestly, "and I am grateful to the bottom of my heart for all that you have done for me. I would not complain about the clothes. Or my hair."

The Welshwoman thought that over. "They are right to ask a boon of you in their prayers," she said finally. She stuck out a clenched fist. "When I open my hand you must pick a stone."

"A stone?" Constance shifted the bundle to her other arm. "Is it soothsaying?" she asked, looking into the other woman's face. "I do not have much faith in it."

But she exclaimed when Llwydd opened her fingers. "Ah, how pretty! Where did you get them?" They had come to a stop in the middle of the road so she could see the stones. "May I pick them up?"

Llwydd's eyes were hooded. "Only one, willow maid. Only one."

Constance picked up a white stone, a silver-streaked pebble smoothed by the running water of a stream. "This one, then." She turned it over in her fingers. "Does it mean something?"

Llwydd let out her breath, then intoned:

"What your heart wants it will surely lack,
What your heart cherishes it cannot take,
What your heart fears will make it break,
Your heart's happiness gone, will yet come back."

"Is that my fortune?" Constance handed back the pebble. "I had thought first to pick up the reddish one."

Llwydd snatched back her hand. "Not the red." Muttering, she put the stones deep within her cloak and started toward Thierry. "Never the red. Not for you."

Constance shrugged and went after her.

It began to snow. The wind had died, and at first the snowfall was pretty, with large, whirling flakes falling out of a grey sky to coat the fields and the winter-bare trees. A group of merchants on horseback passed them, staring, then galloped off. They caught up with a solitary villager with a wagon and donkey and asked about the next village, which he told them was miles to the north. Then, because Cenred suddenly did not like the open fields on both sides of the road, they headed toward the woods.

They had no sooner left the road than they

heard the sound of horses. Cenred listened, then motioned them to run. They ran, their feet kicking up clouds of fallen snow. Breathless, they fell into a gully short of the woods.

A long column of knights in black and red tunics over their mail and carrying lances topped with gonfalons of the Clare colors trotted by on the Cirencester road.

They lay on their stomachs, watching. Thierry whispered, "Where are they going?"

Cenred squinted at them. "If I had my guess, Wrexham, and then Castle Morlaix. They're a hundred and more by the look." He waited, then said, "If I were Robert fitzGilbert I would send the bastard of Nesscliffe to seize the countess's manor at Bucksborough, and reinforce the Castle Morlaix garrison with my own."

Constance put her hand to her throat, thinking of Julien at Bucksborough. "My children!"

He did not look at her. "Be glad they are girls. If they were boys they would already be dead."

At her low moan Llwydd put her hand over Constance's. After the troop of Clare knights had passed they got to their feet and crept toward the covering wood.

That night they slept in a hedgerow. With the drover's wife's good supper of bread and turnips and cheese they were not hungry, but it was bitterly cold. Dead leaves on an oak tree gave them a natural bower and kept off the snow. Cenred and Thierry scraped a shallow trench and Constance and Llwydd slept between them, sharing cloaks and coverings.

Constance put her head on Cenred's chest. Only her feet were cold. In the morning they had nothing to eat—they quenched their thirst with snow and started off in the still-falling flakes.

It was a journey that Constance would long remember. They had no food and could steal little in the villages. Llwydd found them something to chew on by stripping the bark of trees, and they dug up roots in streams gurgling under a coating of ice. Thierry went looking for more widows, and left a hamlet pursued by a pack of dogs instead. But he had salvaged a stolen loaf of bread. Then they lost the road and spent a day searching for it in a heavy snowfall, Cenred carrying Constance on his back.

"We are going to die," she told him, putting her mouth to his ear. It was not uncommon for travelers to perish on the roads in winter, and all knew it.

He said nothing. Dully, she wondered how he could keep going, although now he put her down to rest more and more. He wore a strip of sacking tied on his head to keep his ears from freezing. His hair and new beard were frosted white. He looked, she thought, when he set her down at a stone roadside cross, like some shaggy snow giant from the children's tales. She knew she looked no better.

She put her rag-wrapped hand to his face. She could feel nothing but snow and beard. Yet his eyes blazed like the blue sky. "Cenred," Constance whispered through frozen lips, "remember that I love you."

Tears came oozing from her eyes as she said it. He had made no pretense to her of where his heart lay.

And he gave no sign that he heard.

They started again in a world of dizzying white. They were alone—no one traveled the road in such weather. They seldom spoke, saving their strength. Finally Thierry, trudging ahead of Llwydd, croaked, "Witch-woman, tell us, are we going to perish here?"

Llwydd shook her head. It was hard to tell whether her answer was yes or no, she was so bundled against the cold.

Night was coming in the gray haze. Constance tried to get Cenred to put her down by kicking her heels, feebly, against his sides. But he bent his head and kept on.

They came upon a rail fence, and knew they had wandered from the road again. Constance could not hold back a sob.

Then, in the maze of whiteness, someone was calling. Cenred stumbled ahead. Whatever it was loomed like blurred shadows in the whirling snow.

"Who are you?" voices shouted.

Constance could hear Thierry behind them,

trying to answer. Coming close, a bearded face under a broad-brimmed hat peered at her.

"It's a boy," the face said. "We are looking for a party coming north on the road from Basingstoke."

Constance began to struggle. She heard Cenred's croaking voice asking, "Who the devil are you?"

"It's not a boy." Another face peered at her. "Countess, I am Sir Winebald of Mallon's groom, and we have two of his horses with us."

She felt Cenred bend to let her slip from his back. She was so stiff she almost fell. Their hands held her up.

The same voice said, "You do not know us, but you gave aid to our brother Durand Ivorson of Badderly Fell, who could not feed his girl children this year."

The bundled shapes stood looking at her. "I know nothing of this," Constance managed.

The other voice said, "Yea, milady, you gifted the convent of St. Hilda's, where your aunt is the lady prioress, with silver for Durand's girls to enter there."

Cenred and Thierry turned to stare at her.

"We have brought horses to take you into the village," the first voice said. "We almost did not find you in the storm. We have been down the road twice and were turning back when Wulf saw something by the fence."

"Horses." Thierry started toward the gray shapes. "St. George save us, they really have horses!"

Constance peered through the snow. He said he was a lord's groom, so the horses belonged to the lord. She could not remember giving any silver for someone's girls to go to St. Hilda's, but she supposed it was true. She staggered when the snow-covered figure that was Cenred took her by the shoulder.

"Give them your thanks," he rasped in her ear. His face was a mass of hair and ice—she could only see his eyes, but the familiar devilry was in his voice. "Or by the Holy Mother's tits, St. Constance—I believe they will start praying to you!"

Twenty-five

"Well, I'll tell you, there'll be no more use for miracle plays now until Easter. In this month of February and well through March, times are always slim.

The manager of the troupe of players who had stopped their wagons at the Wrexham inn stepped out of the way of the local lord and his mounted hunting party. The young man, a vassal of the Earl of Hereford, and his friends cantered their horses through the inn's courtyard with a great blowing of horns, followed by the houndsmen with several dozen dogs already baying and straining at their leashes.

It was not stag-hunting season—in late winter that was over; the earl's vassal and his company were out to chase wild boar, in particular one that had attacked a woman gathering wood in the border forests not a week past. *A huge, hungry monster,* the villeins had described it. But then everything was hungry now that winter was coming to a close and spring had not yet brought in its fruits.

The manager lifted his felt cap respectfully as the hunters went by, then turned back to Cenred.

"What goes best now," he went on, "is farce. Folks wants to laugh in bleak, cold times, makes them forget their miseries. As for a scholar—" He surveyed Thierry without enthusiasm. "—I can't say, I've never used one. Unless he's got some good, spicy recitings, that is. Village folk like that. And they pay, too, you know, as much as the lordlings."

His look passed on to Cenred. "And I've already got a jongleur—he's my nephew, my sister's brat. I can't hardly get rid of *him,* now can I? But I can always use a good-looking boy. That's a nice lad you have there, fine-featured and slender, very pretty."

He took Constance's arm and squeezed it. "Can you play sweet maids, boy? Listen," he said, looking sharp at Cenred, "I'll take him off your hands permanent, if you say so."

Constance opened her mouth but Cenred's big hand had already covered the manager's and lifted it away. "No, take all of us," he said softly, "including the Welshwoman."

The man took a step back, eyes narrowing.

"Ah, so that's the way it is." He stared pointedly at Constance. "All the world to its own tastes, as they say right enough. Well, he's comely enough, although I wouldn't be making a fool over him, myself. And the other?" He gave Llwydd a strange look. "Hounds of hell, man, what would one expect to do with *her?*"

"She tells fortunes," Cenred said, his expression bland. "Soothsaying's very popular with the village goodwives. We split the fees half to half."

Constance ducked her head to hide her smile. Cenred could out-bargain a London whore, as the saying went. Still, the look on Llwydd's face was comical. Casting her soothsaying stones with a traveling show, and for money, plainly came as a surprise.

She watched Cenred talk to the players' manager with his hands out, palms up, charming and persuasive. Freshly clean-shaven, his long hair trimmed, wearing a blue woolen jacket and black chausses and his gaudy boots, Cenred was so handsome the inn's cooks and servant maids had slipped into the courtyard just to ogle him.

Beside Cenred, Thierry wore scholar's grey with a red sash. Of them all, only Llwydd stuck to her battered black cloak, although her gown under it was new.

And she, Constance, was as nicely dressed as any of them in her boy's shortcoat, hose and heavy cape, and a cap with a long cock feather. She told herself she'd been so comely that she'd almost got a place with the troupe on her own. It had pleased her to see how quickly Cenred had seized the man's hand and flung it away.

It was now almost the Feast of Saint Agatha. They had been on the road since the great snowstorm after the Feast of Epiphany. Four weeks. If it had not been for the gift of clothes from the weavers of Shrewsbury, they would have been worse than ragged scarecrows by now.

After Sir Winebald of Mallon's grooms had brought them to the borders of the Earl of Hereford's lands, they had met two women and a man traveling the road in a mule cart. The weavers at Morlaix village had sent a message to their brothers of the Shrewsbury clothmakers' guild to search for the Countess of Morlaix on the road from Cirencester. The women knew at once who Constance was, and couldn't stop exclaiming over her boy's garb, her shorn hair, and the group's starved and ragged condition. They knew, of course, about Everard and the girl, Emma.

It was the first time Constance had heard her name. It was still a marvel to her, how Everard had come to Morlaix village looking for a girl, the cow in tow, and how he had bedded the weavers' pretty girl and won her, and then been attacked. Her knight captain had always been so stern, so fierce, so much her protector, Constance had never thought of him as someone's lover. She understood that the weavers' girl, Emma, was very devoted to him. For some reason this gave her a small pang.

The message was that Everard was recovering slowly, as was to be expected with broken bones. He assured her of his devotion, and urged her to God's care. It was delivered by way of the clothmakers with a much-needed sum of money collected from the weavers, Morlaix's smith, and other people of the town.

Cenred and Thierry had made no jokes about the clothes or the money; the aid was heaven-sent. And in spite of Cenred's mordant tongue, they well knew that if it had not been for Sir Winebald's grooms that night in the storm they might well have perished.

The weavers at Morlaix sent word that they were loyal to her, and also all those in her fief, in spite of the Clares' garrison of knights at the castle. All beseeched her to return as quickly as possible and reclaim what was hers.

Which they were doing, Constance thought as she watched Cenred, as fast as they could. After their brief sojourn with the Shrewsbury weavers they had kept steadily north. At the Feast of St. Agatha the Martyr the winter corn was greening, but the cattle and villeins were gaunt and hungry-looking from the long winter. Still, traffic was heavy on the muddy road. They had passed many freemen and even some country villeins going south in the hope of becoming footsoldiers in King Henry's war against his nephew, Robert Clito, in France.

Constance waited patiently with Thierry and Llwydd as Cenred, talking fast, cajoled the fat manager into hiring them all.

Every night for the weeks they had traveled she had slept in his arms. They had made love in barns and in the fields when they could snatch a moment, once even sharing a haystack with Thierry and Llwydd, so close they could hear the rustlings and whispers and moans of their coupling.

In spite of the hardships and danger it had been a golden time. Her wild jongleur was ardent and tender, lustful and impatient, daring, impetuous, outrageous and wicked—she could not think of some of their times together without blushing madly. But more than once after their lovemaking she had looked down at him while he slept, and longed to cry out to him to forget his beloved Heloise and love *her* instead.

Even now she hurt, knowing that even to say such a thing was futile and senseless. Even if Cenred loved her, and she knew that he did not, he would still leave her. He had never promised otherwise. At Wrexham they were only a few short leagues from her own lands at Morlaix.

And this time they had together was perilous in more ways than one. She had seen the looks on the faces of the cloth guild weavers from Shrewsbury. It was stupid to think the weavers would not know what was going on, would not gossip about what they guessed at when they looked at her, the Countess of Morlaix—and then at the tall, surpassingly handsome singer and juggler with her.

They could not have each other, Constance told herself. It was in the faces of the people around them. It was in the little Welsh witch-woman's eyes.

"What your heart wants it will surely lack,
What your heart cherishes it cannot take,
What your heart fears will make it break."

The words made more sense to her now, if one believed in such pagan things. God and the saints knew she feared parting from him. No, *dreaded* was more like it; her heart was torn. And what she feared would surely make it break.

Beside her, Thierry muttered, "Ah, Cenred is closing the bargain. Good for him. The troupe will take us now." He turned and saw her face. "God's wounds, what is the matter?"

Constance shook her head.

Cenred strode to them, carrying a cloth sack and what seemed like a bundle of bright straw.

"Come." He was smiling but he was angry. He took Constance by the hand. "Let us get away from this quacksalver mountebank before I strangle him. I have had to promise him the damned moon and stars to get him as far as Morlaix village."

"Morlaix village?" From the look that passed between them she knew they had planned something. "What is it you haven't told me?"

"Hush." He dragged her away from the wagons. They left Thierry in the inn's courtyard, and started down the road. "We are going to Morlaix with the mummers. Keep your voice down."

She tried to pull her hand out of his. "Let me go. You can't scheme like this and not tell me. I will not go to my castle with anyone until you say what this is."

"*Your* castle." He looked sidewise at her. "Yes, but Robert fitzGilbert and your bastard brother are there, squatting on what they have taken from you, and hoping you will not show up to challenge them. At least, not before the Clares can get you wed somehow to fair Robert."

The thought made her sick. "Stop, I want to talk to you." He paid no attention; she had to run to keep up with him. "What is that straw thing in your hand? What is in the sack?"

"Wait a moment until we get out of their sight."

He loped down the road, half-dragging her. In another moment they had to jump aside for more of the hunt—nobles and their ladies—galloping to catch up with the rest.

Constance stared after them. "I hunted here on Hereford's land last winter." Now she was that same woman. And also one of the faceless people she had seen by the roadside then, as she galloped past.

Cenred gave her hand a tug. "They mean nothing to us." He jumped over a stone wall and waited for her to follow.

The field had lain fallow for that year and had a soft carpet of dead grass. With the stone wall at their backs there was no wind. The winter sun was almost warm.

"Here." Cenred pulled her to him and fitted the bunch of hay over her head. It was snug as a cap. He held her at arm's length. "Ah, you'll do. Now I can see why they call villeins hay-heads."

Frowning, Constance tried to take off the straw wig. He stopped her. "Listen." In the bright winter sunlight his chiseled face was intent. "There is a mummer's turn called Jack and Little Jack. It's famous at fairs in the south."

He opened the sack and took out a pig's bladder blown up to twice normal size. He tucked it under his arm.

"Little Jack walks like this." He moved away from her, using his long legs in a droll countryman's stiff-kneed hobble. "Can you do it?"

Constance lifted her hands to touch the wig. She did not take it off but a thousand questions welled up in her mind. The set look on his face stopped her. He was not being comical now. Far from it.

She hesitated. "I will try."

She stumped across the grass, trying to imitate him. It was not as easy as it looked.

He watched, eyes narrowed. "Sweet baby Jesus, you may have a talent. Do it again, and don't roll your arse."

She looked startled. Then, concentrating with her tongue between her teeth, she jerkily walked back.

Without warning, she saw him draw back in exaggerated dismay. She heard him cry, "Dolt! You have ruined my pigpen!"

Then the pig's bladder hit her.

The shock and surprise of it took Constance

from her feet. She stumbled and fell flat on her back. In an instant Cenred was over her, pinning her.

"I will kill you," she spluttered, spitting hay from the terrible wig out of her mouth. She was even more enraged when she felt his big body heaving against her with laughter.

"Constance, my sweetheart." He followed her violently twisting head with his mouth, trying to kiss her. "You were magnificent. The troupe is going into Morlaix castle," he said as she fought him, "and, God willing, you will play Little Jack to my Farmer Jack until such time as the Morlaix knights who are inside can secure the portal gate. Then we will take fitzGilbert's garrison knights and pretty fitzGilbert himself, and your treacherous bastard brother while they still sit gawking at us."

She stopped struggling and looked up at him.

He pulled the wig from her head and kissed her lightly on the mouth. "When your loyal knights are all within the hall, you will pull off Little Jack's hay head, jump up on the high table and reveal yourself. St. George save us, I couldn't have written the thing better myself! We will play it to the hilt. Then all that is dear to you," he said huskily as he looked down at her, "is finally won, countess, once more."

He released her hand to smooth her tumbled hair, picking stalks of hay out of it. "My brave, beautiful Constance," he murmured. "God help me, you are my heart and my conscience—I do not mock you, truly. Your people love you. I wish to God someone loved me as they do you."

There was a moment when she dared not breathe. She looked up into his face. "I love you," she whispered.

His face changed. "Constance, no."

She threw her arms around his neck and pulled him down to her. "I could run away with you—I don't want to go back! I could make your wandering life mine. Don't leave me," she begged, "I never wish you to leave me. In all my life I have never known happiness like this!"

He gave her his crooked smile. "Live with me, as we have lived and starved since Basingstoke? What a fine life for you, my beautiful countess. And what of your children?"

Her children.

Her lips trembled. Ah, Holy Mother, he knew she could not leave them. She turned her face away.

"Constance, dear one, don't weep." He leaned over her and his lips gently touched the tears on her cheek. "Believe that I would not destroy you as I once saw—as others I knew were destroyed. I can give you nothing, only misery and want. You belong to your people and your children and your knights and your manors and your damned castle. One would have to be blind and deaf not to know it."

"No," she moaned.

"Yes." His hands were under her coat, caressing her breasts, sending rivers of fire into her flesh. "Ah, sweeting, it matters not what you or

I want—you are no mad, wandering jongleur's doxie, and could never be. You are my fair Countess Moon, proud and kind and wondrously brave. And much too good for what they have done to you, King Henry and the God-cursed Clares. But you have conquered them. As you," he whispered in her ear, "have conquered me."

She clutched him, tears running down her face. He did not have to say that this might be the last time they would have each other.

He had unbuttoned her jacket. Now he pulled up her tunic. "I want to see your beautiful breasts." His mouth touched hers hungrily, his tongue invading her lips. "I want to see all of you while I take you."

In the harsh sunlight their naked flesh was unexpectedly white. She pulled his hose down around his hips and laid her hand on him, already huge and straining. He groaned again.

"Come, sweetheart," he whispered hoarsely, "let me take you to paradise here in the Wrexham field, in the warm sun." He fitted his mouth over hers and kissed her so deeply that fire flowed into her in silky waves, smouldering and spreading.

He took her hand and drew it to his mouth and kissed each finger separately and then the palm, his tongue stroking lightly. "I can't stop thinking of you, Constance. This is the way I want to remember you, every part of you, as I have dreamed of you every day these past weeks."

His soft words whispered across her skin, across her stomach and thighs as he pulled her clothes out of the way. And then when she was moaning for it, the curve of her breasts. Gently his lips followed their fullness and at last seized the aching pink centers. She writhed under him, trying to press him closer as his mouth and tongue took them strongly. His hand slid down to the warm, silky patch at her legs' joining, opened it with a touch of his finger and slipped inside. He heard her gasp, then her loud moan of desire. He stroked her softly, watching her flushed face, her half-closed eyes.

"Ah, God, Constance, how much I want you. How damned sweet you are like this, letting me touch you. I dream of it. I think of you, I can't get you out of my thoughts!" He held himself over her, his body shaking to match her own fevered trembling. "Touch me now."

A rough sound, almost a sob, broke through his lips as she took him in her hand and stroked him, adoring his bursting power.

He kissed her deeply, murmuring urgent words against her wet, opened lips. "Do you still love me?"

Eyes drowning in his, she nodded.

"Then say it, my sweet one. And move for me while I'm inside you. I want to remember this, how much you love me."

Constance was sobbing as she moved her body in an ecstasy of love and desire. He held himself still, his forehead pressed to hers, face contorted with pleasure and pain. Her hands roved over him, caressing the muscles of his back under his shirt, the contracted strength of his buttocks, his arms, until he began to move. Long, forceful strokes that demanded her passionate endurance. A blackness swept over her. She sank her teeth into the soft skin between his shoulder and his neck and heard him moan raggedly. "Ah, Constance—Constance," he whispered, "give me this to remember."

Then there was the sound of her name over and over as a deep, raging madness overtook them. With their hearts thundering, time and the world fell away. They had found each other, possessed each other, and there was nothing more. After the firestorm of their mindless desire, they lay exhausted in the sunshine. Cenred rolled to one side and lay still, his arm flung over his eyes, still shuddering.

It took a long time for Constance's own trembling to stop. She reached out and put her hand against his stomach. He quickly put his hand over hers. "We need to plan what we're going to do," he said.

She raised up on her elbow to look at him. "Cenred—"

He took down his arm. "No, don't speak of it." He wouldn't look at her. "I can give you nothing. We have settled that."

He sat up and yanked up his hose to cover his groin. "We need to go to that damned black dog of a Gascon you prize so much. Get him out of his stinking love bed and on his feet to rally the knights in the castle without rousing the Clares."

He got to his knees, still not looking at her, and raked back his bright gilt hair with both hands. "And we need someone to spread the news that the Countess of Morlaix perished in a winter storm after Christmas, and that her body has just been found in a melting snow-drift. I had thought of sending Thierry, but I fear the Welsh witch will want to go with him. The last time Llwydd was in Morlaix she was chained with me in your prisoners' wagon; I doubt the people there have forgotten."

Constance sat up and stared at him. *I can give you nothing.* That was what he'd said. His manner now told her that was the way he wished to end it. She ran her fingertips over her mouth, swollen and wet from his kisses.

He turned and looked at her. "Did you hear what I said?"

She lifted her head and nodded. She saw him get to his feet and pick up the sack. He put the straw wig and the pig's bladder into it.

He was going to leave her, she told herself. For all her frantic desiring, there was nothing she could do. Everything he said was true. She could not follow him on the roads, she was no wandering singer's trull. And he knew her well, that she could not leave her children. She wanted to weep, to scream, but her eyes were dry. Her face felt as stiff as wood.

Then she saw something over his shoulder. Her muffled gasp made him whirl.

A head and shoulders thrust up above the stone wall. Black, curly hair, dark eyes. A hunter, carrying a huntsman's long bow. He laid it on top of the wall.

"Milady?" Uncertain, he peered at them. "It cannot be. They told me at the inn—" He stopped and looked at Constance with widening eyes. "Yes, it is she," he breathed. "By the tripes of St. David, it looks like a boy but it is she, the lady of Morlaix."

Before they could stop him he laid one hand on the stone wall and vaulted over it. "It is as the song says," he cried. "The Lady Moon, so fair, so far above—"

"God's face!" Cenred blurted. "How long have you been watching?"

Constance looked to him, then back at the hunter.

"My lady, do you not know me?" he asked. "You heard my case in your manor court in the matter of one who is now my loving wife, the daughter of the smith of Neversby."

"Jesu." Cenred stood with the mummers' sack in one hand, his mouth twitching. "Tell me, Countess, is there no damned end to them?"

The other favored him with a withering look. He fell to one knee before Constance. "Milady, I am Ralf the serf, huntsman to my lord the Sheriff of Repton."

Now she remembered him. The black, curling hair, the fierce, unserflike manner.

"Lady," Ralf was saying, "I owe you my life and my good fortune. My wife and I now have a child, a sweet babe for whom we beg your permission to give the noble name of Constance." He shot a warning look in Cenred's direction. "Give me some task, I beg you! Any task that I may do for you in unworthy payment for all my life's happiness that I owe you."

Wordless, Constance could only stare at him. Beside her, Cenred threw back his head and laughed.

Twenty-six

It was snowing again.

"Do we have to wait outside?" Constance was cold, and snowflakes were beginning to collect in the huge straw wig.

Cenred pulled her against him for warmth, his hands at her waist. They had been standing for some time in the castle ward just outside the kitchen, along with the troupe of mummers waiting to entertain Julien, the fitzGilberts, and their guests inside. It was a big feast: the triumphant Clares had invited their marcher allies, and those of the nobles of the north and west who were not with the king in France. The ward and the grounds beyond the castle walls were filled to overflowing.

Beyond the group of players the Clares' knights stood talking around small guard fires. Constance looked around covertly, knowing that Everard was somewhere in the castle. The weavers plotted to get her commander inside during the feast dressed as a villein, so he could rally the Morlaix knights.

"Don't complain," Cenred told her softly. "There's no room in the kitchen. But it is always an entertainer's fate to stand waiting in the rain or snow, summer or winter, and pray that the act already on is not good enough for a blasted encore."

Around them the mummers seemed unconcerned by the snowfall, brushing the flakes from their costumes as they stood talking. The sweet maiden, a boy whose cheeks were thick with paint and the shadow of his first sprouting beard, held a small, shivering dog. The manager's nephew, the jongleur, practiced throwing his silver balls high, rotating them in combinations of fours and sixes.

Constance pressed against the reassuring warmth at her back. "Pray God we will succeed," she murmured. She was tense with nerves. She could not bear to think of what would happen if they failed.

He tightened his arms around her. "It will succeed," he whispered, reciting in her ear:

> " 'Glory is never a trivial thing
> If only I do it right. And Apollo
> Hears my plea and comes to my aid.' "

He looked down at her. "A nice line, although it's the Georgics, and Virgil was talking of bees."

She had to turn then, and smile up at him.

"That's better." He smiled back. "It is only

the usual players' skittishness which attacks you. Think of what we are going to do. You have done it all before, we have practiced it together, and it will work."

Yes, it will work, Constance told herself. When he said it, she believed it.

She looked around the ward. There were plenty of Morlaix knights—many of them would have recognized her had her face not been hidden by a mop of straw wig—although not so many troops. The bailey was crowded with wagons and military horses. From time to time she'd glimpsed the castle people, servants, the bailiff's staff, workers from the armory, going about their duties with their eyes red with weeping.

They grieve for you, Cenred had said.

It made her feel strange. Ralf the huntsman had done his work well in spreading the false news of her death.

There were sudden roars of laughter from within the hall. A dancing bear was entertaining with his master; something they were doing was apparently very funny.

Nervous, Constance gripped the handle of her bucket. It was heavy, with a false bottom filled with sand to weight it down. Dear Holy Mother, she had never in her life dreamed of herself as a knockabout comedy player in her own castle! Her role as Little Jack was to be the speechless, fumbling assistant to Cenred's oafish farmer trying to build a pig pen.

She had the bucket, and soon Cenred would hand her the board she would carry. They had been practicing for days—how she should dimwittedly swing the beam she held across her shoulders when she turned, and when he should duck. She was still in mortal terror of really hitting him.

She took a deep breath. At that moment she saw the bailiff and one of the Morlaix reeves crossing the yard.

Constance could not move.

It was Clarembald, her own bailiff, coming straight for the players huddled by the kitchen door. Cenred felt her stiffen and tightened his arms around her. "Steady," he murmured.

The bailiff went up and down the line. Constance held her head down, the straw wig effectively hiding her face. Looking at the ground, she saw the bailiff's shoes stop in front of them.

"What's this? What's this?" Clarembald's voice was sharp. "We'll have none of that here!"

She felt Cenred's hands drop from her waist. Constance was nearly faint with fear. God and St. Mary, they thought Cenred was fondling her! They'd both forgotten how she was dressed.

"My sister's boy," Cenred said smoothly. "The lad's cold."

"Hah." The bailiff's hand was on her shoulder. "Let's have a look at you."

He tilted her head back.

Constance stared up at him, helpless. She had known Clarembald since she was a child. She would wager Castle Morlaix and all that was in it that he could not help but know her. Even if he had been told she was dead.

But if Constance thought she saw a flicker of something in the old man's eyes, it was quickly gone. He gave her shoulder a shake. "See that yon big lout keeps his hands to himself, hear me?"

She nodded, numbly. Even if her life depended on it she could not have spoken at that moment.

The castle reeve stepped forward. "All right, all right, hurry on now," he shouted. He made herding motions with his hands. "Into the kitchen with you!"

Cenred pushed her along. As they crossed the kitchen and its mayhem of cooks and roaring fires, he said in her ear, "I have written a thousand poems to you in my head, and, God take my stupidity and lack of anything to write on, I have put none of them down."

She stumbled in surprise, and turned to look at him.

"Keep going." he told her. He put his hand in the small of her back and guided her to the door of the feast hall where the rest of the players stood waiting.

The manager flapped his hands at them. "Hurry up, hurry up. You go on right after the bear."

"Poems?" Constance twisted to look up at him.

"Yes." He quickly bent and kissed her on her lips. "Remember me, Constance," he said huskily.

"Why—"

Her question was lost as he thrust the board into her hand. The manager grabbed her wrist and forcefully slung her out into the hall.

Constance reeled out into the space before the high table, bucket in hand and the oak beam across her shoulders. As she staggered, the board's weight carried her around in a circle. A loud burst of laughter rang in her ears.

Cenred charged up behind her, shouting that she was a lazy, stupid oaf, and they would never get a day's work done.

Dazzled, Constance peered around her.

Morlaix's feast hall was packed. On all sides a sea of faces in the foggy, smoky air was fixed on her. The murmuring, rippling, amused noise of a crowd waiting to be entertained assailed her ears. And she was so close to the nobles at the high table she could have tossed an apple into Julien's lap. Her half-brother sat at table next to Robert fitzGilbert. Both of them were staring right at her.

Mouth open in horror, Constance stared back. Her expression seemed to convulse them.

She could not believe that they looked right at her but did not know her. She was still gawking when she heard Cenred hiss at her. When she turned, the board nearly caught him on the side of the head. The hall screamed with enjoyment.

Cenred pushed back his villein's cap and gestured threateningly, berating her for her clumsiness. While she stared at him, aghast, the crowd howled.

Under his breath he said, "Constance, drop the bucket."

Dear God, she needed to do something right. Her nerveless fingers let it go, but his foot somehow managed at the last moment to be under it. The bucket landed on his toes with a thud. Cenred let out a howl and danced about on one foot, holding the other with both hands.

Constance watched him with a sudden return of her senses. They'd practiced this. *Watch me,* he'd said. *Follow what I do.*

Now, big and lithe, his golden hair flying out from under his red countryman's cap, he hopped madly about, squalling in mock pain as the hall brayed its delight.

Constance had seen him like this before, at Christmas, when he'd taunted King Henry. Now she watched, fascinated, as Cenred stopped short and stood and scowled at the howling crowd. He waited long moments, hands on hips, glaring at them. Then he shook his fist at them.

Delighted, they roared back. Constance, her hands steadying the board across her shoulders, watched him.

She was finding that while she could only stumble about, genuinely playing the farmer's dolt, Cenred had the feasters in the great hall in his hand. He glittered with energy and devilment. He was the bright-haired lord of misrule, the magnificent king of mischief. She had the strange feeling he could do anything—*anything*—and they would like it.

He came striding back to her.

"Stupid oaf, you have ruined my pig pen," he yelled, and pointed to a spot on the floor. "Put the board *there!*"

Constance whirled to look. As she did so the end of the board swung around and hit him.

Really hit him.

She heard the sound of the blow to his head. Then Cenred jerked back and fell sprawling. She threw the piece of wood from her and raced to him.

She threw herself on her knees beside him. "Cenred," Constance cried. His eyes were closed and the long length of him was stretched out limply. The world had come to an end. She had really hurt him. "Oh, Holy Virgin, what have I done!"

He opened one eye and winked. The sound of the howling audience beat in their ears.

"The high table," he said without moving his lips. "I am going to chase you."

Constance sat back on her heels and stared at him stupidly. She could hardly hear what he said for the noise.

"Constance," he reminded her urgently.

Dazed, she got to her feet. He was not really hurt, she told herself. Even now she didn't quite believe it.

She looked around. At the front tables the nobles were laughing so hard they were gasping, holding their sides. She started for the dais uncertainly. He was depending on her to do as he said.

Somewhere in the hall her Morlaix knights,

if all had gone well, were waiting for the moment to fall upon the Clares' forces, Robert fitzGilbert, and her wretched brother.

It was Julien she made straight for.

Cenred was right behind her, still playing his part, swinging the oak board like a club and vowing at the top of his lungs to wreak terrible vengeance if he ever caught her. Out of the corner of her eye Constance saw a tall figure in a black cloak and a white bandage about his face, lunging to meet her.

It was Everard.

Longspres, the castle constable armed and mailed, was not far behind him.

When they met before the high table, Everard reached out and lifted Constance up onto it. She felt plates and cups scattering under her feet. She yanked off her straw hair.

The crowd was still laughing and shouting. Constance tried to find her footing among the remains of the feast. She lifted her voice to scream, "Hear me, I am Constance, Countess of Morlaix!"

Her voice was lost in the noise. Down the board her steward, Piers de Yerville, had gotten up from his seat and was hurrying to pull her down. Her half-brother Julien still stared up at her, an entertained smile on his face. On his other side Robert fitzGilbert held up a cup of wine in salute.

Everard hobbled forward to place himself before the high table, his sword drawn, the constable with him. At the sight of Morlaix's feared knight captain, the crowd changed. A hush fell.

In the silence, Robert fitzGilbert's voice suddenly cried, "Christ crucified, it's her ghost!" Then he fainted dead away.

The entire high table rose then, shouting and shrieking, and stampeded down from the dais. The Morlaix knights came from their seats with a roar. At the back of the hall someone flung open the doors and the villagers, waving rakes and hoes, poured in.

Constance looked down at Julien. He leaned back on the bench despite the uproar, not moving. "What now?" he shouted at her. "Come Constance, will you kill me?"

Kill him? She remembered the dagger Cenred had given her. Even now, hating Julien, remembering the misery of her injury and sickness and imprisonment, and that he had tried to steal her fiefdom, she did not think she could bring herself to use it.

She licked her lips. In front of her Everard was beating off a knight, swinging his sword awkwardly with his left hand.

Two Morlaix knights quickly sprang to his aid. She could see the Clares' knights making a stand at the center of the hall behind a barricade of overturned trestles. Heart pounding, she searched for some sight of Cenred.

He was gone.

I swear by heaven's stars, by the high gods,
By any certainty below the earth,
I left your land against my will, my queen.

The *Aeneid,* Virgil

Twenty-seven

The Count of Souilly's provision barge went slowly up the winding River Seine, traveling under sail when there was enough wind and oar power when there wasn't, sliding steadily through the greening spring countryside.

At the Forêt de St. Germain the boat caught a steady easterly and the sails were set for the first time that day. The crew shipped oars and rested, watching the eastern reaches of English King Henry's Norman domain glide by.

Cenred, who was working the oars as a boatman for his passage, peeled off his leather shirt and leaned back against the rowers' bench, letting the warmth of the pale sun sink into his skin.

Spring was warmer by far here in France than in England. By their looks the crabapple trees on the riverbank would be in bloom in a few days, and the winter corn was already knee-deep.

The tubby little boat made progress slowly,

wallowing in the currents coming down from melting snows in the mountains to the east. All around them the river was the earthen color of the spring freshets that emptied into it. One could not drink it; the boat's cook drew a bucketful of river water each morning and then, cursing, threw it back again. The water the crews drank was, thankfully, that which they carried in casks filled in Rouen.

Closing his eyes, Cenred threw back his head and let the sun soak his face. They were not, he knew, far from Paris. Along the riverbank the burned skeletons of villages passed by, the remnants of the fighting of the previous summer that would resume again now when the weather turned fine.

It was not easy to go up the Seine into the domain of the French king when both parties were at war. One way was to ship aboard some great lord's household supply boat carrying provisions to his town house in Paris, as Cenred was doing, and hire on for the price of the travel.

And even to ship as an oarsman one had to be blessedly strong, able to row for hours, especially when outrunning the river pirates that infested the upper Seine. Their cargo was valuable. At Pont de Arche the count's boat had taken on sacks of grain worth their weight in gold now in the winter-hungry city, baskets of trussed fowl, and two swineherds and their flock of red Flanders swine that the captain shouted for them to hold in the stern well to windward, so as to keep the stink out of the sailors' nostrils.

Cenred yawned in spite of himself. He had done more rowing coming up from Rouen than he had done in a lifetime. His hands that he used for juggling and the all-important art of writing and composing verse, were full of blisters that had finally hardened into rower's hornlike callouses.

He leaned back against his bench and flexed his tired shoulder muscles. He was grateful for the oarsman's seat on the boat and the chance to get up the Seine without paying a fare as he was in his usual moneyless state, but God knew time passed slowly. He could never become a sailor. It was a dreary existence, requiring a dullard's mind and oxlike strength in the face of perverse wind, water, and weather.

His seat mate, a bearded Fleming from Rouen, suddenly tugged at Cenred's hand, holding up a piece of black bread. "Eat, now that we're resting," the sailor said. "Mightn't get this chance again afore Paris."

He shook his head. He hadn't felt hunger, hadn't felt the need for anything except haste since he'd left England.

For the thousandth time he told himself it was a damnable folly to get this close to everything he despised and that was dangerous to him. When one came right down to it, he had no reason to be in France except for the one reason that he could never deny. Heloise.

She had the power to drag him from the far

corners of the earth. And from what he had heard, she needed him now. Christ, they would never let her alone, these churchly vultures!

The thought made him groan out loud.

The Fleming sailor turned to him. "Ah, what is it now, a shoulder cramp? That's what you get for sitting so in the wind like that, shirtless and naked. That'll cramp a man's back every time, no matter how big and strong he is."

Cenred managed a smile. "Nay, no cramp. An inner pain, you might call it."

He made his body unbend, following the slip and wallow of the boat as it clawed up the river against the current. He had to give the thing a rest. If anyone knew the furor of his thoughts they would truly think him mad.

But he knew how much she was hated. Not just for what her enemies saw as tempting, even ruining, Peter Abelard—a thorn in all their sides, as that put the lie to the hair-shirt wearing, flagellating, fasting hypocrites that they were—but because sweet Heloise had many friends in the church who loved her. And wanted to help her still.

It was said the convent school at Argenteuil was even more famed under the new abbess. Many pupils had been drawn to it, more than could possibly be enrolled.

Plainly, so much love and success could not be tolerated. Such notorious sin, as the church saw it, could not be rewarded. It was necessary to make Heloise suffer. To put her in bad estate for all the world to see. To give her no measure of small happiness, even with the convent school. She must be made to lose the last things that were still dear to her.

They would do it, too, the bastards.

He had picked up the news by accident from a wandering friar in the fenlands in the east country, at a cloth fair. They had sat down together to share a flagon of ale given to the friar by a big-hearted tavern cook, the friar offering Cenred half of it in Christian charity. Cenred, hungry as he was, hadn't refused.

The talk had fallen to gossip of church affairs, as it always did when one was with monks and friars. This one wanted to tell about the great reforms Adam Suger had brought about at St. Denis. At the name of Peter Abelard's monastery, Cenred had pricked up his ears.

"So it was as Peter Abelard had said," the monk told him. "St. Denis was a most vile and corrupt place after all, as Adam Suger discovered when the Pope sent him there. But no one believed Abelard's accusations at the time, of course, his own scandal was too great—it dazzled men's thoughts, they could think only of that." He'd handed Cenred the flagon, urging him to drink. "You have heard of Peter Abelard? Ah, that is a story—it has set all Christendom agog. You know, it is hard to make up one's mind about Abelard, even now."

Cenred wiped the ale from his mouth with the back of his hand. He'd said only, "Yes, I have heard of Peter Abelard."

The friar told him that Abelard had gone

into the east of France to found an oratory he called the Paraclete on some land given to him by some noble friends—the king was thought to be the main contributor. But then the Paraclete had been abandoned after hordes of Peter's followers had descended upon it and the landholders around had complained of the mobs and the disorderliness of the students. So Abelard had elected to go back to Brittany to assume the post of abbot offered him, strangely enough, at a wild, uncouth Breton-speaking monastery there.

Cenred had not been much interested in that; what Peter did with his life now that he was a monk did not concern him. But he gave him his attention when the friar mentioned the papal envoy, the fearsome Adam Suger, the churchman who was restoring discipline to St. Denis, Peter's old monastery.

"While he was reforming the chapter house there, Suger unearthed a charter," the friar said, "that declares that all the land that the convent of Argenteuil stands upon belongs to St. Denis."

Cenred had been holding the ale pitcher to his lips. The effect of the friar's words was such that he forgot to put it down. He sat stiffly, staring into space. It took a long moment to understand what the other man was saying.

When he could speak, he said, "They are scheming to destroy her."

The friar had looked disconcerted. "The Abbess Heloise? I don't know. Why do you say that? All I know is what I hear, that Adam Suger has petitioned the Pope to declare this document of ownership valid, and demand that the nuns leave Argenteuil. And raze the convent, eventually. I do not understand why the place has to be destroyed, myself, but they say that Suger urges the Pope to eliminate the place completely, tearing down the buildings to the ground. The nuns will be offered dispensation—they may return to secular life if they wish."

The words continued to beat in Cenred's head. *Raze the convent. Dispossess Heloise and her nuns.* For seconds he was not able to hear, to think of anything else.

He had heard of Adam Suger, a monk who was as virulent in his hatred of women as the saintly Bernard of Clairveaux. And Bernard had dragged his own sister from her horse in the public road and beaten her severely because she had dared to marry and have children.

Now this Suger, as the arm of the church, the representative of the Pope himself, was going to inflict more cruelty on Heloise and her nuns at Argenteuil!

On the shore, a band of ragged children was following the course of the provision boat as it navigated the shallows near Les Andelys, on the borders of the French king's domain. Cenred rested his arm on the oar locks and laid his chin against it, watching them.

All that had been weeks ago. Now he was on the river Seine, making his way toward Paris.

At nearly every bend of the river, castles looked down with their water locks below, their toll gates to be paid for and passed. The waterway from the sea up to the city of Paris had known little peace: The war among English King Henry and his nephew, Robert Clito, and the French king, who supported Robert, had left its familiar mark. They had seen many small riverside towns that in better days had supported themselves by fishing and barging and were now burned out, boats sunk, docks crumbling into decay.

"Look at the destruction," Cenred muttered, "the waste. It is no wonder I prefer to be a singer and a jongleur."

The sailor turned and raised his eyebrows. "So that's what you are, is it? Well, that's not a bad thing. Entertaining the folk is better now, ain't it, than pushing a oar upriver like this?"

Cenred watched the shoreline slide by with a somber look. "I was trained for war since a boy. But I hated it then, as I hate it now."

The other nodded. "Ay, you have that look, a big man like you, to be a fighting man. But you had no stomach for it, eh?"

Cenred turned hooded eyes to him. "Jesu, who would? You see it before us now on the riverbank—the starvelings, the death, the ruin. I am not a priest but I swear I could not love war, hard as I tried, nor love those who would teach me its arts. So I became a poet, a juggler, and when I am lucky, a fool." He paused, and a hard smile touched his lips. "That has caused no end of trouble, as you can imagine."

The other man's look was appraising. "So, a knight's son, are you? What wouldn't take up the sword as your family wanted? I've heard that story before. I bet your old pa broke his heart over it."

Cenred had to laugh. "My father was a man of iron and did not have a heart to break—anyone who knew him will tell you that. And if my sire thanked God for anything it was that at least I did not become a monk." It was hard not to think of Peter Abelard. "I had a friend," he said more softly, "the firstborn son of a knight, and the family was sure he would take up the profession of arms, as is the custom. But philosophy was my friend's passion. He would go to the schools in Paris or die, he said. And so he persuaded the second son, his younger brother, to take up knighthood for him. But now that I think of it . . ."

He stared across the water at the shore for a time.

"Now that I think of it," Cenred said, "it would have been far better for the world if Peter had taken up the sword. No churchman's heart beats in that breast, for all the brilliance of the mind. And Abelard's heart is hardly a Christian's, meek and mild. It was a sorry day when he took minor orders to teach and read philosophy. No one could have known then what misery he would cause—far greater than as a knight, merely slaughtering his fellow man."

The sailor hadn't been listening. He suddenly pointed to a sheer bluff ahead. "You see that ripple of current comin' out there by the point? Well, lad, keep awatchin'—"

They saw two boats slide out from behind the bluff and turn into the current to pass downstream, toward the count's provision boat. Under his breath, the Fleming cursed.

"Watch it there!" the bargemaster shouted.

The low-sided boat with its sails full of wind was trying to maneuver close to the provision barge to take advantage of their surprise. The count's barge, heavy-laden, was clumsy and hard to turn in the current.

Cenred looked across the water and saw the faces of serfs in the other boat, from grizzled old men down to beardless boys, a whole village with a ravenous look that said they would kill for foodstuffs and leave no survivors.

"Pirates!" The sailor beside him was trying to fend off the hooks the others threw into the benches to lock on and pull alongside. "The devils are for us!"

In moments they were fighting for their lives. The bargemaster at the steering oar turned the barge and drove it toward the shore, knowing their best hope was to beach it and fight on land.

Cenred had no stomach to battle a boatload of starving villagers; his mission was elsewhere. Fortunately, that was not too far away now that they were so close to Paris.

He jumped onto the pebbly strand as soon

as the boat went aground. As he turned to look, the count's boat people seemed to be holding off the hungry serfs for the moment. If he was smart the bargemaster would buy off the pirates with a part of the food they were carrying. But most likely, Cenred knew, they would fight until one or the other was slaughtered. That was the usual thing.

He ran up the hill that overlooked the river, took one last look at the boat careened on the strand with its fighting sailors and pirates, and loped away.

Argenteuil was located on the land in one of the great meandering loops of the Seine north of Paris. The day was warm. Keeping a steady jog up the hill from the river, Cenred raised a sweat before the convent came into view at the end of its avenue of chestnut trees.

At the sight of it he could not forestall a feeling of foreboding. Something was wrong. At the main gate, where there should be a crowd at all hours of the day waiting for food and alms, there was no one. A wrecked wagon, one wheel missing, was drawn up in front of the door. It could not have looked more abandoned.

He leaped the last few steps and threw himself against the oak door, at the same time grabbing the knotted rope that rang the bell.

" 'Ware, 'ware," he shouted. The bell clanged

loudly. "In the name of God and His Holy Son, come to the gate!"

The gate bell subsided slowly. Then there was a silence, no sound of anyone approaching within. Finches flew in and out of the chestnut trees, twittering in the sunshine. Cenred rested his arm against the wooden planks of the convent door and put his head against it. Somewhere in the fields around them a cow bellowed.

They couldn't have left yet. From what the friar had said the bishop had yet to rule on the dissolution of Argenteuil. That should take months. Shouldn't it?

At last the bars in the grille in the door slid back and a shadowy head appeared behind it. "The convent is closed," a voice said.

"Sister." He strained to see, but the iron bars were made so as to conceal the person standing there. It was not Heloise, he knew; not her voice. "I wish to speak to the abbess," he said hoarsely. "Tell her it is—tell her it is Cenred. Whom she knows from the schools at Notre Dame."

It was the only thing he could think of. He did not wish to say Abelard's name.

The voice said, "Did you not hear? We are closed by order of the bishop and the Abbot of St. Denis. There is no longer an order of nuns here."

Cenred brought his fist down against the oak planks of the door and, thick as it was, it shook and rattled on its hinges. The figure behind it made a muffled noise of alarm.

"Go and fetch her or I will tear this damned thing off," he shouted.

The shadowy head disappeared. Cenred leaned his head against the door, eyes closed.

If it was true, and that filthy devil in priest's clothing, Adam Suger, intended to turn out the nuns here, and they would be given dispensation to return to secular life . . .

He ground his eyes against his forearm. He could save her. If all this was true then everything that he could have hoped for would be his. She could be free of the church. Free of Abelard. Together they could go to Brittany and take her babe from Abelard's sister, and then they could live someplace. There was always Rome. England. His throat tightened until it felt there were iron bands about it.

He started, then lifted his head quickly when the familiar, silvery voice said through the door, "Ah, it is true, Cenred, dear friend. It is you, after all. After so long a time."

He knew he was trembling. She was so close. He couldn't see her through the grille; for a moment he considered putting his fingers through it to see if he could tear the bars away.

"Heloise," he whispered. "God in heaven!"

"Shhhhh." He heard a rustling as she turned her head, looking at him through the metal grille. "You frightened the gate mistress."

"God's face, tell me—what have they done to you?"

There was a moment, then he heard her sigh. "Ah, friend, you cannot come here like this—there are too many who wish to make much of every small thing that happens here, to our detriment. Now here you are, my dear, beautiful friend who comes crashing at our gate in his pity and concern."

He said, "You know I could never pity you."

"No?" He heard the sad smile in her voice. "Surely yes. There are times when I pity myself. It is not a nice thing."

"Heloise—"

She interrupted him.

"Come now, at last
Have done, and heed our pleading, and give way.
Let yourself no longer be consumed
Without relief by all that inward burning;
Let care and trouble not forever come to me
From your sweet lips. The finish is at hand.
I forbid your going further."

"I cannot," Cenred said, his voice strangled. "I cannot say poetry with you now."

"Nay, you know the lines, it is Jove speaking to Juno, remember? At the end of the Aeneid. Dear Cenred, you must remember it, and its message." She paused, then added, "But perhaps I should not remind you of the innocent woes that Virgil has brought to me."

"They say—I have heard—it can't be true, that Suger will turn you out."

There was a silence.

"That the nuns here may return to a secular life," he plunged on. "Come out, Jesus in heaven, come with me. I will love you and look after you, as I always promised."

"Cenred."

Now he did put his hands at the grille, trying futilely to find a finger hold to rip the thing out. If he could just see her.

He felt rather than saw her pull back.

"Nay, I took holy orders by his command," that soft, clear voice whispered. "You were there with him, in the back of the church—you saw it all. I will not leave the church now."

"I have money. Give me a day or two," he begged. "I will secure more money than we will ever need to live well in some far place. Heloise, I will take you and the boy to Rome . . ."

"Dear Cenred." He felt the warmth of her hand pressed against the grille on the other side. "Peter knows our plight. He does not have much, but he has offered us the Paraclete. Remember the oratory he built in the mountains to the east? It is somewhat a ruin, they tell me, after his students left and he abandoned it to go to Brittany to be an abbot there. But we will be allowed to establish a chapter house. Most of the nuns here now will go with me, and we will be very poor, but we will survive."

Cenred's hand had found a grip. He wrenched at the bars.

"Heloise, I beg you, leave this living hell," he burst out. "I know there is not enough religion in you to endure what Abelard has forced you to do—shut yourself up like this. Let me make you happy. Jesu—how long must this go on? How long will you take to prove your love to him?"

He pressed his face against the grille, but there was no answer.

After a few minutes he knew she had gone.

Cenred let go of the bars and staggered a few feet, then sat down in the roadway before the convent gate. He could not go any farther. God knows he could not move until his agony abated somewhat. He put his elbows on his knees and cradled his head in both hands and pressed them together, hard, against the pain.

A cold dread had wrapped itself around his soul. How long would Heloise take to prove her love to Abelard? He knew the answer.

Forever.

His thoughts roared through his head like furies. Heloise would follow Peter Abelard to hell. He had heard it said many times, had said it himself. Now one had only to hear her voice speaking of him to know it was true.

The finish is at hand. Christ in heaven, he knew he could never recite that line again without choking on it!

And to make sure that all this was so, an unkind Fate had let Abelard at last come forward to take care of her, to give her the few ruined buildings of his oratory, the Paraclete, and land for her and her nuns.

He heard a click of metal behind him and knew someone was at the grille, opening it. Watching him. Not Heloise. The nun who had come in answer when he had rung the bell.

He knew she was standing in there watching him as he sat in the road, a big man without his wits, pressing his head between his two hands as if to squeeze his brains out and have done with it. Have done with the world and life itself.

She could not know that he was only trying with his two hands to hold death and madness away. A monster God had showed him the truth, and he could not bear it. Heloise was lost to him. Not only to him, but to all those who loved her.

He moaned. He could not help it.

Then something came into the blackness of his mind like a tiny light. Shining there in the darkness, so small one could hardly realize it was there. And it comforted him.

Not only comforted him, but loved him.

God help them all, the finish was at hand here at Argenteuil as Heloise had said. But it was not the end. If he had asked her, he knew she would have said that was so.

Cenred sat for a long moment thinking about it. About love. About its unyielding grasp on a human heart. Then he got to his knees, to his feet, and reached around to brush the dirt from his hose and jacket.

He stumbled the first few steps going down the hill and then he stopped, staring at the ground, thinking. Then suddenly he put his head down, and began to run.

Twenty-eight

Brother Welland crossed the castle ward, lifting his habit to jump the bigger puddles, and made it to the abbess's side in time to help her down from her palfrey.

"Milady abbess," he said breathlessly. Welland, a serf's son, was still much in awe of nobility within the church. Taking her arm, he steered the Abbess of St. Hilda's around a small lake in the middle of the bailey. "My mistress is still at her accounts and does not know that you have arrived. Our new steward, Sir Everard Saujon, is with her. But I will fetch her now that you are here."

"Nay, no need to see my niece," she told him. "If you can show where I am to sleep, I will go there. Traveling in a road that is no more than a bog for half a hundred leagues is never restful. I am sore weary."

The clerk looked over his shoulder to where two young girls in novice's garb were unloading the abbess's baggage from their mules. The convent girls wouldn't lack for a certain kind of attention, he thought, not with so many lusty young knights billeted at the castle.

"And the bridegroom?" the abbess wanted to know. "What's his name—Morsehold? Is he here?"

"Yes, my lady." It was from Sir Thomas Moreshold's knights that the St. Hilda's students were getting the most attention. Welland put himself discreetly in between so the abbess could not see.

"Not much changed here," she was saying, looking around. "Morlaix does not change. Only we do." Her little face was suddenly bleak. "I was a child here, you know. The earl, Gilbert de Jobourg, was my brother."

Brother Welland did know. "But there are changes, reverend lady," he assured her. "There is a new building, the New Tower—"

"Yes, yes, never mind." She gripped his arm. "I have heard poor de Yerville was hanged."

Reluctantly, Brother Welland nodded.

He supposed Abbess Alys had also heard that her niece, the Lady Constance, had not inflicted the customary torture for traitors on her former steward, a procedure that usually went on for days. The countess had even been loath to witness the hanging, although her subjects, or at least a good many of them, would not have understood any unwillingness on her part to be there to savor her full revenge. Nevertheless, those closest to her knew that it had been an ordeal for her; the countess did not like to see men die. And de Yerville, like so many there at Castle Morlaix, had known her since she was a child.

"What now of the other one," the abbess asked, "the Clare who wanted to marry her?"

Brother Welland made his expression properly circumspect. "Lord Robert fitzGilbert is now serving with King Henry in France. It is even said he is betrothed to a niece of the Montgomerys of Avranche."

The abbess snorted. "Hah, the useless are hanged for their sins, and the powerful marry!"

Welland lowered his eyes. "As you say, reverend lady."

He led her through the bailey to the Old Keep where, on the second story, there was a room set aside for the abbess and her novices. Two gaunt-ribbed hounds from the smith's shed came out and sniffed at their heels. Brother Welland kicked them away.

In front of the feast hall, wagons from the countess's fiefs in the south were filled with foodstuffs for the coming wedding. A group of the Abbot of St. Botolph's knights in purple tunics lounged around them. As they recognized the old earl's sister they came to attention, knuckling their helms.

Robert fitzGilbert's fate had come as no surprise. No king's court would punish one of the powerful Clares unless the king willed it, and King Henry had prudently sent no message from France. The countess's would-be bridegroom, sufficiently chastened by the collapse of his relatives' intrigues, had promptly left the Welsh marches with all haste to serve in the war under the command of one of his many Clare uncles.

At the lower door to the Old Keep two servant women came hurrying out, one carrying a cup of hot wine. The abbess took it gratefully.

"Milady," Welland told her, "if you will excuse me go to the countess now to tell her you are here."

She waved the wine cup, indicating she was not through with him. "Tell me what I heard on the road is not true. That my brother's bastard, Nesscliffe, has escaped."

Brother Welland looked uncomfortable. "Ah, most miraculously, lady abbess," he said, "Julien of Nesscliffe having been imprisoned in this very keep before us, in the part used for prisoners and hostages, since his capture at the feast for Lord fitzGilbert. I believe you know the story."

"And?"

He cleared his throat. "After some time awaiting his—er, fate, the bastard devised a plan to—to lower himself from above, from that barred window, a most daring feat, and make his escape."

At his words they all, including the maidservants, looked up, although there was nothing to be seen. The barred window was as it had always been.

"Daring?" The abbess looked at him. "A fool's tale is more like it. Confound the girl, I knew she could not hang him!"

"Milady abbess!" Brother Welland kept his voice down. "Do you—it is never—on my most holy oath to the Blessed Virgin, no one here would say that Julien of Nessville was helped—allowed—"

"Pah! That's a cock and bull story—I'd be a ninny to believe it. I've known my brother's bastard since he was a babe." She tossed off the rest of the wine and handed the cup to the servant. "Well, well, come now, tell me—how is she?"

The countess, Welland thought. Another difficult subject. "She is—ah, ah, well, I would say, reverend abbess. She is, after all," he said lamely, "about to be wed."

"Saint George save us, don't stammer so. To listen to you one would think the whole world is in love with her. I have heard Moreshold is a good man—and more to the point, does not praise himself that he succors her. No matter what King Henry may say." She turned away. "You, here," she said to one of the maids, "have you a soft bed for me in this stone pile, properly warmed? I am cold to the bones after so much travel. And send for my girls. They are somewhere out there gaping at the knights when they should be bringing my boxes."

The women led the abbess into the tower stairwell. Brother Welland could hear the Abbess Alys giving orders as they ascended the stairs.

He stepped back into the ward and looked at the barred window high up on the side of the Old Keep. The knights who had guarded the countess's half-brother the night of his escape had since been given duty in the east at Bucksborough Manor. It was said Gisulf and Aimery, good men both, had never heard the noise of the bars being wrenched from the stones of the window frame, nor the prisoner making his descent. Or the dogs barking in the ward. Or the hail of the garrison guard, or any other probable event.

The scrivener clasped his hands behind his back and sighed. Then he bent his head and started for the countess's solar, to tell her that her abbess aunt was there.

A few minutes later Constance heard his footsteps on the stairs. When the lay brother came in with the news that her aunt had arrived, she motioned for Father Bertrand to finish what he was doing and gather up the vellum rolls of the Morlaix accounts.

She sat back from the table with Father Bertrand, Everard, and the bailiff, Humphrey, and rubbed the ink from her fingers.

They had been working to bring some order to the tallies of Morlaix, some of them as old as the Conqueror's famous Domesday counting. As she'd suspected, when compared with the old records the castle and fief was not as rich as it had been in the days of her grandfather.

Beside her Father Bertrand somewhat loftily showed Everard again how to make his mark, a scrawled "SJ," a sign Brother Bertrand felt more seemly for the steward of her western lands than an "X" that any villein could make.

Constance knew they did not much care for each other—the hardbitten but no longer able-bodied Gascon knight and the overly refined, Bec-trained Benedictine monk from Normandy. But since Sir Everard did not read or write like most of his class—indeed, like many stewards—they were forced to work together. She had charged them with it, and made them swear their oaths.

"There, it is done." Everard put down the goose quill and looked at the blurry gashes of his mark. "Christ's wounds, this is the worst of it, the scrivening."

Brother Welland leaned over his shoulder. "It will come easier, only the "S" should stand up straight," he advised, "not lean as if it was falling in battle from a mortal blow."

Everard made a growling sound.

Humphrey the bailiff put in front of Constance the draft for the knight serjeant Carcefou's family in Falaise to be paid a sum for his honorable death in her service, and she signed it. Next came the list of the Morlaix tenants' work shares.

In a normal year, three days out of every seven were set aside for work for the lord's demesne, the same allotment for villeins and sokemen. Many of the villagers contributed finished work rather than services, as in the case of the smith and the miller. The weavers' taxes consisted of a percent of their woven cloth or, occasionally now as coinage grew more popular, were paid in silver or gold.

A silence fell.

They were reminded again that with Constance's marriage all that she owned would now pass to Sir Thomas Moreshold. In a few weeks a lawyer would arrive from York in the north, where the cathedral school specialized in law, to set up the girls' dower lands. These, with her own dowers, were the only things she could rightly set aside.

Her gaze met Everard's. She did not expect her new steward to feel as loyal to Moreshold as he did to her, but she wanted no challenges on it. From any of them. In the long run, if a husband were provoked with their resistance, he could replace her staff with his own.

Somehow it seemed that Everard had grown even more fiercely devoted to her and her affairs, as if his marriage to the weavers' girl, Emma, had brought out some sort of guilt in him. Although the saints knew with their babe coming he could never be accused of not doting on her enough.

"The stores brought from Sussex, milady," the bailiff said, putting the lists down.

She held back a sigh. She had drawn heavily in the worst of times for shortages, early spring, on her Sussex fiefs for the wedding feast. William de Crecy and Earnaut fitzGamelin, too, would have a new liege lord in Thomas Moreshold; perhaps after this they would be happy to get rid of her.

The bailiff and Brother Welland were tying up the vellum account rolls when they heard her children coming up the stairs to the solar.

"Maman! Maman!" Her youngest, in a riding cap with a feather on it and the blue stone necklace Constance had bought at Christmastime, ran in followed at a more sedate pace by her older sister. Two hunting dogs furtively pressed in behind. Then came Thierry de Yners, looking exceptionally handsome in black wool jacket and hose.

"Maman!" Her youngest daughter threw herself into Constance's lap, heedless of the ink pot, which fell to the floor. "We are going riding. Come!" She tugged at Constance's hand. "Come now!"

Hodierne came to the table. She looked down sidewise, trying to read the accounts. "Thierry has said I may ride my pony, maman." Thierry was currently Hodierne's god. "It is a reward for writing my prayers four times today without error."

Constance lifted her eyes to the scholar and smiled. "It makes me happy to get such a good report."

She got up and the men stood when she did. She had been dressed for their ride since tierce, but she had sat at the accounts so long she was stiff.

Hodierne took her hand as they started down the stairs. Behind them Thierry, guiding Beatriz, wanted to know if Sir Thomas would go with them. She told him no.

The bad weather had held them within the castle for so long it was a great release to be able to ride in the woods where the trees were like green lace with new buds. She planned to take the girls down along the river. Workmen had begun her new chapel there, dedicated to the Holy Virgin. Constance wanted to see how it was going.

Her sister Mabele, her baby in her arms, was waiting for her at the bottom of the tower stairs. "Constance, where are you going?" she wanted to know. "Are you going to ride? I must speak with you."

Constance stopped to peer at her niece, a very pretty baby in layers of embroidered linen inside a red woolen bunting, who had been named Elisabet. Constance was her godmother.

The babe was asleep, she saw, smiling, its tiny mouth pushed out in a milky bud. Beatriz danced around them, wanting to see her, but Mabele held the baby high, an impatient frown on her face.

"I can't go back with them—you must understand that." Mabele, too, was lavish in her dress: she wore a tight-fitting surcoat, elegantly trimmed in beaver and coney, and a length of green silk veil bordered with lace floated from her braided coronet. "It's unbearable! Constance, listen to me—you must let me stay here for a while at Castle Morlaix. Give me my old room and I will be well content. I know Gildwith and my old maid will help with my babe."

They came out into the ward. Constance's mare was waiting and she saw with some dismay the grooms had put on the fancy new red and gold tasseled bridle that was to be used for the procession after the wedding.

"You will not be content here," she told Mabele. "He hasn't beaten you again, has he?"

Everard stepped forward and took the mare's reins. "I will send them back to change it."

"No, I don't want to wait." She supposed it was unlucky but she really didn't care. He handed Beatriz up to her. Constance put the little girl before her in the saddle. The mounted groom cantered up, leading Hodierne's pony.

"Constance, you aren't listening to me," her sister said. "I'm with child again. Now I must have a boy, he says. God is my judge, Elisabet is not three months! I should have fed her myself and not given her to a wet nurse, but his mother and sisters—"

"Mabele." Constance wanted to talk of this some other time, not when there were grooms standing about, listening. Hubert de Warrenne and his father were out hawking with Thomas Moreshold and many of the guests who had come to Morlaix for the wedding. That was another thing Mabele complained of—that Hubert spent little time with her except when they were in bed.

Constance looked around the ward. "Where

is Bertrada? Why do you not join her in the solar with the de Clintons?" If she could find a de Clinton servant she would send for Bertrada and tell her to come and attend to Mabele, a task she knew Bertrada would greet with little enthusiasm. Her youngest sister and her husband did not get along with the de Warrennes.

Thierry had put Hodierne onto the pony's back. Constance was amused to see the expression on Hodierne's face as she preened herself, looking up at him.

Of a sudden that look reminded her of their snowy, starving journey in the winter and how Thierry desperately diddled any widows he could find for something to eat. And then, how in the terrible storm he had asked Llwydd if they were fated to perish there on the Cirencester road. Llwydd, a mass of frozen rags, had nodded an answer that was no answer, because they couldn't make out what it was.

Thierry handed Hodierne her crop and straightened up, holding the pony's reins while the groom mounted his horse behind them.

Constance still stared at him.

They had never talked of it. She had given the scholar shelter and fed him in those first days of chaos after her return to Morlaix, and then finally made him tutor to her girls. They had liked young, handsome Thierry and it was a comfort to her to know that someone other than nursemaids looked after Hodierne and

Beatriz while she was busy with the near-ruin of her affairs.

Even then, countering the Clares' challenge over her ousting of Robert fitzGilbert and Julien, they'd meet in the halls or in the bailey on an errand and she'd feel a bursting need to ask him about Llwydd—if he knew where the Welshwoman had gone, if he'd felt anything for her beyond the hedgerow coupling of their long winter journey.

Or if he knew of Cenred.

She sat her fidgeting mare, knowing why she did not dare speak of it. All the memories, the grief, the desperate longing for the one man she had ever loved, and who could not love her, would burst from her in a torrent of tears and anguish that would demean them both.

Why, she had asked herself over and over, must his heart be with a woman he could never have, and who loved someone else? And who was now beyond the reach of either of them in the arms of the holy church? While she—all that she owned she would willingly give to him: Morlaix, her Sussex fiefs, Bucksborough, gold, and lands.

All of which Cenred, she suddenly remembered, thinking of what was most important to her, had restored to her. As long as she lived she would never forget their last mad dance in the Morlaix feast hall as Farmer Jack and Little Jack.

No, Constance thought, she could not grab

Thierry and howl her heartbreak. Those who knew her would never believe her capable of it. They would be horror-struck. So she supposed they would go on living like this in a most civil manner, the countess and the tutor, making do with what was left to them. Trying not to remember that desperate time when their lives—and their lovers—were all they had.

Thierry had lifted his head. Their eyes met. The groom and Everard were waiting.

Mabele said something. Everard stepped to her mare, his hand on the bridle, frowning. "Countess?"

A tear rolled down her cheek. She was mortified. "I have dust in my eyes." She pulled the bridle from his hand.

There was no dust around them in the ward, only mud. "We will talk later," she promised Mabele.

She did not look at Thierry as she guided her horse past them, the groom leading Hodierne's pony, and out toward the gate.

They went down toward the river from behind the castle, a slope filled with the shacks of itinerant workers from Wrexham and other towns who had heard that the fief of Morlaix was a place one could look for work in the fields.

Not so this year, Constance thought. Still, the ragged hut-dwellers came out to watch her as she passed, and some shouted good wishes for her coming marriage.

The sun was warm through the budding tree branches, but the path to the river was spongy. Spring had been extraordinarily wet right through Lent, and now in the week after Easter it was just beginning to dry. Behind Constance, Hodierne had persuaded the groom to give her the pony's reins. She galloped ahead of them to the riverbank.

"Come back," Constance called. Beatriz squirmed in the saddle, saying something about wanting to get down and go to the river to see the fish. Constance held onto her youngest daughter as the mare shied and danced uneasily. She motioned the young groom to go after Hodierne.

They paused by the brown, swirling waters. Standing still, the pale sun was hot on their heads. The weavers' village was somewhere out of sight on the opposite shore. It was there that Everard had been waylaid by Julien's men who had hoped to kill him and leave him for the weavers to bury. A sense of time pressed on Constance like a weight.

After the wedding she would go north to live on Thomas Moreshold's lands for a while. He was a good man, and under the circumstances King Henry had not been able to deny her.

"Come, let us go down to the new chapel," Constance called. The groom had seized Hodierne's bridle and was trying to turn her pony.

Constance had already turned her mare's head to go upstream toward the grove where the workmen were building her chapel. She did not see the flash of white, only heard Hodierne scream.

When she turned, a column of mailed knights, white tunics fluttering, was thundering toward her. The knight in the forefront had the reins to Hodierne's pony, pulling it after him.

Constance clutched Beatriz, unable to utter a sound. As she watched, the lead knight in a plumed barrel helmet reached down and scooped Hodierne from the stumbling pony and threw her across his saddle.

Constance turned her mare around as they stormed past. Holding the reins in one hand and her baby in the other, she kicked the mare. The startled horse reared, nearly unseating her. Beatriz shrieked.

"Stop!" Dear God, where were they taking her little girl? She was suddenly in a melee of white-clad knights. Someone seized her reins. Even in the frenzy of plunging horses' she remembered thinking she had seen them somewhere.

Pulling her along with them, they galloped through the woods and out onto the village road toward the bridge.

"Stop!" Constance screamed. They were on her land; they must be mad, whoever they are, to think they can do this. They would never get past the village.

She was fighting the knight who held her

mare's reins, trying to wrench them free and hold onto her screaming daughter at the same time. At the bridge she saw a figure coming toward them. In the sunshine, a tall man with bright hair in shabby clothes. And fancy boots.

For a moment her face, her thoughts, and her very voice were frozen. When she would have shrieked his name, he saw them.

The troop of white-clad knights bore down on him. They would kill him, Constance knew, frantic. She could see he knew what was happening. His eyes found her, saw Hodierne over the knight's saddle.

She saw him stop stock still. Then with a roar he charged toward the knights racing down on him.

She remembered screaming like a madwoman. He was defenseless, unarmed against a troop of knights—he didn't even have a sword! He was going to kill himself, the brave, mad fool—sacrifice himself to save them. It was useless. They would slaughter him where he stood.

The knight holding her mare jerked at the reins and her horse stumbled. Clutching Beatriz, Constance tried to keep from sliding from the saddle. When she looked up Cenred had run to one of the knights in the fore, reached up, dragged him from the saddle, knocked him to the ground, kicked him, and wrenched away his sword.

The column reined in. The little mare slammed

into the horse in front of them. In her arms, Beatriz squalled hysterically.

She would have screamed herself, but her breath was coming in hard, hurting gasps. She wanted to close her eyes. She wanted to pray.

She watched as Cenred swung the sword, shouting in some strange tongue, wading into the horsemen. They began to slide from their saddles. They lay in the muddy road in their glittering mail and white tunics, facedown before him. He struck them broadside with the sword, kicking them and cursing. He strode to the biggest horseman and dragged Hodierne from his arms. The knight came down heavily from the saddle and knelt before him in the mud.

"You damned swine!" Cenred was speaking German Saxon—she could understand only that much.

Holding a wailing Hodierne in his arms, he took his booted foot and put it on the big knight's back and pushed him facedown into the muddy earth. He gave him a kick on the side of his plumed helmet for good measure.

Dazed, Constance walked her mare through the dismounted knights groveling in the road. Beatriz, her fingers jammed in her mouth, was still shaking and sobbing.

She looked down at Cenred. He was as she always remembered him: big body, gilded hair, blazing eyes, handsome as a god. The murderous rage that had gripped him was only just ebbing away. A moment before he could have killed them all. She had seen it.

He tried to put Hodierne on her feet but she clung to him, screaming. He lifted her back up.

"I was coming back to you," he said over her oldest child's howls. "I was coming back, Constance."

Twenty-nine

"His name is Sigurd of Glessen." Cenred gave the big knight in the plumed helmet another kick. "He is Emperor Henry's man—as are they all. They would not leave me alone in Paris when I was a student, and even after Abelard's disaster they followed me. This time they have been lying in wait on the roads, searching the hamlets, damn them, but never clever enough to catch me. Until this piece of dirt—" he said, giving the knight another kick on the side of his helm, "—in his brilliance decided to bait the trap. With *you.*"

Constance's eyes devoured him. She hardly heard what he said—his other words were still echoing in her mind. *I was coming back to you. I was coming back, Constance.* Blessed Mother, she could hardly hold still. She wanted to cry, to laugh—she wanted to throw herself in his arms!

The young groom, bloody-faced, came galloping up, leading Hodierne's pony. He gaped at the big knight on the ground who had not moved in spite of Cenred's blows. All around them the other knights lay in their dirt-splattered white tunics in various attitudes of obeisance.

Constance leaned from the saddle and handed Beatriz to the groom. Then she slid down the side of her mare to her feet.

She drew in a deep breath, so close she could almost touch him. Ah, she remembered the blue woolen jacket, now frayed and not so clean, that the Shrewsbury weavers had given him, the black hose, the red boots she knew Llwydd had stolen for him some long time ago. His effect on her, as always, was powerful. His eyes, the sense of his body inside those clothes, made a sudden warmth rush over her.

She whispered, "Bait what with me?"

He looked down at her. "Any trap. Glessen knew I would come for you if you were in peril." He set Hodierne on her feet. "I was coming back," he said, huskily, "to be your jongleur, your singer, your love poet, your swineherd, your fancy man, Constance, anything you desire. I have found my senses. I know now it is you I want, that it is you I need. I thought my heart was pledged to another, but it was not. Only my anger, and pity."

They could see a group of men hurrying toward the bridge from the village, shouting and waving rakes and scythes. The leader of the emperor's knights raised his head. Cenred promptly kicked it back down again.

Constance shut her eyes for a moment. Everything her heart had yearned for was coming true. Just to hear him say his usual outrageous, impossible things, that he would be her love poet, swineherd—dear Blessed Mother, *fancy man*—made her faint with happiness. Out of the corner of her eye she saw the villagers roar to the far side of the bridge to rescue her and then, finding the troop of white-clad knights lying prone in the road, come to a stop.

He was back, Constance was telling herself, because he said he had found what he wanted. His heart was not pledged to Heloise, sweet Mother in Heaven—only his *pity!* It was what she had longed to hear. But before she let pure joy consume her, she knew that was not all of it. She could see it in his face.

"But they will not let me," he said. "Nor will your king." He lifted his booted foot and rolled the Saxon knight over on his back and looked down at him disdainfully. "Get up and tell her, Glessen."

Lying there, the big German reached up and pulled off his helmet. His face was tanned, his eyes paler than Cenred's.

He slowly pulled himself to his knees, moving the heavy sword to his back. Then his mailed hands worked at a leather bag the size of a man's head tied to his belt.

Constance drew back instinctively. The white-clad knights were also kneeling around them.

The leader reached into the leather bag and pulled out a thick, hammered-gold crown of ancient make set with scarred purple stones. It gleamed dully in the light.

He held it at arm's length above his head. It was a portentous moment, the sun splaying through the trees, striking the heavy gold object held high. The other knights, kneeling, bent their heads.

"Prince Conrad," their leader intoned in guttural Norman French. "All hail to Prince Conrad, Duke of Saxony!"

Constance stared at them, openmouthed.

The object of all this leaned on the big sword, the tip dug into the soft ground, looking cynical. "My older brother, the former Duke of Saxony, is dead," he explained. "Of a sickness, oddly enough. It is a family in which we mostly murder each other. Yours is like a band of angels compared to mine."

Constance turned to him, her face slack. "He—the knight—said you are a prince?"

He shrugged. "Now Duke of Saxony as well. My uncle, Lothar, desires to be the next Emperor of the Holy Roman Empire. After Emperor Henry is dead, of course. They both want me in Germany, not roaming England's roads living the life of a wandering minstrel. But it has taken these dolts a year riding from one end of Christendom to the other to find me. They know I do not want it, that I would see them all boil in hell first."

Constance was stunned by his calm, his irony.

A moment before she had been the happiest woman in the world to offer him her castle, fiefs and manors. She was even prepared to defy King Henry himself to take him as her lover. And he just as wildly had offered himself as her poet, her bedmate, her fool.

Tears welled up in her eyes. None of it was true. She had forgotten how cruel he could be. Why had he come back to taunt her again with something they could not have?

He was watching her. "Poor Constance, you have done nothing to look so. Sweet Jesu, don't cry!"

She drew herself up, chin high. "I am not crying."

Behind them a troop of Morlaix knights was coming at full gallop down the road from the castle, the new knight captain, Longspres, at their head. The emperor's knights, kneeling in the middle of the road before the bridge, did not move. Longspres came as close as possible before lifting his hand to cry halt.

"Milady," he shouted.

Cenred smiled his crooked grin. "They will not move, even though your knights hack them to pieces. It is the way they are trained. As *I* am trained. Know this, Constance, I have tried to live otherwise, but I am still as savage as they. Watch."

He lifted the sword over the head of the leader who knelt, still holding the crown in his hands. "Countess, I am going to cut off his dog's head for daring to touch you and your children."

Before he could bring it down Constance

sprang forward and grabbed his arm. "Sweet Mary, *no!*"

He paused. He held the sword high over the big knight, who still had not moved. "No?"

"Dear saints in heaven, don't kill him," Constance blurted. She felt as if she were going mad with Saxon knights all around them kneeling like statues. "I don't wish you to kill anyone. God's wounds, he is a well-made man! If you would punish him make him—make him a serf, put him to work in the fields!"

He lowered the sword. "Make him a *serf?*"

"Yes." Dear God, what was the matter with him? She saw Longspres pushing his destrier through the kneeling men to come to her. Distracted, she waved her hand at him to stop.

Cenred rested the tip of the Saxon sword in the dirt. "Dear countess, you want me to make the famed crusader Sigurd of Glessen a serf, so he can labor profitably in the fields? My fields? Or whatever fields there may be?"

She nodded, despairing. She knew now that he would go back to Germany; if any man was tied to his fate it was this man before her. This was the mystery she had always seen in him, his power and fire and arrogance that did not fit any jongleur, even a mad one. And to think she had once thought him a ruined monk or discredited knight.

"I know that you—you will rule well." Her voice sank to a whisper. What an idiot she had been, not to see what had been there all the time. "Ah, it is true, you will have a cultivated court with m-music and fine things: it is within your power as no one else's. And you are learned, and know the common folk from having lived among them—"

He stepped quickly to her then, and put his arms around her and drew her to him. "Constance, kiss me."

When his lips touched hers she thought she would weep—she could not bear to give him up. But then she drowned in it. His kiss was warmth and tenderness and violent desire. It left her reeling.

When she opened her eyes he said softly, "I will only go to Saxony with you. This is what I came for, Constance. Surely you did not think otherwise?" When she stared at him he went on, wryly. "Consider, there will be no peace for you with King Henry, anyway—you are too rich and beautiful. And the devil knows I will have none with my relations—they will pursue me forever: they have a dozen baby virgins waiting in Saxony for me to consider. But it is *you* I want."

He paused, and said more soberly, "I have learned a lesson in love, Constance: it endures above all reason. I did not understand that before. But now I know it at last, that you are my heart and my life—with you my soul is at rest. It is a great gift."

"Cenred—"

"Nay, I will tell you about it later. It is enough now to know that you love me." His wicked azure eyes caressed her. "You do love me, don't you? It's what you said. Don't tell me you lied."

She looked up at him. "I did not lie."

"Good." He smiled at her. "Now, I will take you to the emperor, and you will keep me sane in Saxony, and punish my subjects by turning them into serfs to work at a great profit, and manage my estates and keep my accounts, and deal with my uncle. Dear Christ, how Lothar will hate you."

"Milady," Longspres was calling, "do you wish me to capture this ruffian?"

Constance licked her lips. "You cannot mean any of this. It is one of your jokes."

He grinned. "Jesu, woman you have only seen the good side of me! I do not always play the Christmas Fool and Farmer Jack so sweetly." He dropped the long sword into the dirt and lifted her, his big hands at her waist, and swung her around. "Come with me, Constance, you will not be lonely for your wealth—even before attaining the dukedom of Saxony I was richer than you by far! I have fiefs and peasants without end, and you may lavish them all with charity, and make marriages, and arrange schooling for all the beggars' brats. I only ask that you love me and stay with me always. I will have great need of it. And I will not go to Germany without it."

Uncertain, she laughed. Yet she knew him well enough to know when he was serious. "Put me down. God's face, my children—the whole village is watching!"

"Say again that you love me."

"Yes, I love you." Hodierne, standing beside them, was watching, big-eyed. "Put me down."

He set her on her feet. The groom brought up the mare. "Shall we go to Morlaix and begin there?" he said.

Wordless, she nodded. Cenred lifted Hodierne onto her pony and the Saxon knights got to their feet with a jingling of spurs and mail.

He turned to the still-kneeling knight and took the amethyst crown from his hands. "Let me come to your demesne properly, then." He lowered the massive circlet and put it on his head. He moved it once to settle it, then stood there, looking at her.

He should have been, by the way he was dressed in his shabby jacket and worn boots, a common sort of man. But nothing could dim his size, the way he held himself, the blaze of those brilliant eyes. And now the presence of the ancient crown. At the back, the Morlaix knights exclaimed in surprise.

"Come," he told Constance.

He made a basket of his hands and boosted her up on her mare. Her cloak swung back a little and she saw his quick look, eyebrows raised. He said nothing, only smiled.

She closed her eyes and said a quick prayer. There was so much to be done she did not know where to begin, she thought as she settled herself in the saddle. She really could not go to Saxony—she was to wed with Thomas Moreshold in three days. Her sisters, Mabele and Bertrada, needed her, and dear saints, King Henry would punish her, she dared not think how! She would lose her lands, Morlaix, everything. Cenred had already said his relatives would hate her. She was so happy she could have laughed aloud.

They turned up the castle road. Longspres moved his knights behind them, the Saxons with their white tunics and gonfalons following, the noisy crowd of villagers bringing up the rear.

Cenred had mounted a Saxon knight's horse. Now he looked back over his shoulder. "Constance," he shouted.

She kicked the mare closer to him and he reached out his hand. "Stay with me," he told her. His grip on her fingers was strong. "That is all that needs to be done, now, that you will stay with me."

"Yes," she told him, her heart full.

She knew that he had guessed what she had to tell him. What Thomas Moreshold, that good man, had accepted with her grateful thanks. The child she carried would probably be a boy, she told herself, the very child the others had striven for so mightily. And she knew to him, this golden, cross-grained, wonderful man she loved, that boy or girl, it truly would not matter.

All that needs be done, he had told her, *is that you stay close to me always.*

He turned his head and looked at her and grinned. And Constance smiled back.

Author's Note

Abelard and Heloise lived into their sixties, she as an abbess, he in his chosen role of embattled philosopher. Although undoubtedly brilliant, his works are notable now mainly in the context of medieval church dialectic. Their correspondence, especially Heloise's frank and unrestrained letters, is famous.

Abelard was on his way to Rome to defend himself against charges of heresy brought by his chief antagonist, Bernard of Clairveaux, when he died.

Their son, Peter Astrolabe, was dedicated to the church apparently while still a child and died, a monk, in his twenties.

Heloise, one of the most learned and accomplished women of the Middle Ages, achieved stature as an abbess, but was never reconciled to her fate.

"Stealing Heaven; the love story of Abelard and Heloise," a novel by Marion Meade, is highly recommended for those who wish to read on. "Peter Abelard," a novel by Helen Waddell, largely reflects a biased, establishment-oriented view of the subject.

Lothar of Saxony succeeded Henry the Fifth as Emperor of the Holy Roman Empire in 1125.